BOOMERANG

Raymond Q. Armington
and
William Donohue Ellis

WARD & WARD

First Printing — September, 1988

Copyright 1988 by Raymond Q. Armington
All rights reserved

Manufactured in the United States of America
1988 Printing
Publisher: WARD & WARD CO.
West Geauga Trail
Chesterland, OH 44026-2898

Production, R. & E. Ward/ Graphics, Thomas F. Theus/

Research-Manuscript, Nancy A. Schneider/

Editing, Dorothy Couzens

Library of Congress Cataloging-in-Publication Data

Armington, R.Q. (Raymond Q.) 1907-

BOOMERANG.

Includes index.
I. Ellis, William Donohue. II. Title
PS3551.R466B66   1988   813'.54   88-26156

ISBN 0-9621126-0-7

ISBN 0-9621126-1-5 (pbk)

Other works by the authors:
MORE: The Rediscovery of American Common Sense
THIS WAY UP

FOR A BETTER WORLD

In memory of
Elizabeth Rieley Armington

Prologue

Concorde Flight 102
Washington-Paris

E.J. Fash's head inclined forward and canted slightly inboard away from the sighing of the engines so he could eavesdrop. He knew from his preparation that this dialog was the most important assignment in his 22 professional years. He had a sense that it was far too big for him. So he strained to hear each exchange.

Despite a glint of gray at the temples, seasoned Ed Fash was changing ... backwards. He hid that from colleagues on the *Miami Herald* by sustaining his savvy sports desk parlance. But when they shifted him to financial, Fash changed. Even after several years on the new assignment, he approached it with a cub's impressionability, and just occasionally a flicker of that freshman pretension of improving the world with the pen.

A protective cynicism about his desk drawer of walnut-backed wall plaques left him still boyishly surprised to find himself seated in the lounge of the Concorde bound for Paris. His boss had explained, "It could be the biggest event since the war. And I'm paying for you to ride that fancy French sky bus because you may get more of the story in-flight than in Paris." Then he had growled, "Besides, I want you to get a little jump on those CBS pretty boys and girls. I'm sick of them reading your financial pages, then acting like they're really in the news business."

At first Fash was struck by the fantastic coincidence that he recognized all of the dozen other men and one woman in the aircraft's lounge with Senator Justin A. Forte. Out of 260 million Americans, how could so many on one flight be recognizable public figures?

However as he eavesdropped on their arguments, he realized they must all be part of Senator Forte's wildcat committee. They had to be giants to be chosen by Forte.

Forte had no authority to form the committee for this

trip except his own stature on seven major senate committees and subs dealing with trade. He irritated senate colleagues and Commerce and State with what they slurred as "The Forte Mis-guided Tour." However, not one journalist labelled it a *junket*.

The European Commission, executive body of the European Community, had reluctantly yielded to Senator Forte's pressure to hold an "information meeting" in Paris, clarifying its overwhelming new program, "Europe 1992."

Forte had avoided all controls by raising private funding for the trip with just five short phone calls. He drafted his delegates with short notes. You might fight Forte's ideas, but not his invitation to listen. He had invited his ideological enemies to show them the threat firsthand. "I'll risk your impatience," he told them now in the flat tone of a discouraged professor, "by repeating what I said in my note. I know we're all scan readers at your levels.

"The huge program, 'Europe 1992,' could open up genuine world free trade. But more likely ... it will become 'Fortress Europe,' shutting out all imports. That can shut down the world and bring back 1933."

Massive-shouldered, Michigan Senator Drummond challenged, "All due respect, Justin, what makes you free trade types think we Americans are going to have any say-so in whether 'Europe 1992' goes 'Fortress Europe' or otherwise? We don't make European policy."

"Yes, we do. Particularly you, Drum."

"Me? That's crazy."

No one paid any attention to the eavesdropper, so E.J. Fash was free to jot notes in a flexible notebook as if he were a business traveler updating his expense account:

> Drummond - Senator. Mich. Dem. Wants to be U.S. Pres. Could be, too. Labor backs him 100% for his protection stand on the Trade Bill. Very little interest in substance of most bills. But fascinated by legislative politics. And good at it. Extremely shrewd w/media. Cuts no deep tracks on ideology.

> Forte - Senator. Missouri. Rep. Opposite of
> Drummond. The hell with P.R. Knows foreign
> trade cold. Adamant free trader. Brainy scholar
> type. No good in rough and tumble with real
> people.

Forte answered Drummond, "I think 'Europe 1992' may be a direct response to the massive protection *you* and your crowd are amending into S.B.115."

The Canadian, Margaret MacDonald, nodded. "Amen."

Fash noted:

> Margaret MacDonald - Canada. Three trade
> committees. Looks 33ish. Gracious, but bluntly
> resents U.S. slowness in implementing famous
> US/Canada free trade agreement.

Forte said, "You all know why I picked you for this trip. You each influence thousands. Most of you disagree with me. Now I want you to see firsthand the threat of the massive project 'Europe 1992.'

"If it becomes Fortress Europe, I think you know what that will bring. At best a 1933-style world depression. At worst ..."

Several of them nodded. Vanwert, the former German, completed, "War. Like twice bevore. Next time vorse."

Fash noted:

> Axel Vanwert - former German Kaiser Werks
> V.P. Came to U.S. to head Kaiser subsidiary
> here. When he got his US green card, jumped
> Kaiser ship to ——?

Fash was robbed of the continuing dialogue by a flurry of loudspeaker announcements and refreshment serving. He used the conversation blackout to fill in the cast, what little he knew:

> Braxton - pres. of Biz. Roundtable, CEO's of
> big corps. Aggressive. String puller. Talks free

trade, but wants tariff protection for machine tool biz. He's pres., Militech Tool. Cinci.

Fisher - heads some machinists union. Wants to kill imports of forgings/castings. Hates Braxton for constant automating of machines.

Rivera - Peru. Finance. Educated US. Handsome. Self-assured. Came on duty after huge Peru loans from US. Resents same. (Why did Forte invite him?)

Sukuto - Trade Dept. Japanese Embassy. Very savvy re Wash DC personnel. Rivals Forte in trade savvy. Polite, but tough. Forte must have invited to show Japs Europe 1992 threat to Nips also.

Adam Flitch - No real clue, but suspect he's sales type. Probably brought along for ... why?

When the crew gave the flight back to the paying customers, Fash could hear Forte, "Sure, we're unofficial and theoretically we're going over there just to listen, but with the stature you represent I would hope you would voice a message of our own - 'don't build a fortress Europe.'"

For the first time Sukuto spoke. "To voice that, we will have to promise convincingly to get our own houses in order."

Braxton was a man whose thoughts were close to his mouth. "Just what the hell's that mean, Mr. Sukuto?"

"I only mean — why permit U.S. special interests to interfere with free trade in your trade bill S.B.115?"

"Like what special interests?"

"With all respect, Mr. Braxton, you machine tool companies, for example. Through your ASME and your Robotics Institute, you lobbied through a tremendous tariff against large Japanese stamping machines in S.B.115. At the very time when U.S. badly needs Tashoba stamping presses."

"Why yours?"

"Because the molds can be changed in six minutes instead of four hours. Same production line can make different models without shutdown. With that, your citizens could have had a good car for under five thousand dollars. Why not give your citizens a break?"

"Why dont' **you**? Three hundred Japanese farmers just dumped seven truck loads of California oranges in Tokyo Harbor squawking against American farm imports. Why not let your people have cheap American oranges, rice, beef? Clean up your own house."

Sukuto nodded. "I said 'both our houses,' plural."

Fash felt that Sukuto, representing the most powerful economic nation, was working hard at an apologetic courtesy. He wondered how long that courtesy would last. Another year? Two?

Fash missed a few mumbled exchanges but Drummond's bass voice rumbled through clearly, "Why should the U.S. be the one to tolerate a huge negative balance of trade all the time? Why can't we say to you guys — you can sell us as much as you buy from us? A straightforward common sense balance of trade?" He was aiming at Sukuto, "Would you do it?"

Sukuto smiled and turned up his palms. "We're a small country. How much can we absorb?"

"Well I mean suppose we said you four Asian Tigers leagued together can sell us all you want, so long as you buy that much from us?"

Sukuto suddenly leaned forward and pointed at Drummond, "That could work, but you won't let it."

"Why won't we?"

The group focused on Sukuto's answer, "You won't supply what the world wants to buy."

Drummond grinned conspiratorily at the group as if they had all heard something ridiculous. Sukuto, to seem unaware of that, talked to his open hands, but apology fell from his manner, "Put it this way, Senator: Why does the U.S. try to protect your obsolete, uncompetitive industries ... soaking your citizens for it in rip-off prices? Instead — why not let your people have more for their money when the product is available better and cheaper — from elsewhere? More for all ... via expanded world trade?"

The group went silent. Into that silence came a composed contralto voice. Margaret MacDonald had seemed too young and too chic to be here, until she spoke, "Or if you're going to subsidize, as in the case of grain, milk, sugar, tobacco, why not do it visibly and honestly rather than hiding it in a protected high price of the goods?"

Drummond challenged, "You talking about U.S. farm supports, Madam?"

She turned a beautiful and expressionless face to him. "Senator, I mean U.S., Canada, Germany, France, Italy. Without all these farm subsidies the whole world could eat ... cheap ... and still feed Africa with leftovers. Doesn't that makes subsidies insane, Senator?"

One of Drummond's strengths in politics was that, when bested, he could turn on a great electric grin and back off with no hard feelings.

Fash was interested that Forte did not interfere. The Frenchman, Pierre Masse, was aboard as a guide and host from European Community and 'Europe 1992.' He had the urbane confidence of the perennial staff type. "What you are talking, balanced free intercontinental trade, sounds well. But in all history, continents beggered their neighbors. Why try to go against ancient history?"

The truculent Vanwert asked from a leaning-back position, "Do you mean to say you don't really know?"

"You do?"

"Yes."

"Then why?"

"Ancient history's spears had a range of sixty feet. Today — three thousand miles ... in minutes. When nations are beggered, they will fight."

The group turned thoughtful. None were old enough to have lived WWII, but all were missile literate. And only last week a summit of African prime ministers had issued a joint manifesto that it was "a natural right of human beings to eat. The earth's fertility belongs to all continents."

The thoughtful spell was broken by Fisher, the chunky redhead of the Machinists Union, who protested, "What I don't see is how the U.S. came out on the short end of this stick?"

The question was apparently too basic to earn a response from people at this level. Fisher augmented, "I mean — we start 1950 strong. We're Marshall Planning Europe. We set Japan on its feet. We're sending foreign aid to the whole damn world. Now suddenly those people are shutting down our plants and firing our people. How come?" He looked at the German with the U.S. green card.

The silence continued. Finally the tired voice of Senator Forte said, "Wrong question, Mr. Fisher." The senator did not look at Fisher but at Drummond. "Your question should be — why should a nation consume its own wealth, even borrowing to consume beyond that, thereby becoming an impoverished borrower, losing its leadership position?"

Now Forte looked at the Machinists Union executive. "It's a human mistake. Rome did it and fell. Spain did it. France. But we don't fix it, Mr. Fisher, by adding your tariff against foreign semi-finished castings and forgings. If they don't come in as raw forgings, that metal will come in as parts of trucks or boats or tractors."

Drummond snapped, "Not if I can help it!"

Forte said, "If you're going to protect that comprehensively, we're going to pay for a huge bureaucracy to keep score on the imports. Why have a foreign trade policy that requires an army to police?

"One reason the 14 E.C. countries are going to a free trade 'Europe 1992' is to dump the choking regiments of red-tape bureaucrats. Right now a truck crossing a border checkpoint in Europe is into an hour and a half of frustration and a half pound of paperwork. If our S.B.115 passes, we'll be worse."

A Concorde steward sidled up to the ear of Pierre Masse and talked. Masse nodded. The steward left and returned with a phone which he plugged into the forward bulkhead. Masse went to the phone. Fash found that interesting and watched. The Frenchman seemed to be protesting but finally acceding to something. He hung up and returned to the group. Fash thought he looked like a man suddenly longing for the simpler times of boyhood.

Adam Flitch, veteran foreign sales manager for a large U.S. fastener supplier, addressed Drummond, "Why don't you slow down the anti-trust activity to let our companies compete with foreign? Get our prices down?"

"I don't see how anti-trust hurts a fastener supplier, Mr. Flitch."

"Plenty. The Koreans like our heavy-duty bridge fasteners. But they want us to use these fasteners to partially fabricate some bridge sections with steel from our plate division. Soon as we put our own bolt through our own plate, our government yells restraint of trade; and the contract goes to Laval of France. Right, Mr. Masse?"

Masse's head snapped out of a reverie. "Pardonnez. Sorry. I was not listening."

For the first time Forte smiled, "I think Mr. Masse has a problem on his mind."

"You are perceptive, Senator. I do. Can I speak to you en prive?"

"No need. Tell all of us."

Masse leaned forward, making a steeple with his hands, "We-ll, messieurs et madame, this is very ..." He was struggling. "This is very, very awkward. You see, suddenly..."

Forte said, "Let me spare you, Mr. Masse. That radio call was from your people, cancelling our meeting."

"Well, not cancel. Postpone. They want to be really ready for you. And suddenly, and unfortunately, the right people came unavailable by emergency."

Forte nodded. He glanced at his group to see if they were studying Masse. They were.

Masse struggled on. "But they realize the tremendous time and expense you all ..." Drummond was about to sound off but Forte lifted a finger to let Masse continue. "...they have arranged a special very informative commercial-industrial tour of ..."

Forte raised a hand, "Thank you, Pierre. Thank you. But call your people and cancel the tour before they spin a lot of wheels."

"But then your whole trip will be a total waste."

"No, Pierre. If my group has been alert," — he looked around at them — "then what just happened may be more informative than anything we would hear in Paris."

Masse seemed puzzled. "But what will you do? Turn right around and go back?"

"No. We will go on to Europe Community headquarters in Brussels and chat with the 'Europe 1992' fellows there."

"But they will not be expecting you."

"True. That could be even more informative."

"But I meant they might not be ... uh ... available."

"Well, Pierre, even though we're not an official delegation, when you consider the make-up of our group, they ought to see us. For example, there are only a hundred U.S. senators in the world, and two of them are right here. They wouldn't keep us sitting in the lobby, would they?"

"Of course not! Still, I must make some arrangements." He rose.

"No, Pierre. No arrangements. We'll just wing it this time."

"Wing it?"

"Ad-lib it."

"Well, I should cancel the industrial tour they're arranging."

"No. Let it alone. How much arranging could they do so quick anyhow?" Masse sat down. "And Pierre ... no need to accompany us. We'll find our own way."

Forte signalled for the attention of his group. "Gentlemen and Miss MacDonald, does this say anything to you?"

Margaret MacDonald looked at Masse, "Amen."

Flitch said, "Now this trip could really amount to something."

When the principals went on to discuss the new plan, Fash filled in his notes:

> One hour from landing, Paris, looks like Forte mission could become first alert re Fortress Europe. Most of U.S. asleep. Unaware what Forte trying to tell us. Only few journals even discuss Europe 1992.

> Pluses: Forte knows all nuances internat'l
> trade. And has guts and clout.
> Negatives: Forte not good sloganeer. Does
> not excite, arouse.

Fash was aware that the very self-possessed young redhead who had dropped into the lounge seat next to him was exercising strong restraint to veil interest in this note taking. Fash wondered what such a young man was doing on such an expensive flight. He was not in the mold of the precocious executives aboard. He wore a conservative enough blazer, but a soft roll open collar. Fash surrepticiously noted the oversized TV producer-type wrist watch with practical stop watch and display of three timebelts.

The young man's coffee was delivered by the steward who refilled Fash's cup, creating just enough mutual interruption to excuse an introduction even on the Concorde. "You're Mr. Fash of the *Miami Herald*, aren't you?"

To Fash's unconcealed surprise the stranger explained, "Your photo on the business page." He offered a hand, "Red Graves."

Fash asked if he was from Florida.

"No. New York. In and out of TV production." He was one of the new breed of independents who found stories for TV network news. Worked on a fee basis. "I line up the stories for network prima donnas. This time CBS. They're in the back getting their beauty sleep.

"I'm sure you despise us TV types ... because we cause the national leadership to divert their main attention away from the basic issues to ... how will it play on the tube?"

"I did; but I changed."

"Why?"

"Unintentionally ... you guys are creating an unofficial daily referendum."

"Huh?"

"Even at your worst ... you force the leaders to be aware of the public. The public has a chance to respond quick."

"Even when we hoke up the news?"

Fash smiled. "They'll catch you at that someday."

Fash asked how Graves was familiar with *Miami Herald*.

"I'm not. Only the business section. We use it to find stories before they become stories. I figure since you're here, this one is a big one."

Unlike his boss, Fash was not cynical about TV news. He enjoyed it. Felt complimented. "Well, I don't know, Mr. Graves. This Forte mission may abort."

"Whether it does or does not, Mr. Fash, you wouldn't be covering an unofficial trip like this unless you believed there was something very heavy at stake. What is it?"

Fash studied the young stranger. "Just about everything, Mr. Graves. Everything."

1

VISCONTI

Sarnia Fuel Dock
Sarnia, Ontario
It's a long scramble from deck to pilothouse. For MacDougall, 30 years.

In open water, MacDougall ... and MacDougall alone ... was truly master of the 604-foot *Nelson Moran* and her cable-taut schedule. But now he and his vessel were prisoners of the unhurried refueling crew at Sarnia dock on the Great Lakes. Fuming on the dock side of his pilothouse, he looked up to the racing pilothouse clock and down to the molasses-paced refueling crew.

The only reason the 60-year-old *Nelson Moran* was not laid up, scrapped or converted to grain storage like all other small Morrell class mid-size iron ore carriers killed by foreign imports in the 1990's was Captain Robin MacDougall. A short wiry enduring type like his boat, he pushed her for four extra season turnarounds between Duluth and Toledo. With cheating some admiralty law, that piled up 50,000 extra tons which the office could not ignore. She was small enough to get up into the small river mills that the new thousand-foot monsters couldn't touch. He always had her hatches uncovered before she came under the loading chutes at Duluth. And after unloading at Detroit or Toledo, even before the discharge boom was secured, he was casting off. He raced other vessels for position at the Soo and the fuel docks, making enemies but making schedule. **His** schedule.

What drove him was the sickening sight, every time he passed Detroit docks, of mountains of Japanese steel coils. That could beach his boat.

Now at the Sarnia dock, even before the men finished

1

securing the bunkers, he ordered the bowline off.

The first mate objected, "Cap'n, the third engineer is still ashore for that spare gauge."

"We'll run on the standby. He can catch us by bus in the Detroit River. Cast off now ... or we'll all be ashore for good. The country's awash in Jap steel."

Seville, Ohio

At the small Dart Industries plant producing acrylic plastic skydomes, Edith White looked out the second-floor office window at quitting time watching her brother come on duty on his bicycle, plant night watchman and gardener. On the north side of 40 with a May Queen face on a bulky body, she was the stay-at-home daughter, inheriting the care of her parents and her slow brother, Ned. When she landed him this job at Dart, her life blossomed. But for how long?

She had just seen the skydomes on the construction site for the new high school gym. Not Dart domes. Made in Germany. She scolded Bob Morton, the builder. He turned up his palms, "Edie, I never would have bought foreign. But your school board required I get three bids. Those domes are half the price of Dart's. I don't see how you'll stay in business."

Edith could always get another job in another town, but not if locked to Ned. How could somebody in Germany reach out and wreck the only factory in Seville, Ohio?

Massillon, Ohio

Gian M. Visconti, head roller, Specialty Steel Company's Number 3 Mill, stowed his safety gloves and goggles in the company locker, banged it shut, and punched out at 3:30. In his card slot was a green card: "Number 3 mill will be down 2 weeks. Report back Wednesday after Labor Day."

Visconti the elder had seen the stack of Korean slabs building up in the yard. They worried him until he and Jim Peco decided they were only special alloys for one special order.

Two weeks off could be good. He could better enjoy the family reunion over Labor Day. If he had to lose two weeks pay — hell — the company had been good to him. Twenty years with a lot of overtime had educated three boys and a girl. And what kids! Margaretta had a big job now with the company front office. And Gian A. Visconti, the younger ... he was something else. A star. Ever since high school football. But dammit, he was the one kid that never came home.

Chicago
United Machinists Union Headquarters
John Visconti, the younger, did many things very well. One that he did especially well was concentrate ... even in a crowd. His associates joked about it, not affectionately. When they would see him chew the inside of his cheek and drift into that thousand-mile gaze, one would elbow another and point.

One thing he did not do well was sustain interest in any action which was not his job. So when the executive committee meeting, Chicago Region, United Machinists Union, moved on to subjects which others should handle, Visconti pulled out of his folder and concentrated on two conflicting newsclips which gave him a hard problem:

(*Iron & Steel News*)

SEN. JUSTIN FORTE MOBILIZES
SENATE OPPOSITION TO SEC. 19
OF S.B.115 LIMITING
IMPORT OF METAL CASTINGS

St. Louis Aug 10 — The Senate's stalwart anti-protection leader today declared war on protection for U.S. foundry industry. Foreign castings come in at near net shape, requiring minimal machining which is devastating the ranks of the United Machinists Union, already at low ...

3

Despite his youth Visconti had been assigned by United Machinists to confront and turn around formidable Senator Forte on that part of Senate Bill 115. Visconti had the knowledge, the poised good looks, and especially the nerve for the job. There was something else about him, too, a kind of threat, even as a stationary presence. It followed him all the way from Massillon football, where he was loved during the games but not afterwards.

He knew he needed extra time to prepare for this Forte confrontation. However, the *other* newsclipping, even more urgent, would rob him of that time. It presented a personal opportunity to unload ten years of guilt, a chance finally to repay his family.

His great gift to them would not be appreciated at first; but later. He could wait some more. For the kind of deception he must now attempt, the occasion cited in the clipping was just what he needed. This would be his worst yet conflict-of-interest mission.

He restudied the *Canton Repository* clipping his sister had sent with a note: "Gian, your family P.R. is worse than ever, but if you could come home for this event, it would be a chance for Mother and Dad to show you off. They've never had that chance since you became such a big shot. And they've earned it. The family is assembling."

(*Canton Repository*)

LABOR DAY HOMECOMING.
MASSILLONEXPECTS RETURN OF
MANY DISTINGUISHED ALUMNI

Massillon Aug 15 — Features of the huge Massillon homecoming on Labor Day, besides the exhibition game between Massillon and Canton McKinley, will be several dinners, including one working dinner for leadership of several unions to consider three plans for revival of the city's metalworking economy which is flattened by import competition to the degree that ...

Visconti could make it to Massillon and still get to St. Louis the following Wednesday for his showdown with Senator Justin A. Forte. He would have to do his S.B. 115 preparation in flight. But that would be easy compared to preparing to meet his father, Gian M. Visconti, senior roller, Specialty Steel Company.

He scrawled a note to his sister: "Margaretta: will be there August 29." He added the address and slid it down the table to Janet Hoff who nodded and stepped out of the conference room promptly.

He was just leaving the office building when he was stopped by Ed Fisher, region president.

"Miss Hoff told me about your trip to Massillon. John, you've got to postpone that to get ready for Senator Forte. We've got everything riding on this."

Visconti had been selected to lobby because Forte, leader of the anti-protectionist corps in the Senate, was known for his cerebral approach to international trade. He had studied it from Marco Polo forward.

Visconti was nearly his match. The sign on his door at United Machinists, Chicago, said *Public Affairs*. That was to umbrella anything they wanted him to do. At 33 he was already tagged for high union office. Not because they liked him; they needed him. He knew that.

"Ed, the trip home is something I've got to do. You want somebody else to handle Senator Forte?"

"John, we have big plans for you."

"So do I."

"The reason we've handed you the big assignments ..."

"... is because I deliver."

Visconti did not fit comfortably as protege under the wings of even the new 1990's type labor executives. There were none of the old 1980's mission type labor men left at regional headquarters. Few even in the plants.

At headquarters the new leadership was realistic, educated in economics, unemotional ... efficient. Labor was now not a *cause*. It was an agentry business like real estate, advertising, stock brokering.

Visconti was the 1990's archetype. Educated in economics, business, and some law, he was never off balance in his

5

world. Assigned to call on political leaders early, offering or withholding union support, he was already armed with the knowledge that the mightiest put on their pants one leg at a time. However, he recognized that Senator Justin Forte might be different.

Visconti's youth was seldom noted; his knowing ice-blue gaze equalized negotiations. Although the high boned face was finely sculpted, it was flush at the ears with a muscular neck. He had one advantage over other staffers: he had worked summers in a rolling mill where the elder Visconti worked. He knew the heat, the noise, the conspiratorial camaraderie, the truculent emotional wall, thicker than the partition between the plant and the office.

But nothing prepared him for the upcoming meeting with his father, Gian M. Visconti.

Margaretta met him at the Akron-Canton Airport.

Neither the initial greeting nor Margaretta's banter could bridge the long separation nor sustain for the drive to Massillon. He quickly realized she knew more about his career than he about hers. And he withheld the questions that would reveal how he had shut out everything in concentrating on his job.

She was very bright. "It's all right, Gian," she grinned. "We could read about your life. I'll tell you about mine later."

After silence for a half dozen miles, Margaretta asked without malice, "Gian, why did you come? It's not for this town homecoming."

"Why not?"

"Because you didn't come for your class reunion."

"I had charge of a union stewards seminar."

"You even missed the reunion of your state championship football team."

"They had me moving the headquarters to smaller space that weekend."

"Always the indispensable man."

"Ever occur to you I came for the *family* thing?"

"No."

6

"Why not?"

"You missed Christmases — weddings — christenings. Why now?"

"Margaretta," he framed his reply carefully, "you remember I always wanted to do something really important for Mother and Dad? *Really* big?"

"Yuh. Your guilt gift. You always wanted to bring a new car with a big ribbon on it."

"But by the time I could do it ... they didn't need it. They outgrew stuff like that."

"I know."

"Well, I'm bringing something bigger."

"What could be bigger than the lump of cash you sent for Danny's special therapy school?"

"This is bigger ... but related."

"What is it?"

"I don't want you involved in it, Marge. They're going to hate it ... at first."

"Then why not try some simpler gifts ... like an occasional visit?"

"Look. It hasn't been all my fault. You remember how they drilled it into us — *achieve*. Right? Well, there's a price."

* * *

John Visconti had not remembered the home place being this small.

And he remembered his father larger. But the arm and shoulder muscles still strained the seams of the senior Gian Visconti's lumberjack shirt. The body was still well south of 60. It was the confident face that was lined for 75, a road map of decades in the rolling mill heat, the last ten as head roller in the slab mill. When he grinned the vertical wrinkles flared horizontal, pushing up to close his eyes into slits and deepen the crow's feet. These were from squinting at the speeding white hot blooms he maneuvered back and forth, closing the rolls some after each pass until he had a glowing orange slab, then cherry red, then pink, then gray.

His big knuckled claw landed on his son's back. "Gian! We're proud of ya!"

He flattened out the *Canton Repository* and pointed to the paragraph his wife had marked:

> Among the distinguished Massillon sons re-
> turning for Homecoming is Gian A. Visconti, son
> of Gian M. Visconti, head roller at Special
> Steels. Some will remember how young Vis-
> conti, wide receiver, would concentrate on the
> ball with such intensity that ...

"Gian, the steward brought me a message from Harri-gan, president of our local. Wants you at that working dinner to say a few words about the future of metalworking unions."

"Dad, I'm not prepared on this region."

His mother had been standing in the rec room doorway with a small tray, openly enjoying the sight of him. She beamed, "Hey. From you he wants a *national* picture! Not region!"

"I don't want to ad-lib some unprepared ..."

"Hey! He invited your old man to go along with you! Y'*gotta* go!"

"But I read that it's a *working* meeting."

His father said, "Sure. Tell us what the metalworking union leadership is doing for us to shut out the foreign stuff ... like your upcoming meet with Senator Forte. Ten min-utes is all."

Two days passed while John looked for an occasion when the right members of the family were together for his announcement. He rose at 5:30 mornings to prepare for his Senator Forte meeting. Meanwhile he learned more about his brothers.

Frank had worked his way up off the foundry casting floor into the office. Doug was production manager, ham-mer division, of a forging company. Mostly crankshaft for diesels.

Finally the right combination came up. His father and two brothers were down on their knees on the rec room floor assembling some parts. John walked in and watched. Gian, the senior, cocked his head so his cigar smoke missed his eye while his arthritic claws aligned the holes in two angle irons. "Frank, shove that bolt through. No; the washer first. And you a metals man!" To John he explained, "It's a special combination chair and bed for Danny, with wheels. Frank designed it. Danny's good arm can turn this crank to move it. We hope he can steer it with his good leg. We're gonna beat that spina bifida disease."

The boy was now in the hospital again.

John knelt to grab the two angle irons forming the other side. "No, Gian. Go do your work on the Forte thing so you'll be free to go after supper up to the square for the homecoming stuff."

"Dad ... I didn't come for the homecoming." The purposefulness of his statement stopped the construction project. The brothers and Gian, senior, rose.

"I came home to see you and Frank and Doug on something that ... to say it ... I have to be looking you in the eye."

Gian, the senior, broke out a wide grin. "It's going to be cosmic, gentlemen! We'd better get cigars." He passed out his specials and indicated chairs, "Pro-ceed, Sir John!"

"Dad ... Frank ... Doug ... do you think I'm in the best position in this room to know what's going to happen to the metals companies? Or not?"

Gian, the senior, queried Frank and Doug with a glance, then turned his cigar hand palm up, "H-e-y! No contest! With that education we bought you at Wharton school for super bookkeepers, you oughta know the big picture best. Frank and Doug wear suits to work now, but just barely; and I'm still rank and file." He winked at his other sons.

"Then let me pay back for that tuition money; I know I got the lion's share. I'm speaking from what I *know* is going to happen. Not what I *think*. What I *know*." He looked down at his shoes. "Dad, I want you to get out of the mill. Frank I'm telling you to get out of the foundry. Doug ... I want you to get out of forging. They're going down. And what remains viable is going to move to new geography and new technology."

He did not look up. He waited.

Margaretta stepped into the room with a tray, saw the silence and withdrew.

The mechanicals of the house were suddenly audible, the air conditioner, the refrigerator, the traffic outside, the flag cable slapping the flagpole in the wind.

Suddenly a great roar of laughter burst from the senior. "Hey Gian! A great gag! I've got to pull that one on Harrigan!"

Without looking up John said, "No joke, Dad. This is the one big thing I can do for my family."

The grin lines in the senior's face sagged vertical. He leaned forward, "What did you say?"

"I know you heard."

"This *is* a joke, Gian."

John did not answer.

"Very poor, Gian. Very, very poor joke."

Frank cautioned, "Dad, when did John ever make jokes?"

"I do not believe I am hearing this." The elder was on his feet, pacing. "I do not believe you come home to tell your brothers and your father to get out of the jobs that have provided for us." His arm wave referenced the whole house. "Take this home place ... a new bath and closed-in porch. A 1990 Buick and a '91 Olds in the garage? And your sister's fancy little ... whatever brand that is? Doug ... he's got a boat. Your sister works in the mill office. A big promotion. What's so bad with metalworking? Those checks I sent to help you through Wharton ... did you think they were from an 1880's mill hand? With only normal overtime I brought home 50G's some years."

"That's part of the problem, Dad."

"Oh-h-h! I wasn't worth it? I was overpaid?"

"What I'm saying ... the metalworking jobs will **not be there**. Your jobs. We simply are not competing with foreign. And metalworking is going to go down now very, very fast. Hammer forging will die. Foundries ... the same. I want you to get out and get new jobs before the crowds."

"Gian! We got you so educated you got dumb. You don't understand about steel."

John Visconti knew what lecture was coming. He would not interrupt. Despite watching the disastrous decline of

10

the steel industry, the older steel men all believed as Gian Visconti, the senior:Steel is the backbone of the economy. The companies are now stripped down to fighting weight and on the way up. There is no way the United States is going to let the metalworking industry go to foreign ... and leave us helpless in case of war. The industry is going to be protected by tough import restrictions. The union leadership is working to that end. "That's what we pay you guys for! So of all the people in the world who should believe that ... and work for that ... it is you young punks at the big desks in the union offices. I can't believe you are spreading this poison!"

Young Visconti looked into the wet eyes of the senior who dropped into his chair, breathing hard. "I'm not spreading it. This is the only time I have ever told *any*one. And the last. It cost me to tell you this. I made the trip just to tell my family, *only*. On my job, I talk your way. It's my mission with Senator Forte."

The senior was on his feet again, pacing. "So this is your big gift to the family?"

John nodded.

"You don't think we can handle ourselves? We've got pension credits. We've got skills. Experience. Why suddenly do we need this big favor from our Wharton School executive type?"

"Only one reason."

"Explain to us please."

"Young Danny."

The room stilled. It was Frank's boy, possibly the brightest Visconti ever born, offset with a tangled body.

Frank finally asked, "You been doing some arithmetic, John? What do you come up with?"

"A million and a half."

"Dollars?"

John nodded.

"How do you figure?"

"Medical and therapists ... about 400 thousand. Special education ... 200,000. College ... six years at 25 thousand a year ... 150 thousand."

"That's not a million and a half."

"I know. But allow for inflation maybe 40-50 percent over his years."

"Forty! Who's gonna cause that?"

"Me, for one," he said with resignation.

"You?"

"I will be one of the union people lobbying through the protectionist legislation. If my record means anything, and the leverage I have behind me, I will succeed on my part. If my counterparts in textiles, wood products, food, and chemicals also succeed in shutting out imports, prices will go through the roof. We'll need a million and a half to get Danny through."

The senior cut in, "The metalworking business will get us the million and a half."

Long seconds of silent estrangement ticked by. John looked at his brothers. "You guys are letting me carry this load alone. Do you know I'm right, and don't want to face it? Or do you believe like Dad?"

There was no answer.

John did not look up. "Frank, tell Dad whether it's true or not that the U.S. Army is now importing castings for the tanks. And is GE importing castings for the tank engines?"

"True."

The elder Visconti betrayed some surprise.

John asked, "Frank, how long a backlog of orders at your foundry?"

"Week to week."

John asked, "Doug, what's the backlog at the forge?"

"There's work for the two automated electrohydraulic presses and for the ring rollers. But the hammers ... spotty."

"Next question," John said. "What is Margaretta's new promotion at Specialty Steels?"

Doug hesitated, "Something new in personnel."

"Frank, do you know Margaretta's new job?"

"Yuh."

"Say it, Frank?"

"Outplacement manager."

Gian, senior, sat up straight, "What's that mean?"

John nodded to Frank. Frank said, "It's a new position.

12

A new type of work."

"So? What *kind* of work?"

"Dad, I'm not sure," Frank answered. But John stared at him and he gave in. "Okay. The job is helping people find new jobs when they're ... let out."

The senior said, "Margaretta said it was the 'human resources' department."

John said, "Dad, I'm trying to get you and Frank and Doug to see the facts and make the change *now* .... before it's too late. Ahead of the crowd that will be looking for work."

Visconti, the elder, strode over to look down on Visconti, the younger. "You are being paid out of metalworking men's dues; and you don't believe the industry will survive. How do you live with yourself?"

"With great difficulty."

"I should think so."

Margaretta paused in the doorway. "Look, you big strategic types. Mom has looked forward to this. She is making a landmark dinner. Don't any of you cosmic debaters spoil this for her!"

The elder addressed John, "For Mother, you make this nice. But don't tear up what I built. I carried a big load bringing this family through this far. I still got a load to carry with Frank's boy. I don't need Frank and Doug quitting their jobs now. All they know is metal."

He walked to the phone and tapped in one digit. "Ed? This is Visconti. Say, y'know Harrigan wanted my boy, Gian, to give a talk at the seminar? I'm sorry to tell you, but he won't be able to do that. Conflicting commitments. Sorry."

John walked out into the backyard. He remembered when his father had brought home the small billet of steel with the hole drilled in it as a socket for the flagpole. He looked up now at the flag his father flew for Labor Day.

* * *

At the bus station lunch counter, John Visconti took up two places, one for his doughnut and coffee, the other for his briefing materials on Senator Forte. Suddenly there was a hand on his shoulder, Margaretta's. He stood up. "Look, Marge, the bus is no problem. Gets me into Akron. Cab to the airport."

"I know that, you dummy. Come on, I'm illegally parked."

They talked of many things, but when she let him out at the airport he held the car door open. "Marge, get out of the mill."

"Hey, it's no tragedy if I get fired. I can get a good job like that." She snapped her fingers.

"That's not what I mean."

"Then what? You think I won't recover?"

"Not from what I'm worried about."

"So how bad could it get?"

"You could wind up having to discharge Dad."

"Hah," she laughed. "He'll be the last man out."

He closed the car door softly.

2

FORTE

Even when he was unprepared Visconti was better prepared than most men heading into a showdown. He bought a first-class ticket only to better spread out his papers.

He organized a stack of telegrams, commitments from other metalworking unions authorizing him to offer Senator Forte conditional support ... or otherwise ... depending upon whether the senator would back off fighting the metals section of S.B. 115.

However Visconti's thus-far success had been in knowing his opponent. He rescanned a sheaf of clippings about the senator, then saved for careful restudy a *N.Y. Times* profile:

> He walks the senate corridors with a messy handful of papers plus a battered ancient briefcase, head down like some ivy league dean of history, followed by a handful of men straining to hear his mutterings. But he is Senator J.A. Forte, briefing the staff of a Commerce Subcommittee which he thus far rules by sheer knowledge. This reporter is in the straggling entourage. Forte mutters to the committee staff, "Now for Thursday's expert witnesses, I want real production floor castings buyers who *use* the castings in manufacture. Don't bring me purchasing agents. And for foundrymen, I want real production floor managers. Don't bring in here any association types. And no P.R. men recycled as public affairs. You got that?"
>
> As the entourage reached the committee room,

the staff filed in, but a handful of press interrupted the senator's progress. Tymer of New
Republic said, "Senator, with your Missouri
hurting from imports in shoes, beer, textiles and
automotive, aren't you the wrong one to lead the
Senate anti- protectionists?"

"Yes. Can you get somebody else to do it for
me?"

There were grins among the media. Tymer
pressed, "But unions have returned you to the
senate several times."

"True. But do I let them tax all the non-union
citizens an extra three thousand dollars a year
via higher prices protected by this bill?"

"But why pick on this foundry protection
section so extra hard? Citizens don't buy castings or forgings."

Tired, as if from saying it a hundred times,
Forte did not raise his voice or his eyes. "Because
a casting or a forging that needs machining is
the main frame of most everything that rolls,
floats or flies. If we have to pay top dollar for
those, nobody can build anything important in
this country competitively."

He moved toward the hearing room, fielding a
few more questions.

When he took his seat on the committee dais,
even though he studied some notes without
looking at the crowd, he became the focus of the
chamber. The man's formidable grasp of foreign
trade was known throughout the Congress.

One other characteristic commanded curiosity of the political and media world. It kept the
media in suspense ... when would it crack? It
gave senior professional politicians a study to
watch — would Forte's method of building a
power base be cheaper than the constant time-
consuming attention to large voter blocks? Young
political professionals privately debated, as if
discovering a new phenomenon — is Forte's

thing a viable career strategy?

They referred to Forte's towering integrity, a Pike's Peak rising in the flat District of Columbia.

It is well understood Forte is kept in office not by voter affection, but voter trust.

A handful of legends circulate. The most recent is his vote against the Mississippi River Improvement bill which would benefit his own Missouri. He calls it 'The bandit's relief bill.'

The Air Force dubbed him "Senator Separate Checks." In his capacity on the Armed Forces Committee, he had occasion to lunch with defense contractors. He always told the waitress, "Separate checks, please."

Visiting the AVCO wing assembly plant in Kentucky, the company sent a car for him at the airport. Upon arrival at the plant he presented the startled vice president with $30 and asked for a receipt.

"But, Senator, we pick up any plant visitor in a company car."

"I am not *any* visitor. I am the United States Government. We do not accept free rides from suppliers."

Visconti made notes on 3x5 cards which he shuffled and reshuffled to get a certain sequence.

He checked into the St. Louis Regent, ordered dinner in the room, and settled into a night and day of solid study.

By Wednesday morning few men outside the senator's staff knew more about Justin Forte than John A. Visconti. That included knowing this would be the encounter of his career. A man who won't accept even a camouflaged compromise is trouble.

He walked slowly to the senator's office, reviewing his strategy. It was a long-long shot. It required seeing the senator alone. That would be a problem.

It was a large suite of offices, extra heavily staffed because, as leader of the anti-protectionist free-trader corps, Forte needed a tremendous amount of data on every industry. He had a computer room accessing industry and university data banks, and he needed enough staff to receive lobbyists from industries and nations.

While being ushered in silence by two staff people down a corridor to a small conference room, even the worldly Visconti was reminded that however many powerful men one might encounter in life, a United States senator is one of the world's handful, one of a hundred elected from 260 million. Even if from a small state, his impact is enormous.

Visconti noticed the senior staff man, DeLancy, studying him, puzzled that he had no briefcase, no display material. He asked, "Are there others joining you, Mr. Visconti?"

"No."

Besides that, Visconti knew that any young labor man in a high position attracted curiosity today.

When Visconti was deposited in the conference room, awaiting the senator, the staffers also took seats, confirming that Visconti would have trouble getting to talk to the senator alone.

When the staff men suddenly put their yellow pads on the table, Visconti sensed they knew the senator was approaching.

He trudged into the room, head down, studying the top sheet of a handful of papers. His other hand held a styrofoam coffee cup. He put the coffee down at the head of the table, then walked to the other end, extending a hand.

"Mr. Visconti."

"Senator."

The senator trudged back to the head chair, sat with elbows on the table, a fist in a palm, his shotgun eyes getting the drop on his visitor. "Mr. Visconti, I know you want to make the most of the 15 minutes you have with us. So I will tell you what you do not need to use your time to establish. We..." his hand encompassed his staff... "already *know* your union's position on S.B. 115. We *know* how many registered machinist union voters you can influence in my state ... either for or against me. We *know* you can put together a pretty strong coalition of *other* unions." Then he

smiled, "We *know* your personal stature in your union. So
..." the senator placed a pocket watch on the table ... "does
that save you five minutes for better use?"

Visconti grinned back, "Yes, sir. And I thank you."

"So shoot."

"But Senator, with due respect to your staff, I need to see
you alone."

The senator's light went out, "My staff is me. You don't
think I can process all this information alone."

"Senator, you notice I bring no briefcase, no notebooks
full of data, no flip charts? No helpers."

Forte slapped the table and laughed. "Thank God! But
what nerve you have, coming practically naked."

"I do have nerve, Senator. And I come without paraphernalia or colleagues because it's well known to nearly everyone that your staff would have dug out the data and
anticipated my whole presentation ... if it were conven-
tional. I would not have come if only to state what you
expect."

"How come it requires privacy?"

"I can't afford to have anyone else hear because it is not
exactly what I am sent to propose. If you don't like it, you
can throw me out. But if I can't tell you in private, I might
as well leave right now."

From under scraggled awning eyebrows Forte stared,
"You *are* different. I'll hear it." He nodded to the staffers
who left.

"Well?"

John Visconti took a deep breath. "Senator, we both
have an economics background. We both know your position against S.B. 115 is correct."

Forte straightened up, "You admit that?"

"Of course. We both know the Smoot-Hawley protection
bill plunged the world into the Depression of the '30s. We
both also know protectionism today, carried all the way, is
surefire depression, unemployment, and brutal inflation."

"Then you admit I've got to strip S.B. 115."

"No."

Despite twenty years in the Senate, Forte found his attention riveted by the cold rationale spelled out by the younger man. "You admit I'm right? And you still want S.B. 115 to pass with the metalworking section?"

"Senator, you are the backbone of anti-protectionism. Without you and your three-dozen free traders, all-out protectionism will bubble up through Congress like a volcano. To stop it, you have to get re-elected. You and Senators Boar, Butus, Bain, and a dozen other leadership types."

Visconti, without referring to a single note or card, spelled out Forte's Missouri constituency — 5000 brewery workers threatened by imported beer, 17,000 textile workers threatened by imports, 22,000 automotive component workers threatened by imported parts. He recited the thousands of threatened workers in the Missouri shoe industry, machine tools, wood products, and agriculture.

"Yes, yes, Visconti. And you're telling me you can lash together a coalition of these unions against me."

"No."

Visconti studied the wood grain in the tabletop until he was sure of the Senator's curiosity.

"You said *no*?"

Visconti nodded.

"Then why are you here?"

"Senator, compared to the protectionist pressure that's going to come, S.B. 115 is small potatoes."

"So?"

"*So ... let S.B. 115 go through so that you get re-elected and come back to fight the big ones.* If you let S.B. 115 pass, we will swing a large part of the metalworking industry behind you; and my own union will stay out of coalition with other industry unions against you."

"Visconti! How did you get up the nerve to propose this to me?"

"Because it is the only proposition you can accept, and your only chance to stay in the Senate to win your fight."

"Whether that's true or not, you like to scare people, right?"

Visconti shrugged.

"Visconti, how do you live with yourself?"

"My father asked me the same question."

The senator rose. "Mr. Visconti, it has been interesting; but you knew up front that I cannot accept your proposal."

"Not yet. But later."

Visconti now rose, pulled a previously written 3x5 card from his pocket and laid it on the table. "My home phone."

John Visconti sensed that the senator would like to shake hands, but couldn't. So he nodded respectfully and walked out.

As he was about leaving the front office the senator's receptionist handed him a message slip: *Call your sister. Urgent.* "Would you like to use a phone, Mr. Visconti?"

"Thanks. But I'll need to think first."

In the elevator Visconti thought about Margaretta. And the word "Urgent." In the lobby he found a quiet pay phone. He sat there thinking. Then he slid plastic into the slot and heard the phone blink-blink 36 digits, opening a connection he dreaded.

Her breathing preceded each word, "Gian. It ... already ..." There was a long pause. He felt her working for control. "Gian. It ... already ... happened. And they say it's my job to ... to notify ... notify ..." She struggled. "They're keeping the bar and rod mills. But closing down Dad's slab line. They're going to buy the alloy slabs from Dae Woo, Korea."

"All of them?"

"All. Gian, you've got to come home."

"Oh sure. To say 'I told you so?' Margaretta, there's nothing I can do now. That's why I came home *before* — to tell Dad to grab the separation pay buy-out, and get out."

"There must be something you know how to do. You're a professional. There are rules about job termination."

"No more, Margaretta. Besides, I'm not in that union."

"But you know your way around unions."

"Can Dad bump the roller on the rod line on seniority?"

"He wouldn't. It's our neighbor, Jim Peco."

"Damn!"

"What do I do, Gian?"

"You've got no choice. Quit, today."

"Quit?"

"Yes. You cannot live the rest of your life knowing you fired your own father."

"He'll ask why I quit at supper tonight."

"Tell him you got to thinking about what I said. So you quit."

"I don't know, Gian. I don't know. I wish you'd come."

"Margaretta, what good if I came? In fact, it will make it worse. Quit your job right now. Be out of the building by three o'clock."

* * *

On his telephone recorder in his apartment back in Chicago was a message from his assistant, Janet Hoff: "Hi. This is you know who. They've scheduled a meeting with you Monday a.m. to hear your results with Senator Forte. Fisher's office. They're on the edge of their seats. Apparently they got funny backdoor feedback from somebody. Something about Forte's staff walked out of your conference, mad. Be prepared. But then you always are. Till Monday then."

3

HAMILTON

Unsure whether they were a welcoming committee or an inquisition, the four men sat facing Visconti uneasily.

Fisher was saying, "John, you're not giving us much to go on. I can't tell if it was a plus or a minus or neutral."

"A success ... long term."

"How long?"

"Until the Jovanovich survey proves to Forte for sure how many of his brewery and textile and auto parts constituents are out of work from foreign imports. He has a strong, young opponent who can rally the Missouri unemployed and their families against him at the polls. The company managements will withhold fund support. He'll need ten million at minimum for his re-election campaign. And he doesn't even have time to campaign."

"You say your visit was a success. Did he commit to back off his opposition to S.B. 115?"

"Of course not."

"Not?"

"This is a rare bird."

"Why rare?"

"He won't buy votes by punishing the whole population with high prices to protect the jobs of a few. So he's got to be against S.B. 115."

"Then we don't see what you accomplished, John. And we hear you sent his staff out of the room, mad."

"Nobody but Forte tells Forte's staff to leave a meeting."

"So why did Forte send them out?"

"Because I said I had brought a proposal he might wish to first consider in private."

"And the proposal?"

Visconti summarized the proposal: That to complete his

free trade mission Forte had to get reelected. If he would back off on the metallurgical protection of S.B. 115, United Machinists would stay clear of any consortium of unions opposing his re-election, and would assist his election in the usual other ways, including substantial campaign funding."

"You committed *us* ...to *that*?"

"Yes."

"Who gave you that authority?"

"You. The authority goes with the assignment."

Fisher stared at Visconti, "We-ll!"

The others in the room held silent. Fisher finally broke it. "So the bottom line is — we got zero."

"No."

"So what did we get?"

"We got a thinking man to think about a way to survive to accomplish his mission. Re-election is no longer Forte's main mission. Free trade *is*. I told him that if he ever needed our deal ... to call."

"Don't hold your breath."

Fisher reached into his briefcase and pulled out the *Chicago Tribune* business section, folded it in half and slapped it down in front of Visconti:

FORTE TELLS COMMERCE COMMITTEE SB 115 IS ENTERING WEDGE TO KILL U.S. HEAVY MANUFACTURING

Washington — Senator Forte told a Commerce Subcommittee that "because machining is basic to all major metal manufacturing, SB 115, protecting high machining wages against imports, will raise all metal manufacturing costs."

He was "surprised that the machinists cannot understand that this bill could ultimately drive component machining offshore. In fact, already ..."

Fisher said, "Now do you really think Forte is going to

call us?"

"He'll call."

* * *

Hundo Sukuto was very personable, very informed, and very strategic, "Senator Forte, I'm aware we have besieged you with Japanese delegations, to the point where you had to stop receiving us; so I appreciate this audience."

"Mr. Sukuto, I'm seeing you because I am told you can get action. I'm for free trade — yes. But I cannot sustain resistance to protectionism here unless you quit blocking American products. After the election you probably won't have me here to push free trade unless you can dramatically open up your markets to us. I mean dramatic!"

"Senator, I have brought you a report of our free trade study commission, which ..."

Forte put up the flat of his hand. "No! No studies. No committees. No more joint conferences! Action only. Emphatic. Specific. And quick! Or I assure you the U.S. goes protectionist against Japan."

"That's against all you stand for, Senator."

"Protectionism is gross stupidity, Mr. Sukuto; but I will not sit here and condone disguised protectionism on *your* side."

"Disguised?" Sukuto looked wounded.

"You have a lot of phony rules that keep our goods out of Japan more effectively than a tariff."

"You ask *us* to be specific. Will *you* be specific?"

Forte did not go into the fact that Japan forbids import of U.S. rice which they could have for $180 a ton while they paid Japanese farmers $2,000 per ton. He did not point out that U.S. wheat, sold to Japan for $130 a ton, was resold to Japanese millers for $550 a ton.

Forte pressed a desk intercom, "Mrs. Rider, bring Mr. Sukuto that telegram from Missouri Sports Goods — about the 500 surfboards."

Sukuto read the telegram explaining that 500 American surfboards were impounded in Tokyo.

Forte leaned forward. "Why?"

Sukuto said, "I know about this case." He grinned. "I was afraid you'd mention it."

"So why?" Forte repeated.

"It is a matter of safety. Japanese people fall off of surfboards and get hurt."

Forte rose and moved quickly to a table where 16 legislative bills were laid out, each three to six inches thick. He grabbed one, opened it to the middle. "Now we're getting somewhere." He laid the open document in front of Sukuto and dashed a pencil line down one full page. "Americans fall off of Japanese three-wheel all-terrain vehicles and motorcycles and snowmobiles! You are looking at a proposed law saying all your terrain vehicles and snowmobiles will enter the U.S. through Bangor, Maine, where they will be inspected and tested for safety over a 30-day period. I may have to vote for that if you can't show me you can get action."

Sukuto grinned. "I would say you have got me over a surfboard, Senator. Will you continue to work with me if I can demonstrate some action on this?"

"Damn right. But ... quick!"

"Yes. Therefore, and only for that reason, may I use your phone?"

Forte handed it across the desk, "Dial nine."

After Sukuto stated his credit card number and reached his party, courtesy gave way to command. "Mr. Hatachu, I am in the presence of Senator Forte. When I hang up from this call I want to be able to tell him that the 500 surfboards now held up for safety reasons in Tokyo, shipped by Missouri Sports Goods, will be released by 11:45 tomorrow Eastern Standard Time; and that his secretary, Mrs. Rider, R-i-d-e-r, will receive a phone call from you ... saying that this has been accomplished. This is your top priority. No excuse will be acceptable."

There was a pause as Sukuto listened to the phone. Then he said, "No! The senator probably already knows that Coke has 90 percent of our soft drink market, and Max Factor sells more in Japan than in the U.S.; and he knows we're a huge market for Xerox and Kleenex. He wants surfboards cleared. Do it." He spoke a phrase in Japanese, then, "Thank you. Good-bye."

He rose, handed the phone back to Forte. "I'm aware there is no comparison, Senator, between the dollar weight of surfboards and motor vehicles. But I'm trying to start earning your respect for Japanese action in a small way at least."

Forte smiled and extended a hand. "Keep it up. Maybe we can work."

Sukuto did not point out that U.S. Commodore Perry opened up the Japanese market to U.S. goods in 1854 with seven threatening black ships. Now America was crying when Japan opened the U.S. market with quality and price competition.

* * *

Charlie Hanlon's retirement job at Hamilton Machine in Dayton, Ohio, was night security.

At 11:30 p.m. he walked to the pay phone by the time card board and dialed the union steward. "Fred, you said I should call no matter how late."

"Yuh-yuh, Charlie. What?"

"They just rolled in. Flatbeds with big machines, most with tarps."

"Those are the robots all right. How many trucks?"

"Three."

"How many machines?"

"Looks like nine."

"What else is going on?"

"Some management types are down here to receive them. Backing them into the new building and unhitching."

"Thanks, Charlie. You did just right."

At 11:45 the steward phoned Sam Hennessy, president of United Machinists' District Lodge 111, "Sam? They just rolled in the computerized machines at Hamilton Machine. It's time."

Hennessy hung up and immediately began dialing. His

27

wife came into the kitchen, "Sam, our guests."

"Just this one call. Very brief."

However, it required three tries. It was not until 12:45 that he reached Ed Fisher in Chicago. "Ed, the imported machine centers came tonight at Hamilton Machine."

"Oh."

"Now Ed, you said we would get help from national headquarters if they brought in these machine centers."

"True."

"It's got to be *effective* help right now if I'm going to be able to swing Local 111 votes for your re-election."

"It will be effective."

"Who you sending?"

"Parsons has been studying your Hamilton Machine battle for months, by assignment."

"I don't want Parsons."

"Parsons has detailed knowledge about every step in this hassle."

"He has the knowledge, but not the guts. I want Visconti."

"You don't want Visconti."

"Why don't I?"

"Visconti can make you more trouble than you've already got. And you can't handle him."

"I don't want to *handle* him. I want *him* to *handle* the Hamilton problem."

"Visconti seems to be drifting away from our customary solutions."

"That's why I need him. Look, Ed, you don't seem to get the picture about Frank Hamilton. This is a guy who will lay everything on the line. This is showdown time. I mean for the industry. And for *you*, Ed. Don't send me your usual staff-type negotiator."

Fisher dialed Visconti periodically. At 2:30 a.m. he reached him. "John, where were you all night?"

"Aren't bachelors allowed to be out until two thirty?"

"Sorry. Dumb question. I'm calling late because I need to see you in the office early tomorrow morning."

"You forget I'm going to Massillon. My sister..."

"That's why I called. You've got to postpone it, John. The

Hamilton Machine case. The computerized machine centers came into Hamilton tonight. We've got to move."

"That's Parson's assignment."

"I have to give it to you."

"Ed, this isn't right."

"Maybe not, but, John, this is make-or-break time between Hamilton Machine and Local 111."

"It's a critical time also between my family and me, Ed. My father got let out. They want me in Massillon."

"If you choose Massillon, John, then I guess it's make-or-break between you and me as well." He hung up.

Visconti dialed Margaretta.

* * *

Under the world-wary countenance you could still make out on the face of Frank Hamilton vestigial traces of the enthusiastic young engineer who had started a machine shop in an abandoned gas station and built it into a high-reputation job shop with 68 employees. The quality of the machining work was so good, much of their work was machining prototypes for new products. He said to Visconti, "What's your national union headquarters doing — getting into a little local squabble like this?"

"Our local asked for help."

"Sure. But do you go running to help every local that's in a fight with a small shop like this?"

"No. Just this one."

"Why?"

"Because of your reputation."

"What? As a sweat shop?"

"No. As possibly the finest job shop in the country; and one of the few such small shops that is really reaching for robotization."

Visconti explained that United Machinists knew the backbone of American manufacturing is the hundred thousand small job shops that supply three quarters of all machined parts used in the big products. Small business employs the majority of all skilled labor. "And yours is a pivotal shop. What happens here will affect all machinists ... and others."

"So because we're so good — you penalize us."

"Yup."

"Doesn't that strike you as outrageous?"

"Yup."

"Visconti, I'm so sick of this mess that before I'll put up with any more hassle out of this union against automating I'll shut the place down, sell the machinery, rent out the building, and go sail on my boat."

"No. You won't."

"Who says?"

"Because you are already fighting off a perfect chance to do just that right now."

"What are you talking about?"

"You don't think I came here without doing my homework."

"So?"

Visconti looked around at Hamilton's staff. "I'll explain if you insist, but I think you'd prefer if we talk alone ... unless your whole staff already knows."

"You damned ferret."

"True."

Hamilton turned to his staff. "Please excuse us."

The two men left the office. Hamilton pointed to the local union president. "Then he goes too."

"Fair enough." Visconti nodded. "You too, Sam."

Hennessy left.

Hamilton challenged, "So what am I fighting off?"

"Take-over by White Engines."

"So what's new? Somebody's always trying to take us over."

"True. But White won't quit."

Hamilton sagged. "How do you bastards find out?"

Visconti ignored the question.

Hamilton now leaned forward and pointed at Visconti. "Look. Three alternatives all with the same damn fool outcome. If I buy your local's deal, this plant will lose half its business to Mexican shops overnight. If I continue without the new machine centers, we'll lose half our business in a year on price. If I sell to White, your men have a worse employer to deal with. Why can't you boys understand those simple facts?"

"I do."

"So why are you here?"

"To show you how to fight off White Engines, continue robotization, and remain the leader."

"Huh? What kind of union guy are you?"

"You didn't take the time to do your homework on me, as I did on you. But I can show you what to do."

Hamilton slouched back, studying Visconti.

Visconti outlined a plan for Hamilton to make such a high-dollar contractual commitment to the union that White Engines would back off. The dollar commitment would be an intensive, sophisticated, expensive education program for training the machinists to manage new machining centers and the robotry. The education program would cost double digit millions to cover staffing and machine time.

"Why would that stop White? They could swallow such costs better than I can."

"Even if they could afford the dollars they can't afford it."

"Why not?"

"They would then get pressure to install the same education in all their plants. United Machinists will see that they know that."

Hamilton finally smiled. "You know, Visconti, you're a really creative troublemaker." He sobered, "But even with that kind of education, we have many men who cannot be retrained for this."

"True. If they don't pass, you can let them go. And most will pass because you don't have a bunch of metal benders and grinders."

"True. But even of those who do pass, we won't need them all."

"Right."

"You know that?"

"Of course. You will establish a placement service and place all the graduates."

"How am I supposed to set up an in-house employment

agency?"

"With the union's help. It's an appropriate role for us."

"What's the trick?"

"No trick. If you go out of business to foreign competition, we lose all the jobs. If White buys you, we probably have to go out on strike."

"You're not demanding raises?"

"The education is the raise. The biggest you ever gave."

"Will your national back you on this?"

"I am national, remember?"

There was a lot more to be argued. But in four days, Visconti was on the road to Massillon, then back to Chicago.

(*Machining Digest*)

HAMILTON MACHINE STARTLES MACHINING INDUSTRY WITH UNPRECEDENTED UNION DEAL

White Engines Expected To Back Off Hostile Acquisition

In a surprise move Hamilton Machine quickly settled its nine-month hassle with United Machinists and created a new type of labor agreement.

Surprisingly the national headquarters of United Machinists agreed to an unheard of trade-off.

White Engines, hearing the details of the settlement, immediately cooled efforts to acquire Hamilton Machine.

The agreement which thwarted White Engines was ...

* * *

The strong applause which followed Visconti to the podium to address the assembled presidents of all the United Machinists' locals at the Leadership Meeting was not from affection, but anticipation. He was usually at the tail end of the program and gave it a lift because he was always well prepared, crisp, to the point, and brief. This meeting had droned on about the need to pressure the political base for protection against imports. There had been long profiles of the particular legislators in each region who should be pressured. The national president had reported that the meeting of G.A.T.T. (General Agreement On Trade and Tariffs) assembled in Geneva had folded on free trade and ended in a protectionist mood. He optimistically described the 34 senators most aggressively demanding strong protectionist stands and he concluded, "There is a protectionist landslide starting out there. And the free trade politicians are going to have to leap on our bandwagon or be buried in landslide elections. Let's get out there and help bury them!"

Applause was perfunctory because to the assembled leadership the oratory gave no help from slowing foundries and machine shops back in their home districts.

But cold-blooded young Visconti never talked rhetoric. He might have some solid strategies they could take back for their rank and file.

Up in the projection control booth the audio visual director, Irving Shultz, muttered to the projectionist, "Watch your script close. This guy is different. He doesn't ad-lib around, and he wants those charts on screen right on the cue. I mean *right* on."

On the podium was a thick loose-leaf notebook containing the speeches. Visconti opened it to his own and delivered the opening paragraphs which restated, as had all talks, the showdown challenge of imports. But he was more specific about numbers.

Then Irving Shultz from his high angle view saw Visconti close the big book. He hissed to the projectionist, "Hey. Stay alert. I think he's going to wing it."

Visconti was saying, "Gentlemen, we do have a showdown battle on our hands. But it is not the one we have been fighting. Our big battle ... is to undo our teaching of the last thirty years ... overnight. We have been teaching our members the wrong lessons, and for the last few months we have known it." He pointed to the audience, "You knew it. I knew it. We studiously avoided teaching our own members real world market economics ... so that they could protect themselves and make shrewd decisions. So that they would have seen that twenty-eight dollar an hour metalworking men here can't survive against equal quality seven-dollar-an-hour Japanese and four-dollar-an-hour Koreans."

In the projection booth Shultz stood up, "Holy Cow!"

Visconti said, "Oh, we taught, all right. We taught them the competition is management's problem, not ours. If we hold their feet to the fire, management will find a way. So keep the pressure on the bad guys.

"And all we really taught was the good guys vs. the bad guys. We taught it only half right. It's the bad guys vs. the bad guys. In the open market — sure, management will try to pay us as little as they can. And we'll charge them the most we can. Fine. It's a good system ... provided one side is not handicapped by its own leaders ... kept in the dark.

"When did we ever really brief our people on the competition, naming names and numbers and what U.S. customers foreigners shanghaied? When did we ever really brief them on the costs in our industry?"

In the control booth Irving Shultz said quietly, in amazement, "He is killing himself. Absolutely. He's shooting himself dead, right out in front of everybody."

The projectionist asked, "Why do you say that?"

"Are you *listening* to him? *Listen!*"

Visconti was saying, "So we need to change our basic function."

He then outlined the new union as an employment agency, with active service to members — get them jobs, then better jobs. To do that requires training the member for his field, and retraining if necessary. "That means we need schools. I mean *real* schools. It will cost money. But this is what we have got to do."

The house was as silent as a mothballed lathe. Visconti outlined a new type of union. The dues would leap. The members would be clients of the union and would own it, demanding of it educational facilities, the usual pension benefits, and stock in the companies where they worked in enough quantity to have a collective voice.

A central feature would be professional financial counselors to work *individually* with the member regarding personal finance and investments, arming the union member for shrewd handling of his career.

He pictured a new type of union in which the member is the client.

Visconti concluded, "Let's do it, do it right and do it now."

He began to leave the podium amidst thick silence and the outraged glares of Fisher, Parsons, and Halsey. As he passed their chairs, Fisher said, "It's been nice knowing you, Visconti."

Suddenly a belated, hesitant island of applause broke the silence from the very back of the hall. It gradually grew and rippled forward. Then it broke out in spontaneous support of Visconti's traitorous message.

Monday morning Visconti found a note on his desk: "Meeting. Fisher's office - 10:00 a.m."

When he entered, they were already assembled, Fisher, Halsey, and Parsons. There was no fourth chair. Fisher began without greeting, "John, the board met. You don't seem to be with us. You ad-lib new policies without even conferring. So turn your active projects over to Parsons. Clean out your desk by noon. Don't take anything from the files. I'm sorry, John, but you did it to yourself."

* * *

On the 11 p.m. news, Visconti heard a 40-second segment about Senator Forte's re-election trouble. When the weather and sports ended, Visconti's phone rang. "Mr. Visconti?"

"Yes."

"Justin Forte. I realize you and I have opposite missions. However, you correctly assessed the fact that mine will fail if I don't get re-elected. I am still vigorously opposed to S.B. 115, but I am experiencing severe re-

election problems in my St. Louis region. The big
brewery had to lay off two thousand more because of
beer imports."
"I just heard on TV."
"You once made a proposal ..."
"Senator, I..."
"... that your organization might be of important assis-
tance if I ..."
"Senator."
"... if I were to ..."
"Senator, I probably can't help now."
"What?"
"I've just been ... fired."

* * *

(Wall Street Journal)

Executive Changes

Chicago — John Visconti, highly effective officer
in United Machinists, is no longer with the
organization.

4

STRAUSS

(*Women's Wear Daily*)

S-MART FASHION CHIEF TO HOST
NOT-SO-FRIENDLY SUMMIT MEET
OF GARMENT MANUFACTURERS
Invitation Considered
Command Performance

It is believed that M.B. Strauss, Fashion
General Merchandise Manager for the now
dominant S-Mart chain, has summoned his
fashion suppliers to a top-level meeting. Legendary for his coercive buying techniques, rumor
has it that he has invited only the garment
manufacturer CEOs; and that he will offer a
proposition they 'can't refuse.'
He is holding the meeting not at S-Mart
headquarters in Chicago, but at a hotel. No
media has been invited.
Strauss' sometime vendetta against garment
makers is well ...

They were assembled nervously in a very small but
plush meeting room, seated theater style.
M.B. Strauss, a powerful presence in any group despite
his short stature, was groomed appropriately for the head
of S-Mart retail fashion marketing. He worked his way
from the back of the room forward with a very slight limp,
shaking hands with the garment manufacturers in the
aisles who half rose to shake his hand. He well understood
their gesture was a puzzled combination of sympathy for

his slight stoop from a fused spine to correct spinal arthritis, forcing his head to look up at them, and partly a worried respect for him as the third-largest chain buyer of garments for 2300 large S-Mart stores.

They wanted him to make his way forward. Even the younger garment executives knew the Strauss legend. Melvin Strauss began in the West schlepping a line of work pants and gloves among small towns in four states in a third-hand yellow-gullwinged Ford SunBird because it had a big trunk for his wheeled cases. On straight commission with a low end line and the towns so far apart and calling on the economy trade, he couldn't make the medical bills for his ailing wife. He could not push the towns closer together, but he felt he could double his sales if he could also in each town call on the better store, the one which did not carry work clothes.

He tried to persuade his manufacturer to sew a few superficial accent items on the work clothes so he could present them as dressy casuals to the snakeskin boot trade. They turned him down. He took his idea to a competitor. Reluctantly Gray Stag Work Pants made up a sample line. They put a red bandanna lining in the pockets and slash cut the pocket so the red lining winked as the pants walked. They put a leather beading down the side seam of the whipcord work pants and added a rope belt with a leather buckle. Now when Strauss drove into a town, he had two lines — economy and upscale.

His instinct was so right that Gray Stag could not make enough pants.

Strauss told them they were scratching the surface in the West. Would they send him to New York and let him open a tiny Gray Stag ("Drop the work pants name") showroom? They said, "No." But he went anyway. He couldn't afford a showroom. But he schlepped around to the big store buyers in the days when you lined up in the buyer's waiting room for a five-minute audience. And you'd better have your cases partly open when you crossed the threshold. The buyer continued his paperwork while you showed your line, looking up now and then, maybe nodding, maybe waving you to hurry it up, and if you were lucky with one item, he might growl, "How much a gross?" But usually he'd say, "Gray Stag has no name in N'Yawk. No shtus. Call me when you've got some brand recognition."

In three months of that Strauss ran out of money and retreated West to build some savings. But he had observed some things about New York retailing. In a year, he returned wiser. Avoiding the giant stores, he watched *Women's Wear Daily* for stores in trouble. He "walked" these stores. Then he went to a buyer, not to present a line of garments but an idea. "Take a corner of your men's department. Make it a casuals boutique. Put these casual pants and shirts in as the core line. Then surround it with casual shoes, hunting jackets, fishing boots, outdoor casuals. Put in some fishing gear. Call it 'Outdoorsman's Corner.' I'll put in the stock on thirty-day consignment. Let's see what happens."

Gray Stag could not keep up with the orders.

Strauss moved to a different manufacturer. Women's wear. Again — he did not sell garments, but merchandising ideas. "Older women don't like to buy from young women. Staff your senior line with older women. The reverse for young women customers."

Strauss was on a roll. He was called by other manufacturers, moving up with each change. Still never selling clothes, only merchandising. "In your dressing rooms, get rid of those wire hangers and put in a hand mirror so the woman can see the back, and put soft lighting, not those fluorescent tubes. And put in a velvet covered chair."

Gray Stag had a young new management. They called Strauss back as vice president, marketing.

It went like that for eight years. Then he got a call from the chairman of S-Mart. "Melvin, you ever been in the women's wear departments of our stores?"

"Of course, Mr. Blumenthal."

"Can we do better?"

"Of course."

"For you to tell us how — takes what?"

"Put Gray Stag line in all your stores."

"Your lines I don't want. I want you. Any chance?"

Strauss went with S-Mart. At a rate of 20 stores per

month he converted S-Mart's harshly lit, piperack clothing departments into softly lit, exciting wonderlands. A woman didn't go there "to pick up a blouse." She went for an adventure. In every S-Mart town Strauss revolutionized fashion retailing. Competing stores had to shift into high gear. Strauss began to mandate what merchandising aids suppliers must furnish with their lines. He was coercive on cooperative advertising. To get your line into S-Mart was a prize worth everything. "And it cost you just about that," complained Abrahms of Londonderry Rainwear.

Now the room in Chicago quieted as Strauss reached the front of the group.

He abjured the slightly raised stage and podium and microphone which he did not need. Expensive tailoring somewhat camouflaged his bent posture, but the forward-inclined handsome head still forced his eyes to look up at his audience.

His opening was urbanely friendly. Then suddenly the light went out of the face and the room, "I confess disappointment that in a few of you larger garment companies your CEO chose not to accept my invitation, but instead sent a representative. I don't blame you representatives for that; it was not your decision. However after you hear what I have to say, you may wish to step to a phone and relay my message to your presidents ... unless you can speak for them. Since I will ask for your response to what I will say here."

Strauss allowed a long pause, then "Gentlemen, you really stuck it to us retailers in the garment section of S.B. 115 which you lobbied into that bill, adding 40 percent to our costs on imported garments.

"All right. You achieved it. The bill will probably pass. You won. So that's behind us. I'll not go into what that will cost us retailers ... or the public. Vudeu? I've invited you here to tell you ... *what we are going to do about it.*"

Some manufacturers not in Strauss' immediate vision risked a quick questioning glance at each other. Although they were competitors, Strauss was making them allies.

"We are going to give **you a chance to work** with us to

offset the damage. If you do what we ask ... in twelve months ... we will continue to buy your garments. If you don't, we retailers will make other plans, which can include manufacturing for ourselves. I am speaking for my own company only, of course, but with our 2300 stores, I think you know S-Mart's influence in the fashion retail industry trade associations."

He did not need to mention his own presidency of Fashion Retailers Institute.

"Here is the deal. It is a way you can retain S-Mart's business." The rag trade is accustomed to extremely direct talk, shorn of niceties or vagaries even at board level. Strauss, during his career rise, shed some gross vocabulary but retained the clarity. "You gentlemen are supposed to be our friends. Your fathers understood that we were their meal ticket. But you forgot. Hence — gefutzevit."

Strauss recapped the fact that it takes American manufacturers 66 weeks to deliver garments to the retailer's shelves, including the time to make the fiber, then the fabric, then the apparel.

"That means you force us stores to order next year's seasonal garments before we even know what is selling well this year. So we naturally make huge mistakes in ordering. So if we have a loser — costly mark downs, high inventory costs.

"If we have a winner, we also lose. In a week we're out of the popular styles and sizes, and reordering from you is too slow. So in lost sales and inventory charges, your slowness costs us retailers, as a group, twenty-five billion a year. Farpotshket!"

"Forty-five weeks you boys can cut out of that pipeline and deliver to us in 20 weeks." He pointed out that the Koreans, Taiwanese, and Chinese can do it now; but S.B.115 would kill that.

"This would mean lower inventory costs for us, and we could predict more accurately what styles are moving before reordering. We could even place just half our seasonal order, observe how it sells, then place the other half ... smarter. Every day that passes before we must reorder, we get smarter for reordering.

"And you can get that delivery down to 20 weeks. You've got to invest in new equipment. You've got to robotize. Chrysler can do it. You can do it."

Judd Hobart, Sports Apparel, Inc., courageously interrupted, "Mr. Strauss, sir, a robot can pick up a stack of stiff steel sheets. But a stack of cloth swatches ... once you pick it up, how you going to lay them out flat again?"

Strauss held up the flat of a fat hand. "Don't insult me, please, Judd. Engineers we're not. But we both know Wingspread Corporation in New York put in CAD equipment to deliver sweaters in days instead of weeks."

Hobart protested, "Even if we could, our textile vendors have all recently put in big looms that need long production runs of the same fabric to pay out."

Strauss said, "Judd, we know it will take large investment. It gets down to — are you apparel people going to make that investment ... or we retailers?

"If you can't accommodate us on this, one of two changes will happen: Either you create your own retail outlets to sell your clothes or we create our own manufacturing. Since we already own your ultimate customer, the lady who walks into our stores, it is easier for us to get into manufacturing than for you to get into retailing.

"If we must come to it, we are not without plans."

He nodded to a smartly dressed advertising woman who undraped a panel displaying a large apparel label — "S-MART FASHIONS."

The young woman then removed the hyphen and slid the "S" close to the "M" so that the label read "SMART FASHIONS."

The room smoldered. Strauss let the audible murmur rise. Then he said, "Gentlemen, I consider that I have done you a favor. I thought it important enough to come in person. I'm sorry some of your senior people did not, for example Mr. Abrahms of Gray Stag.

"I have not come to debate, so I will leave you to discuss what I have said. I hope you will join me at six in the Windsor room for dinner. And I hope you will then have a response for me." He limped back through the silent garment manufacturers. No eyes met his.

* * *

(Women's Wear Daily)

STRAUSS ULTIMATUM JOLTS INDUSTRY.
GARMENT AND TEXTILE ASSOCIATION
EXECUTIVE COMMITTEE TO CAUCUS.

The GTA is corralling the association trustees to plan response to what they now consider an impossible challenge by the nation's third-largest fashion retailer.

Some trustees have said Strauss' demand would require a retooling investment which would break the domestic industry. The figures nearly approach start-up costs as ...

At GTA headquarters, twelve stunned trustees listened to the Arthur Anderson consultants whom they had engaged to estimate the costs of retooling just one hypothetical vendor label to cut delivery time to 20 weeks. The estimate outstripped their own ball park estimate.

Garment industry executives are different. While other industries listen quasi-reverently to their outside paid consultants, rag trade brass argue among themselves about the presentation concurrently with the presentation. It's a tough pitch. But the veteran vendors to the trade know their chattering listeners hear everything.

The Anderson spokesman concluded, "Questions?"

Judd Hobart said, "Yes. You explained you paid Battelle Research Institute to help with those probable costs. But since some of that machinery doesn't yet even exist, you bought science fiction?"

"No, sir. They already have a garment client for something very similar. They only had to extrapolate some."

In unison snapped two trustees, "Who's their client?"

"Protected information."

Chairman Abrahms pushed himself up out of his chair heavily, "It doesn't matter. The numbers we have just heard totally rule out the retooling." He waved off the

43

consultants. "Thank you, gentlemen. If you'll excuse us, we have matters to discuss. Send the bill."

Packing up their easels and charts, the accountants were totally ignored as the trustees swiveled their chairs toward Abrahms. "Is there anyone here who thinks that kind of retooling money remotely possible?"

They didn't even bother to answer.

"Is there anyone here who thinks the accounting consultants overestimated?"

No one spoke.

"Is there anyone here who thinks Strauss of S-Mart is bluffing?"

There was no answer.

"Then, gentlemen, I appoint Hobart, Levinson and Berkley as Task Force S ... for survival ... to reconvene with us here in 15 days and present us a plan to handle Strauss' threat. A plan we can present to the full membership. It may be as simple as telling Strauss we need three years instead of 12 months. And hope he retires. Or it may have to be something drastic."

Judd Hobart said, "Meanwhile, we've got to answer Strauss ... that we're working on it. You should carry the message, Mr. A, because of Strauss' former Gray Stag connection."

"No. Mel Strauss always felt he should have been given stock in Gray Stag. He's not friendly to us. You are our best delegate to Strauss, Judd."

"No-no. My company is too small to count."

Levinson agreed. He said the only delegation Strauss would listen to would be the presidents of the three largest garment manufacturers. It was agreed. And the plea would be for more time.

Abrahms said, "We will reconvene here on the 20th of the month ... to hear the task force's plan. That could be the most important plan this industry ever had ... or ..." Abrahms' commanding eyes scanned the board "... or, gentlemen ... it could be the last."

(*Women's Wear Daily*)

SPECIAL GTA TASK FORCE
TO MEET RE: STRAUSS CHALLENGE

By now it is known throughout the trade that S-Mart has given an or-else challenge to the garment industry to reduce delivery time to 20 weeks.

A special GTA task force has been assigned to design a response. *Women's Wear* hears that the costs of achieving 20-week delivery have staggered garment executives who consider it impossible.

What possible solution the task force might propose is inconceivable.

With the help of several assistants, Judd Hobart completed the task force presentation to the GTA trustees, "In a nutshell, gentlemen, we launch a sweeping grass fire *Buy American* campaign so intensive that the retailer cannot buck it without peril."

Garment executives in session brush aside rules of order, are volatile. The trustee's meeting exploded into a babble of objection.

"Been tried ten times!"

"Never works!"

"Didn't work for autos."

"The Garment Workers had that *Buy American* TV commercial for years. It bombed."

"Is that the big brainstorm you're bringing?"

Chairman Abrahms pushed himself up out of his chair and moved heavily to the podium. Hobart started to leave the dais, but Abrahms held his elbow. Whenever Abrahms merely stood up in front of the vociferous trustees, law and order returned. He ruled this obstreperous association by periodically threatening to quit. Members wanted to keep him in office because they trusted him. He would not let the large corporate members vote to fund projects of no use to the smalls, nor vice versa. He had something else ... a sense of the industry heritage.

He did not raise his voice. He asked, "Ted Bricker, what is your idea of a solution?"

Bricker answered, "We-ll, I wasn't involved in ..."

Abrahms asked, "Fred Jarvis? Your suggestion?"

Jarvis shrugged.

"Jed May?"

May turned up his palms.

"Anyone?"

Abrahms said quietly, "Then we will let Mr. Hobart outline the details on *how* his task force feels *this particular Buy American* campaign can succeed, even if others have failed. His plan is different. No canned TV commercials. No print advertising. No speeches. A true grassroots campaign. Give it your full attention."

He pushed the podium over in front of Hobart, then lowered himself into a chair facing the trustees. A granite mountain backdrop for Hobart.

* * *

Three miles outside the little town of Hanging Limb, Tennessee, Red Graves parked his sleek Firebird in a dirt road entry to an abandoned trousers factory. He changed from his suit to blue jeans, locked the car and walked downhill into the center of town. This was the tenth town he had studied for his employer, Action Promotions, which was doing a project for GTA, the Garment and Textile Industry Association. Already he felt this would turn out to be the right town.

The rambling two-story clapboard shirt factory was nearly all dark except for a hundred feet on the ground floor. That's how badly The Tennessee Shirt Company had lost out to Asia.

He entered Agnes' Hanging Limb Restaurant. It was midmorning, yet the place was still full of men idling over coffee. Prices were shockingly low. Graves wanted to surprise the work-worn owner-cook-waitress with a large breakfast tip, but he needed to avoid display.

Later he saw a group of men coming out of the post office, so he walked in there. He noticed the wire wastebasket nearly full of torn brown envelopes with windows in them. The whole population must be on unemployment.

It was in the one-story Mountain Department Store that he first found what he had been told was down here somewhere. Over the shoe counter hung a ten-foot slightly sagging canvas banner. Lovingly sewn onto it in red, white, and blue strips were the words — "American Goods."

Smaller signs with the same legend were on stakes over the other merchandise sections. In the lower right-hand corner of each, Graves saw a small credit line: "Courtesy Hanging Limb Buy American Committee."

Over in the hardware store the loungers studied Graves as he entered. He fingered some pipe fittings of different sizes in a row of bins, a position which let him scan the store. They had the signs, too.

The store owner at the same time was scanning Graves, "Hep you, suh?"

"I'll have to measure my pipe and come back," Red said.

He walked back uphill to his Firebird and drove to Memphis. He checked into the Hotel Tennessee, arranged long-term storage for his car, then strolled used-car row. Spotting a row of ancient pickup trucks under a sagging string of lights, he crossed to the opposite side of the street to a filling station and repair garage.

He watched for a while until he identified the young overworked owner-manager-mechanic. "Could I pay you $20 to step across the street and tell me which of those old pickup trucks is in best shape — engine, transmission, brakes — never mind appearance?"

The young manager redistributed the grease on his hands with a black rag. "I don't need to go across, and you don't need to pay me. That Chivvy, third from the left. Looks worst, but its the best. Young Larkin kid had to give it up after he put a lot of love into it. Re-did the whole engine and transmission ... used my tools in exchange for working the pumps."

"Thanks. That's worth the twenty."

"No. Just get your gas here."

"I won't be in the neighborhood. Take ten at least."

"No. Now when you make your deal across the street, make sure you get both spare tires. Larkin had two."

Across the street Graves priced the truck.

"How's $850, suh?"

"Seven-fifty ... if I get both spares."

The salesman looked startled. But he said, "I'll get the otha. How will ya be payin' for this, suh?"

"Cash. Providing you get all the paperwork and title and tags by 9:30 tomorrow morning when I pick it up. Otherwise you still own it."

"Deal."

That night Red got what he knew would be his last good hotel dinner and bath and night's sleep for a long time.

In the morning he took delivery on the pickup, gassed up across the street, and headed back to Hanging Limb.

* * *

In Hanging Limb, Graves slept the first night in the truck. But at 5:30 a.m. he drove to Agnes' Hanging Limb Restaurant. Agnes arrived on foot at six to open up.

Then she carried in the eggs a farmer had left. She turned on lights and Graves could see her rushing around, getting burners lit and sugar shakers filled. When he saw her getting ready to scrub the floor, he picked up the bundle of newspapers and brought them in.

She said, "We're not open yet."

"I know it. I got the time. You got work to do. Give me the mop."

Suspiciously she released the mop. But watching the energy with which Graves went to work on the floor, she put on her apron and went to mixing batter.

When the floor was mopped, Graves took the chairs off the tables and set them upright. She handed him a tray of silverware, and nodded with a tired smile.

Finally she sat him at the counter with a mug and filled it with coffee, "I never been ready this much ahead before. I thank ye."

She poured herself one. He asked about the restaurant. "I hate it. I was collars and cuffs at the shirt works. I loved the work, bein' with people all day. They said I was good. Sewed twenny, twenny-five an hour. Survived three big layoffs. Then one day they said we lost the S-Mart work-shirt orders. S-Mart went Korean and Taiwan. What's Taiwan got to do with Tennessee?

"Anyway, I got let out. I went on the gover'mint draw, but I got my father to look after. He has the black lung, but not certified. So I had to get more money. All I knew besides collars and cuffs was cookin'.

"But this is the first time I had the place ready to open, with a chance for a quiet cup of coffee for myself. (I have to get my dad up and dressed and fed first.) So for that I'm gonna make your breakfast."

"I want more than that, Miss Agnes."

Her smile erased. "What?"

"I'll get it ready to open every morning and wash all the dishes and wash those windows, for board and a place to sleep in the back."

She thought about it solemnly. Then she looked him in the eye, "How do you like your eggs?"

In 30 days Red Graves and his beat-up truck had made friends in six towns around Hanging Limb, and had been adopted by the Hanging Limb *Buy American* Committee. He explained his presence by saying that he was unemployed and would have to leave soon to find work.

That left him time to nurture the *Buy American* Committee with ideas which they liked. He did nothing so overt as making a campaign plans book. Just casually mentioned a steady parade of ideas, spontaneously. "Hey, what if we put on a *Buy American* Parade in four-five towns around here?"

Nobody really added up the escalating list of Red Graves' suggestions:

- lapel buttons, bumper stickers
- get merchants to label "foreign goods"
- spread the committee to six towns
- get the *Mountain Herald* to do a special *Buy American* edition

- *Buy American* sales discount sale days
- store front signs: American Goods Sold Here

Finally, without saying good-bye, Red Graves drove out of Hanging Limb to Memphis and into the service station opposite used-car row. He coaxed the young manager out from under a panel truck, handed him the keys and the title to the Chevy pickup and grinned, "Call that Larkin boy who put all that work into this truck and tell him it's his lucky day. For twenty dollars, he can have his truck back. And you keep the twenty."

The mechanic said, "Are you jokin' me, Mister?"

"Nope. Here's the registration and signed title. And both spares are in the truck."

"Gee! Will he ever be ... hey ... can I do somethin' for you?"

"Yeah. Drive me to the hotel to pick up my own car I left in storage."

In New York, Graves talked to his former colleague, the producer of the "American Scene" network TV show. "Here's the pitch, Irving. Next Thursday the mayor of Hanging Limb is scheduled to take delivery on a small, but brand-new, Hitachi fire truck built in Japan. They bought it because it was the only one the town could afford. But because of the *Buy American* campaign I described to you, they wrote and phoned the supplier, canceling the order. The vendor refuses to cancel the order or return the down payment.

"They are going to make delivery next Thursday. The mayor, backed up by a committee of citizens, is going to refuse delivery."

"Well, what's going to happen then? Will they leave it or not?"

"Who knows? But either way it's got to be fantastic TV. Then surround it with shots of the grassroots *Buy American* campaign spreading in six towns around there, and you've got a fantastic and significant 20-minute segment. Stick that hairstyled, trench-coated pretty boy of yours down there interviewing the mountain people, and their comments will make him look almost as clever as he thinks he is. Send a couple of your pretty twinkies on remote into the surrounding villages. You'll have a guaranteed winner. And when you get your Emmy, you don't even have to credit me ... because it's not the best thing I ever did in my life."

"Aren't you coming with us?"

"Nope."

"Well, Red, I think you put us onto a good one."

"Just remember that when I bring you my next one."

On Thursday morning a small sparkling red fire engine drove up to the town hall in Hanging Limb, Tennessee, towing a return vehicle. The driver stepped out and was startled to find himself facing the mayor and a delegation of citizens and two CBS mobile units with TV technicians scurrying around with cables, cameras, and lights.

The segment CBS aired, thanks to the judgment and skill of the producer and the natural dialect and appeal of the Hanging Limb people, drew a tidal wave reaction across the country. ABC's director of documentaries got a call from the vice president of programming. "What are you doing about getting us in on this *Buy American* thing? It's hot."

ABC went into the Hanging Limb district of Tennessee looking for new angles, interviewing laid-off women from the shirt factories. They also interviewed the part-time mayor who made a sincere and eloquent statement, "I think if every town and county government, states too, did like our town ... and insisted on buying American goods with American tax-payers' money, we'd be halfway to lickin' this import shoot-out. We got an ordinance now ... all town purchases got to be American made."

The governor of Tennessee ordered all state purchases be U.S. built.

Across the nation, councilmen and state legislators raced each other to prepare and present legislation mandating that government purchases be American made —

trucks, graders, snowplows, landfill dozers, water and sewer pipe, meters, typewriters, computers, sign post angle iron, school construction materials, calculators, and busses.

American Legion posts picked up on the television shows and started *Buy American* campaigns in many midsize cities.

The periodicals, getting onto the story a month behind the television network, sought out these other local campaigns.

The swiftness of acceleration of the *Buy American* drive is what astonished politicians and pollsters. In the space of 30 days it had become a phenomenon.

(*Chicago Tribune*)

DETROIT POLICE HEAD FEARS
ANARCHY IN THE STREETS

"We Are Looking At The
Making Of Another Watts-Type
Burning Of Cities"

Detroit—Assigning extra patrols to Woodward Avenue, Commissioner H.G. McNamara expects chaos from the Buy American fervor erupting in the streets. Detroit demonstrations take the form of burning slum houses. "The city's housing problem is already severe," he warned.

(*Women's Wear Daily*)

BUY AMERICAN GROUPS
PICKET 150 SELECTED
S-MART STORES

Carry Signs
"Foreign Goods Sold Here"

In an obviously syncopated move, pickets selected the very largest S- Mart units to ...

(Wall Street Journal)

CANADA UNIONS LAUNCH
"BUY CANADIAN" MONTH
DESPITE FREE-TRADE PACT

(Wall Street Journal)

CONSUMER PRICE INDEX RISING
AS NON-LEGISLATED PROTECTIONISM
SPREADS

Then it alarmed law enforcement people.

(N.Y. Times)

CROWD SMASHES WINDOWS
OF THREE 42ND STREET
IMPORT STORES

Spill Foreign-Made Cameras,
Recorders, Radios, Binoculars
Out Onto Sidewalk. Looting.

New York — In an obviously well-coordi-
nated operation, a *Buy American* group struck
three import stores simultaneously at three
o'clock, pulling onto the street the ...

(*Los Angeles Times*)

TRUCKLOAD OF JAPANESE
TV SETS ATTACKED
LEAVING DOCK

Truck Opened. Sets Smashed.

Ten young men carrying a banner halted the truck as it came off the dock ramp at ...

(*Dallas Morning News*)

TRUCKS STOPPED BY ROAD GANG
TO SEARCH FOR FOREIGN GOODS

Colinas — A planned assault, 14 trucks were stopped and searched on Highway 36 by 46 motorcyclists wearing *Buy American* jackets which ...

(*Columbus Dispatch*)

U.S. FLAGS MARK CERTAIN MACHINES
IN MANSFIELD GM PLANT
Flagged Machines Work Well.
Unflagged Machines Plagued.

Mansfield — A giant press in the General Motors plant in Mansfield stamps out 800 Chevrolet roofs per hour. Suddenly it has developed mysterious problems.

This press, built by Ishawawjima- Harima, was brought on a caravan of trucks from the Cleveland port to Mansfield. A fleet of Mansfield autos attempted to stop the caravan, but it was escorted by police cruisers and helicopters.

GM management protested that they wanted

to buy American but they could not find anything comparable. This Japanese sequential press allows changing to a new die in five minutes as opposed to six hours on an American press.

Throughout the plant Japanese and German machines dominate. Here and there is a lonely U.S. machine to which operators have affixed small American flags. These machines are carefully maintained by the crews, while the newer foreign machines mysteriously break down.

In a stand-up conference in the Senate corridor, free trade Senators Forte, Butus, and Boar disagreed. Boar said, "We ought to try to get S.B. 115 out of committee and onto the floor for a vote. In this *Buy American* furor, it will be far too mild to satisfy, so the vote will kill it."

Butus was emphatic, "No. If that bill gets to the floor, they'll start loading it up with amendments until it is a real monster."

Forte proposed, "Let's try to keep it in committee until Congress recesses."

* * *

At Action Promotions on Madison Avenue, New York, Red Graves finished cleaning out his desk and packing six cardboard cartons with his personal belongings. One was covered with newspaper and magazine clips of the *Buy American* campaign, and congratulatory letters from Abrahms and Judd Hobart of Garment and Textiles Association. He was just taking these down when the President of Action Promotions opened the door and charged in. He looked around at the packing boxes. "Red, I just heard! What the hell are you doing?"

"I was going to tell you, Arch. I've got to quit."

"Quit?"

"I've got long thoughts, Arch."

"How long?"

"What right have media types like you and me got, starting movements like this? People are getting arrested and put in jail, and a guy was killed in Houston in a hassle over import TVs. In Detroit they're burning houses."

"I see." Arch Kilburn sat down. The thought was not a stranger to him. He had set out from college to be a CBS foreign correspondent. Then he drifted into this. Found it exciting.

"Well, Red, you've made a bundle. You can afford to quit. But before you haul a load of guilt on your back, let me ask you to face something. Media is no longer an incidental part of America, or the world. It's not a side effect. It's right up there with the other branches ... legislative, executive and judicial ... and now media, a fourth branch of government. It's the first branch of commerce. It's the first branch of religion. It's the first branch of fashion, international relations.

"And crummy as it is ... it is in a way the whole shootin' match. And ask yourself ... is that a bad thing? It's pure democracy. Give the people information and let them decide. It turns the nation into one big debating society. Every side gets a voice."

He waited, letting Graves think, which he did.

"Arch, you're right except ... we stack the deck."

"Red, I agree. But how else? Does an attorney stack the deck for his client as best he can? Does a senator stack the deck as best he can? Does a salesman tell his product's best features? Do the Jets put in their second-best quarterback to be fair to a weaker team?

"Red, I can't change the world for you."

Graves put out his hand, "Arch, I learned a lot working with you. I don't say you're wrong. But I've got to get out."

"Can we call you for certain jobs ... on a selective basis?"

Graves shrugged.

5

REMBERG

(Women's Wear Daily)

S-MART'S STRAUSS CHARGES
GTA WITH DESTRUCTIVE
BUY-AMERICAN CAMPAIGN

Cites Garment Makers Damage to Retailers.
Vows Retaliation By Stores

(Wall Street Journal)

S-MART'S M.B. STRAUSS PROPOSES
FASHION RETAILERS INSTITUTE
MEMBERS BREAK FROM
U.S. GARMENT MAKERS

Retailers Threaten To Better
Garment Making

Over at Garment and Textile Association the trustees
were in special session. Except for Abrahms who slouched
at the end of the table, thinking, with his head in his hand,
twelve of them were talking at once around a huge boat
table. The Strauss threat was not idle. Retailers had
already started several clever manufacturing operations
on a very limited but promising scale, carefully clear of
anti-trust regs. One such operation, making children's
clothes, was a large well-organized cottage network, in

which women at home moved materials from house to house for various operations ... cutting, sewing ... button holing, pressing. Another was a customer do-it-yourself kit operation. Several others were small manufacturing operations suitably arm's length from the retailer fiscally, but otherwise retailer directed.

Some of these competing operations were in the back yards of these battling garment manufacturer trustees.

The din lowered, A. B. Abrahms was rising from his chair at the head of the table. At the moment that he reached his full height the room reached silence. "Gentlemen ... we may have made a mistake. Let's say it's my fault, if that helps, and move on. Vuden?

"We are in trouble with our own customers. Now, when our industry has been in trouble before, what is it that has almost always saved us?"

There was no reply. Abrahms said, "Lev ... what do *you* say?"

Levinson throught for a moment. "The designers."

Several heads nodded "Amen."

"We have raised prices under the protection of *Buy American*, and thus reduced the market. We have offended our retailer customers to the point where they ... who own our consumer customers ... are intent on going around us. The retailers will become the manufacturers. They won't build plants; they'll farm out the needle to wherever. They will also import components, assemble here, and label it American made ... Yankee Brand.

"In my opinion we have one choice. We must come out with new designs with such overwhelming appeal that the retailer has *no choice*. Our individual labels have not done that. We have got to have a hula-hoop; hundreds of different ones. The executive committee recommends that this association take on this mission and fund it, and license out designs to our individual member companies for manufacture. Details to be worked out later...on who gets what."

The trustees liked the idea. It fit their experience.

But the meeting ran beyond midnight because the big question on everyone's mind was ... who? What designer could turn around a whole industry?

Almost to a man they came up with one name. But all the telephoning they did that night could not locate him.

* * *

The Garment and Textile Association Task Force, still nicknamed Survival Force, finally traced aging Lou Remberg's address to Hartley Hill Road, Saxton's River, Vermont.

People in front of Saxton's River Hardware stared at the powder-blue stretch Cadillac which pulled to the curb.

Levinson lowered the window and beckoned over a young farmer. The young man just grinned. Bradley murmured to Levinson, "This is Vermont. They don't beckon. Get out of the car."

Levinson asked, "Where does that road go?"

The young Vermonter's grin stretched. "Lots of different places."

"I should have asked, 'Could you tell me where Mr. Remberg lives on Hartley Hill?'"

"Sure." But he did not move.

"Well, *would* you?"

Lou's place was an ancient Vermont farmhouse, constantly under renovation on the outside. Inside, it was fully remodeled, Appliance Park Modern.

Lou sat surrounded by the paraphernalia of distinguished old men; leather books, wall-hung awards, framed sepia photos, and three daily newspapers strewn beside his chair. His shave had left some islands of whiskers over abrasions from previous shaves.

The committee laid before him the need for a design revolution to save the U. S. garment industry and force a *Buy American* grass fire. They put it to his industry loyalty, his religion, his patriotism, both U.S. and Jewish, to come out of retirement and make it happen.

"Why do I need this?"

"Lou, the budget is whatever you say."

Remberg's open palm referenced his comfortable surroundings, "Do I need money?"

Levinson asked, "What do you do with your life?"

"What all old people do—work at staying alive. I'm ten hours a week with the goddam doctors."

"It could be money for your Israel Children's Scholarship Foundation?"

"Millions I've raised for them; let somebody else."

"This job you could do in six months."

"Like hell. Twenty-four months! Maybe three years!"

"What's three years, Lou?"

"Y'damn young fool! That could be fifty percent of what life I got left!"

"What else would you do with your life?"

There was no answer.

Levinson said, "Lou, what we're talking about is saving the industry that made you...and put your kids..."

"And I did nothing for the industry?"

"Hey, Lou, that's why we need you. We all know you converted the ugly sweatsuit into high fashion, and your casual suit made millions for the industry."

Levinson then recited friends of Lou Remberg who were still in the thick of rag trade battle, and losing.

"Jack is in trouble, too?"

"On the edge. His Spring Show bombed. About fifty big pencils didn't even come."

"And Sol?"

"Going chapter eleven."

"Suppose I got lucky...like Fairyland...and came up with this superman line of clothes already, then how you going to divide up any such super line among the association labels? Who gets what?"

"The Association will auction or assign. They'll accept. They're desperate."

"They'll compete like sharks."

"They'll cooperate."

"It's *that* bad?"

"Worse."

Lou rose and went out to the kitchen. He returned with a coffee for himself only and sat down. He centered a cigar in purple lips and scratched a wooden match to it.

"I'll need fifteen months, three cutters, and four sewers.

I want the three Levine brothers."

"Anything."

"Ship all the industry fabric swatch books to that old bar on this property."

"Sure."

"And I need a sculptor."

"A what?"

"A sculptor."

"What in the world do you need...right, one sculptor."

"And the rule is — you can drop any item from the line. But no changes."

"No changes."

"And I want a young demographer."

"You mean a market analyst?"

"No! Those types only take history's numbers and add ten percent. I want a real demographer, and a young one that knows she don't know anything yet."

"*She?*"

"Yes. I want a woman with some sensitivity. Don't send me some tennis-playin' witch out of Vassar. I want a country girl from a big family that worked her way through Hunter or some other hard-knocks college.

"Also a mannequin builder I want."

"Lou, we can ship you all kinds of ready-made..."

"No."

"Why not?"

"Reasons."

Lou Remberg had a list of other demands. He specified a secretary who knows the rag trade and "knows that needs doing before I do"; and he specified that one-quarter of one percent of the wholesale price of every garment go to Israel Children's Education Foundation.

Levinson reported back poker-faced to the executive committee of the association. When he presented Lou's more eccentric demands, Chairman Abrahms said quietly, "Lev, no disrespect, but did Lou seem ... uh ... you know? He *is* 81."

"Hard to tell. I do admit he asked me two-three times the same questions."

Berkley said, "That could be only hard of hearing."

Abrahms drilled Levinson, "Lev, we're betting the whole works on this. You sure Lou is not...farfufket?"

"I think I'm sure."

"Then we better come up with everything on Lou's list...in spades."

But after a month there was no communication out of Remberg, except calls from his secretary with demands for more bolts of cloth, and he wanted a young anatomy professor sent to him part-time, and he wanted a sculptor, and a particular one at that...William McVey out of Cleveland.

"Why McVey?"

"Mr. Remberg says because he's the great sculptor who did the Winston Churchill in Washington."

"I *know* who McVey is. But what makes Lou think we could get *him* for *this* kind of work?"

"Mr. Remberg said you'd ask that. He said ... with all the junkyard welding statues being bought, the *good* sculptors probably need work."

The executive committee worried. A sculptor? An anatomy professor? A demographer? Abrahms called Levinson. "I'm concerned, Lev. Before the next committee meeting, you and Sherm Berkley better make a trip up to Lou's studio in that barn. Take a look."

"We did already."

"And what?"

"We-ll...nothing."

"Nothing?"

"Oh, the activity is tremendous. He has that whole staff hopping, but...uh...no designs yet."

"Then hopping about what?"

"He said he'd tell us when he knows more. He's also traveling some. Said he's got to see what people are doing in their clothes today."

"What would they be doing?"

"Same as always I guess."

"Lev, I'm antsy. Do you think Lou would come and give a progress report to the committee?"

"Nope."

"Why not?"

"He sent the report with me."

"What?"

"He said tell 'em, 'Look, you guys want a fashion revolution. So revolutions take research. I got to see what's going on today in the world."

Sally Jergenson, Remberg's secretary, had a very difficult job. The most difficult part was trying to get Remberg off the studio floor to take calls from the association. He would always anticipate what they wanted and tell her what to answer them. He usually guessed right, but the association officers wanted to hear it from Remberg's own voice. She could tell they did not understand why he was so busy.

She tried to explain to them that he was working with the demographer and the anatomy professor and the sculptor and mannequin builder. When they asked, "What's the sculptor doing?" she was required to reply she was not allowed to say, for security reasons.

Sally never had trouble getting through to the top brass in the garment industry. Orders were to put her through pronto anytime. But, being aware of the power, stature, and importance of top rag executives, she had trouble delivering the brief, demanding messages from Remberg. And since he restricted how much she could say, she had trouble getting the executives to believe them. She reached Levinson just as he was leaving for lunch at Seventh Avenue Club. "Remberg needs w-h-a-t?"

"He needs one hundred yards of very, very lightweight navy blue gabardine, Mr. Levinson, impregnated with thermally reversible polyethylene glycol."

"W-h-a-t?"

"P-o-l-y..."

"I can *spell!* But what the hell for?"

"Mr. Remberg said it was to prevent foreign garment companies making quick knock-offs of the line."

"How in hell will that ... I'm sorry, Sally, I forget you have a tough job. Did he say where I get this stuff? Who makes it?"

"Nobody makes it yet, Mr. Levinson. Mr. Remberg said — there's a small home insulation company in Chicago, Thermofiber, that uses Polyeth ... PEG. Get them to impregnate one hundred yards of gabardine with it."

"That is utterly ridicul ... you got it, Sally. Never hesitate to call."

Levinson dialed A. B. Abrahms, "Al, you may be right about Lou's ... uh ... stability."

"What happened?"

Levinson explained. There was silence on the other end. Then Abrahms reflected, "Lev ... you remember back in 1970 we thought Lou was nuts when he came out with kids' jogging suits with fluorescent stripes? Then we had to put the stores on allocation?"

"I forgot."

"Find already that polyethylene glycowhatever."

Levinson sent Murray Stone, a young fast-track middle manager, into the fringes of Chicago, looking for Thermofiber Company. It had moved several times. Finally he tracked it to a couple of Irishmen working in an abandoned car wash. When he called on them, he had the wit to first discuss only their insulation, getting an explanation about how PEG soaks up heat quickly in a warm environment, then releases it slowly in a cold environment.

"Could you soak this stuff into cloth?"

"Cloth? That would be awful expensive insulation."

"I s'pose. But could you?"

"Why not? Where do we get the cloth?"

"I'll send it to you."

"Who are we doing this for?"

"Can't tell you. I'll pay in cash ... if your price is right."

The impregnated material was ultimately shipped to Remberg's farm studio in Vermont.

But Murray Stone kept thinking about it and a month later asked his boss whatever happened to it. Levinson phoned Remberg. Sally Jergenson said Remberg was away.

"Where?"

"Canada."

"Doing what?"

"Testing some garments."

"Why Canada?"

"He said that's confidential."

Levinson phoned Abrahms the news. Abrahms was silent a moment, then quietly, "Lev, ask Lou if he would come to New York and give us a progress report."

Levinson reminded Abrahms that Lou had twice refused.

"Then we better get five of the trustees and go up to visit his studio. Unannounced."

Remberg's studio security was disguised as a sagging farm gate, but the fence was chain link under a coat of fast growing vines. The young un-uniformed guard wore patched jeans and appeared to be painting the gate. But the instant the stretch Cadillac rounded the bend, he jumped in front of the gate, the paint brush and bucket his only weapons.

The occupants in the back seat tried to overwhelm him verbally, but he returned each assault with the air of a Vermonter who has the support of his boss.

Finally Levinson said, "You tell Lou we've got to see him."

"Tell him yourself."

From the back of the crooked mailbox, the guard pulled a cordless phone and dialed. When he had Lou on the other end, he handed it to Levinson. When Levinson finished talking, he handed the phone back to the guard who listened and then spoke to Levinson, "He said, 'Come on up; but hide the big car behind that little shed and walk up.'"

The four visitors were stunned at what they saw in the open studio. The sculptor in one corner was making a miniature statue of a fairly ugly bent-over old man with feet splayed out. The mannequin builder carefully referencing the statue was building a life-size mannequin to match the statue.

Across the back of the studio were other mannequins of bent-over men with quite realistic heads. Some were black, more erect, and skinny.

Lou Remberg offered no coffee or chairs. "We gotta lotta work to do in a short time. So I'm only going through this once already. Start with this old man here." He pulled an elderly mannequin out to center floor. "And start with his pants. Old men are either skinny or fat. If skinny, they bend over forward. What happens? The pants we give him now

65

bubble up in front because he's bent, and stretch tight across his butt. The wife tells him to stand up straight. He does for 15 minutes. Then he's got droopy drawers in the back. Also...we build the pants for young men with big thighs, so an old man's skinny legs let the pants flap around. All dressed up—he looks crummy.

"So what are we going to give him? (Benny, bring out Number 7, with the pants. Good.) Okay, we're going to give him skinny pants to make the most of his good feature, thin legs. And we're gonna bend them a little right here, and tight across the seat so he doesn't have an old man's saggy stern. And we go slim on the cloth in front so he doesn't have a balloon front when he bends over.

"Now, for the brief moments when he stands up straight— when his daughter visits or a good lookin' woman goes by— this spandex V in the side seams accommodates."

"Lou," Levinson had the temerity to interrupt.

Remberg ignored him. "Benny, get the shirt. Put it on him and tuck it in."

"Lou," Levinson stepped forward.

Remberg helped Benny put on the shirt.

Levinson persisted, "Lou, what are we doing with all these old man mannequins?"

Without turning from dressing the dummy, Remberg yelled, "Maggie! Come out here!"

From one of the side offices came a young woman in faded blue jeans and a white shirt. With a square, handsome face, even unadorned, she stood in country dignity holding a notebook. Remberg put a tie on the mannequin, "Maggie—the demographer, tell them why we're starting with old people."

Maggie read from her notebook the staggering statistics of the elder population, with spendable income projections. Lou nodded—she could go.

The four visitors looked at each other. Levinson said, "Proceed, Lou. Sorry."

"Notice the shirt does nod taper. Even skinny old men are straight down. Notice the collar; the higher rise hides the turkey neck, and the big tabs with the soft roll frames the old man's face gently. Put a short rise, small tab collar on a young man with a bull neck, he looks good. On an old man, he looks like a 1928 bookkeeper.

"Benny, gedda jacket. One old style, one new senior style."

He and Benny put the old style jacket on the mannequin, "Nodice. The old style on a bent man, the front slants out ahead of him. Nodice also the bony shoulders make bumps in the coat shoulder.

"So what do we do? Benny, the new coat."

When Benny put the new coat on the mannequin, it was cut away more sharply in front so it did not bell out. The shoulders had rigid padding and lay straight. There was padding in the center of the back so the shoulder blades did not deform the coat.

"Now what you got to do," Remberg pointed at the visitors, "you got to introduce new sizes with the old numbers. A young man, 41 long, for the rest of his life orders a 41 long. He won't admit he shrank to a 38 regular. So you got to call your 38 regulars '41 seniors.'

"Now we talked about old skinny men. Next old fat men. Benny!"

Benny brought out the heavy-set elderly mannequin and they proceeded to dress it, with a running fire monologue by Remberg...how the lapels were set high and belled outward to form a straight line with the paunch...how the bi-swing back enhanced a heavy man's rear view...how the inside chest pockets were set high so the wallet didn't fall low to exaggerate the bulging belly...how the vertical pleated panel in the sleeves opened and closed with the movement of ham-like upper arms, and a spandex junction in the armpit prevented the coat shoulders from climbing up to a fat man's ears when he crossed his arms.

The visitors stood increasingly spellbound.

Remberg sensed it, and he softened some. "Sally, geddem a coffee and some chairs yet while Benny and I get the women mannequins."

They did not realize how long they had been standing until they sat. They talked among themselves.

Levinson turned up his palms in wonder. Berkley's eyes rolled to the heavens. "Leave it to Lou." Levinson's head nodded ever so slightly back and forth and he held his voice down. "He's hit it. He *has* hit it. *He has hit it!*"

"Has he?" Berkley asked. "Or do we just need a hit so bad that we *think* he's hit?"

Remberg covered some of his new work for elderly women, not yet complete.

Then he moved into young career women's fashions, ending with what they all knew would be a show stopper. He brought on a young woman model in a suit with briefcase, wearing jogging shoes. "Now, notice in the cities the young career women are wearing jogging shoes to commute to work. Then in the office they change to nice shoes. So here's what we're gonna give 'em." Remberg attached with hook and loop fasteners to the model's jogging shoes a small sharp-looking wraparound boot top in white leather. Then he showed other such attachable boot tops in shaggy carpeting material and some in black patent leather.

Lou's young studio staff enjoyed the stunned expressions on the four visitors while Lou moved from design to design.

Levinson had brought along young Murray Stone as a staff assistant. He now spoke up. "Mr. Remberg, sir ... that gabardine impregnated with polyethylene glycol — what was that for?"

Remberg stared at him, then at Abrahms. "You said very tight security on all designs. Only trustees. Who's he?"

Abrahms said, "Lou, he's not a trustee, but he works for Lev; and he heads the association government relations committee. He's 100 percent okay."

Remberg said, "Benny, you and Ed bring in the competition's overcoats." While waiting, Remberg explained that in the line they needed a lot of items "the foreign compeition can't knock off in 60 days. And we got to start looking ... what the people are doing. They show us what they want. It was the people showed us they want jogging shoes to go work in."

The bulky overcoats arrived on a wheeled rack. Remberg took a heavy tweed overcoat off the rack, "You take a hundred-pound woman and you hang this monster on her;

it's all she can do to stand up — along with a bag of groceries or a briefcase."

He tossed it to Benny and grabbed a man's overcoat. "You put this on a man, he needs two seats on a commuter bus." He grabbed a trench coat bulked out by an inner liner. "Brooks Brothers still wants us to button in this fat liner. You can hardly bend the coat to sit down." He balled it up and plunked it on Murray Stone's lap. "You go to the theater, you got a Newfoundland dog of a coat on your lap." Remberg went through a whole rack of winter coats, ending with a quilted, air-filled long coat. "This coat is nice and light, but look what it does to a woman with a good figure. She's a stuffed sofa."

Remberg said, "Benny, tell Caroline already come out in the new coat."

A willowly model strode onto the open studio floor in a fine-weave gabardine so light it flowed with her motion like a dress.

Remberg explained it was the gabardine impregnated with a polyethylene glycol. It stores heat from the closet in the house; out in the cold it releases stored heat. "Sure, the heat only lasts two hours. We tested in Canada. But Maggie, the demographer, did a study; nobody but footballnicks are out in the overcoat two hours."

The model pulled out of her pockets and held up gloves of the same material.

Abrahms, with an enormous smile that bulged his jowls, handed Levinson a big cigar and lit them both. "Lou! Never utter the real name of that chemical again. Just call it 'Heat Memory.' Beautiful!"

Abruptly, Remberg said to the visitors, "I got to have a nap. Maggie! Tell them where they can go and buy themselves a sandwich." He walked away. Berkley and Levinson charged after him. Levinson said, "Lou, it's fantastic. Fantas-tic!"

Remberg waved him off. "Later already. I got to get my pills and a nap. The goddam doctors run my life now."

* * *

The Garment & Textile Association executive committee argued about how to roll out the line. With a big splash? With a full media break-out? Test markets in L.A. and New York?

The ascetic Berkley prevailed. "Look, we wanta revolution so bad, we maybe sold ourselves we got one. But maybe we got another Nehru jacket. I say...do four very exclusive sneak preview shows in four secondary cities. Stay away from New York, Miami,and L.A. Do like Pittsburgh, St. Louis, Sacramento. Invite only a half-dozen top pencils. Then if it bombs, we go back to the drawing board; no damage. If we're a hit...bring it in to Broadway, wide open."

(*Women's Wear Daily*)

REMBERG RETURNS!
FOUR SNEAK PREVIEW SHOWS
KNOCK OUT THE BIG PENCILS

"Heat Memory"® Line A Super Hit
Stores Accept Allocation On
"Seniors" Line.

St. Louis—The new Rembergs shown here drew raves and orders.

What the select audience saw was not only a line of smashing designs, they saw a major design method shift. Remberg has gone beyond style aesthetics to something new in fashion — basic research.

These lines were designed not for models, but for ordinary people who bulge, bend and stoop. And the clothes are not for the runway, they are designed for living.

Remberg has smashed through all the usual tinkering with bows, belts and ...

6

VISCONTI, THE ELDER

The attendant knocked on the glass window of the racquetball court, holding up a cordless phone. Visconti reluctantly came out of the court, "What?"

"Sounded urgent."

Urgent after they had fired him? Then he remembered he had given Margaretta this number ... in case.

Her words did not scare him as much as her attempt not to scare him. She stated up front that their father was all right ... now. Outside the plant gate, he and about thirty discharged senior men, including several first-line supervisors, had blocked two flatbeds hauling in German alloy slabs. They invited the drivers out of the cabs, then released the restraining chains. With a fork-lift they unloaded the slabs and stacked them, barricading the plant gate. During the arrests, Visconti and three others were injured. After hospital treatment, the three joined the others at the police station. Their father faced three assault charges plus resisting arrest and trespassing and property damage.

"How bad is he hurt?"

"Broken arm. In a cast. He's not the problem. It's mother. She can't eat, sleep. Won't talk. She's scared."

John Visconti knew why his mother was scared. Gian Visconti, the senior, was a traditional padrone...head of the house...which he would protect recklessly. His house extended to his children's houses, and now to his fired co-workers. They would thrust the leadership on him as naturally as they would breathe.

Back in 1988 when he was steward, he led a wildcat walkout of one shift against orders of both local and national. He lost his stewardship and was suspended six weeks. Back in 1987, the millwright on Visconti's shift received a shocking invoice from a surgeon, $13,000 beyond the $6,000 the insurance would cover. The millwright had exhausted all appeals. The young surgeon, son of a Specialty Steel senior executive, was suing the millwright. He couldn't concentrate on his work. Visconti said, "Bring me the bill."

He took a half-day off the job and marched into the surgeon's waiting room, then past the startled office manager into the warren of labs and offices, opening every door until he found the most ornate office.

"Dr. Carlisle?"

"Who are you?"

"Never mind that." He placed the millwright's invoice in front of the physican, "Write out a new invoice for six thousand."

The doctor reached for his phone. Visconti's paw slammed down on it. "Write!"

The doctor wrote.

Visconti knew he could be fired.

When he clocked out, Harrigan told him, "That doctor's father is waiting for you outside. Carlisle."

He was, but what he said was, "It serves the kid right. Don't worry about it."

Margaretta said, "What shall I do?"

"Did you call Harrigan at the union?"

"Yes. He said the company's got them cold, and the new management is going to make an example of this."

"Where are Frank and Doug?"

"When there's real mean trouble, Ma said call you. What do I do?"

"First—get cash and bail Dad out."

"None will come out unless all come out. Dad has turned bitter. He's in the 'Buy American' thing. What do I do?"

"I can't tell from here. I will come home."

"How come suddenly you can leave your job?"

"Because I have none."

"You?"

"Yes. So I will come."

"No. Tell me what to do, but don't come. Gian, you're

not...it's like the whole thing is your..."

"Fault?"

"Yes. Because your warning came true."

"All right. Get me a room at the motel. I won't come to the house."

"What will you do?"

"I won't know till I get there; then I'll work on the project."

"Project? Gian, this is your *father*."

"Sorry. Force of habit."

He told her to save any newspaper accounts so he could study them. He went to his apartment, packed a bag, and phoned Janet Hoff. "Just kind of want someone to know I'm gone and where I am."

She chuckled, "When you big operators lose your jobs, you're like lost lambs."

"In wolf's clothing?"

"Yes."

"Anyway you're right. Step out from behind that title on the door, you're two feet shorter. I found out quick."

"You'll always be ten feet tall, John. You're too mean to fail. Call me."

Visconti consulted his union directories and phoned the president of the Massillon Fraternal Order of Police. He introduced himself and asked for a professional courtesy. "Arrange an appointment for me with the police chief day after tomorrow."

"I think I can. But about what?"

"I'm not sure yet. Can you do it blind?"

"You don't make it easy. But I'll try."

In his motel room in Massillon, Visconti studied the newsclips Margaretta brought. The elder Visconti figured prominently, in a leadership role. John studied one large newsphoto of a close-up of his father's face yelling at a young policeman with the reckless abandon of an outraged man.

Visconti searched the newsclips for names and job descriptions of the other fired steelworkers. He made a few phone calls to City Hall, asking questions about the city

73

financial picture.

The police chief had now connected the names ...Visconti the son, Visconti the father. When John walked in, the chief had with him, standing, a man and a woman he introduced with reserved civility as arresting officer and recording stenographer. "I thought it will help to have them present in this litigious age, Mr. Visconti, if you don't mind."

"Captain, I'm not here as adversary. I have some professional counsel I think will be important to you. But you should hear it alone first, then decide whom you want to tell."

"Oh? And the subject of this counsel?"

"Labor relations. That's my business."

The chief nodded to the officer and stenographer who left.

The captain leaned back. "So?"

"Captain, in my work I have recently visited 28 metalworking towns. Massillon is just heading into a long hard siege."

The chief scoffed. "Hey, steel will come back strong. My father..."

"Forget your father, Captain. Forget my father." Visconti's demeanor and ice-blue eyes had long commanded the attention of his seniors. "When steel comes back in Massillon it will be thin two-inch imported slabs which require no smelting, coking, and very little rolling. Mini-mills will come, using continuous casting from melted scrap, not ore. Grass will grow in the employee parking lot."

"Suppose you're right. What is your big secret message?"

Visconti traced the history of descending steel towns: closed mill, reduced employment, reduced tax base, pressure on city government to slash costs. First cuts are on street maintenance, then parks, then rubbish collection, then fire. "Then comes police manpower economies...at the very time, Captain, when your crime will skyrocket."

"Logical. So?"

"So you will have a bigger job to do with fewer men."

Visconti explained the pattern in other towns had been to cut paid staff, call in the free auxiliary. And the next step had been to call for free volunteer deputies. "And the best

74

deputies that you will want, who can command respect and control people, are those very men you have in jail. Your best move is to let them out...now...before you alienate them."

"They don't much want out. This will blow over. They'll forget and forgive."

"True. But not their wives. Do you think their wives would let them volunteer for the chief who kept them in jail?"

"You have a point." The chief turned thoughtful. "But I'll never get the Company to drop charges."

"Wouldn't they respond to what we just discussed?"

"No. They need to make an example, or chaos will set in all over the mill and in their other plant in Canton." The chief rose. "I'm aware of your reputation as a negotiator, Mr. Visconti; but I'm afraid you're off your turf this time."

(*Youngstown Vindicator*)

HOUSE OF REPRESENTATIVES USES "Buy American" FUROR TO LAUNCH ITS OWN TRADE BILL

On The Rising Protectionist
Tide, Presidential Hopeful, Slazer,
Launches Severe Protectionist
Trade Bill

Washington—Waving a newsphoto of 30 fired steelworkers in Massillon being loaded into police cars and three into an ambulance, Representative P. L. Slazer (D-Oh) declaimed to the House of Representatives, "Thirty steelworkers from my district being hauled off to jail for trying to save their jobs from German steel! That makes it time for action!"

With 170 co-sponsors in the House, Slazer introduced the long awaited HB 1010, subtitled *Trade Emergency And Export Promotion Act.*

With the introduction of this bill, creeping

protectionism leaps full bore. The preamble states the purpose "to reverse the enormous shortfall in our balance of trade."

This bill, much more severe than SB115, mandates a 30 percent across-the-board duty against any major trading partner whose exports to the U.S. exceed its imports by 65 percent, excluding oil.

It mandates counter subsidies for agricultural exports against nations which subsidize their agriculture exports.

Slazer, on the House Ways and Means Committee, capitalizes the momentum of the "Buy American" sentiment behind...

Senators Forte, Boar, and Bain were meeting in Forte's office concerning the competing House Bill 1010, waiting for Senator Butus who was late.

Forte said, "Let's start without him."

Boar disagreed. "We need him. See if he's en route."

Forte had Mrs. Rider phone him. She said Butus wanted to talk to Forte. The others could only hear Forte's end of the conversation, "No. The speaker phone is not on. We'll wait for you."

* * *

"Bute, you can't back off now. We need you."

* * *

"But we've only got forty senators fighting S.B. 115. If you back off, there's only 39."

* * *

"Sure it still matters, despite H.B. 1010. That house bill will become so extreme it'll never pass. That'll leave S.B. 115. And 115 will become more severe as the Senate tries to match the house bill."

Sure you've got election trouble at home. So have we all."

"Well...we were counting on you, Bute. But...so long."
Forte put down the phone slowly and said to the others,
"You heard. Bute buckled. We just lost a strong man."

Visconti asked Margaretta to get the name of Specialty
Steel's local bank, and that local bank's large city correspondent bank, which turned out to be Toledo Trust.

He phoned for an appointment and was referred to a vice
president, Richard Lempke, who seemed a jovial type. "I'm
sure if you want to drive all the way to Toledo to talk to me,
it must be important, Mr. Visconti. But it's hard for me to
make the connection between my bank in Toledo and thirty
men in jail in Massillon, even if they were fired by our
correspondent's customer."

"Understandably. But if I make the trip from Massillon
to Toledo for a five-minute talk, it may save you a trip from
Toledo to Massillon."

A great laugh boomed in over the wire, "Young man, you
make an intriguing approach. Come ahead."

"Thank you."

"Do you mean you only need *five minutes*?"

"Maybe only three, if you would do one thing before I get
there."

"What's that?"

"Check out my credentials with Mellon Bank in Pittsburgh with regard to the steelworkers' bank boycott a few
years back."

"I'll do that, sir."

Visconti was shown into the large office of Richard
Lempke who proffered a fat shirt-sleeve arm and a big grin,
"Mr. Visconti!"

It was a conspiratorial grin that brought a mirrored

response, even from the humorless Visconti.

Lempke seemed to tacitly enjoy postponing the subject at hand as they sparred around with introductions. Finally Visconti leaned into it. "Well, since I only asked for five minutes I'd better state my proposal."

Lempke held up two pudgy palms, "No need, Mr. Visconti. You already did that."

"When?"

Lempke grinned broadly. "Even tenderfoot bank vice presidents aren't that obtuse, Mr. Visconti. You told me to check your credentials with Mellon Bank in Pittsburgh. I did. You stirred up that union boycott of the bank...opposing plant closing.

"Now you are about to make a proposition to me that, since we are a prime lender to Specialty Steel, would we influence them to drop charges against thirty men in a Massillon jail...to prevent a boycott of Massillon Bank by steelworkers, which you have probably already arranged with Mr. Harrigan, the high priest of that local."

Visconti grinned.

Lempke returned it. "Have I left out anything?"

Visconti allowed himself a rare laugh. "I couldn't have said it better."

"Now, Mr. Visconti, since a lot of the money we lend to Specialty Steel comes from the deposits of steelworkers, originally paid to them by Specialty Steel, your proposition tends to command our attention."

Visconti nodded.

"But everything we just said, you could have said on the phone. So why did you make this trip?"

"To show seriousness of intent."

Lempke chuckled. "All right. Now, Mr. Visconti, I'm a fairly low-level v.p. We've got two layers of 'em above me."

"So I've got to go up the chairs, right?"

"Nope. I did that. And we are willing to make the request to our customer that they drop those charges. And we expect to prevail."

"You could have told me that over the phone. Why did you let me make the trip?"

Lempke laughed, "My boss said, 'Let's wait to look him

in the eye and judge how serious he is.'"

Margaretta drove her brother to the airport. She explained her mother's relief. Visconti asked, "What did Dad tell her about how he got out?"

"What do you think?"

"I think he said something like ... 'The union came through again. Harrigan got us out.'"

"Almost verbatim. Except he added, 'And he'll get our jobs back, too.'"

Visconti nodded.

Margaretta put her hand on his arm, "Thank you, Gian."

"Sure. But, Margaretta, get the family to take off the blinders."

"I can't."

"I was serious that we'll need three million for Danny. It will take all of us working."

"You're the uncle Danny doesn't like. How come you're the one worries about him most?"

Visconti thought about it. "I guess it's because I know what they all expect of him. The poor kid."

7

MORTON

Seville, Ohio

At 5:10 a.m., Monday, Cpl. Hurd, driving owl patrol on Old Western Reserve Road in Seville, Ohio, pointed out to Sgt. Cramer lights in the quonset hut out behind the Dart Industries plant.

"Should we check them out?"

"No. That's just Jason Dart fooling with his pet project out back of the factory. Worries the whole town. He's not tendin' the main business."

Jason Dart was no big name in industry. But, for at least five towns around Seville, he was.

Fairly late in life, after a half-dozen trial-and-error businesses, he started this company in an old quonset hut making acrylic plastic skydomes and skylights, residential and commercial. He expanded to decorative acrylic panels for room dividers in restaurants and bars. Carried up on the postwar construction boom, the line expanded to interior modular office wall systems — plastic panels in extruded aluminum frames. Built the big factory in front of the quonset hut.

The company became the important employer in Seville and beyond. Then the gout crippled Dart. He turned active management over to his son, Roger, who brought in a new young team.

Old man Dart spent more time out in the old quonset developing something or other.

Cpl. Hurd asked, "They got sales of two hundred mil a year and the chairman's got to work nights?"

"He says it's because he's running out of time. Arthritis, the degenerative kind, and the gout is gainin' on him."

"So why not relax and enjoy what he's got?"

"He's got to get his pet project launched. Thinks it'll change the nation ... scrunch the inflation and let everybody own a house."

"What could do that?"

"He doesn't say."

"Could we go have a look?"

They swung into the back entrance and braked. Hurd pointed to a weathered gray pickup. "Bob Morton's truck. How come he's here?"

Inside, Cramer nodded to Bob Morton, local builder, and to Jason W. Dart, chairman of Dart Industries, "Just checking, Mr. Dart."

Dart thanked him; said everything was okay.

Hurd asked, "All right if we watch, sir?"

Dart nodded, pointed to the coffee maker, looked at his watch and quickly rejoined Morton at the side of an eight-foot-high metallic and wooden structure, a large box, 15 feet long by twelve wide. On top of it were two parallel I-beams which projected far beyond the length of the box.

Morton said, "You didn't tell me why you asked me to come here ... and so early, Mr. Dart."

"Bob, I know how you hustle, and I didn't want to interfere with your regular work schedule ... in case you tell me what everybody else does ... that this won't work, won't pay, and won't sell." Then he added, "And I want to pay for your time, Bob ... as a consultant."

It hardly took much explanation of the prototype for Morton to catch on. The old man said, "Haven't got a marketing name for it. Just been calling it the Utility Cube. You drop the whole unit into your basement excavation, the I-beams rest right on top of your foundation walls. The Cube becomes a center support member for the house."

Built into one side of the Utility Cube were the furnace, air conditioner, hot water heater. On one side was the washer-dryer, set tub, food freezer, and electrical service breaker panel. Inside the Cube was hollow space for servicing.

Morton, already a veteran small builder at age 38, was not an impressionable man. But he was already slowly nodding his head. Quietly he muttered, "W-o-w." He did not know why Mr. Dart would call him here to see it. He knew Dart only from a respectful distance. Dart could hire some *real* consultants. The best.

Morton still wore his plasterer's whites and drove an old pickup to his various job sites. He started as a plasterer. Took over a partly finished house as payment from a defaulting builder for whom he had dry-walled a street of houses. Then he bought two half-finished houses from another builder who went under in the wave of bankruptcies. Then he took over two houses bankrupt at the foundation stage and finished them. Later he bought 16 acres and put in a street of houses. Then he built a warehouse for lease. And when Jason Dart started his pet project, Morton remodeled the interior of this old quonset hut. Only the bank and the realtors and the local building trades knew that Morton's net worth was astonishing. They argued about the secret of his success. Some said it was because he talked small and he acted small. His office was still his truck. His conference room with local trades was early breakfast at the corner table at the Deli. Small one-truck contractors for electrical and plumbing and cement work would drop in there for coffee to see if Morton had work for them, or they'd leave messages for him with Bobbie-Jean, owner-operator of the Deli.

What looked to his accountant to be a chaotically casual operation was really the tightest-run ship in local construction. During coffee at 6:30 a.m. with the local trades, he could schedule them so close that a half-hour after the plumbers were done, the electrical man started, and no trade was stumbling over another or undoing previous work. On a Morton job, the electrician was never ripping out new plaster board to install a junction box ... or somebody would hear plenty about it at the Deli next morning.

Morton didn't park a big dumpster at each building site for the tradesmen's scrap. His deal was — each tradesman hauls off his own scrap. Exception: lumber. Morton salvaged all lumber scrap, sawed it, and stored it. When they finally rolled the grass sod on a Morton house lot, there wasn't $300 of waste and the house was priced to sell in a week.

So while high roller builders were closing down or shifting into remodeling work, Morton was expanding ... and he knew the merit of what he was seeing in the quonset hut. "Mr. Dart ... if we could have had this 15 years ago ..." He didn't finish. "Ah ... and here's where the central plumbing comes in. And the gas line. And that hole is probably for a rubbish compactor. Right? And what's this blank space here?"

"For a computer control synchronizing all heating and cooling appliances to spread the energy load. You know — prevent the hot water heater running while the air conditioner is trying to cool the house, and so forth."

Morton nodded. "And we could drop this whole unit in a basement excavation and probably connect it all up in a half-day."

"That's what I was hoping you'd think. Then I figure you could save another ten-fifteen man-hours if you add the appliance wall."

"Huh?"

Dart limped over to a support beam and punched a starter button.

Startled, Morton looked aloft. Lowering by crane came a solid wall of appliances locked together — range, refrigerator, dishwasher, and kitchen sink. Dart slowed the crane to inching mode and the appliance wall settled on top of the Utility Cube.

Dart limped up a stepladder. "Now y'see, Bob, you just connect these twelve large bolts and ..."

Morton nodded, "And hook up the water and electric. *Man!*"

Morton climbed the other stepladder and studied. He came down thoughtfully. "But what if it's a one-floor plan?"

"Okay." Dart raised the crane. "Then we take the I-beams off the top. Set the Cube on your concrete pad."

Dart started the crane and moved the utility wall laterally, rotated it ninety degrees, and lowered it along the other side of the Cube.

Morton nodded, "Or you could ship it already attached?"

Dart nodded.

Morton said, "So what do you want from me?"

"Three trial installations in three of your houses?"

Morton walked around the unit thoughtfully. He handled the tags on the units — Carrier air conditioning, Westinghouse panel boards, Sears water heater.

Dart said, "Bob, I could change the brands to suit you."

Morton shook his head and continued walking around the unit. Dart studied his face. "Bob, could you just put in *one* unit for trial?"

Morton grabbed the electric cable from the panel board and matched it up to the cable harness going to the kitchen appliances. "Gee. A two-minute connection." But he looked depressed.

Dart said, "Bob, for a trial installation, I'll modify it to your house plan."

Morton's expression was severe. He idly connected up the flexible hoses from the sink and dishwasher to the Utility Cube. "Gee," he muttered, "another two-minute job."

He walked glumly to a boxed dishwasher and sat.

Dart said, "Bob, I'll pick up all costs for a trial if you ..."

Morton put up the flat of his hand and looked toward the door where the officers were just leaving. Sergeant Cramer waved, "So long, Mr. Dart."

Dart said, "What's the matter?"

"Mr. Dart," — Morton leaned over his hands and studied the concrete floor — "you've invented a revolution." The aging engineer hung on the long pause of this youngster in more suspense than he had experienced during his oral exam at Case Tech. "I could take five thousand dollars out of the cost of a house. Maybe six ... seven ... maybe eight ... ten."

"So?"

"But I can't touch it, Mr. Dart."

Dart nodded sadly, "Building code?"

"I've spent ten years building a get-along policy with the building inspectors and city halls in Seville, Lodi, Creston, Wadsworth, Akron suburbs. Very costly. They'd kill me with this. There's no code for it."

"If I used company lawyers, could we get the code

changed in just one town?"

"Yes. Figure five years."

"Bob, I haven't got five good years left."

"Didn't you think about code, Mr. Dart, when you started this?"

"Yes." Dart was an engineer. He had learned *some* of the politics of business. "But usually when I came up with a real improvement, it has bulldozed through the objections."

Morton studied Dart, marveling at the naivete of bright men.

Dart asked, "Bob, if I could find an even smaller town somewhere, and make a donation to the town to change the code, would you build a house there with this unit?"

Morton shook his head.

"Even if I'd go the whole cost?"

Morton shook his head.

"Why not?"

"I only told you the half of it. You know the other half."

"Cuts down work for the trades?"

Morton nodded. "The trades would shut me down all over town the next day."

"That's why you shut me up a minute ago?"

"Well ... Corporal Hurd moonlights some sheet metal work on my houses; his father does electrical for me."

Dart rose and extended an arthritic hand, "Bob, I understand. I appreciate your coming."

* * *

At about 5:30 a.m., Thursday, Sgt. Cramer was handling the owl patrol alone. Cpl. Hurd had called in sick. The Thursday owl shift was always quiet. Cramer did not put in for a sub.

By habit he scanned the Dart Industries plant. All quiet. Even old man Dart's car was not there. He bent the patrol car's headlights around the wooded curve onto Old Mill Road and glanced at the quonset hut.

Suddenly he grabbed his radio. "Patrol Six. Dart Industries. Fire!"

85

Bob Morton was eating lunch at the corner table at Bay Deli, reading the *Akron Beacon Journal*:

FIRE AT DART INDUSTRIES
LEAVES MAIN PLANT
UNTOUCHED

Seville — Assessment of damage from an early morning fire at Dart caused no loss in the main plant.

It did destroy some prototype models in the quonset hut behind the ...

Bobbie-Jean refilled Morton's coffee, "My sister works there. She said it hurt nothing important because only three old men work in that quonset on ..."

"Bobbie, hold the coffee." Morton put some crinkled dollars on the table and left.

His truck pulled up to the Dart main office. He noticed Jason Dart's old gray Buick in its slot.

The receptionist was new in town. She looked at Morton's dust-outlined footprints on the carpeting, "Maintenance office is over..."

"I want to see Mr. Dart."

"Which one?"

"Jason."

She studied his plasterer's overalls. "Have a seat. And the name?"

"R.L. Morton."

Reluctantly she dialed, then reported, "Mr. Dart is in a meeting."

"Try it again, and use the name *Bob* Morton."

She did and reported, "The secretary wants to know what is this in regard to?"

Morton was used to being underestimated. He calmly reached over and took the phone, and in a quiet voice said, "Take a piece of paper in to Mr. Dart's meeting. Just write on it 'Bob Morton.'"

To the surprise of the receptionist, a prep-clad Vassar type arrived in the lobby quickly to lead Morton upstairs and right into the meeting. Amid the stares of the executives, Jason Dart rose, shook hands with the plasterer and turned to his son, Roger. "Carry on."

He limped out with a hand on Morton's shoulder. In Dart's office Morton said, "Was the fire an accident?"

"I suppose."

"I doubt it. It could be my fault."

"Yours?"

"Corporal Hurd saw the Cube. And he saw me."

"You can't help that."

"Does the fire kill everything?"

Morton was surprised that Dart was leaning back smiling. "Bob, did you see that old hand crank mixer in the lobby on a pedestal, in a lucite cabinet?"

"Yup."

"Well ... I started the business with that mixer out in the quonset hut. As the business grew, it went broke three times, and three times I went back to that hand mixer. So ... the fire is just one more setback." Dart's smile suddenly faded. "Of course, this one is different; I'm running out of time."

Morton asked, "How much time to build another prototype?"

"If there's any reason ... a month."

"There's a reason."

Dart sat up straight. Morton pulled a much folded blueprint from his back pocket and spread it on Dart's desk. "Jason," — and the first name suddenly came naturally — "I agreed to build this fancy hunting camp for an Akron man up in the Allegheny foothills of Pennsylvania."

Dart stood up and flattened the blueprint. Morton said, "It's a dirt road no-man's land. Minimal type township government, run by the county seat thirty miles away. If you'll build a one-floor model, and sneak it in there at sundown onto my slab, I could have it all boarded in by daylight before any inspectors or union bother me."

Dart smiled, then clouded up. "You're still taking chances, Bob."

"You, too."

Then Morton explained, "But it's a one-lane winding mountain road. Can you haul the unit in there?"

"Bob ..." Dart leaned across the desk and offered a hand. "I'll put it on the North Pole if you'll install it."

8

JASON DART

J.W. Dart's elbow leaned on the executive committee meeting table with his head on his fist, like a man holding back. He was.

Jason Dart was not a natural-born executive. He was a natural engineer, founder, builder. His executive skills were acquired laboriously. The beauty of that was — he knew it. Therefore he was working hard at doing one executive process right ... the transfer of decision-making to the corps of capable young out-of-town managers Roger had brought in.

Therefore he held back when they voted against buying the new hot mold press in favor of landscaping the plant and paving the parking lot.

He held back when they elected to take the Dart franchise away from the first really large distributor that star salesman Tom Dougherty had signed up to handle Dart skylights and wall panels. Dougherty's concept of marketing through big wholesale distributors instead of through hardware stores, mill houses, and lumberyards zoomed the business to whole new levels. Dougherty had moved westward state by state, signing up top-notch distributors. When he reached California, he got drunk.

Dart said quietly, "You gentlemen realize, do you, that that distributor was the one who first lifted us out of the sandlot league?"

Marketing Vice President Snagle said, "Yes, sir. But now his son is running it; and losing us market share in Chicago."

Dart nodded. "Proceed."

He held back when they proposed receiving a delegation from Pittsburgh Glass interested in friendly acquisition of

Dart. However, he did ask, "Do you feel they really want this *plant*? Or just the *brand name* and our network of 160 top-drawer distributors established by Tom Dougherty?"

Snagle asked, "Why wouldn't they want our plant?"

Dart said, "Pittsburgh Glass could build a more modern plant than ours in three months out of petty cash. But it would take them ten years to build a distributor network and a brand name."

The young comptroller asked, "Do we really care if they move us to a new plant ... if the price is right?"

"Well, to the people around Seville we're the main employer of ..." But as Dart looked around the table, he realized suddenly the new managers were all imports from out of town.

The production vice president said, "Mr. Dart, our preliminary talks thus far promise an infusion of funds to modernize our plant."

Dart nodded. "Then I want any further talks we have with them to be contingent upon also funding intense R&D for our Utility Cube and Appliance Wall."

The men around the table looked down at their note pads. The production manager finally said, "All right, Mr. Dart."

Dart held back when they came to discussion of personnel. Some of his old friends in the plant were being considered for early retirement. But Dart held back.

Then they came to Tom Dougherty. Vice President Snagle said, "Now I know this is going to hurt because Dougherty is a company legend." He nodded to Jason Dart. "But, sir, we've got to bite the bullet and get it over with, quick and clean. There'll be blood all over the floor. But it will be over in a week."

They all looked at Jason Dart. He said mildly, "Are you younger men aware that Tom is the one who made us national? Worked his way west state by state, establishing distributorships for our products?"

"Yes, sir." Snagle did not look up. "But by the time he reached California, he had become an alcoholic. We took him back three times and tried to help him. But now he's wrecking the sales force. He's a super salesman hero figure to them. Taking them the wrong direction."

Roger Dart addressed the old man. "J.W., at our national sales meeting in Dallas, the veteran distributors all clamored for Tom to get on stage and make a few remarks. When he got to the podium, his speech was slurred. He got maudlin on the platform. Got mixed up on some product features."

Dart said, "Gentlemen and Miss Anderson, the product was never what they bought from Dougherty."

"What then?"

"Prosperity."

"We-ll, sir, I don't see how one salesman..."

"Dougherty created a swath of prosperity in his wake," Dart explained.

"How?"

"He would charge into town out of breath, with the aura of a man who has just left a prosperous distributor customer in the town behind him...and was on call to a thriving customer two towns up the road...and business must be picking up everywhere. And you'd better grab onto Dougherty's coattails and join in the prosperity.

"So they would buy a larger order from Tom than they planned. And when he left, the air was charged. And once they had the goods in inventory, they had to resell it; so they stepped up the effort and they *did* resell it. And so business did really pick up in a wide path behind Dougherty's car."

Dart said, "You men are making the decisions."

They voted to retire Dougherty from the sales force; and were moving to other business. Jason Dart said, "Gentlemen, when you dismiss Tom from Sales, transfer him to our Research and Development Department."

Snagle said, in all sincerity, "Mr. Dart, that's very generous; but do you really know what you're in for?"

Without emphasis, Dart said, "It's not generosity. I need him ... to sell the Utility Cube."

Roger Dart said, "J.W., if *you* haven't been able to sell it ..." He didn't finish.

Dart, senior, pushed himself up from the table. He slid a single sheet of paper across to Roger, "Gentlemen, I've noted the rest of the agenda and the recommendations. I'll be satisfied with those. Let me know if any changes. Excuse me."

He grabbed his cane and left.

* * *

At 6:00 a.m. Thomas X. Dougherty was vigorously stripping his apartment. He yanked books off his shelves, uncovering bottles. He poured them down the shower drain and turned on the water to kill the wonderful fragrance.

Even today Dougherty was 185 pounds of explosive energy, just as he was when his name stood for the game-breaking Notre Dame halfback; a name that opened customer doors wide for years. By the time the name was not remembered, Dougherty had substituted solid product knowledge and sales skill.

He had charged across the country in a marketing tour de force legendary in the building supply industry. A gregarious salesman who entertained with irresistible charm, he drank heavily during long absences from home. Beyond his vigorous charm, his strength in establishing distributors was that he in turn showed the distributors how to resell the Dart products ... working with their salesmen intensively.

How Dougherty achieved all that was partly his furious pace. He was always bumping into photoelectric doors which didn't open fast enough, overpaying restaurant checks to avoid waiting for change, and getting speeding tickets.

Sometimes Dougherty's rapid approach to people caused them to perversely slow down until he learned to turn on his electric grin which would melt glaciers. It recruited people into a complicity with him for what he needed done.

Dougherty ripped open the pocket on his racquetball bag and threw out a pint. Out of the record cabinet, a fifth. From his shaving kit, a half pint. He poured this one into a tall glass which he placed on the coffee table. He took the empties down to the rubbish and returned to stare at the glass on the coffee table. "I can take you or leave you, you son of a bitch." He talked to himself a lot since the divorce.

Next he made instant coffee, and sat drinking it while staring at the glass of bourbon. Then he shaved.

By 7:45 a.m., arriving at the quonset hut, Dougherty braked the subcompact so it rocked. He walked inside.

Amid the strong odors of charred wood and damp ashes mixed with new pine sawdust, Dart was in a stand-up meeting with Emile Hoffstetler and Frank Hood. Dougherty waited until it ended. Then he walked up to Dart and stood arms down at his sides.

"Jason ... thank you. I guarantee..."

Dart held up his hand, "Tom ... don't make any promises."

The old man walked to a large empty wooden crate, pulled it over on its side with the handle of his cane. He grabbed a phone from a box on the floor, blew ashes off it, and placed it on the crate. He tossed beside the phone a map of the U.S. and some color photos of the Utility Cube in the hunting camp in Pennsylvania, then waved Dougherty toward the crate.

"Your office, Tom. Can we do it again?"

"Give me two months, Jason. We'll sell some."

9

WHITE

But two months was nothing.

Dougherty smashed head-on into village building codes and construction trades. Large builders had developed an accommodation with both. A Columbus tract builder explained, "You might save me ten thousand per house, but you'd cost me ten million in hassles."

Dougherty did manage to sell a few hand-made units in very remote rural areas. The costs of these few sales, however, were staggering.

There was still a small sign in the parking lot at Dart Industries - "Reserved for J.W. Dart."

When he went to using a cane, Dart came in three full days a week. When he went to crutches, he came in three half-days.

Senior employees always glanced over to see if his old Buick was there. It wasn't that he couldn't afford better, but machinist Emile Hoffstetler had rigged this one with hand controls.

They watched for his car because, on the days when he came in, a certain relief from the new systems of the new management pervaded the plant. The old man strode ignorantly through some new systems and protocols; no one felt up to educating him.

But his crutches took him all over the plant, and an employee could still get his ear with a special problem; and changes could still happen.

Before he toured the plant, however, J.W. always went out behind it to the quonset hut skunkworks to tinker on the Utility Cube with Emile and Frank and sometimes Dougherty.

On the morning of December 15, Edith White, formerly

J.W.'s secretary, now transferred to personnel, was summoned to young Dart's office. En route she looked out a window and saw J.W.'s car in his slot. Crossing the lobby toward young Dart's office, she encountered Vasilov, the head designer of Modern Interiors. He was ordering an assistant, "David, get that old guy's portrait off the wall so I can see how much room we got for the new logo."

Edith White froze in her tracks as she watched a workman take down J.W.'s portrait and put it on a pile of other discards. She moved closer to Vasilov who talked to two assistants referencing an artist's concept, "Now here is the effect I want. Dark earthtone carpeted walls match the carpeted floor and the carpeted reception desk, destroying all perspective lines. The receptionist behind the desk in a red blouse will be like she's floating in space ... and when a visitor comes in he'll be momentarily disoriented ... impressed. It will take his breath. Got it, David?"

"Gorgeous!"

"The only other visual will be the new logo, horizontal, in light piping clear acrylic, on that back wall from there to there."

"The words 'Dart Industries' won't fill that space."

"No. But it's going to be 'Dart Division of American Glazing Company.'"

"What?" It was Edith White's involuntary gasp.

Vasilov only glanced at her and turned back to his people. "Pull that old machine out of that alcove. We'll use the alcove for the switchboard and screen it by erecting a carpeted theatrical flat. You'll never see it."

Edith White explained, "The receptionist always handles the switchboard!"

Vasilov grinned at her. "Where have you been, honey? This will be an automatic board. This place is going 21st century — fast. And first class."

"It's already first class! Dart skylights are the industry standard."

"Ma'am, you don't seem to be plugged in to what's going on here, and we've got work to do. David, haul that old cider press out of that alcove."

Edith snapped, "That is not a cider press."

"No?"

"That is the hand mixer that started this whole business."

"Whatever. David, move it."

Edith said, "Three times when we went broke, Mr. Dart went back to that mixer."

"How nice for you."

"So we put it in that display case on that pedestal to remind us ... not to get too big for our boots."

Vasilov looked down at her boots, containing plump legs, and grinned, "Well, it looks like you did anyhow, honey. Now ... mind if we work?"

"Yes." She saw the one called David tipping the old mixer and display case onto a wheeled dolly. Without thinking she walked to him and straightened up the cabinet. He tilted it onto the dolly. In tears, she straightened it again. He tilted it back. Involuntarily she slammed her clipboard against his knuckles. It broke and threw a splinter up into his face. Blood flowed.

Vasilov charged over and stanched the blood with his shirtsleeve. "All right, lady. Now you're into old-style assault and battery! What's your name?"

In the old Dart company, Edith White never panicked. But changes were coming so fast ... so many new people, new titles. She froze, staring at the blood. The lobby wallpaper music interrupted with a message, "Edith White to Roger Dart's office, please."

Vasilov barked, "What's your name?"

Edith fled out into the plant. She almost ran into the tool crib foreman, "Is J.W. in the plant?"

"No, Miss White. Out in the quonset."

She started to run. He mounted the electric cart and caught up to her, "Hop on if it's that urgent."

Dart was chalking a diagram on the cement floor for Emile Hoffstetler, "Make a masking device that will screen off the furnace. Like a rolltop desk turned on its side, running in aluminum tracks. It should look like paneling of narrow slats."

Edith interrupted, "Jason, I think I'm in trouble."

Dart concluded to Emile, "You know what to do. Just be

sure you get those tracks machined at Hamilton Machine down in Dayton." Dart took the crutch Emile handed him and turned to Edith White, "What happened?"

"I was called to Roger's office to meet with those American Glazing men when I ..." She explained the whole confrontation. "They're going to sue me."

"Well, Edith, I'm not the head man anymore. But let's go see. I'm due in the same meeting you are anyway ... with the American Glazing men ... about funding for the Utility Cube."

He signaled the tool foreman, "Give us a ride up to the front office on that thing."

As they entered the lobby, the decorator pointed to Edith and yelled, "There she is!" He beckoned to an assistant, "Denise, get her name for the lawyers."

The assistant stood with pencil poised as Dart's crutches approached. Vasilov demanded, "What is your name?"

Edith began to answer, but Dart put his hand on her shoulder, "First, young man, where is this wounded warrior of yours, and how bad off is he?"

"Look at the blood all over the floor!"

"I see it. Where is he?"

"In the company first-aid station."

"Thank you." Dart called over to the new receptionist whom he did not know, "Young lady, dial me the aid station."

She handed him the phone.

"Miss Hart, how bad off is this decorator fellow?"

He listened, then repeated, "A large Band-Aid? Thank you."

He turned to Vasilov. "My name is Dart. We will not bill you for the medical treatment, provided you repair the display cabinet for that old mixer to Miss White's satisfaction."

On the way to the meeting she said, "They're making it look like New York."

"I know, Edith. But you and I have got to adjust to some changes."

In the conference room Roger Dart said, "Miss White, where have you been?"

Jason Dart said, "She has had a very upsetting experience, which has to do with the American Glazing transition; and since that transition is the purpose of your meeting, we will get to it in due course."

Edith White handed Roger Dart the clipboard of personnel information he had requested.

The three American Glazing men and one woman sat together along one side of the table. The leader, Alton Moore, who would be the new comptroller of Dart Division, graciously rose and walked all the way around the table to shake hands with the newcomers. Then he turned to Edith White. "Whatever it was, Miss White, we want to fix it. I have told all our American Glazing people to respect the Dart traditions and to remember we did not acquire a good company to disrupt it. And we are all aware of your long personal association with Dart."

The young comptroller who would be "AG's man" here, was a master; and not insincere. But when they got to the agenda item, "Funding for Utility Cube and Appliance Wall," Moore had a hard task from which he did not shy. "Jason, we're in trouble on this one, sir. As a businessman, you understand we had to put our own Market Research Department on this."

Jason nodded, "And?"

"We came up very negative."

Jason Dart said, "Never mind that, your development manager, Ed Carson, made me a direct promise of funding for the Utility Cube. Don't you honor that?"

"Jason ..." Obviously Moore hated what he had to say. "Ed Carson is no longer with American. And I have to say it is because of some other promises he made ... which turned bad."

The table watched the founder take the surprise. Dart was what he was. He took a deep breath, exhaled and, as if alone in the room, stared ten miles out the window contemplating corporate promises.

After a respectful delay, Moore said, "But, Jason, before we scrap it, you're certainly entitled to hear our market research conclusions. You might have valid counter arguments." He pointed to his colleague, "Estelle Anderson brought the findings. Shall we?"

"No." Dart continued to stare out the window. "I think I know what your market research lady found. Building code opposition — trade union opposition — a lack of exclusivity." Miss Anderson was checking off items on her list. "Right, Miss Anderson? Despite the patents, it is not hard for a competitor to nearly replicate. It is, after all, only an assemblage of existing components. Right, Miss Anderson?"

With genuine reluctance, she nodded.

Moore said, "Jason, that's why we had to back off. But we certainly want to listen if you have stronger reasons why American Glazing should fund Utility Cube."

"I do have one, of course, but it's not one you can sell back at your home office."

"Try me."

"Simply that the division now *needs* it. Needs a major new product."

"Why? Your existing product line is exactly what we bought."

"I know. But there is good reason the company ... the division ... needs this new product. For survival."

Instead of rising to the opportunity to make a full bore pitch, Dart spoke quietly as if tired. The table leaned in to hear. "Very soon now, foreign plastic companies ... probably ICP first ... will discover that skydomes are economical to ship across the oceans because they are light and they nest into each other compactly for shipping. A stack of a hundred domes" — he pointed to the credenza — "can be a package no higher than that. Acrylic sheets for sign-making or room dividers also lie flat and compact. One shipload could supply eastern U.S. for a month."

The table was silent. Finally Alton Moore spoke, "Jason, if that's true, that's like telling me to go back to the home office and tell them they've made a horrible, strategic mistake."

"Oh no. There is a lot of business to be done before that becomes a threat. But I suggest you not build a new plant somewhere else, you ought to keep production here and upgrade the machinery."

Moore nodded. "Jason, that brings me to the next point. American Glazing can hardly afford the drain of the Utility Cube. We'd like to spin off that operation. Do you think you could find a buyer?"

Listlessly Dart said, "How could I find a buyer?" He finally smiled. "With the negatives Miss Anderson just cited?"

Moore nodded. He turned to the head of the table, "Roger? Any ideas for a customer?"

Edith White excused herself from the meeting.

Roger Dart said, "I doubt we could sell it as a going operation, but the land and the building..."

Moore shook his head. "Miss Anderson? Did your market research suggest a buyer?"

"No."

The meeting continued exploring possibilities until interrupted by an urgent phone call for Jason Dart. The assemblage listened to Dart's end of the call which was a series of uninformative monosyllables.

He returned to the table without comment. The meeting continued to explore increasingly unpromising possibilities, even after Edith White returned. Dart let the meeting run until they came down to a resolution to advertise it for sale.

Now Dart straightened up at the table and his voice was deeper, "Gentlemen, Miss White has been making some phone calls, and we now have a special opportunity. A potential buyer, whose failing health puts a very, very tight deadline on the offer, empowers me to act. The offer is modest, but firm. It is to include patents, land, building and contents. It is for $300,000."

There was some relief but not enthusiasm on the American Glazing side of the table, as the dollars were so modest.

Moore said, "Well, that's the best yet. I'll take that offer back."

"No, Alton. You'll make bigger decisions than that on this job. There's a tight time limit on the offer."

"How tight?"

"Sixty minutes."

Seeing Moore's mental struggle over clearing this with his American Glazing management, Dart said, "Alton, I think all you would need do to get American's quick approval would be to send them the phonefax ... right now ... a copy of Miss Anderson's market study plus a picture of a check for $300,000. Ask for a return reply by phone."

"Are you saying the check would be that quickly available?"

"Yes."

"May we recess five minutes while I place a call?"

When the meeting at Roger Dart's conference table resumed, Alton Moore said, "Jason, the management favors the 'disacquisition.'" He smiled apologetically. "That's the new word. But they say $500,000. And the purchaser agrees to stay out of the acrylic business."

Dart looked out the window, thinking. Finally he said, "That's high. But could it include the buyer borrowing Emile Hoffstetler and Edith White and Tom Dougherty three half-days a week?"

Moore worked a minute with a pocket calculator. "Okay on Hoffstetler and White. But the buyer would have to assume the whole Dougherty salary because ... uh ... Jason, Tom Dougherty probably will not be on our payroll after Friday."

Dart studied the bird in the tree outside the window. He said, "Alton, you drive a hard bargain. But the buyer is running out of time for negotiating."

Edith White opened a slim briefcase. They all watched her take out a cash management checkbook and begin to write in it.

Dart said to her, "Make it a binder of ten percent."

He turned to Moore, "Start the paperwork."

* * *

The meeting over, Moore followed Dart out to his car, "Jason, are you going to come out okay? It's obvious that buyer is *you.*"

"Not entirely. Those calls Miss White made were to Hoffstetler and Dougherty and Bob Morton. They each want to put a little money into it."

"But I know that after the fire you put a lot of your own money into fixing up. So I'm worried about you coming out of it okay."

Dart put a hand on Moore's shoulder and grinned, "We're going to be selling Utility Cubes by Christmas."

But by Christmas ... Dart was in a nursing home. He had fallen and broken a hip. The immobilization for that repair had left him weak. The gout prevented him from doing the therapy exercises. A downward spiral set in.

Young doctors saw no urgency to resuming the recovery therapy for an old man who dozed, watched television, and muttered about getting released from the nursing home ... as if he had some mission in life. The physician, on periodic visits, patted Dart's shoulder. "Relax and get a lot of rest, Jason."

Dart's daughter came frequently from Cincinnati to visit. She handled all arrangements with the nursing home and the doctor.

Edith White deflated Utility Cube Corporation and set it on a shelf in two briefcases in her apartment. She paid the periodic taxes; and wrote a moonlighting check semi-weekly to the night watchman at American Glazing to check the quonset hut now and then.

* * *

In Washington, a layer of very high-level government personnel attend two or three pre-Christmas parties nightly. Then, above this level, is a small layer of giants who have graduated from this career imperative. Three of these now met in the nearly vacant Senate Office Building. Late in the night these three worried about the republic ... Senators Forte, Boar, and Bain.

Forte said, "We lucked out. Neither S.B. 115 nor H.B. 1010 will get to the floor before recess. But we all know what's going to happen when they reconvene. Drummond and Slazer will immediately reintroduce their bills. And Drummond will work like a bear. He wants to run for president."

Boar worried, "The trouble is ... Drummond will expand his bill to include the 200 separate protectionist senate bills and Slazer will do the same in the House. So we'll have two super protectionist omnibus bills on track. And they'll pick up all that special interest support."

Bain said, "That may not be so bad. They'll have a lot of support ... true. But they'll also have that much more nit-picking to slow them down."

"I'm afraid you're wrong," Boar argued. "I think it will roar through town like an express train."

Forte said, "So it's going to take a bridge washout to stop it. What have we got for the plan?"

"Nothing," Boar said.

10

RUOFF

(*Wall Street Journal*)

TOLEDO GRAIN ELEVATOR FAILS, ROCKS EIGHT GRAIN BELT COUNTIES
Bankruptcy Court Freezes Creditors

New Canadian Duty Against
U.S. Corn And New Campbell Soup
Mexico Process Plant Partially
Blamed

Toledo-Judge Millard C. Trout signed the decree Thursday, appointing a creditor committee headed by J.L. Barstow, president of _____

Wyandot County, Ohio.

It was the first day dry enough for the land to take the machine weight for disking corn stubble.

Alongside Grayson Road, Benjamin T. Ruoff's aging John Deere 6620 pulled the side hill harrow to the end of a row. He cut off the 145 horses, creating a stunning quiet. He climbed down, straightened up his six-foot-two slowly, stretched off four hours in the saddle, and watched the dust trail on the field road materialize into the pickup driven by his diminutive woman, Sheila, bringing lunch. Why so early?

His troubles with Toledo Grain Elevator faded as he gazed out over the land. He could look an hour in any direction and see nothing but land tended by four generations of Ruoffs. Despite these three bad years, the land will be here, and there will be more Ruoffs on it.

Moose Ruoff, 46, strode over to the pickup and took the lunch basket out of the back. Sheila reached up to his shirt pocket and pulled him down to kissing level. His dusty beard split in a laugh. "What was that for?"

"You'll need it today."

"Need it?"

"Judson True from the bank called."

"Oh-oh. On *Saturday*? What about?"

"You know how Jud is with women. No business talk. But Sunday our interest payment will be 90 days over. Prob'ly some computer buzzes all 90-day delinquencies."

"So when does he want me?"

"Today, he said, if you could."

Shirtsleeved Jud True unlocked the bank's front door. "Thanks for coming in on Saturday, Moose. I knew you'd be helping over at Steve's Monday. And I can't wait till Tuesday."

He led Moose behind the oak rail to the one desk cluttered with paper. Following True, Ruoff noticed for the first time, to his surprise, that his high school classmate walked old. The high forehead went right over the top and partway down the back.

In Wyandot and Crawford Counties, on any six-digit farm matter, business is family and family is business. So you start with family. Jud True asked if Medicare would handle Gran Ruoff's recovery from the fall. Moose grinned, "No. She's doin' too good. That throws her care into mere maintenance, not therapy. So it's not covered."

True asked if Ben Jr. would stay dropped out of Ohio State Ag another year to work the farm, or go back.

"We're hoping we can spare him. His school record is so good. So Sheil's going to work half-days at the new doctor's office."

It burned Judson True. The new medic in town rents cheap a tiny $500 a month office too small for his patient load, works four days a week, and hauls in $300,000 farm dollars a year. But Moose Ruoff, in charge of a three million dollar asset seven days a week, can't count on bringing home a living.

"Moose, my board tightened down on me ... is why we need to talk. You know the situation on your present loan. And you prob'ly know what kind of additional loan you need for this year. I know it doesn't fit your rotation plan to crop your hundred south of Clayton Road next year. But I was wondering if you could see your way to squeezing out one more year of corn on that piece before going to grass. To help your cash picture."

Ruoff noticed Judson had lost weight even since the last Corn Grower's Association meeting when he spoke on farm import threats. "Jud, that piece is corned out. I got to build it up. Why'd you ask?"

"Moose, this year they're making me show a realistic repayment schedule on every account. Besides the old loans, you'll need some new money; so you and I got to figure out more net income for you."

Moose pulled a small sweat-stained, 69-cent ring binder out of his chest pocket. "Jud, I'll have three thousand some odd coming from calves. Ought to clear a thousand. I should clear six thousand on the dairy, even payin' for the new concrete yard the government wants. Jesus! And six thousand on land rental to Varney."

True did a quick total and looked up ... waiting. The big farmer leaned across the desk. "But here's the good part, Jud. I've got twenty-one thousand coming soon from the government price on last year's corn. I plan to use most of that to pay back interest ... plus penalties. That let's you renew my note. Then, the best part — I've got that thirty-one thousand bushel of soybeans in Toledo Elevator. If I even get three dollars a bushel, I've got ninety-three thousand dollars. I can use sixty of that against my old notes. Right, Jud?"

Jud True's bony face was lined from sweating out the finances of Wyandot and Crawford County farms. Some farmers he had to turn down, and his wife had to sit beside their wives in church. He resigned as church usher.

106

Passing the collection plate to farmers he knew he would not be renewing was too much. His wife, Marci, drove over to Galion to shop. She could not bear to be seen spending money.

True said, "Moose, that plan won't fly."

"Won't fly?"

"Your ninety-three thousand soybean money from the elevator may be five years coming; and then ten-twenty cents on the dollar."

"What!"

True explained the beans were tied up in the elevator bankruptcy, with all the other creditor money.

"No! I'm not a *creditor*! I'm a *customer* of the elevator!"

"You *were*. Now you're a creditor. You hold receipts for thirty-one thousand bushel."

"Jud, you don't mean *all* of us with grain stuck in those elevators got to stand in line with the elevator's regular creditors!"

True nodded.

Moose stared at the painting on True's wall of a field on Clayton Road. "Jesus!"

True asked if Moose could sell off the 300 acres south of Clayton Road. Moose still stared at the painting, mute. True repeated the question. The deep timbre was gone from Moose's voice, "Who would buy?" True opened his Ruoff file and handed over a clipping:

Holiday Inn Reported
Seeking Property Near
Interchange

Moose scanned it and slid it back. "Jud, those are *my* soybeans at Toledo Elevator!"

True explained the bank's lawyers had talked to the judge. He had been through this same thing with eleven other stunned growers. The elevators were sealed by federal marshals. The beans would be sold to satisfy the elevator's debts ... as in the cases of 32 previous elevator failures.

"Jesus!"

True said, "Moose, we *are* going to work out something on your loan. Would you consider selling that piece on Sudbury Road?"

"Jesus!"

True outlined other possibilities.

"Jesus!"

True suggested leasing out some more land. Ruoff asked for the names of the other growers with grain impounded in the elevator. Then he stood up abruptly and told True to unlock the front door and let him out.

"Jud, those are *my* beans!"

There was no use trying to stop him.

* * *

(*Toledo Blade*)

PROMINENT WYANDOT COUNTY
FARMER
ARRESTED IN TOLEDO
ELEVATOR BRAWL

Charges Include Trespass,
Assault, Attempted Grand
Larceny

Toledo — Angry Benjamin T. Ruoff and his son, Benjamin Ruoff, Jr., and two of their employees arrived at Toledo Elevator Sunday in four trucks to retrieve Ruoff's soybeans from the bankrupt elevator.

The new Canadian duty of $2.00 per bushel against U.S. corn, combined with Campbell Soup's moving its processing from northern Ohio to Mexico, triggered the failure of Toledo Elevator. The year's grain production of hundreds of farmers is impounded.

The gatehouse security denied admission. Ruoff became insistent, demanding immediate return of his beans for which he showed xeroxed copies of receipts. The guard said the receipts were irrelevant now, and dialed for security back-up which arrived on the run. The younger Ruoff left his truck and joined his father.

The chief of security, A.L. Teague, tried to reason with them inside the gatehouse, displaying a copy of the bankruptcy order.

The elder Ruoff balled up the copy and threw it to the floor. "That's a piece of paper! The soybeans are a year's work!"

He told the son, "Start up the trucks. The gate is only wood."

When the son left the gatehouse, guards started after him. The elder Ruoff blocked the door, imprisoning security personnel inside. The guards rushed him, in the course of which, they later told police, they were assaulted by Ruoff.

The farmer denied this. "All I did was raise my hands up for protection and they ran right into them with their chins."

Two guards pulled the younger Ruoff out of his truck.

The elder Ruoff, out on bail, will appear in State Street Court in Toledo in two weeks.

11

SCHLICTER

In the Ruoff kitchen Ben Sr., striding for the breakfast table, was interrupted by Sheila, who held up a clean white shirt. "Take off that denim, I need it for the laundry." He leaned over and she tugged the pullover shirt off his massive torso. Grabbing a shoulder before he straightened up, she planted a kiss above the fur line on his chest.

"What for?"

"For protection."

"Do I need it?"

"Martha called from the bank."

"Before breakfast?"

"Late yesterday."

"You forgot to tell me?"

"No. Didn't want you tossin' all night in bed. Maybe crushing me to death. They asked if you'd come in today."

"Oh. That's why it's a white shirt day."

"An *ironed* white shirt. Don't get it all wrinkled before you get to the bank. Don't sweat."

"Is it bad news at the bank?"

"The bank ever good news?"

When Benjamin Ruoff stepped into Bucyrus Trust, he sensed something unfamiliar. It might be only that for once he was using valuable *morning* time to come to the bank instead of worn-out afternoon time. Then he noticed it was quieter. The floor was shinier. There was a new young fellow in the first cage. But Martha was at her usual place. "Jud in, Martha?"

He was striding right past her when she rose, "Ben, could you wait here a minute? There's somebody in there."

He lowered himself into the visitor chair, splayed the magazines around looking for the *Ohio Farmer*, but there were new magazines. He fanned pages of one called *The Economist*, and tossed it aside. Martha said, "Ben, you'll be seeing a Mr. Schlicter."

"Schlicter? Where's Jud?"

"Well, Ben, it was very sudden. Very sudden. The bank's been bought by Toledo Trust."

"*Bought!*"

Just then dairyman Charlie Herndorf came out of the manager's office. He looked at Ruoff, "Hi, Ben." He looked at Martha, shook his head, and walked out.

Martha dialed one digit. "Mr. Ruoff is here."

Ben started to rise, but Martha apologized, "Just a minute more, Ben."

While he sat studying the ceiling, the walls, the teller windows, Martha studied Ben Ruoff. She was struck by seeing him idled. Martha Cushman suddenly realized that except in church she had never seen a Ruoff male seated, idle. Had always seen them in action, sledging fence posts on Clayton Road, directing the commission milk truck backing up to the milk house, directing volunteers erecting the gazebo on the public square ... constant, graceful, powerful motion. Idle like this ... he was diminished.

As she thought about it, that was the depressing change in the whole town—Garver, the greenhouse man, now seated part-time at the fire station, a different person. Brinkley, the once quick-striding farm implement dealer, spending more time now seated at the restaurant. Matt Filson, the crop duster, now stationary, clerking part-time at NAPA Auto Parts.

She suddenly realized that was what had always been depressing about Sundays ... seeing these men sitting still in church in their unaccustomed suits, brown leather faces below untanned foreheads. Take away motion, these strong graceful men were awkward.

Martha's phone lit up, "Yes?"

She nodded to Ben. He sprang up and strode into the head office. But he paused just inside the doorway because of the sudden changes. Instead of the clutter of Judson True with pictures of Marci True and the Bucyrus basketball team captained by Danny True, he saw newly paneled

111

walls, a new larger desk, totally bare of papers but for a single 3x5 card with a cryptic formula on it. He was confronted by the back of a well-barbered head and a flannel suit. Schlicter was working the computer behind his desk. Ruoff could read the top green line on the screen: "Benjamin T. Ruoff." The lines below that were rows of digits and capital letters, as if the bank was talking about him in code.

Schlicter finally swiveled around, "Mr. Ruoff."

The directness of Schlicter took Ruoff by surprise, "I know you're aware of the condition of your loans. Which parts of your farm do you feel would be most saleable, to raise this back interest and at least half the principal to bring this loan down in synch with your farm's potential?"

Ruoff, still standing, was speechless.

Schlicter gestured toward the guest chair. "I'm sure you realize we've got to come to a positive resolution of this problem."

"What problem? My farm has paid interest to this bank for a hundred years."

"Not *this* bank, Mr. Ruoff. It's logical you wouldn't have noticed the new sign. It's so similar, 'Bucyrus Trust Corporation, a wholly owned subsidiary of Toledo Trust.'"

"Since when?"

"Seventy-two hours ago."

Moose Ruoff slapped his work gloves down on the desk, powdering it with a large hand-shaped penumbra. Schlicter looked at it, then explained, "This bank must now operate as a free-standing profit center. And under my system each account must now carry its own weight. Keep current." Schlicter did not pick up the 3x5 card but glanced at it. "In your case we're talking about over 90 days arrears in interest, plus penalties, on two hundred ten thousand. That's why you and I need to figure out, Mr. Ruoff, what you can sell quickly enough. Then structure a new smaller line of credit."

"Slow down, Mister!"

"Schlicter, Warner Schlicter."

"My deal is already made, Mister. Where's Judson True's new desk?"

Schlicter put his forehead in his hand for patience to answer the same question again. "Mr. True is no longer manager here."

"Jesus."

"Nor employed here."

"Anyway, Judson and I settled my deal with this bank! He knows my situation! And he knows me! He knows I pay!"

"But you see, Mr. Ruoff, I don't."

"That doesn't matter. You can't switch on me now. My deal is sealed."

"With a handshake, Mr. Ruoff. There's no new paper on it. I know that Mr. True could make a generous renewal with you based on long acquaintance and a handshake. You and many others. I'm not that lucky."

"Judson wouldn't let this *happen* to us."

"Well, you will remember that even Mr. True, to make renewal palatable to his board, let stand the 'on-demand' clause on half of your debt."

"*On demand?*"

Schlicter nodded.

"You ...."

Ruoff grabbed his gloves, leaving their powdered outline. Martha rose as he came out.

"Martha, what did Judson do to us?"

Moose pushed the rusting pickup out County 262. When he crossed Sandusky River bridge he could see all the way to the True house. Blue and red lights strobed in front of the house on a paramedic van. A handful of neighbors' cars were in front of the house. People stood on the lawn.

Somebody was being carried out on a gurney. Close to the house Ruoff pulled onto the berm and joined the Herndorfs. He asked Charlie, "Something happen to Marci?"

"No. To Jud."

"Heart attack?"

"No."

"Stroke?"

"No."

"What?"

"Doc wouldn't say."

(*Toledo Blade*)

FARM BANKER TAKES OWN LIFE

Bucyrus — Judson True, manager of Bucyrus Trust,had 25 years of farm banking experience. "The last ten years had been pure hell for Jud," explained Steven Varney, a diversified farmer. "Jud worked closely with all of us trying to hold down the rising farm bankruptcies."

In a ten-year balancing act of counseling farmers on land sales, trades, crop shifts and refinancing, Judson True helped farmers stay barely afloat.

Triple Blow

However, three sudden blows struck northwestern Ohio farms. "Jud's finger in the dike could no longer stop the flood of farm failures," Varney said.

Using a loophole in the free trade pact, Canada slapped a $2.00 per bushel duty on U.S. corn. Ohio corn movement slowed to a trickle.

The nearly coincidental transfer of Campbell Soup's processing operation from Ohio to Mexico further stifled the movement of Ohio crops. Those farmers who had not accepted the government lockup price were suddenly stuck with no market for a year's work.

These events triggered the failure of Toledo Elevators, thus impounding farmers' crops during bankruptcy proceedings.

True Could See
No More Solutions

Judson True had worked out scores of ways to help farmers stay marginally afloat. But the grain elevator bankruptcy overwhelmed his clients.

True, no longer able to sit beside his troubled farm neighbors, resigned from the school board, from his church vestry, and from two lodges in which he was an officer.

He told his wife, Marcia, "Two out of four farms are going to go under. And I can't stop it."

Services will be private. He leaves, besides his wife ...

12

THE SALESMAN

"I'm out of choices." To a group of growers in Jo-Ann's Diner, Moose Ruoff showed a formal foreclosure notice from the bank. "They're gonna take my place, sell it to satisfy the debt, and give me back any change." They passed the notice around gingerly. "I got sixty days; pay or get out. And the lawyer says they can do this to me."

Charlie Herndorf said he was in the identical situation, "But they'll never sell our places in this market, Moose."

"Schlicter says they already got a buyer for mine."

"Who'd buy today?"

"Four doctors in Toledo."

"Damn."

"What I'm saying," — Ruoff looked at each man —"I've got to get my thirty-one thousand bushel of beans out of that Toledo Elevator to pay off the loans. You're in the same elevator. So I'm going to go get the beans. How many want to come?"

Herndorf said, "We'll get our money from the elevator before our sixty days are up."

"Jud True said no. It could be two-three years."

"Evenso, if we get there with our trucks, we don't know how to unload the elevator. And they got the excess stored in idle iron ore ships. We couldn't get the beans out."

"I've got to. Some way."

* * *

116

The Ohio Farmer
Editorial

The Big Boomerang

The second and well-planned raid by 22 Wyandot and Crawford County farmers against the Toledo Elevator to retrieve their product ended in bloodshed and serious injuries. The farmers, driving their trucks by different routes to avoid alarming officials, were foiled. Someone in Bucyrus, probably hoping to avoid bloodshed, tipped off federal marshals who arrived in force.

Who is the culprit?

Yes, we can blame the farmer for greedy land expansion, overproduction and excess debt.

Yes, we can blame the government for subsidies, enticing too much land into production.

Yes, we can blame the bankers for misguiding farmers eager to go into excessive debt.

All these contributed to the bloodshed last week.

But the elevator bankruptcy was triggered by the Canadian duty on U.S. corn. Now — responding to last week's disaster in Toledo — Ohio's senators have persuaded the U.S. president to use his executive prerogative to raise the duty 100 percent against Canadian shingles, lumber and newsprint. This will immediately shut down some Canadian operations, causing Canadian unemployment,and raise prices of shingles and books to U.S. consumers.

But the Ohio senators will earn plaudits from Ohio farm voters, while both senators know they have created a boomerang that can ultimately kill the free trade pact and impoverish both nations.

* * *

117

Sheila Ruoff rolled the sleeve neatly up over Moose's left arm and hand cast. She had slit the sleeves of several shirts and hemmed the edges after the second raid on Toledo Elevator.

"Thanks, Sheil. Where's my sample case?"

"Ben put it in the Bronco."

The bank had ordered them out of the house, but allowed them to occupy the old trailer camper they once had used for fishing trips. They could keep the four-wheel Bronco to try to make a living.

Moose lifted her up with his forearms, cast and all, "Sheil, today I am going to sell four sets of encyclopedia, or I won't be home."

"Put me down. And you get your hulk home for six o'clock supper. Sale or no sale!"

She watched the truck lay a dust trail up the field road. Young Ben, preparing to paint the exterior of the camper, saw the wet on the back of his mother's hand that brushed her eye. He bent down to her eye level, "Now lookit here, little miss. Just 'cause you got a son that can't paint straight and a husband who knows from zilch about sellin' encyclopedia, don't you give up on us. We're very fast learners."

"Baloney." Despite the wet eyes, her grin had the calm of a woman loved by strong men. The sheer breadth and bulk of Ruoff men was reassuring. "You're a couple of dumb oafs."

"On the contrary, we're the brightest men in your life and borderline geniuses."

"Prove it."

"Case one. When they invited us off the farm, Dad first went to selling farm machinery for Ed Brinkley. Quickly learned nobody's buying. He quit that. Took to selling insurance. Quickly learned he knew nothing about that. Now he's selling encyclopedia. He goes out of town first to rehearse his sales pitch on strangers. Then he's going to bring his act right back here to Broadway, Bucyrus, Ohio. That's pretty savvy, isn't it?"

She smiled. "And you. Prove to me you're not a dummy, wanting to stay out of Ohio State another year."

"Here's why that's such a brilliant move. I'll get a job at the air tool factory over in Bryant. That'll give us some survival income. And working indoors all day will be so hateful, plus bailing Dad out of scrapes with the Toledo Elevator will be so hairy, I'll appreciate college all the more when I finally go back."

She slapped him with the dish towel.

"And ... listening to Dad's sales-pitch rehearsals about encyclopedia will drive me back to college."

With his sample case Moose Ruoff walked up to a dairy farm in Freemont, Ohio. He reviewed the instructor's repeated admonition, "Attempt to close at the earliest chance, and then repeatedly throughout your presentation." He could tell the kitchen door was the main door. He could tell by the three rope swings suspended from the oak tree, with the grass scuffed off below, the house had youngsters who could benefit by an encyclopedia set.

The doorbell didn't work, but the German police dog inside hit the door hard enough to serve the purpose. He could hear the lady's voice settling down the household so she could answer the door. While he waited he could tell this farm had once been a Class I farm. The White 3000-W tractor with the A/C enclosed cab package was once a sixty thousand dollar rig. But one drive tire was gone. To replace that would be a thousand dollars ... used. He could tell the two GMC trucks on blocks were being cannibalized for spare parts.

The dog unbarred the door at a quiet command from a young woman. A guarded expression on her face had not totally wiped out a habit of welcome. She had a toddler on her arm and she looked down at the sample case, then up to the face of the towering Ruoff. "Yes?" The careful "yes" was the way Sheila Ruoff had begun answering the door when the bill collectors started coming in relays after the bank takeover news.

Ruoff swallowed his tongue, "Uh, Ma'am, I wondered if you would be interested ... I mean, could I have a glass of water?"

She smiled finally. "Come in out of the hot."

She said to her son, "Get the gentleman a glass of water. Put ice."

She placed the toddler in a high chair with a bottle and took the empty glass back from Ruoff. She smiled, "You did well for a man who wasn't really thirsty."

Ruoff stood like a kid in a caught fib. She nodded to his sample case. "You didn't carry all that in for water. What changed your mind?"

Ruoff turned up his palms and his beard split in a grin, "I'm a farmer. I saw you need a new thousand-dollar drive tire before you need these five-hundred-dollar encyclopedia."

She looked out the window thoughtfully, "I'm not so sure." She scanned her brood. "Not sure lately."

She put a coffee cup in front of him and pointed to a chair and sat opposite. "Show me."

Moose opened a sample volume to the section on "forestry." There were full-color pages of leaves of different tree species. She pointed to one leaf. "I always wondered. Shaggy bark hickory." She motioned her boys over, releasing them from their good behavior tableau. Moose opened the "W" volume to "whales." The boys leaned into the illustrations.

While she watched the boys hungrily take over the whales, the woman said, "Is there a cheaper binding ... than the five-hundred-dollar?"

He told her about the four-hundred-dollar set; but through the window he saw her husband replacing the jack under the tractor's tireless hub with a pile of 6x6 timbers. He began packing the samples, "Why don't we wait six months to see if they bring out a three-hundred-dollar set? Give you and your husband time to talk and think about it real good."

He U-turned the truck and was heading out when the German police dog hit the driver side with a bang that suggested Ruoff stop. The dog was followed by the woman. She held out a twenty. "For a deposit. You bring the four-hundred-dollar set, tomorrow."

Ruoff looked over at the farmer, then he told the woman he didn't need a deposit. "And wait until we investigate if there's a cheaper set." She said, "We had our chance buying tractor tires. The boys need their chance. You bring the books."

Her face ventured a smile, "And you can tell it at home tonight what a forceful salesman you are!"

"I can't do that, Ma'am."

"Why not?"

"They know this is only my second sale."

13

LEMPKE

(*Wyandot County Courier*)

DEAL FALLS THROUGH
FOR OLD RUOFF PLACE
Customer Backs Off. Cites Canadian $2.00
Bushel Duty On U.S. Corn Imports And
Campbell Soup Construction of Mexico Process
Plant.

Upper Sandusky — Warren Schlicter of Bucyrus
Trust announced that the bank's sale of its
foreclosed Ruoff farm fell through. He said the
property is back on the market at a reduced
price. This embattled farm, idle now since ...

Steve Varney wore a black patch over his left eye from
a childhood tractor accident. As his Jeep came to a stop on
the shoulder of Clayton Road, he studied the Ruoff place.
Jimsonweed was spreading. Kudzu vine was taking over
the woodlot. Standing hay was flattening down. Varney
was only 35, but his eyes were full of years. A third-
generation farmer in the Bucyrus area, he had always
admired the Ruoff farm, and Ben Ruoff.

Spotting the bank's caretaker man on the foreclosed
farm, an unemployed auto worker returned to the corn belt
from Toledo, Steve Varney leaned on the Jeep's horn and
motioned him to come over to the fence. Young Varney's
gestures had a precocious natural authority. When the
caretaker arrived, Varney said, "That pond water level is
too low for the cattle in this heat. See that galvanized box
on the side hill? Ben Ruoff had a gate valve inside there that

raises the water level."

"I know that. Mr. Varney, isn't it? But it's padlocked. The bank lost the key Ruoff gave over."

"Damn!" Varney dug into the Jeep for a fence cutter. "Take this and cut the lock. Get it back to me sometime. I've got to go into town right away."

Varney walked up to the polished oak railing in the bank. He took off his cap, revealing a white forehead over the browned face. "Miss Martha, is Schlicter in?"

"Yes, Steve, but ..."

Varney continued right on in as he had always done when Judson True managed the bank.

Schlicter stiffened. But there was about Varney a preoccupation with essentials that trivialized protocol. Schlicter knew who Varney was.

Varney put a faded DeKalb Seed cap on the desk and sat, "Mr. Schlicter, I've been watching the Ruoff place. Shame to see it running down. I'd like to manage it for you. I'll put a farmer on it ... a family."

"We have a man on it."

Varney's hand brushed that away. He outlined a simplified management agreement, fees and commission, explaining that he knew that property well and the others the bank now owned. He could bring the farm back into moderate production. But his main object would be to preserve it in workable condition. "That will hold the value up ... and the price you'll get."

"Be cheaper for us to drop the price than pay your fee for the man you'll put on the farm."

"No. There are families who just want to be on the land. Salary is not their priority."

"Who would you put on the Ruoff place?"

"You deal with me. Who I put on is my business."

Schlicter leaned back and smiled. "You really figure me for a city hick, right, Mr. Varney?"

"I s'pose. Same as you figure me for a country one."

Despite his MBA degree, Schlicter had learned one polestar truth about management, "The one control I need to retain, Mr. Varney, is *who* you put on the farms."

"Fine. Then you go ahead and put doctors and lawyers on them...and unemployed auto workers."

Varney picked up his cap and walked out.

* * *

A month later Varney slowed the Jeep and studied the Ruoff place. The offset tandem disk harrow was left in the rain with only 14 rows of corn stubble turned. The erosion gully on the slope had not been contoured closed. It had opened up more, exposing broken drain tile.

On the next field, cut hay lay unbaled after two heavy rains. It would have to be turned and dried again. Evenso, it could be unfit even for stall bedding. Of course, it could be disked in. That field could use the tilth.

He drove slowly toward the barn complex. The new boards Ben had bought to close in the wind damage to the barn lay on the ground weathering while the gap remained. The silo was still half painted the way it was when the marshal put Ben's family out of the main house.

Then Varney saw the mailbox. "Damn fool!"

The mailbox post had been straightened up, reinforced with a 4x4, and painted!

Schlicter's car was parked by the house. Varney drove in and stopped to watch. The banker was supervising a crew of Dister's painters and some out-of-town carpenters. The side of the house was being painted. On the front, already painted, the carpenters were hanging decorative shutters. Two men from Schuler Appliance were bringing in a new kitchen range.

Schlicter walked over to Varney's Jeep, "What are you doing here?"

"Trying to figure what *you're* doing."

"Isn't it obvious? Putting this farm in shape."

"Uh-huh."

"Packaging is important, Mr. Varney."

"Uh-huh."

"You disagree?"

"Uh-huh."

"Why?"

"On a working farm, you paint the barn first. If there's anything left over, you paint the house ... maybe."

Dister, the painting contractor, passing close behind Schlicter, caught Varney's scowl. Dister farmed 50 acres himself on the side. He shrugged to Varney.

Varney started the Jeep engine and said to Schlicter, "I don't know what your paint job is costing you; but that unbaled hay lyin' out there is gonna cost you two-three more passes over that field. Did you put that in your computer?"

He U-turned out of the drive.

* * *

Schlicter was relieved. He was driving to the Holiday Inn to meet Lempke for the final breakfast meeting before the big man left town. Big Dick Lempke hadn't been the fearsome inspector after all. The enormous executive vice president whom Toledo Trust had brought aboard during the farm emergency had been in Bucyrus three days now. He had been sent to monitor Schlicter's performance of course; but he had presented the trip as a collegial visit. This upcoming six thirty breakfast was a pain, but a small price to conclude an evaluation visit from headquarters. Schlicter was willing to accept there must be some good reason Toledo brought aboard such a jolly, harmless buffoon with no distinguished fiscal credentials.

Lempke had met everyone in the bank and, although the staff chuckled some at his loud and bulky joviality, they too were relieved. While the bulging Lempke asked a lot of questions, he made no suggestions. He complimented Martha on her customer handling. He complimented the cleaning people and took the clerical staff to lunch. Maybe Lempke's executive vice presidency of Toledo Trust was a form of quasi-retirement for over-the-hill executives of the bank. No. They had pointedly brought Lempke out of retirement from the grain elevator business. Well, whatever.

Schlicter said to the motel dining room hostess, "I have

a table for Schlicter and Lempke." A hand from behind landed on his shoulder like a bag of coins, "Mornin', Warny!" Schlicter stiffened at the diminutive. "I cancelled your good reservations. I'm takin' you to a different restaurant. It's on me. Okay? Leave that imported tennis club vee-hickle of yours parked here. We'll take my car."

His car was the plainest subcompact rental. Although Lempke's huge body compressed the back cushion, he had to raise the steering wheel to clear his belly. His huge hands and fat arms concealed the wheel. He looked like a man driving a toy car.

Lempke fired up a short-stemmed, big-bowled pipe and pulled onto the highway. Smoke filled the subcompact, but Schlicter aborted a move toward the window switch.

"Go ahead, Warny, open her up."

The big man was surprisingly *aware*.

Schlicter opened the window and relaxed, "Mr. Lempke, since this is your last morning here, what else can I show you to ... uh ... complete your ... uh ..."

"Mission. *Mission* is what we've got, Warny. Mission to keep your bank from failing. Mission to keep these three counties as customers when the pendulum swings back. When the farmers are kings again."

"Kings? You really think the American farmer will ever come back, Mr. Lempke?"

Lempke drove a mile in silence, then, "Warny, you ever study much history?"

"No, sir."

"Well, banks are going to go through a lot of hell because we're only water boys. But the farmers will be back."

Obviously Lempke's generation, without benefit of macro economic studies, like those from the National Bureau of Economic Research, had little chance to outgrow agrarian sentimentalism. A losing debate with a dinosaur executive vice president was no part of Schlicter's career plan. Successful turnaround of this Bucyrus farm bank would give him combat credits on the firing line which should earn him recall to Toledo headquarters office as a precocious young line vice president, on target for age 35. Then he would be very recruitable as a medium-sized corporation comptroller. "Well, back to my question, Mr. Lempke, what else can I show you?"

"Nothing more, Mr. Schlicter."

The *Mister* caused Schlicter to sit up straight, puzzled.

"It is now my turn, Mr. Schlicter, to show you some things about running a farm bank that's in a foreign trade war. Having observed you, I think you can learn it in the next 90 days."

"The choice of 90 days is because ...?"

"Because that's what you have, Mr. Schlicter."

This Lempke transformation was a jolt.

"You are a very bright man, Mr. Schlicter. Your graduation as number six in your Kellog class proves it. You took four of the toughest electives. In short, you are a brain."

Schlicter felt naked. Lempke kept his eyes on the road.

"But you got a late start compared to your bank customers."

"Late start?"

"Yes. They begin their trade at eight or nine, bringing the eggs from the henhouse. At ten, or whenever their legs can reach the clutch pedal, they are pulling a 22-foot cultivator and cultipactor in front of their daddies who were following on seed drills. Then when they were 15, they were planting 50 acres a day at six miles an hour. They sat at table every night with at least one parent who knew that particular soil since he or she was eight.

"By the time you were entering MBA school, your customer was often already taking charge of an investment of a half million dollars in land and a half million in tools and sheds, and entering the world's most complex business. While you generally only need to know two numbers ... what you pay for money and what you rent it out for ... he is into an infinite mathematical complexity of changing chemical formulae, complex botany, purchasing, law, politics, marketing and, worst of all, meteorology. He is about to support his own young family and his parents and grandparents ... and *you*, Mr. Schlicter. He supports you. So do you know that customer, Mr. Schlicter? And how to help him do all that?"

Schlicter shrewdly kept silent.

"I am going to *help* you learn that. But it will be up to you to learn very quickly. The first step is easy. Take off your suitcoat and tie ... *now*."

Schlicter did so in the cramped car.

"The degree of difficulty accelerates, but the next few steps are also easy. One ... sell tomorrow that tennis-club car of yours. Get a brown American subcompact. Two ... put your secretary in your office, and you sit at her desk out in the bullpen where you can see your customers and see out the window to Main Street.

"Three ..." — Lempke swerved into the dirt apron of Jo-Ann's Diner — "eat breakfast here every day, and lunch."

When the car stopped, its wake of dust flowed over it, further powdering the once red facade of Jo-Ann's Diner.

"Don't lock it." Lempke preceded Schlicter past the heat of the bug-covered radiators of a couple dozen pickups and cars with splash patterns of dried Crawford County mud.

Inside was alive. Except under the tables, the design on the linoleum was worn off in pathways, and down to the wood by the cash register. But the hurrying waitresses, two high school age and two mature women, were crisply clean. Jo-Ann raised a tray above her face to say, "'Morning, Mr. Lempke. There'll be room over by the jukebox. Jim and Neil are about leavin'."

Schlicter noted that Lempke had already made himself known here.

The newcomers waded through the frenzied scene to the table which had only one chair. On Jo-Ann's return trip with a trayful of empties, she dragged another chair into place. "Careful of that chair. One wobbly leg. Be with you d'rectly."

Lempke took a dime from his pocket and tightened two screws in the chair. Hardly seated, they were handed menus by a scrub-faced high school girl on the fly who pointed to a Coca Cola wall blackboard, "There's today's Special. Be right back."

That pace sustained through the ordering and serving.

While talking, Lempke kept his head inclined to his pancakes. "Now, Mr. Schlicter, eat slow. I'm giving you a chance to learn your market. What do you see?"

Schlicter looked around the crowded tables, mostly

farmers. To his credit, he seriously studied the crowd. He now knew Lempke was a mystery. There was something important here. But what? At the unmanned cash register he saw two farmers taking toothpicks. One called out, "Jo-Ann, how much were those sausages?" She called back, "Two seventy-five." The customer put money in the cigar box and took out change.

Schlicter noticed some men on their way out paused to put an ear close to a radio at one end of the restaurant, others did the same at the other end.

Lempke finally said, "You'll get the hang of it. There are several of these restaurants in your territory. Find them. Use them. It's your Ph.D. course." Schlicter's attention was riveted. "For example, notice the tip left on this table by just two men before us? Generous, don't you think?

"Next — you notice how fast these waitresses move? They know their market. These farmers need to get on the fields before the dew burns off.

"Next — notice the men pause at those two radios? That one is tuned strictly to a weather station; the other, to the farm market. What station is that, by the way, Mr. Schlicter?"

Lempke expected no answer.

"Next — listen real close for a minute and tell me what you hear."

The diner was a jumble of voices. But Schlicter now took Lempke very seriously. He concentrated harder than he ever had at Kellog lectures. He gradually picked up a few snatches ... "lost all his pre-blight spray to rain" ... "Campbell's will also quit domestic tomatoes. All Mexican..." ... "Canada's two-buck duty is to offset our price supports" ... "Ed's taking the government price" ... "That new Monsanto systemic needs less water ..." ... "Jo-Ann, has Steve been in yet?" ... "wants $900 for a rebuilt transmission." ... "Has he been in yet?"

Schlicter fed back to Lempke what little he heard.

"Not bad ... for a novice, Mr. Schlicter. You may succeed. Now, you've been in this territory quite a while. Who is that fellow in the white shirt sitting with those fellows near the door?"

Schlicter shrugged.

"That's Snelling, the best trusted surveyor in the area. More work than he can handle lately. Why?"

Schlicter shrugged.

"Farmers trying to survive are selling and swapping and renting land. Requires surveying. So Snelling knows what's going on. You need to know him."

Lempke next pointed out a lawyer who specialized in land law, a drain tile man who drained fields, and a land leveler specialist "who works with him." He pointed out the new Ag Department entomologist.

"This, Mr. Schlicter, is where they make their trades, buys, swaps, and get professional information. And this is where they learn whether the curculio worm has crossed Route 231 or not. This is where they tell each other who is a good supplier and who cheats. And this, Mr. Schlicter, is where they discuss you and me. This is where your world turns."

Schlicter took a thoughtful look around. "How did you learn all this in three days?"

"I didn't. *Three decades.* Every farm community has two - three places like this. Find them. The people you need are here."

"People I *need*?"

"Yes. For example, did you see those fellows at the counter move over to that crowded table?"

"No."

"That's because a fellow named Steve Varney came in. You know about Varney?"

"Somewhat."

"Then you also know he's something special in these counties and in fact in the Midwest."

"In the Midwest?"

"You need to know these things, Mr. Schlicter. You do know he's the youngest man on the state Ag Commission and may become next president of Midwest Corn Growers Association. I trust you subscribe to the *Ohio Farmer*?"

"Uh ... well ..."

"Well, do so."

"I know a little about Varney."

"Then you know he's a problem-solver. Looked to for action."

"I'm not so sure."

"No?"

"He brought us a proposal to manage some of our foreclosed farms."

"And?"

"It wasn't right. We would lose too much control. No sound fiscal organization can give up that much control."

"What kind of control for example?"

"For example, what farmer he would put on the Ruoff place. He said it was none of our business who he puts on it. That farm is a three-million-dollar asset."

"Asset, Mr. Schlicter? Or liability?"

Warner Schlicter studied the hand of the girl refilling his cup.

Lempke said, "Steve Varney is the third generation on Varney Farms and considered one of the shrewdest young farmers in the county."

"That's easy when he inherits land already paid for."

Lempke had read the *Ohio Farmer* profile which explained that Varney's two older brothers had been given the Varney farm to run. The oldest married a city woman who persuaded him to move off the farm. The father had to come out of retirement to operate the spread. The second brother took it over, but he overspent and underproduced. The father again came out of retirement. Then he noticed what he had not seen for years: His youngest was the farmer, Steve.

Lempke explained this.

Schlicter said, "Well he still took over a sound farm."

"So did many others. Whom, by the way, in our infinite wisdom we encouraged to overexpand and go into hock to us at 12 to 15 percent. Not Varney. He rents expansion land. Never buys. Rents a lot of his machinery. Buys little. I trust you knew all that, Mr. Schlicter, about the most distinguished young farmer in your market?"

Lempke stacked his dishes and rotated his finger as a command, "Country courtesy. Helps the girls."

Schlicter stacked his dishes but said, "Considering the

acreage he works, I'm not impressed with Varney's sales volume."

"Young Varney early made a bold trade-off. He went organic. Sacrifices some yield for low costs. When foreign competition moved in, he lucked out."

Lempke's shirt pocket was stuffed with pens and pencils and papers. He pulled out the papers and shuffled through until he dealt out a folded wilted clip from *Ohio Farmer*. "Just read the part I marked ... later."

Lempke drove the younger banker back to the motel, both men in silent thought. The young man got out. Lempke leaned over the passenger seat to say good-bye adding, "I was hard on you only because farm lending is a high skill. The economy will not forgive our mistakes. Forty percent of farm banks will go under. And I know you don't want yours to be one of them."

"No, sir."

"Then there is one way out for you."

Schlicter bent down to hear.

"Do I have your full attention?"

"Yes, sir."

"Mr. Schlicter, you need to contact Varney and offer him the management of as many of your delinquent farms as he will accept."

"Sir, I'm sure he won't accept any...from me...now."

"Mr. Schlicter, I recommend that you persist, insist, beg. You have 90 days, sir."

* * *

Calling Varney was a new experience for Warner Schlicter. He was accustomed to a business where both suppliers and customers traveled to the bank to do business, and both returned his calls promptly. But trying to reach Varney by phone was exasperating. Varney had learned to control his own time. "Sorry, he's over at the Sudbury Road place this morning." "Sorry, he just left for the dairy barn." "Sorry, he's in Columbus at the Ag Commission."

However, in the course of two weeks, Schlicter managed

to talk to Varney six times. Varney was polite. He knew that in a farm community you're going to need everybody at sometime in your life. He simply said he could not take on management of the Ruoff place, he had too big a load right now.

Lempke phoned twice to ask about progress.

"None yet, sir."

"Study your man, Mr. Schlicter."

The banker later got out the clipping Lempke had given him:

> ... and while Varney suffered in his early years from the slower soil restoration of organic farming as opposed to the instant fertility of chemicals, he is now being rewarded. Compared to chemically treated soils, Varney's tilth is gaining, containing 5 to 6% organic materials as opposed to 2 and 3%. Varney's fields can absorb a six-inch rain without runoff.
>
> He must work the ground more before planting to control weeds, but his fertilizer bill (microbial) runs $50 the acre as opposed to $300 for the chemical farmer.
>
> While his corn yields may be 120 bushels per acre against his neighbors' 140 to 150, his costs are way down.
>
> Why doesn't everyone do this?
>
> Varney is no born-again organic Messiah preaching to his neighbors whom he serves in several farm organizations. "I was lucky. I started young enough, before inflation, when I could afford the slow build-up of soil, with lower yields. Today you can't start this kind of farming and pay your loans."

Schlicter, having traded his rag top for a brown subcompact, drove several times to Varney's office in the barn on the Sudbury Road place. Varney's wife-secretary (and high school girlfriend), sensed that Schlicter felt awkward waiting for Varney on the barn apron, trying to stay out of the way of the farm's traffic. She took him into the barn office by the side door and poured him a coffee, "Steve is only down taking a new irrigation pump to the men working at the pasture. Back any minute."

Varney came an hour later, trailed a hand across Joan Varney's shoulder as she pointed to the messages she'd scotch-taped to the back of his chair. "The most urgent are the top ones." He nodded, then motioned Schlicter to a chair.

Schlicter said, "I'm here for the same thing we talked about before. I made a grave mistake in turning down your proposal."

Varney peeled the messages off the back of his chair, shuffled them into priority, and gazed out the window as if trapped. Then, in full sincerity, "Warner, I'm very glad you turned me down. I'm fighting for minutes. Just can't take it on now. I've got to help a bunch of us corn men. We used to sell a lot of our high sucrose corn to Canada. But Canada's two bucks a bushel duty hit us hard on top of Campbell soup's gone Mexican."

Schlicter said, "The bank can now offer you, besides the commission on any possible profit, double the flat management fee you named."

"I need money very badly, but I need time worse."

Schlicter nodded. As he left, Joan Varney's gentle eyes showed sympathy for him, and for all the people caught in the farm trouble. Everybody's troubles bruised Joan Varney.

14

VARNEY

Moose leaned across the coffee table in Varney's house. He had the sample encyclopedia volume open in front of Joan Varney, across from him. She had called Steve in from the barn office. Moose was showing Joan how the transparent plastic overlays against the basic world map tracked the sequence of creation of new nations in the world and the changes in boundaries of old nations.

Joan was scrutinizing these changes. Steve was scrutinizing Moose, a man who had excelled at agriculture since age 13 when he took six 4H blue ribbons in Columbus.

Joan said, "Steve, I think we need this set."

"You're right. How much is it, Moose?"

Moose was about to explain it was cheaper without the optional cabinet. That caused him to look for enough empty space in Varney's bookcase beside the fireplace.

Suddenly he packed up his samples. "Joanie! Why didn't you tell me? You don't need this!" He pointed. "You've already got Britannica, the best one."

Joan's soft voice assured him, "That's obsolete, Moose. Nineteen eighty-five. For example ... doesn't have these new countries you showed us."

Moose snapped the sample case shut. "How bad are you going to need to know international stuff?"

"Real bad," Steve said. "Ecuador is shipping in high sucrose corn to Cargill, one of our oldest customers. And I'm not sure where Ecuador is."

Moose rose, grabbed the sample kit, slapped Steve on the back and laughed, "It'll be in the newspaper, buddy! What am I doing in this crazy business? So long now!"

He walked out briskly.

* * *

When Varney returned to the barn office, he found Schlicter waiting. The banker said, "Steve, hear me out. The parent bank in Toledo authorized me to make you a spectacular offer." Varney merely kept his eyes on Schlicter. "For every farm you will manage for us, you would receive, in addition to the fees already offered, a three percent commission when we sell it. Real money!"

He waited. But Varney wordlessly shook his head.

"You can't mean that. You'd have no sales work. The commission is all bonus! *We* do the selling."

"That's part of the problem, Warner. You only need to recover your loans plus interest. So you'll dump the farms cheap to some absentee owners who will overcrop it and wear it out. More excess production ... hurts us all."

"You're managing three farms for Prudential Bache. Why not for us?"

"I told you. No more time. Plus ... I don't want to be associated with the bank. You're destroying friends of mine."

"Me?"

"For example, you made a great farmer into a terrible book salesman."

Schlicter said, "You're not consistent. You *don't* want us bringing more land into production, but you *do* want your friends back in production."

Varney wiped a hand over his eyes. "I never said it was simple. That's what killed Jud True. We need help, Schlicter; and you're not giving us any."

Varney let the banker leave without a good-bye. Suddenly he called after him, "Schlicter, there's one way I'll do it." Schlicter returned quickly. "But I don't think you could deliver your end."

"I'll bet we can."

"I mean *you* ... personally."

"I'll bet I can."

Varney looked at his watch, then picked up a shovel and led the way to the silo, "We're short-handed and trying to get some silage up before weather. We'll talk out there." En route he trailed a hand over the shoulders of a twelve-year-old girl. "Jen, get a pitchfork for Mr. Schlicter."

The two men stood on a four-wheeled cart, shoveling silage onto a bucket belt that took it up into a small silo. Finally Varney said, "The deal I will make is this: I will manage three foreclosed farms at the fees last discussed, if ..." he broke off to tell Jen to tow in another wagonload with the tractor. Schlicter stopped shoveling, "If?"

"If ... you will do the following. You have on your Toledo top staff a shrewd old man, who knows farming and is a pretty good talker. People like to listen to him. He is a registered lobbyist. He has financial experience and brains, too."

"What's that got to do with me?"

"I'm coming to that."

Varney explained that he was leading a delegation to Columbus to testify before the Agriculture Committee in favor of H.B. 703. The hearing would destroy most of a week's time. Maybe two. Maybe even four. Varney wanted Schlicter's vice president to study H.B. 703, then join the Varney delegation from the Corn Grower's Association to lobby the bill through in Columbus.

"What's in the bill?"

Varney explained that H.B. 703 would enable the state and towns and cities to buy back farmland, take it out of production, and hold it against future land shortages.

"And why should our vice president do this for you?"

"That's your problem. Your part of the deal is to recruit him for this."

"But four weeks of a vice president's time?"

"Not *any* vice president; this *par-tic-u-lar* vice president."

"What name?"

"I didn't write it down. You got a V.P. named Camp?"

"No."

"Kemp?"

"No."

Then Schlicter said, "O-o-h, you mean Lempke?"

"That's it."

Schlicter put down the fork. "Then I'm out of luck." He jumped from the cart. "He's my boss. There's no way I give him orders to give up two weeks." Varney tossed the other fork to Jennifer and motioned her to help. To Schlicter he merely said, "I gave you your chance."

* * *

Martha Cushman could not figure out the cause of Schlicter's nervousness. He had her cancel his appointments. He paced his office, seeming to rehearse something. She couldn't know he was nervous because he had lost control of the timing of the phone call.

Schlicter had prepared himself for the call to Lempke with more notes than he had taken into his MBA oral.

He had considered carefully the timing of the call. He discarded just before lunch, just after lunch, just before closing. He had elected the opening of business when Lempke would be fresh. He went over his notes on why he could ask his boss to give up two weeks away from his job. He would lead up to it with situation summaries ... one, two, three. He had these on cards in front of him.

But when he placed the call, Lempke's very efficient assistant said Lempke was not in, "But I'll have him call you promptly, Mr. Schlicter."

Caught off-balance, Schlicter did not say instead that he would call again. So now Lempke might sandwich the call in on the run to a meeting or some other ...

His phone rang. Martha said it was Lempke."Hi, Warny. Got a meeting in five, but didn't want to keep you waiting. Shoot."

"Mr. Lempke, let me call you at a better time."

"No, talk. If it takes more than five minutes, it's too complex for this old boy."

Schlicter started through his prepared talk. At point three Lempke laughed, "Warny, this is me, remember? Skip the warm-up and say it."

When Schlicter finished there was a long pause.

Then Lempke, in a slower, deeper voice, said, "So you are asking if an executive vice president of this bank holding company will take two weeks off the job, maybe three, four — to accompany a young farmer to the hearings in Columbus?"

"Uh ... yes, sir."

138

"And Varney got you to make this call?"

"Uh ... well ... "

"You ever consider putting Varney on your board?"

"Uh ..."

"No? Okay."

"Well, Mr. Lempke, I withdraw the request. It is very presumptuous."

"Sure it is." There was another long silence, then a quicker voice, "But we better do it."

"Better?"

"Yup. Y'see, the young man has the answer. We have eight farm banks, all stuck with thousands of foreclosed acres. This would give us a market for that, save our marginal debtor farmers, and take excess land out of production. It should be a federal program; but starting at the state level is faster. Not bad. Not bad."

Schlicter judiciously remained silent.

"Warny, get Varney to manage as many of your farms as he will."

The phone went dead.

* * *

On Clayton Road, Schlicter suddenly hit the brakes. When the dust overtook his car and cleared, he thought he saw Ben Ruoff stringing fence on the Ruoff farm.

Warner Schlicter was a keen intellect. He worked at putting into practice Lempke's lessons. Therefore he regularly got into his plain brown subcompact and toured the county roads through Oceola, New Winchester, Spore, Brandywine, Lemert, Upper Sandusky, viewing the farms of his loan customers.

But today he was betrayed. He drove to the pay phone at Jo-Ann's Diner and dialed Varney's office. Joan Varney said her husband was en route to the Ruoff farm.

Schlicter floored the accelerator back toward the Ruoff farm, arriving just as Varney's Jeep was leaving. He turned in, blocking the drive, and got out to confront Varney.

"Varney, what in hell are you doing?"

"Meaning?"

"Did you put Ruoff back on this farm?" Varney remained seated at the wheel. "Of course."

"You double-crossed me. You agreed to manage. Instead you're just putting your friends back on their farms."

I'm doing both."

"Putting a failed farmer back on his own farm is managing?"

"Ruoff is a failed financier, not a failed farmer."

"Couldn't you get someone else?"

"Of course."

"Then why didn't you?"

"Get in. I'll show you ... if you can understand."

Driving over the field roads and yelling over the Jeep's porous muffler, Varney pointed to a field corner, "Ruoff knows that corner gets too wet too often for early planting. But it's okay by May twenty." He drove to a field south of the wood lot. "Ruoff knows that field is always best ... for the last eighty years. It's something to do with the trees just north. So he never cuts the wood lot real thin." Varney bumped the Jeep through the creek up onto the stubbled field, "How many years of hay do you think that field needs to produce a good year of corn?"

"How would I know?"

"You wouldn't. But Moose Ruoff knows. He got it from his father who got it from his father."

Varney cut the engine dead and turned to Schlicter. "Now, Mister, do you have eighty years to let me teach some new farmers about these lands?"

"No."

"Then stay the hell out of my way."

15

JUAN G. L. J. RIVERA

Ed Fash shambled into his cubicle at the *Miami Herald*, cleared enough desk clutter to park his burger and fries and cola, and called over the shoulder-high partition, "Mike, did we get a callback from Mr. Bexley at Chemical Bank of Chicago?"

"No. The P.R. guy called and said Bexley was en route to New York."

Fash rooted through the paper debris and fished out two old phone call slips.

"Hm-m-m. Mike, come in here."

Mike Knox came in and said, "Ed, for once eat your lunch, and we'll talk after."

"No. Look." He showed Knox the two slips of other calls. "Oyler of Bank of America is headed for New York. Cowan of Bank One left for New York. Try Ziegler of First Dallas."

"You mean to ask him about the effect on Texas of the stepped-up congressional protection drive?"

"That's what we wanted originally. Now we just want to know if he's *also* going to New York."

Under Ed Fash, the *Miami Herald* had developed a financial section of national scope, way beyond the state's industry and commerce. But the *Herald* knew its readership. From trailer camps south of the Tamiami Trail to the Palm Beach coastal castles, retired people were managing life savings ranging from IRAs to family mega-trusts.

Many subscribed to the *Wall Street Journal* and *Value Line* and all the rest, but Fash had built a business section that focused on his Florida readership. Knowing he was no financial expert himself, he did original research. His manner in interviewing financial authorities was an earnest effort to learn. Later when he knew a lot, he never tried to show the interviewee's how much he knew, nor sought ratification of preconceived theories. He still listened. Although he did not realize it himself, he had become an excellent practical economist. Chief executives instructed their P.R. people and corporate secretaries that his calls should be returned promptly. And if he needed background figures, they should give him the right stuff. And Bexley specifically ordered, "If Fash calls, don't hand him off to some precocious MBA who's gonna instruct him in the big picture."

Mike Knox came back to Fash, "Your burger's turning chartreuse."

"What about Ziegler of First Dallas?"

"He's left for New York."

"Bingo."

Knox picked up Fash's bag of wilted french fries, "You'll get grease poisoning." He looped them into the wastebasket.

Fash said, "You know what I'm thinking?"

"Yup. You're thinking there's an off-camera banker's summit shaping up in New York." Knox took the lid off Fash's burger and covered it quick, as if he'd seen a felony and didn't want to be a witness. "Your next question is, where in New York?"

"Bingo."

"It'll be in the conference room of J. Lincoln Barnes, boy-wonder vice president of Citibank. And you want me to go there and play a country newsman wanting another feature on the cashless society or telephone banking."

"Bingo."

"And then you want me to select some young P.R. bank trainee who really pines to be a real journalist, and take him or her to lunch hoping he or she will show off and tumble the news about this banker summit meeting."

"Bingo. Go."

* * *

On the 14th floor of Citibank in the small deluxe conference room attached to the office of the brilliant 42-year-old

Vice President Barnes, eleven men faced Juan G.L.J. Rivera, about the same age as Barnes, graduate of UCLA and Cornell, now Minister of Finance, Ecuador. The men were exhausted.

Rivera rose from the table and turned his back to the group as he stared out the window. The move interrupted the argument. When the room went silent, he enunciated, "Gentlemen, you've drifted off point. We are not here to discuss restructuring payment schedules for Ecuador. We are here to decide one thing." As the tall Ecuadorian turned to face the table, the sun of the harbor made him a formidable silhouette highlighted in a blinding penumbra. "Default or Abrogation? Which do you prefer?"

The declaration lay on the table like a ticking bomb.

Everyone had thought it would start with Brazil, as it nearly had back in '89. Ecuador!

"I came here to give you this chance to register your preference in case you might give us more favorable treatment under one course than the other. Myself, I favor abrogation. And that is probably the way we will go, but you have the chance to present me any advantages to Ecuador if instead we merely default."

Oyler of Bank of America said, "For your predecessor, we extended in good faith ..."

"Don't talk about my predecessor," snapped Rivera. "You are talking to *me*. If Ecuador only defaults, it leaves open many doors and clouds the issue. If we abrogate, it is clear-cut. The deal is over.

"If we abrogate, it favors you as well. You can get help from your government on the grounds that your banks suffered a huge loss, *not* from poor loan judgment, but from your government's damaging tariff on our beef, sugar, coffee, wool, corn, leather. You bankrupt us. If we only default, you are guilty of loan imprudence. Your government will have trouble bailing you out with tax-payer money."

Oyler's neck veins swelled. "We've got more choices than that!"

"What? Repossess Ecuador, or the city of Quito? How?"

He did not have to spell out what everyone in the room

knew. If Ecuador abrogated, the Economic Association of South American Nations could logically push their request that their interest payments come back to them as new loans. At the least they could all suspend interest payments.

Bexley of Chemical of Chicago finished noodling the total possible Latin American damage to this group on a card that was too small, so he abbreviated. The bottom number was 65. He slid the card in front of Ziegler of First Dallas. "Add nine zeros."

Oyler exploded, "How can you stand there and do this to us? You hired the money!"

"Correction. I did not hire the money. Look at me; I am only 41. My *predecessors* rented the money. I would not have done so. You crippled our nation with loans, just as you did your own farmers."

"We were trying to help."

"Help makes helpless." Rivera paced.

Murphy of Mellon Bank said, "Your government didn't talk that way. They talked social progress."

Rivera spoke quietly, "Please, gentlemen. Banks are not social agencies. They are businesses. You appraised us as a *profitable* loan."

Oyler said, "*We* didn't. We inherited these loans. The men who made them retired."

Rivera smiled. "So, fine. We can both blame our grandfathers. We are even."

"Even, hell!" Ziegler cut in. "You've saddled us with catastrophic loss. You and your neighbors hauled sixty-five billion out of here, not counting lost interest."

"Compared, Mr. Ziegler, to what you've hauled out of Latin America at bargain prices?"

Oyler started to answer, but Barnes of Citibank held up a hand, "As Mr. Rivera says ... let's stick to business. Mr. Rivera, do you realize what abrogation will do to South America's world credit?"

Rivera sat down. "You know we would have considered that carefully, Mr. Barnes."

"And?"

"We think if we default, we do hurt our credit. If we

abrogate, the Middle East and the Soviet Bloc will love us. We become David; you, the giant. Our credit will rise because, with abrogation, we wipe out our previous debt. We start clean."

Bexley leaped in. "Clean?"

Rivera shrugged. "It's the real world."

The table was silent.

Finally Barnes of Citibank asked, "Mr. Rivera, would you go again with us tomorrow to our State Department in Washington to see what we could work out?"

"Thank you, no. I would be ... how do you say it ... 'out of channels.' Our embassy there talks to your State Department. I talk to banks. Are there any questions?"

"How could there be questions?" Oyler snarled.

"Well, there is one question I expected."

"What?"

"I expected you to ask, 'Why now? Why did we not do this a year ago? Two years? Why not next year?'"

"Well, why?"

"We are anticipating the passage of your brutal protection bills being reintroduced in your Senate by Drummond and in the House by Slazer, carried over from last year with new names. Your violent *Buy American* campaign will drive one or the other of these bills through. It will shut us out totally. You will strip us of any means to pay you. We will have nothing to lose from the U.S."

"Why didn't you lead off with this?" Bexley asked. "And seek our influence on our government?"

Rivera shrugged. "Your banks have never exercised prudent economic leadership of the U.S. Not in the panic of 1873. Not in 1929. Not in 1932. Not in 1987. Not now."

The silence was so deep that they could hear the antique grandfather clock slice another hour off Ecuador's course toward default ... or abrogation.

Rivera pulled out of his slim briefcase a Citibank newspaper ad. He slid it across the table to Barnes. "Even your own people you mislead." The advertisement was a photo of a telephone, headlined: CITIBANK HOTLINE TO CONSOLIDATE YOUR DEBTS. "What kind of financial leadership is that, Mr. Barnes?"

Rivera rose. "And unless you have something further, I guess we have done our talking."

Oyler said, "Now just a minute! There's got to be something we can do!"

"There is of course. You can try to head off the Pro-American Tariff Bill. But you don't have the stature nor the understanding."

"Who do you think you're ..."

Rivera interrupted, "Since you may have matters to discuss together," — he turned to Citibank's Barnes — "I will pass up your kind invitation to lunch."

En route to Citibank executive dining room Bexley asked to use a phone. With the time difference to Chicago, he was able to catch his assistant to the president before lunch. "Tell Matheson to call in marginal 'on demand' loans. Do it by phone. Then follow with the required written notices, *hand* delivered. *Today*."

His color deepened. "Yes. Today."

His temple vein throbbed, "Well, get him out of the meeting ... now. Get a message back to me here in a half-hour telling me it's begun. Don't state any details. Just say, 'Matheson has started.' And wait a minute ... tell Hunzinger in P.R. if he starts getting calls from the business press, his answer is — 'It's just part of a routine annual portfolio review, and a prudent increase of reserves.' Move."

At the host's Citibank luncheon table, the other bankers were also late in arriving. Bexley declined everything but the soup. Mid-lunch Barne's assistant walked in with a small envelope for Bexley. He opened it. "Matheson has started." Bexley told the waiter he had changed his mind. He would take a martini and the small steak.

In Miami, Ed Fash received a call from Mike Knox, "The meeting is here at Citibank all right. Or was. But security here is like the fifth *gon* in the Pentagon. Media types all have leprosy here. I'm on a lobby pay phone."

"You got nothing?"

"Zee-ro."

"Zero?"

146

"The TV hounds smell something, too. But they're no better off. They're here in the lobby with pretty anchorettes crying all over the security guys, who are lapping it up but shaking their heads."

"Mike, what's the biggest thing right now that could bring the big banks to talk at that level?"

"Some Third World nation missed a mortgage payment?"

"Bingo."

"I should see if there's a finance type in town from south of the border?"

"Bingo. And call me."

At 4:15 p.m. Fash reached by phone Hunzinger of Chemical Bank of Chicago. "What's up, Hunze?"

"You mean in Chicago finance in general, Ed?"

"Not in general, Hunze; and not Chicago. New York."

"New York? I'm in Chicago."

"Your boss is in New York."

"Ed, you've always been interested in serving your *Miami Herald* readers with accuracy, right?"

"That's why I call you."

"And I've got orders from Bexley never to lie to you, right?"

"That's why I call you first."

"Well, to honor your requirements and also Bexley's instructions, I have no choice but to do what I'm about to do. I hope someday you'll understand, Ed."

Click. The dial tone came on.

* * *

(*Miami Herald*)

GRAVE POSSIBILITY
OF LATIN AMERICAN
LOAN DEFAULT
Eleven Major Bank
CEO's Hold Summit Meet

New York City — At the same time that eleven large foreign lender bank presidents met, Ecuador Finance Minister Juan G.L.J. Rivera was here, ostensibly for ...

(Wall Street Journal)

ECUADOR MAY DEFAULT ON QUARTERLY LOAN PAYMENT

New York — Ecuador Finance Minister Juan G.L.J. Rivera, who assumed that post with the recent change of administration, arrived in New York with a surprise ...

(New York World)

ECUADOR ABROGATES!
Loan Contract Flat Out Canceled

(Commerce Journal)

CHEMICAL BANK AND TEN OTHERS FACE STUNNING WRITE-OFFS

New York — When Ecuador defied U.S. banks Wednesday, Columbia followed 72 hours later with the milder action of passing a quarterly interest payment. Although Chile and Mexico have not yet reacted, they have both requested a meeting for ...

In Chicago, Jack Matheson took the 31st outraged call-back from Chemical's correspondent and subsidiary banks. It was Richard Lempke.

"Jack. Lempke — Toledo Trust."

"Yes, Dick."

"You boys don't mean this, right?"

"It's from the very top, Dick."

"In other words, we backwoods types are going to pay for the mistakes of your hotshots playing international finance?"

"Don't forget we took care of Toledo when Honda and Toyota flattened your automotive economy."

"That was long before my time. The benefits of being one of your correspondent banks are fading fast, Jack."

Lempke hung up and dialed Bucyrus. "Warny, you always wanted to be in the banking business, right?"

"Yes, sir."

"Well, now comes the test."

"The test?"

"Call in all your 'on-demands!' Foreclose your delinquents. Liquidate all foreclosed collateral."

Schlicter was trying to absorb this.

"You there, Warny?"

"Yes, sir."

"You understand it?"

"No, sir."

"In plain English — get liquid quick!"

Warner Schlicter hung up and dialed one digit. "Mrs. Marks, call Clark at Farm Auctions in Upper Sandusky. Tell him we need to see him ... today."

Benjamin Ruoff charged into the kitchen at 5:30, rolled up his sleeves, and scrubbed his hairy arms at the sink. Then he stopped and sniffed the air, "Holy smoke! Brownies! Whose birthday?" He opened the other oven, "A roast! In the middle of the week?" He picked her up and sat her on the counter top. "Who's coming?"

Then he saw the extra-damp eyes, "What's the matter,

149

Sheil?"

"Moose, whatever happens, remember this: As long as we're together, we're going to be okay. You and I and the boys ..."

"Huh?"

She pulled out of her apron pocket one page of the *Bucyrus Courier*. He held it arm's length.

(Bucyrus Courier)

LEGAL NOTICE

Auction-The public is informed herewith that the lands, structures and machinery of the Benjamin T. Ruoff farm located on Clayton Road, Bucyrus Township, County of Crawford, State of Ohio, will be offered at public sale on the premises beginning at 10:00 a.m. on the ...

(Toledo Blade)

67 NORTHWESTERN OHIO FARMS
SLATED TO GO UNDER THE
HAMMER THIS MONTH
Wave Of Farm Auctions
Stuns Farm Communities

At Jo-Ann's Diner, Charlie Herndorf said, "Ecuador! What in hell has Ecuador got to do with Bucyrus!"

He was looking at Steve Varney.

"Everything," Varney said.

BOOK II

16

FLITCH

(*Business Week*)

FORTE'S FREE TRADERS IN SENATE SWAMPED AS CONGRESS SEIZES BUY AMERICAN MOOD TO REMOUNT SEVERE TRADE BILLS

Senate And House Re-Introduce Last Year's Failed Trade Bills Renumbered S.B. 700 and H.R. 776

The Senate's toughest free trader admitted to being stunned by the new bills. "The Senate has rounded up 200 specialized trade bills into one monster omnibus S.B. 700, a new name for last year's S.B. 115.

"This new bill is an economic declaration of war against the world which will counterattack immediately. No ships will sail. Prices to consumers will go through the roof."

Forte said the only bright spot is that "when joint House-Senate committee attempts to meld S.B. 700 and H.R. 776, there may be eighty or ninety legislators on the Joint Committee, which may make it impossible to get agreement this year."

S.B. 700 contains a textile-garment section Forte says will take the shirt off the average American's back. "The section on shoes is so harsh, some of this nation may soon go barefoot."

Beyond a long list of protected products, S.B.

700 strips the president of his discretionary power to negotiate. It mandates punitive tariff increases against nations running a 30% trade balance against us, and ...

(Political Biography Digest)

REQUIEM FOR A BRILLIANT SENATOR
by Jackson Garth

It is now common talk inside the Beltway that Senator Justin Forte has killed himself politically by total commitment to a single issue.

Gossip has it that few Missouri candidates have asked Forte to endorse them or attend their fundraisers back home. In Washington the senator's phone calls are returned less promptly.

It is interesting to note how often great leaders have fallen into the fatal trap of betting their total prestige and effort on a losing cause.

Coincidentally enough, Forte is going down under the same cause that snuffed out the blazing career of Wendell Wilkie who saw the vision of "One World." Forte sees the same vision ... via free trade.

Reluctantly, this writer, in interviewing the senator, felt compelled to ask, "Do you think you can survive this?"

He thought about it briefly. "I have to believe there is some way to wake up the public to the disaster they'll suffer from protectionist extremes."

I then asked, "Why risk everything when you can see protectionism snowballing? Isn't it a waste?"

"No. Every time my finger in the dike delays the bill a month ... that's progress."

"But if it still passes, how will you feel?"

"How would I feel if I didn't try?"

I then asked ...

(Backstairs Digest)

FORTE'S SENATE CORPS SHRINKS

Senator Butus was the first hard core free trader to abandon Forte's ship. A head count of anti-protection senators is now a guessing game, but ...

(Washington Post)

Addressing the Commerce Committee, a fatigued Senator Forte charged them, "Rather than raising tariffs, we should be beefing up our assistance to our own exporters instead of throwing roadblocks in their way with stupid legislation that ties their hands."

Senator Drummond responded that the government has several effective programs to assist exporters.

* * *

The Department of Commerce coordinator of the international marketing seminar in Detroit thanked the panel of experts he had assembled on stage and began to adjourn. The audience gave vapid applause, like people paying a tax. Mistaking this for enthusiasm, the coordinator added, "Now the next Department of Commerce seminar on International Trade is scheduled for next month in Chicago. Do you have any suggestions for that meeting?"

The audience checked watches and remained silent. Finally in the back of the room a hand went up. The speaker pointed to him with relief.

Rising slowly to respond was a chunky graying veteran of the sales wars. The face, still young, already had a granitic authority. "I would suggest ..."

The speaker interrupted him, "Would you identify yourself, sir?"

"Adam F. Flitch. XRW Corporation, Fastener Division."

"Thank you. Your suggestion?"

"With all respect ..." — Flitch's speech was relaxed, as a man not expecting results — "this is the third one of these I have attended with high hopes. I suggest your next seminar feature speakers who have *actually* been involved in international *selling*. We all have staff types who can study out the paperwork A-B-C's presented here today ... the forms, the currency handling, the shipping, the use of trading companies. Many of us come here at great expense ... time and money ... for solutions to the *real* problems."

"Oh? And you consider those to be?"

"It isn't what I *consider* them to be, it's what they *are!*"

"Perhaps you'd enlighten us." The coordinator scanned the audience for signs of how the wind was blowing.

"I had hoped to hear how to handle ... under U.S. rules ... the commissions demanded by foreign government purchasing officials which the rest of the world considers normal practice, but our rules don't. Are there ways we can get around this without the complex, tedious procedures we're now forced to invent?"

The coordinator was dismayed to see the audience now much more alert ... heads turning to the back of the room.

"I had hoped to hear about finding insurers to cover countertrade risk in Indonesia. How to simplify countertrade. How to effectively use switch-trading and buy-backs and offset trading. How to countermove when we get stiff-armed on bidding on foreign public works."

A murmur of approval rose from the crowd.

"We need to know how best to arrange a tax holiday in countertrading. How do you grease the tracks through foreign customs?"

The audience ratification of Flitch's remarks became obvious to the panel on stage.

Flitch said, "In short, sir, we don't need your help with the paperwork stuff and abstractions about Asian culture discussed here today. We need the hard-nosed nuts-and-bolts way to survive our own and foreign governments' restrictions."

Flitch sat down. The audience broke out in applause.

The coordinator muttered to his assistant, "Skip passing out those seminar evaluation forms."

17

DOUGHERTY

Coming home from work one rainy night, Dougherty charged into his subcompact apartment in the routine he had refined since Annie left. Without taking off his raincoat, he punched the range to *preheat*, ripped open a TV dinner, slid it into the oven, set the timer, went back outside for the mail, chucked the ads, dropped the rest by the photo of Annie and the boys on the coffee table, clicked on the 6:30 NBC-TV national news en route to the bedroom, whipped off his tie, shrugged out of suitcoat and raincoat as one garment...and returned to the living room where he sank into a chair for his pre-news ritual. He stared at the half-full glass on the coffee table. "Stay there, you son of a bitch! I have beat you."

He started to slit the mail. Suddenly he quit.

A frenzied off-camera news voice with an accent pulled his attention to a slow pan across a scene he could hardly believe. The scene was mostly roiling smoke, but in the gaps Dougherty could see what were apparently human dwellings, each within three feet of another and some touching. As the camera panned along the smoke, Dougherty made out shadow outlines of women running, carrying children and bundles and pans and chickens. Dogs barked. Foreign voices screamed. The accented news voice was saying,

> "Mexico City, fastest growing North American city, has reached a staggering, unmanageable fifteen million, and is ringed by an impoverished belt of ..."

The camera lingered on a close-up of dwellings, that

brought Dougherty out of his chair closer to the screen.

He was looking at a one-story structure about twenty feet long made of 2x4's anchored in cement-filled five-gallon paint cans. The siding was unpainted cardboard with the words "Westinghouse Lauadeira," "Hooever Barrer," and "Sears Cocinar." The roof was shingled with flattened number 10 cans. As he watched, the building melted.

The camera cut to an American voice and a high angle of roof tops jammed together so tightly that street alleys could not be seen.

"Mexico City is burning.

"For six hours now the Mexican National Guard has been dynamiting fire lanes to protect the center of the city from..."

Dougherty switched to another channel. It was showing a long shot of Mexico City.

"One point two million Mexicans live in the shanty belt, surviving on ..."

The foreground was black smoke. In the distance the bottoms of the clouds were orange.

"My God!" Dougherty switched to several other channels. CBS showed roads clogged with fleeing pedestrians blocking the progress of an occasional ancient automobile overloaded with elderly and infants.

Dougherty charged out of the apartment to the anti-litter urn on the sidewalk and raked through the rubbish. No newspapers. He strode toward a young woman with a briefcase. She shied away. "Lady, I only want to ask if I could buy your newspaper." He reached for his wallet. She handed him the paper and fled.

With pedestrians eddying around him, he read. The whole first page was faxed fire photos. But a small side bar caught Dougherty's eye:

FIRE DELIBERATE
Set by "People for Housing" Committee

Mexico City - After ten frustrating years of broken housing promises by the government, Povo Vor Casa (People for Housing) carefully planned a limited one-block fire. They selected a block where the fire could be limited, arranging for defense against spreading and for evacuating people to safety.

What Went Wrong?

The sight of the fire caused wild gangs of unemployed dissidents, hoping for loot, to spread the fire to other blocks. A forty mph wind came up from the ...

Dougherty returned to his kitchen. His smoke alarm was whining from smoke from his oven. He pulled out the blackened pizza and slid it into the sink on his way to the phone. He dialed Edith White. "Edith, you've been paying the state corporate tax right along on Jason's corporation?"

"Yes, Tom. Why?"

"It's all ready to go anytime he wants to reactivate it, right?"

"Yes ..."

"And you've been sending a bonus check to the Dart watchman to look into the quonset daily, right?"

"Right. But since he lost his wife, Jason isn't the same. No interest in anything. I think he's sinking rapidly. Doesn't even..."

"We're gonna raise him up ... rapidly!"

"Tom, he can't even leave the nursing home. Doctor's orders."

"Whatever happened to habeus corpus?"

"What?"

"Edith, you got phone numbers for Emile Hoffstetler and

Frank Hood?"

"Yes."

"Call them. Find out what they're doing. Tell them to get ready."

"Tom, what is this all ..."

"Edith, I'll call you."

Dougherty stared at the TV. Absently he reached down for the glass of bourbon and drank.

He yanked a copy of *Great Sales Managers* from the bookcase and grabbed the pint behind it. He poured three fingers and brought it to his lips. Suddenly he put it down on the table, shaking. "Stay there, you lousy son of a bitch."

Thomas J. Dougherty discovered early in life a phenomenon in which he had come to put great faith — the game-breaker opening. At Notre Dame, no matter how far down they were by third quarter, Dougherty lived in supreme confidence that, on some carry, a tackler would stumble or look away and the whole field would open up like double doors. Later, in selling, he could endure the weeks of steady turndowns which killed other salesmen, because he knew as surely as sunrise that at any moment...in the next town or the next...there would be a distributor prospect who needed a whole new product line to break open a market. He developed a keen eye for the game-breaker moment.

Dougherty took the newspaper into his car and drove to the quonset. Inside, he switched on only the low bench lights. Emile's hand tools had a coat of dust, the more because he had left them well oiled. But they were lined up on the wall precisely. His measuring instruments had socks on them. The musk of old machine oil rose to Dougherty's nostrils. In the cavernous area beyond the reach of the bench light, tarpaulined prototypes of the Utility Cube loomed in the gloom.

Dougherty untied and opened one tarp partly and looked in. Some metallic parts gleamed in the leaked light and the balsam fragrance of the wood paneling escaped.

"By gosh, Jason!"

A door slammed and a voice demanded, "Who are you?"

Dougherty could not see the questioner behind the

flashlight. "I'm Tom Dougherty. And you?"

The flashlight extinguished. "Oh. Hello, Mr. Dougherty. Corporal Hurd. Just checking."

"Uh-huh. You do that often?"

"No. I saw the light on."

"Uh-huh."

"But I could check it periodically."

"Won't be necessary."

"I guess not."

"Meaning?"

"We-ll, this was always a kind of a crazy idea. Right?"

"Good night, Corporal."

Midmorning, the gardener at Northbay Nursing Home looked up, startled. Usually cars entered the drive reluctantly. But a dusty old blue 1988 Pontiac sprayed gravel turning in and braked so abruptly in the fire lane, the car rocked. A heavy-set man with a newspaper exploded out and headed toward the entrance.

"Hey, Mister, you can't park ..."

The photoelectric door didn't open fast enough and it snagged part of his newspaper. His approach to the reception desk blew the sign-in sheet off the counter. The white-clad receptionist picked it up and glowered.

"Tom Dougherty, to see Jason Dart."

She completed filling out the day's expected physicians list. Dougherty's heart pumped. She signed in a pharmacy delivery man, then looked at Dougherty.

"Dougherty, to see Jason Dart."

"Visiting hours are not until two-thirty."

"Two-*thirty*?"

"Two-thirty." She resumed her work.

But Dougherty remained standing at the counter. Watching the action for a few minutes, he observed a handful of nurses and aides moving the wheelchaired residents to an outdoor garden, each handling two chairs. He chose a senior starched nurse."Nurse, I've got nothing to do until visiting hours. Can I wheel some out?"

The receptionist started, "Sir, that's ..."

But the nurse interrupted, "Darn right, Mister. Bring two at a time. Start with Room 112."

Dougherty strode down a long hall. Chairborn patients waited in limbo in the rooms. He searched the names beside the doors.

He was taken back when he found Jason in his wheelchair staring vacantly out the window. The scalp showed more pink through the white hair than Dougherty remembered. The wrists hung limp.

Dougherty was suddenly slowed. Jason Dart had gotten old.

"Jason!"

Dart turned slowly and smiled benignly. "Tom. How nice of you to visit."

"Jason, this is no visit! This is business!"

"Business?"

"Business."

"Tom, business is over."

"First I've got to wheel you to the garden."

Dougherty pushed the chair down a corridor toward an outside door. "Not that one, Tom. It sets off the alarm."

"Alarm? Is this a jail?"

"There are some Alzheimer's patients. Protection ... so they ... we don't wander off."

In the garden Dougherty pushed Dart to a spot near the padlocked wrought-iron gate. "Jason! The time has come! Mexico City! They need houses! Fast! Cheap! Hundreds of them! Thousands! Tens of thousands!"

It took Dougherty several minutes to explain the fire. Dart had not seen the TV news. Dougherty handed him the newspaper. "My glasses are back in the room."

"The pictures are big. Look. They tell it all."

Jason Dart finally grasped it. He said, "But, Tom, these people probably don't need furnaces or use air conditioners."

"Jason, you can make a simpler model first. Later your regular model. Plenty of middle-class Mexicans got burned out, too."

Dart stared at the flowers, his hand pinching his chin. "Tom, notice these roses. The gardener..."

"Jason! This is it! This is what we need!"

Without looking at Dougherty, Dart thought aloud, "Tom ... there are all kinds of Mexican trade barriers."

"Hey, they're going to be desperate! Barriers can be jumped."

"Besides legislative barriers, Tom, there's a whole mass of customs ... government purchasing agents and a tradition of special commissions to be paid."

"Jason! Remember me? I'm a *salesman*. You build 'em, I'll sell 'em!"

Dart thought silently. Quietly he said, "Tom, there's a problem getting me out of here, my daughter and my doctor, and the house rules."

"Wait here."

Dougherty went from the garden into the nursing home and out through the front door. He walked to the gardener. "Sir, I'm terribly sorry I left my car in the fire lane. I had an emergency. I'll move it right now. Then I need to talk to you."

He moved the car and came back to the gardener. "I sure would be grateful if you'd unlock that wrought-iron gate and tell me what those orange roses are just inside it."

"There's no orange."

"I just saw them."

"There's no orange roses."

"I'll bet you twenty dollars."

The gardener went around to the side, unlocked the padlock, entered, and stooped to the flowers. Dougherty stooped beside him. The gardener pointed to the plants. "See. No orange."

"Well, I'll be darned," Dougherty promptly handed over twenty singles. "By gosh, you win."

While the gardener counted bills, Dougherty moved quickly to Dart, wheeled him out the gate.

"Hey!"

Dougherty wheeled Dart on the run to the Pontiac, opened the door, helped Dart in, slid behind the wheel. The tires spewed gravel.

Dart said, "We didn't get my walker."

"We'll get new."

"We didn't get my glasses."

"With your vision, Jason, you don't need glasses." Temporarily ensconced in Dougherty's apartment for several days, Dart read all the newspapers with the aid of a magnifying glass:

(Special to *New York Times*)

MEXICO CITY ASHES COOLING
Over 200,000 Homeless.
Casualties - 3500. Dead - 150.

Mexico City - The Mexican Office of Housing today released figures on the damage counted thus far (See page 2).

Casualties overflowing seven hospitals are being treated in four auxiliary army tents and two Red Cross hospitals.

Dozers are already moving into the still smoking debris being hauled to a temporary landfill.

The government is under severe pressure from the dispossessed who crowd around the administration building clamoring for housing action promised for six years. Military police have cordoned off entry and exit corridors for government employees who have been attacked by the frustrated crowd, some of whom sleep all night near the government buildings. Lack of food and sanitary facilities have become severe.

US and Canadian airborne medical rescue teams are on the site.

* * *

(*Seville Courier*)

DART REACTIVATES UTILITY CUBE INC.

Emile Hoffstetler, Edith White and Thomas Dougherty Recalled

The lights in the quonset behind Dart Division of Pittsburgh Glass burn around the clock. The tiny company, split off from Dart Division of Pittsburgh Glass, has been ...

The *Seville Courier* explained to a surprised local public that a few flatbed trucks carrying Utility Cubes had been rolling into Mexico City where contractors had already laid concrete slabs to receive the Utility Cubes. The I-beams on top of the Cubes became roof supports. Under the pressure of the housing emergency, Mexican contractors and workmen installed with unheard-of dispatch.

* * *

Dougherty's phone woke him at 11:00 p.m. It was Dart's daughter, Lavinia.

"What have you done with him? I know it was you."

"Lavinia, it's a very important project."

"Oh, yes. More important than his health. I had him safely situated, for daily treatment, and a doctor who cares and cooperates."

"Lavinia, if you could see him! He's into an important ..."

"Oh, yes. Important to *you*. Starting up that damned company again gives you a job ... to support your habit."

Dougherty stared at the glass of bourbon on the table. "Lavinia, until day before yesterday I was off it for months."

"How often have we heard that!"

"And building these house units for Mexico keeps me so busy that I stay clear of the booze. I go to bed early, tired."

"And drunk. Right?"

"Oh, hell." Dougherty hung up. He picked up the bourbon, passed it under his nose. The fragrance had evaporated, but the yellow-brown translucent fluid was beautiful. He sipped it. Then he drank it, straight.

Then he ransacked the bookcase.

Next morning, in the quonset, the phones were ringing from Mexico City for Dougherty. Edith handled Tom's phone. Dart came over to her on his walker, "Where's Tom?"

"He had errands."

"What errands?"

"He didn't say."

"He always says."

"We were so busy yesterday ..."

"Edith ..."

" ... that we might not have heard him."

"Edith ... tell Frank Hood and Emile to go to Dougherty's apartment. Bring him in here."

"Emile and Frank are needed here urgently."

"Same for Dougherty."

18

GARCIA

(*People Magazine*)

Amid the tragic Mexico City fire scenes, one is bringing bemused smiles.

A heavy-set American Irishman named Dougherty and his young American-Mexican colleague, Al Gonzalez, are out in the middle of a freshly bulldozed landscape. With the haste of a man who believes the world could end Friday at 5:00 p.m. Dougherty, through Gonzalez's translation, is showing Mexican contractors where to install short pipe lengths in the concrete pads to create holes for anchor bolts, and to bring in water, sewer and electric service.

The purpose of this special preparation is to receive preassembled Utility Cubes built in Seville, Ohio. These cubes not only contain the heavy appliances, but become the main structural support.

One contractor made a passionate argument to Gonzalez who translated to Dougherty, "They've got no electric here yet. Why a hole now?"

"Tell him — because it's cheaper to make a hole now than later when electric comes."

There was a hasty exchange in Mexican. Then Gonzalez translated, "Tom, he says even if and when electric comes, it won't come from underground. From overhead."

"Sure, but tell him because they're starting from scratch, there's talk ... they may go to underground transmission. So provide for it. A hole is cheap now."

Gonzalez and the Mexican contractor conferred vigorously, the contractor's position being that all his life he has been trying to prevent holes in floors. To make a leak in a floor on purpose is *nao sacredo.*

The explanation to the contractor is necessary because most have not yet seen these Utility Cubes they will install. Only 32 have been received. More are being built. But there are bureaucratic blockages on both sides of the border.

* * *

The meeting of Dougherty and Gonzalez and a very cordial but bureaucratized Mexico City Housing Commissioner, Joaquin Hernandez, was held in a restaurant to avoid the agitated crowd surrounding city hall.

One of Dougherty's many skills in selling was his ability to adjust to his prospect's pace. It was killing him today, however, because Hernandez, although a graduate of University of Michigan, conducted business in stately Mexican protocol, seeming to abhor even mention of specific action as an insult to his mother.

Dougherty reined himself back through the cocktails and the salad and the breadsticks. But when the entree came he said, "Dammit, Joaquin, let's get to it. How many units do you want? And which sizes?"

Al Gonzalez caught Tom's eye and shook his head slightly. Hernandez saw it and said, "No. It's all right to be blunt, Al. Obviously we could use all you could make, but there are problems that go way back."

Dougherty hoped the problems didn't go all the way back to Cortez's landing, but he backed off. He would take his cue from Gonzalez even if it hurt.

Just to get the problems out on the table took three more meetings. One problem was the Utility Cubes were for single family houses. "Uses too much of our space for one family."

"Well, for God's sake if you had said so ..."Gonzalez caught Tom's eye. Dougherty said, "Pass the bread, please." The glacial pace unveiled several other problems and meetings. Dougherty said to Gonzalez, "Al, at this next meeting, you do all the talking. I should be a mummy."

"What was your first clue?"

"Maybe a Mexican can deal with a Mexican."

"I'm an American."

"I think you're reverting."

It was a long meeting. In the middle Dougherty excused himself as if to make a phone call, but actually to give Gonzalez room.

When he came back to the table Joaquin Hernandez was in the middle of an explanation. He cut off as Dougherty approached. But Gonzalez nodded that he should continue.

"Very well. Then understand, you must find a way to make available to what we call ... purchasing officers ... funds which pay for their function in ..."

Dougherty said, "Hey! Why didn't you say so! We understand payola!"

Gonzalez snapped, "Mummy! Remember! Joaquin is saying there must be compensation to defray the costs of the purchasing officers in inspecting and approving incoming goods."

Dougherty was wounded. "Isn't that what I just said?"

Hernandez smiled a warning, "Well, you don't go blundering into it. You feel your way and negotiate on a personal basis with each individual."

Dougherty sighed, "What else?"

The last thing, "Your price is too high for us."

* * *

How a salesman from the Midwest got himself into the Washington office of Senator Knute Boar of Massachusetts startled the senator's staff as they had no concept of the stature, resourcefulness and daring of that little-known

169

breed ... the industrial salesman .. the men who move the output of America's heavy industrial valleys out to both coasts in carload lots through the obstruction of grudging purchasing officers and scowling cost control officers.

The receptionist finally conceded, "Mr. Dougherty, the senator is ready."

A girl who seemed too young to be so at home here led him a long stretch and opened a massive door. The bull-necked senator did not look up. He waved Dougherty to a seat while he continued scratching vigorously on a yellow pad. His pencil snapped. Without breaking stride he grabbed another. Dougherty was pleased to see the desk was a battlefield of stacked paper, and he was pleased to see the wall photos were not signed portraits of presidents but Boston seascapes. He studied the senator whose shoulders and upper arms bulged his shirt. His gray-black brush cut vibrated as the pencil punished the paper.

Before he was finished Boar pushed a button. The same young lady reappeared, waited while he finished the last part and handed her the yellow pad. "Right away, Ellen. Special courier." Boar did not rise or offer a hand. He pointed the wet end of a dead cigar at his visitor. "Mr. Dougherty, you pulled a lot of wires for this ten minutes. Why didn't you see your own Ohio senator? I know you're a salesman.I hope this isn't about government procurement of your product."

"No, Senator, I'm in this office because of this." He placed on the desk a clipping:

SENATORS BOAR, BAIN, AND
FORTE CIRCLE THE WAGONS
AGAINST PROTECTIONIST
ONSLAUGHT IN CONGRESS

"That's true," Boar grunted. "And we're losing. What's that to you?"

"Senator, if you could get some foreign nations to reduce or eliminate their tariffs against some U.S. goods, wouldn't it quiet the congressional protectionist uproar some?"

"Damn right." Boar lit the cigar and studied Dougherty

through the smoke. "How?"

"To save your time, Senator, I brought these." Dougherty laid the newspaper with the photos of the Mexican fire. "Senator, they are desperate for housing." Boar nodded, "Of course. So?"

Dougherty laid beside it photos of four versions of the Utility Cube. He explained how it expedited construction, slashed costs, and formed the major support for a house. He showed the Appliance Wall and how it further slashed time and costs. He explained they had a few of these in place in Mexico City, sold to private contractors. "But if we could be turned loose to really send thousands of these units into Mexico, the Utility Cube could really alleviate the Mexico City crisis."

"So why don't you?"

"Mexican trade roadblocks of three kinds. We thought that with your...influence...you could offer to get our government, maybe even by executive order, to lift some of *our* barriers, *if* Mexico *lifts* theirs on certain products to get these people under roof quick."

Boar rose and leaned over the photos and the pictures of the fire.

Dougherty said, "It would be a beginning for..."

Boar stopped him with his cigar hand. He spread out the photos. He made a few notes.

The wall clock cleared its throat to strike. Dougherty picked up his briefcase.

"Sit down."

Boar read the fire story news clip slowly. He punched his phone. "Reschedule the rest of the morning. Buck my calls over to Ted except the following. See if there is any chance Chris Bain and Justin Forte could meet with me at 6:45 a.m. tomorrow ... here." He pointed the phone at Dougherty, "Can you stay overnight?" Into the phone he said, "Tell them Boar said 'This could be the break we need.' Now get me Ted."

Dougherty moved to retrieve the photos, Boar scraped them together with his other hand. "I'll keep these. Can you be here at 6:45 a.m.?"

Boar said into the phone, "Ted, see if you can get that old

Mexico hand from State to join us at 6:45 a.m. tomorrow. We need somebody who can arm wrestle Mexican trade people. If you can't get him, make a list of second best. By the way, you and I will work tonight."

Knute Boar's abrupt motions, physical mass, bull voice and 20 years experience dominated everyone in his particular Washington path — except Lucy. As he mounted the front steps in Georgetown, he flung away the cigar, sprayed his mouth with a peppermint spray, wiped his feet on the mat and entered. The tiny woman took the bulging briefcase, turned him around to tug the coat off his thick shoulders, "Knute! This is the third late night this week! You're not fifty anymore you know!"

"I'm sorry, Lucy." His voice seemed suddenly squeaky.

He followed her into the small sitting room. She poured him a manhattan. "Sit there. Put your feet up."

"Okay, Lucy."

"I'll bring our burnt pizzas."

He turned on the TV. She brought in a tray, set it between them and turned off the TV, "You don't need that."

"Okay, Lucy."

She let him eat in peace until the coffee. "Knute, you remember we leave early for Boston. Fredericka's one-woman art show."

Boar put down his cup and looked stricken, "Oh, Lucy!"

"You forgot."

"I remembered right up until that Dougherty ..." He explained in full the opportunity that had opened up to cool the protectionist clamor. "But damn! And I also missed Jim's graduation last year. I'll cancel the meeting."

She cleared the tray. When she came back he was dialing the phone. She took it from him and hung it up.

"When the kids are thirty-five, and become human beings, I'll explain to them what their father did for the country. You'll be dead, of course. Meanwhile, tomorrow I will go up to Boston and look at her pictures. I'll get your father to go, too. I'll ask her what the pictures represent, and remind her you paid for four years of art education."

"You're something, Lucy."

"Of course. How do you think you got where you are?"

172

He pulled her over on his tree trunk knee. She said, "You can work until eleven. Period. That's Eastern Standard, not Rocky Mountain time."

"Okay, Lucy."

"Here is how it must be done." Carlos Garcia squeezed his trim gray beard and paced in front of Senators Boar, Bain and Forte, thinking as he walked. Although low man on State's Mexico team, Garcia had the take-it-or-leave-it arrogance of a man who knows the job better than his bosses, but doesn't want their jobs. He already had a pension from selling Ford tractors to Mexico. "The proposal will appeal to the Mexican government with all the housing heat they're getting. But it must come to them from Mexicans."

"Why?" Boar asked. "That'll eat *months*."

"Not with the burnt out mob beating on them. But the middle class workers will fear inundation by American goods inside these what d'ya call them? Cubes. So they can't sell their Mexican built appliances. You didn't think they built any, right? But they do, just south of the border. They have funny names like G.E., Whirlpool and Maytag. We have got to go through Luis Alvarez to get to Echeverria."

Butus asked, "How? Who can do that?"

"I don't know yet. I've got to think."

Forte asked, "Carlos, what are the chances?"

Garcia studied one of Dougherty's photos. "The chances of getting Mexico to lift trade barriers may be better than getting the U.S. to do so. Notice if we reciprocate, we've got to lift barriers on furnaces, air conditioners, copper, steel, hot water tanks, rubber hose and a dozen other items. Mexicans produce those things. They want to ship them here."

Boar turned to Bain, "Chris, are you willing to spend your credits with the president on this one? The president has temporary emergency power to lift certain tariffs."

Bain thought about it. He nodded, "This is probably the best shot we'll get."

Boar turned to Garcia. "So who's our best man to get to this Alvarez?"

"Probably Guillermo Baez ... when he gets back from El Salvador. He's helping with the housing after the earthquake."

Dougherty made a note ... "*earthquake, El Salvador.*"

Boar rose, "That's too late. We got to do this while this mob ..." he held up the news clip ... "is sleeping in the streets by the mayor's house."

Garcia nodded.

Boar said, "Carlos, *you* are our man. Will your boss lend you to the Trade Subcommittee? Are you willing to ask your boss?"

Garcia grinned, "Don't you know, Senator? We minorities don't *ask* nobody nothin'. We *tell* 'em."

Boar finally smiled, "But remember — in Mexico you won't be a minority. You'll have to be polite ... for a change."

"I think I can do the Mexican side. Can you do the American side?" He looked at Forte.

Bain said to the other two senators, "I can get the appointment with the president. But the three of us better go, and we better bring Garfield and Hansen."

Garcia said, "I need a top-notch labor guy with me in Mexico."

That stumped the group. Suddenly Forte pulled a small notebook from his pocket and asked, "Does he need to speak Mexican?"

"I'll do the talking. I need a man who knows labor and knows negotiating."

"Then I know the man," Forte opened the notebook. "Visconti ... John Visconti."

Boar asked, "What's he got on the ball?"

"I can't explain it. He's got a way of ... forcing a card."

"What's his job?"

"Last I knew ... unemployed."

"That's a recommendation?"

"In this case, it may be exactly that."

19

BUCYRUS

Working-type cars, interrupted by only a few of the other type, lined the berm for a half-mile on Clayton Road by the old Ruoff place.

The crowd, most from out of town, milled around the machinery and the buildings, studying the auction items and survey maps of the farm.

Auctioneer Clarke had insisted to Schlicter that the Ruoffs be off the property during the auction, "Or you'll lose money. Buyers don't want to buy a man out in front of his family."

"They're off."

"You sure?"

"I arranged it."

"Do you know all the Ruoffs by sight?"

"I think so. See them around town."

"You know Ben Ruoff *Junior* by sight?"

"I think so. Big. Husky."

"Okay. Then climb up the side of that silo and squint down toward the creek to the lower pasture See if that fellow talkin' to the hosses is him ... with the young lady kinda watchin' him."

Schlicter did so. He then quickly climbed off the silo and got a deputy sheriff to drive him down the field road. By the time they reached the lower pasture they could see the young lady leading two horses up over a rise.

The deputy let Schlicter confront young Ruoff with removing bank *property* from the premises. Ruoff had gotten a halter onto two frisky black colts. Holding onto them both he grinned, "Aw, no sir. Those aren't *property*." He pointed to the two gray horses disappearing over the ridge. "Those are just old pets. Couple old family horses we just kept around because we grew up with them. Nobody'd buy them."

"Well, the ones you're holding are no *old* horses. They're riding horses. And *very* salable."

"Oh, sure, sir, but don't belong to us. Belong to Steve Varney's daughter, Jen. She just pastures them here. I'm just cuttin' them out of the pack to take over to her. Told her she can't keep 'em here anymore."

"How do I know they don't belong here?"

"You have the inventory list."

"Not with me. So don't move those horses until I get it." Schlicter went back to the patrol car.

Ruoff called after him, "I got a way to prove it. Jen's got 'em marked on the hooves."

"Show me."

"Yes, sir."

Young Ruoff raised a back hoof out of wet swale and invited Schlicter to bend over and look close.

"You see the little mark there, sir?"

"No."

Ruoff cleaned the muck off the hoof, "Now?"

"No."

"Here. Take the hoof in hand and lean close."

Schlicter did so. Ruoff straightened up and thwacked the colt on the rump. The startled animal's hooves exploded into the pasture, launching him toward the open gate with the other charging after, leaving the executive kneeling in well-watered pasture.

Ruoff said, "Aw darn! Now look what happened." He reached a hand down to pull Schlicter up. "Well, not to worry. They might show up over at Jen's place ... sometime. You can check them out then."

By 1:30 Clarke had completed that phase in which the total farm, equipment, and livestock were offered as a package. There were no takers. He began to solicit bids for lands, in nine separate parcels, starting with the bank's minimum prices.

He was having some difficulty because of a rumbling noise developing on the road. He was beginning to have some fair bids for the home place with house, barn and sheds when the noise became intolerable. Up Clayton Road came Charlie Herndorf on a 145-horse enclosed cab White 610. It had a serious muffler problem. Percussive noise vibrated the air. When he arrived abreast of the Ruoff place, it was seen that he was followed by Bill McClusky on an old International with an even worse muffler difficulty. Herndorf drove right on by the house and it was then seen by the crowd that in the distance McClusky was followed at 50 yards by Jamison on a loud tractor. Then it became apparent that behind Jamison were nine more tractors ... all with muffler trouble.

Schlicter went to the deputy. "Sergeant, stop this parade!"

"On what grounds, sir?"

"Noise ordinance."

"Don't have one, sir."

"Deliberate obstruction."

"They're on the public roads."

"They're not going to their fields or to do any work."

"Do I know that, sir?"

"What could they be doing?"

"Well, maybe they're all going up to help level the municipal park."

"Ridiculous!"

"Well ... maybe they're all going over to Brinkley Farm Machinery to get their mufflers fixed."

Schlicter went into the Ruoff house to the phone and dialed Martha at the bank, "Miss Cushman, find out where Varney is."

Outside Hearing Room 16 in the State House in Columbus, Steve Varney took a last look up and down the corridors for Richard Lempke. Not finding him, he combed his hair with his hand and entered the hearing room, resuming his seat at the witness table.

The radical nature of the bill to have the government buy back farm lands had drawn a large group of spectator attorneys, bankers, agribusiness types, and rural legislators. The hearings had to be moved to the large committee room.

Especially the radical proposed law had attracted out-of-state media. The latter were intrigued with the contradictions in Varney.

A rural man from a small town called Bucyrus, he should have been distracted by the urban circus in which he found himself; yet he remained oblivious to it, preoccupied only with this H.B. 203, as if he had been in this situation before.

Obviously a young man, he had the self-possession of a senior, and he walked old.

The farm was all over him, the brown leather face under an untanned forehead above the eye patch. Prematurely deep lines mapped the back of his neck. Biceps and shoulder muscles somewhat spoiled the drape of the new style Remberg suit one could imagine his wife may have picked out and brought home. You couldn't picture him going to a clothing store.

Yet his answers to the committee were sophisticated, almost professorial in knowledge of his industry, which he dignified. His strength in the hearing was intense earnestness. The Republican vice chairman of the legislative committee for the bill charged, "Mr. Varney." Experienced, the legislator slowly surveyed the audience and the media, assuring full attention. "The country is in mood swing away from incessant aid to farmers. Yet you come in here representing three farm associations asking for a colossal farm-aid bill."

"No, sir."

"No?"

"Mr. Vice Chairman, it is not a farm-aid bill. The benefit is to the state and the nation. The state can now acquire this land in some cases at distress prices. So the state can only gain."

The vice chairman said, "Where is it written that a government gains by owning land?"

"In our whole history. From the very beginning, government-owned land has been the making of the nation. It began when we had no money to buy a Revolutionary army to fight Britain. We gave each soldier who would sign up for three years an I.O.U. ... a bounty land warrant ... for 100 acres in the Ohio Country. Part of my own farm was originally a bounty farm."

The audience hushed, caught between an interest in Varney's brief history sketch and an interest in how Varney would come to know all this, and what happened to his eye.

The young farmer took the committee through several epochs when government-owned land made the nation. He explained how Jefferson's Louisiana Purchase overnight changed the nation from a vulnerable seaboard strip to a nation with continent-wide expectations.

He reminded that the east and west coasts at one point threatened to become two separate nations unless we could connect them commercially. What gave the railroads the incentive to connect the two coasts by rail was the gift of alternate sections of government land to the railroad builders. The presence of the railroads in turn increased the value of the sections retained by the government, later sold profitably by the government.

"We now face another enormous challenge, Mr. Vice Chairman, in which government-owned land could be our salvation ... if ... if ... government will buy back the land. The present emergency is foreign competition. This is your best investment."

There was a murmur in the audience which tipped the vice chairman that he had unwittingly uncaged some kind of force. He did not want Varney to continue just yet. He suggested adjournment.

He opened the next morning's questions with a severity which suggested that overnight he had put some legislative aids to work researching more ammunition.

"The glaring inconsistency in your testimony, Mr. Varney, is this: You claim buying back farm lands will directly relieve the severe suffering the people of this state are enduring from foreign competition. But the foreign competition which is killing us is steel, automotive, and clothing. Isn't it the fact that you don't care about all that? You're just here pitching a bill to benefit farmers?"

"No, sir."

"No?"

"No, sir. It will work like this: This country used to feed the world. Now we can't compete. For argument, let's say it's the fault of we farmers. But government purchase of the farm land takes the marginal farmer out of the picture. That removes the need for massive annual farm subsidies ... about thirty billion annually ... which burdens the public.

"The remaining farmers could then compete without subsidies and supports. That means our public can eat cheaper. Carried to the full — our public can pay the world market price for, say, sugar ... five cents a pound instead of the price-supported thirty cents. And extrapolate that across every agriculture product, everybody wins.

"Without farm subsidies on *our* side, Canada can lower its subsidies of corn and also the duty against our corn. We remove the duty against Canadian lumber and paper, which lowers the cost of housing, books, newspapers.

"Our remaining successful farmers can afford new tractors, rotary hoes, disk harrows, balers, sickle bar mowers, compactors, computerized milkers, feeders, and cultivators ... all steel, electronic, and automotive-type products."

The vice chairman held up the flat of his hand, "Very pretty theory, Mr. Varney. But let's not make speeches. I want to get to the motivation of whoever we're listening to here."

Lempke had arrived and was seated with the spectators. He used this pause in the testimony to move up to the empty chair at the witness table with Varney. They nodded and waited for the next question.

The vice chairman said, "It is important that this committee know *why* certain witnesses here are saying certain things. If you were to be perfectly honest, Mr. Varney, you do not have knowledge or interest in the rest of the population. You are here for the *farmers* only."

"We're all in it together."

"I was waiting for you to say that." The vice chairman reached his briefcase up off the floor and handed a newsclip to the page. "Take this to Mr. Varney."

The media strained to see what was going on. The vice chairman assisted them, "Mr. Varney, that *Toledo Blade* newsclip pictures a farm auction in progress yesterday and today in *your* home town of Bucyrus. The Ruoff place. Isn't it true that Ruoff is a neighbor of yours?"

"Yes."

"Also a long-time friend?"

"Yes."

"Isn't it true that this is the same lawbreaker who ran an attack on the Toledo Grain Elevator last ..."

Varney leaped up and pointed to the dais, "Just one minute there! Ben Ruoff is no ..."

"I rephrase. Isn't he the same *man?*"

"Yes. But he had every reason ..."

"And didn't you and a few friends come up with the bail money to get this lawbreaker out ... this man out of jail."

"Yes, and I intend to see that ..."

The media cameras came alive.

"And, Mr. Varney, isn't it true that just *yesterday* a bunch of farmers broke up that auction by maliciously running a parade of loud tractors back and forth in front of the Ruoff place?"

"I haven't read the whole clipping."

"I don't believe you need to read the clipping, Mr. Varney. Nothing happens in the farm sector of Crawford and Wyandot Counties, I'm told, that you don't know about ... or *instigate.*"

"Sir, I'm here in Columbus. How could I ...?"

The spectator section broke out in a light laugh. Some journalists converged on the *Toledo Blade* bureau man with whispered questions. The chairman gaveled for order.

"What I'm getting to, Mr. Varney, isn't it true ... you and your farm groups are strictly pushing this bill for farmers? Not for the rest of us?"

Varney rubbed his hand over his good eye, tired. "Mr. Vice Chairman, certainly I represent farmers. And I can see you hold us suspect. Most of the group who came with me to testify for this bill are farmers. But we do have one member of our group who is *not* a farmer." Varney described Richard Lempke's credentials and asked, "Would you let him testify to the merits of this bill from the viewpoint of the varied industries in Ohio ... non-farm?"

The committee conferred off-mike and the chairman

announced Lempke could be queried. The vice chairman eyed Lempke who now leaned forward with his hands clasped, a docile schoolboy, his huge upper arms and torso straining the seams of his suitcoat and raising a ridge of fabric behind his bull neck.

The vice chairman said, "Mr. Lempke, we're trying to fathom the inconsistency of this group's position. On the one hand, the farm population is now down to two point two percent of the population; yet the group you find yourself with is saying there are too many farmers."

"No, sir. Not too many farmers, but too many acres being farmed."

"I don't follow."

"In the first place ... sir ... the two point two percent only includes the Class One through Class Three farms. It does not include the thousands of sundowners."

"Sundowners?"

"Yes, sir. These are the grown-up sons of farmers who work at Bryant Air Tool or General Electric or whatever all day. And the factory work is so restful compared to what they did on the farm as kids, that they come home at sundown and farm 50 acres and five cows, Class Four and Five farms, just to get a little exercise."

The crowd chuckled. The vice chairman fidgeted. What did he have here, some kind of clown?

"But besides that, sir ..." — Lempke was punctiliously polite — "every acre that a tractor won't fall off of is now cultivated by a farmer with a banker on his tail scolding him to raise more than last year. So that farmer is going to do what no other businessman would do — work nights to produce more than he knows how to sell. From the day they put headlights on tractors, things started going downhill. Can you imagine that, sir?"

"I'll ask the questions."

"Yes, sir."

"Mr. Lempke, the land buy-back would not only cost the government enormous initial dollars, it would also lose us the taxes on working farms. It would throw thousands of farm workers and agribusiness workers out ... and we would lose the income taxes from those disemployed armies. You haven't thought this through."

"Yes, I have, sir." Lempke's disheveled appearance and unprepossessing manner had initially disarmed the committee. But suddenly it became obvious that he had been around. After an amiable opening, his face turned severe. "The cost to government of buying the land will be a one-time drop in the bucket cost, while the cost of the present system of buying and storing billions of bushels with each year's record busting crop will bankrupt government. As for taxes lost, you're losing them anyway. Four hundred farms will be foreclosed this year in just Crawford and Wyandot counties.

"You may even sell the land back to farmers at a huge profit twenty-thirty-forty years from now. If we ever have to feed five hundred million people, it will be important to have millions of acres not yet covered with asphalt. The price you pay farmers for land now will be cheap."

"Mr. Lempke, why propose this to the *state*? If you're correct, it should be a *federal* program."

"True. But the federal does not really lead, it follows. So let the state begin it."

"Why not Iowa? Dakota?"

"They're too far gone. They're broke. Too much land to buy. But Ohio could afford it, and the land mass to be bought is not so enormous as Iowa."

"Why should Ohio be the first to spend our state funds?"

"So you'll be first to reap the profit."

"What assures us of profit?"

"History. My colleague, Mr. Varney, showed me how an acre of dollar land in 1800, with ups and downs, of course, reached $4,000 by 1977. But even in today's hard times it averages $1,300."

The vice chairman was patronizing. "And who says it will rise again? You?"

"Oh no, sir. I'm no expert. But the big farm broker in Lima, Ohio, said 60 percent of his farm sales this year were to doctors and lawyers." Lempke grinned, "What more proof that it's a great investment?"

The audience broke into laughter.

Lempke then explained that some small towns, like

Concord, Massachusetts, were already buying back farm land. Why couldn't a state exert such leadership?

The chairman gaveled adjournment.

Varney and the farm representatives agreed to meet at nine the next morning.

The media went to work.

In the corridor outside Room 16 Varney said, "Mr. Lempke, you ..."

Lempke grinned. "So that the committee *thinks* we're on the same side, better call me Dick."

"Dick, I want to tell you how much we appreciate your coming. And what you did today in there was important. You give us breadth. Tremendous help."

"Should we plan our attack for tomorrow?"

"Gosh, I've got to get back to the farm in Bucyrus. Joan said it was urgent. But I can get back here by midnight."

"Wake me up. Room 302, Hilton." He put a heavy hand on Steve's shoulder. "Now ... we're together on these hearings. But at the same time we're at war in Bucyrus, Steve."

"How?"

Lempke grinned. "The Ruoff farm. I'm not going to ask you if you were behind that tractor symphony. And I'm not going to ask you if you're going up there tonight to plan tomorrow's disruption of the Ruoff auction. But someway we've got to work out a truce."

A handful of newsmen and two TV people cornered them with questions. Varney held up a hand, "Folks, could you let Dick and me finish first because we've got a hard problem."

That bought them no privacy. Lempke grinned broadly and held up a chubby hand. "Ladies and gentlemen ... let us make you a deal. Steve's got to get back to Bucyrus tonight to tend some farm business. But he'll be back here tomorrow morning. If you'll let him get going now, we'll spring for breakfast for you all at the Hilton. Seven-thirty ay-em sharp. Deal?"

"What's he going back to the farm for?"

"Prob'ly to plan some more sabotage against my bank." He pushed Varney through the crowd.

The journalists laughed and broke up. But they did not go home.

They went to Bucyrus.

Lempke went to his hotel. He made some phone calls, one to Schlicter in Bucyrus, "How did the auction go, Warny?"

"Had to postpone again, sir."

"Why?"

"Well, sir, it was going well until about ten a.m. A lot of media showed up. Then suddenly a crop duster started work on the property across the road, flying low, and then ..."

"I get the picture, Warny. You ready for tomorrow?"

"Why? Is something else going to happen?"

"Yup."

"What, sir?"

"Don't know, but something."

"Well, do you have a suggestion for what I should do?"

"Yes. Continue learning your trade. But learn faster, Mr. Schlicter."

Lempke placed a call to Washington, the office of Senator Justin A. Forte. He did not presume to ask for the senator. He asked to speak to his secretary. The office was closed, but one staffer was working late, a John Visconti. Lempke identified himself and said, "I'm not in the senator's state, and I wouldn't presume on his time. But would you just ask him if he will start watching the news out of Bucyrus, Ohio, and the state capital?"

"Shall I tell him why?"

"I think it can be very important to him in his anti-protection work."

"You know he gets a hundred calls a week like this?"

"I suppose so. But I'm not a guy who makes many calls like this."

Visconti hung up and turned on the office TV for the seven o'clock news. He saw no items out of Ohio on the national news. Therefore, next morning, he stopped at the out-of-town newsstand and picked up the *Columbus Dispatch* and *Toledo Blade*.

Later he laid on Forte's desk an article from the *Toledo*

Blade:

FARM AUCTION DISPERSED
BY ANGRY CROP DUSTER

State Police Chopper
Signals Crop Duster To
Ground, But He Fails
To Heed Signal

Bucyrus — With scores of farms going under the sheriff's hammer in the region, the population is a tinder bed of explosive emotions.

Farm suicides are no longer uncommon.

Drastic retaliation is widespread, including yesterday's incident to break up the auction of the farm of Benjamin Ruoff. A local crop duster covered the area with a choking fog of 325 mesh lime dust which ...

With that article was one from the *Columbus Dispatch*:

DETERMINED YOUNG AGRICULTURIST
PROPOSES MASSIVE GOVERNMENT
LAND BUY-BACK TO END FARM SUBSIDIES

Holds Ohio Legislature
Committee Attention Three Hours

20

PITTSBURGH

Edith White entered the office of Alton Moore, Dart Division of American Glazing of Pittsburgh. She was received courteously but with surprise. She noticed that he had lost the somewhat intimidating assurance of "the man from Pittsburgh." His desk was a collage of spread sheets. "Mr. Moore, Jason Dart would have come to your office, but besides fighting his gout he's fighting for minutes. Would you come over to the quonset to talk to us?"

"Gosh, Miss White, I'm buried. We're having to lay off sixty people and I'm into marathon meetings with the unions and the pension fund trustees. And Pittsburgh wants me up there tomorrow. Foreign imports of acrylics from IPC are really sticking it to us. They outflanked our distributors through the big builder discount stores."

"Mr. Moore, I assure you any meeting with Mr. Dart lately will be very, very brief."

Moore reached for his calendar, "Maybe Friday ..."

"Too late."

"Look," — he held up his calendar — "today is wall-to-wall layoff headaches."

"If you meet with us ... *now* ... you may have no layoffs."

"Huh?"

"He wants to talk to you about leasing some of your space and certain machines. Or ... about you manufacturing some of our Utility Cubes for us to our specs and specified costs."

Alton Moore allowed himself an ear-to-ear grin, "Miss White, I couldn't possibly make it to your office sooner than three minutes. Is that too late?"

"Almost," she smiled, "but acceptable, Mr. Moore."

He put out his hand. "Alton is what I'm called. What's yours?"

She smiled. "Miss White."

* * *

Powerful in Seville, in Pittsburgh Alton Moore sat like a schoolboy before the group vice president.

Mike Haggerty, although only 41, was currently the favored group vice president because, unlike the other group chiefs, he dumped any division or subsidiary that drew red ink over six months.

He said to Moore. "You first told us we should be happy to be rid of that Utility Cube business for $500,000. Now ... you want $500,000 to tool up to *build* those cubes?"

"Yes."

"And they've only got one market? The Mexico fire?"

"No. Already they have an order to ship a hundred units to El Salvador because of the earthquake."

"They going to get paid in bananas?"

Moore let it go by.

"Look, Alton. Off-site prefabrication of housing is not news. It has no exclusivity for us."

"Mike, I knew you wouldn't believe it from me. So I've got your own residential construction forecaster, Ed Lamb, sitting in your anteroom. Can I bring him in?"

Ed Lamb strolled in with the freedom from awe of a man with the facts. "Mike, Alton is correct. Dart's system *is* new. Previous prefabs concern the outer shell. Roof trusses, wall sections, prefabricated door and window and frames. So they put up the shell fast. Then they tear it apart hauling in and installing the mechanicals; four trades stompin' around in the house undoing each other's work. Dart's concept is ... prefab the mechanical heart of the house and put it in place first ... in one shot ... complete. Then ... hang the house on it."

Haggerty nodded. "Okay, but Moore wants us to invest in tooling to build something anyone else can build. Anyone can buy those components and link 'em up. If it works, we'll be neck deep in competitors."

"Not the way Dart builds them." Moore explained that Jason Dart gets a new idea a week. "If competition should ever catch up, he'll sell out and build something else. Dart is smart."

"Not that smart."

Lamb grinned, "No? Didn't he sell out to us, at just the right moment?"

Haggerty leaned back and stared at the ceiling. "I can get your half million." Then he leaned forward and got the drop on Moore. "Alton, you know my rule: Six months and into the black ... or out."

Moore nodded.

21

SEVILLE

(Forbes Magazine)

EXPORTING HOUSING FROM
SEVILLE, OHIO
A Forbes Magazine Plant Visit

Here in Seville, Ohio, a village near Akron in the industrially devastated Midwest, an infant industrial revolution may be borning.

Elimination of on-site construction work is a long-time dream of practical men. But it has never surmounted the politics. Perhaps finally a country entrepreneur, with a mental quirk similar to that of Henry Ford, may have begun a U.S. resurgence.

While the product of Utility Cube, Inc. is now somewhat well known, very little is known about the company.

Here in an old quonset hut, formerly the manufacturing plant for the Cube, now merely the office (they have a new office under construction), the top staff of the corporation operates on the open concrete floor, still using some crates for desks, though they do have movable acrylic partitions between desks bought from neighboring Dart Division of Pittsburgh Glass which also subcontracts manufacture of the Utility Cubes.

Utility Cube, Inc. also contracts out work to two nearby troubled G.M. plants which were marked for closing and an Akron rubber plant plagued by Michelin imports.

The marketing vice president is a stout, high- octane former alcoholic, Tom Dougherty, whom Jason Dart credits with revitalizing the once-doomed Utility Cube Corporation. Dougherty on the other hand credits Dart with giving him a second chance when he was fired next door.

Flatbed trailers haul the Utility Cubes to Wright Patterson Air Force Base near Dayton where they load onto C5A transport planes for Mexico City. In a dramatic deal for two-way lifting of certain U.S.-Mexico trade barriers, the U.S. sweetened the negotiation by offering the Air Force C5A's to fly the first thousand Utility Cubes into Mexico. The State Department could legally do this under the U.S. disaster relief policy.

Next to Dougherty's small cubicle is another, occupied by Miss Edith White, Dart's former secretary during the time he built Dart Industries. For many years, she did anything that had to be done. She now holds the title "vice president at large." According to Dart, who circulates among the cubicles in a wheelchair, "She's been doing the vice president job for years. We just never noticed it until recently. So we relabelled her."

Uncomfortable in one cubicle is Emile Hoffstetler. With a handful of men he built the prototypes from diagrams Dart chalked on the concrete floor. To this day Hoffstetler cringes when he sees Miss Klaysmith mopping the floor. But today Hoffstetler wears a suit and works from blueprints. He is vice president, engineering, supervising the running changes and relaying Dart's innovative ideas to two-dozen young engineers charged with designing the new functions into the product and devising manufacturing methods.

All staff members are handicapped by the crowded conditions and the noise, magnified by the quonset hut and compounded by the sound of ringing phones rising out of the cubicles.

The Growth Syndrome

Interviewing Marketing Vice President Dougherty about how he is managing such sales growth, the big man grins broadly. "Someday I suppose we'll have to get into the hard sell. But right now its the easiest selling I've ever done."

Forbes: "What is your technique?"

Dougherty: "I sit here and read the paper."

Forbes: "Could you explain that?"

Dougherty explained that he watches the foreign news. He handed this reporter a much-fingered clipping which started a sale:

DOMINION ENERGY MINISTRY RESUMES SHALE OIL EXTRACTION AT ATHABASCA

Will Build Village For 3,000 Workers In Wilds

Canada, like the U.S., is crippled by the return of high petroleum prices. The nation will resume shale oil processing in the wilds of Athabasca. That will require housing 3,000 families quickly in the forest.

Dougherty explained, "So I merely phoned the Energy Ministry. They sent four men down here to look. Jason Dart changed design to put a motor-generator set in each Utility Cube, for electricity. They've ordered a thousand as fast as we can deliver, with a possible two thousand more."

Changing World Trade

Dougherty then explained that he has an unwritten agreement with Senators Boar, Butus, and Forte. Whenever he gets an emergency order from a foreign nation, he notifies them. They arrange for an envoy to strike a deal for lifting certain barriers against U.S. products ... or no Utility Cubes may be shipped.

Dougherty explained that two earthquakes in Central America and a volcanic eruption in Japan accounted for sales of 4,000 units. "We are months behind in shipping."

We were in his office when a problem came up about shipping Utility Cubes to Columbia, South America, where a mud slide rendered over 5,000 homeless. We were invited to sit in the meeting in the makeshift conference room. The trouble was that there is no Columbia airfield large enough for the C5A cargo aircraft. Ground transport is too costly.

Jason Dart rolled his wheelchair around the room, the

others following him with their eyes. He said, "Edith, I hear ocean shipping is way down. That means there should be thousands of those containerization boxes idle. You know ... those things that look like truck trailers without wheels. Find out what it would cost us to buy a hundred of those. Maybe five hundred.

"Then, Emile, couldn't we put a Utility Cube right inside one of those? Cut some windows in the container? Put some room partitions inside it? We can that way ship them whole houses, stacked four high on a ship's deck. When they get the house squared up on a slab, they merely add a thatched roof for cosmetics. And plant some flowers in front.

"Tom, do you think you could sell them on that?"

We looked at Dougherty. He grinned. "Piece of cake."

Dart said, "Emile, get your engineers on that. I think those containers come in twenty- and forty-foot lengths. Check out the forty-footers."

Two competitors have sprung up, one with a porcelain enamel house reminiscent of the Lustron house which was ahead of its time and failed. That company is placing orders for heavy-gauge sheet steel, encouraging to the steel industry.

Jason Dart does not say so; but some investment brokers are saying that exporting housing could be America's next big export surge replacing its lost global automotive superiority, unless the rising severe U.S. trade bill shuts down world trade. Presently the Utility Cube is only allowed into countries which suffer housing emergencies. But so far that includes many nations.

This is how a village in Ohio is significantly influencing the international trade picture with ...

* * *

The new office building, next door to the quonset, was not finished, but overflow staff was already occupying semi-finished spaces.

One room had been equipped with a long table and chairs so that suppliers could make their presentations to executives of Utility Cube, Inc.

Serge Vasilov of Modern Interiors and an assistant were setting up presentation easels with some draped interior design concepts for office decor. They needed some help. He hailed a middle-aged woman passing the doorway. "Honey, could we get a blackboard in here?"

"Certainly."

The blackboard soon appeared. "Thanks. Now could we get another table to lay out some wallcovering samples? We have to make a pitch to Vice President White at nine o'clock ... so if you could hurry it a little ..."

"Certainly."

Another table appeared.

"Thanks. Oh ... is there any coffee around?"

"Certainly."

The coffee appeared. "Thanks. Is this vice president usually on time?"

"Might be a little late today."

"Good." He turned to his assistant. "David, that gives us time to dry run this pitch."

At about 9:15 the same woman re-entered, sat at the head of the table and smiled, "Mr. Vasilov, I'm ready for your presentation."

Vasilov studied her. Then he swallowed, "You are ...?"

"White, Miss White."

"Gee, I ..."

"It's all right. Just be sure your design for the lobby contains a niche to display this historic mixer." She slid a photo of an old hand mixer across the table.

"Yes, Ma'am."

22

MACDOUGALL

As soon as he saw the company courier envelope, Captain MacDougall suspected the message. Otherwise the company would have radioed.

When MacDougall operated the *Nelson Moran* ore carrier on the Great Lakes on the taconite run from Duluth to Detroit and Toledo he wore a tan sports shirt, chino pants, and a baseball cap; but now he took out of his locker his navy blue with the brass buttons to look like what shore people expected.

Downbound on Lake Huron for Toledo, he went up to the pilothouse and told the first mate, "I'll take her into the St. Clair River. Then she's yours. Put her on slow bell to let me get off on the mail boat. I'll rent a car to go to Seville, Ohio. You take her into Detroit. Discharge cargo as slow as you can. Then take her on slow bell into Toledo to give me all the time you can. I'll meet you at Toledo. Don't let anybody screw up to give the dispatchers any alert. But if the company does call for me personally, explain I'm on 'personal emergency' leave."

The mate nodded. He knew the problem. Coming through the Soo Canal, Captain MacDougall had been handed the brown envelope message by the lockmaster: "Tie up for winter berth at Toledo Elevator. You will be met by Brinkman with full instructions."

That was *not* the *Moran's* home port, and Brinkman was *not* the *Moran's* regular shore contact. So MacDougall and the first mate knew what it meant.

Captain MacDougall had managed a desperate phone call to Dart Cube. He never expected to get through to Jason Dart, and he did not. But then out of sheer gall he got Dart's home phone number and placed the call. The housekeeper woke Dart, "There's a Captain MacDougall calling from a ... he said from a ship."

"Ask him to call our traffic department tomorrow."

"Mr. Dart, the man sounded ... uh ..."

"Sounded what?"

"I can't explain it exactly, but ..."

Dart picked up the phone. The gravel voice on the other end sounded as if he had prepared the message very carefully and was reading it. "Mr. Dart, I'm not selling anything. I sail the *Moran* on the Great Lakes. I have an idea you might like. Because the ship will need to go slow downbound in the St. Clair and Detroit River and use two hours unloading in Detroit, I could leave the ship in the St. Clair River, drive to Seville, and rejoin my ship in Toledo before I would be in big trouble. Would you talk to me in Seville ... sir? Fifteen minutes?"

"I hate to have you waste your time. I can't conceive any mutual ..."

"Totally at my risk ... sir."

"Come ahead."

After ten years on the *Moran* and twenty before that on other ore boats, the captain was ill at ease in Dart's office. He spoke with unnatural rapidity, "Mr. Dart, on the long hauls across Lakes Superior and Ontario, and during unloading, there's time to read a lot. I read all about the Utility Cube and Dart Cube Houses going overseas. My crew has been with me ten years. I have the oldest ship in the company and the oldest crew."

Dart noticed the captain was reading from 3x5 cards to be concise. He put up a hand. "Captain ... take your time. I know you didn't make this trip without an important message."

MacDougall pocketed the cards.

"Mr. Dart, they're going to tie my boat up in Toledo and turn it into floating storage for soybeans. There's not enough storage for the huge crop. They'll put a ship keeper on her, dismiss the crew ... and there she sits ... nothing but a silo. Terrible waste of a beautiful 630-foot ship. She was built in 1910, but the six-thirties were a remarkable generation of boats.

"With some more instrumentation and modification she can be ocean going."

"Captain, there's plenty of transportation available to us ... cheap."

"Yes, Mr. Dart, but did you ever see an ore boat?"

Dart shook his head.

"It's a big hollow box." He started to make a ship with his hands. Dart slid a paper pad across the desk. The captain drew a cross section. Then a side elevation—pilothouse way forward, engine room extreme aft, and in the center an enormous hollow box four-and-a-half houselots long, divided into 24 transverse compartments, "and doorways could be cut through those bulkheads, Mr. Dart."

"What for, Captain?"

"Couldn't it be a floating assembly plant?"

Dart sat studying the captain, who finally said, "The newspaper said a lot of countries need your Utility Cubes ... but their import laws won't let you bring in an American product."

"How does your ship help that, Captain?"

"Well ... if you build 'em at sea en route, is it an American product?"

Dart reared back and laughed.

MacDougall said, "It would be from no-man's land."

Dart laughed again.

"Can't it be a ship without a country? Make up a new flag? Or register the ship out of some little island off Africa?"

Dart laughed as he had seldom laughed. "Captain, I can see you haven't had any experience with foreign trade lawyers." His laugh segued to silent thought. "But wait a minute, Captain." Dart pushed up out of his chair and grabbed his walker. He came around to the other side of the desk and looked at the drawing. "Can that ship go up rivers?"

"If I can get twenty-seven feet of water. Even less because your stuff won't weigh fourteen thousand tons."

"So if we could go up a large South American river and let ... say Chile ... supply whatever components they could

... and some of the labor ..." Dart was thinking.

MacDougall said, "They ought to like that, shouldn't they?"

Dart took his cane off the walker and used it to poke a button on his speaker phone.

"Yes, Mr. Dart?"

"Have that young foreign trade lawyer we deal with in New York call me."

MacDougall said, "Mr. Dart, even if you don't do anything, could you have one of your manufacturing hands look at the cargo hold quick? Otherwise it will be full of soybeans and you can't see anything."

Dart caned the phone again. "And ask Emile Hoffstetler to make himself free to go to Toledo tomorrow."

To MacDougall he said, "What makes you think your company would lease or sell the ship to us?"

"It would be more profitable than sitting there keeping the snow off soybeans."

Dart chuckled. MacDougall said, "Mr. Dart, if you should decide it's workable, there'll be better and newer boats than mine idle and available to you; but I'd sure hope you'd use the *Moran*. My crew's too old to get new jobs."

"Captain MacDougall, if by any wild chance this could be done, I'd want the ship run by a guy with nerve enough to bring this crazy idea to me."

They got into more details about the vessel's construction, then MacDougall raced north to the turnpike and cut west for Toledo.

The 630-foot *Moran*, huge in open water, was dwarfed as she lay moored under the towering silos at Toledo Elevator. The elevator chutes extended out over the open hatches of the vessel. Brinkman came aboard. In the pilothouse, he snapped, "Ready, Captain?"

MacDougall scanned the dock for the arrival of Dart personnel, then looked over at the first mate whose head moved, negative. MacDougall said, "No, Mr. Brinkman, we've got a lot more washing of holds to be done. The taconite cargo we brought into Detroit had a lot of degradation. Got iron dust in every crack."

"Well, hurry it up, Captain ... please."

Brinkman was new. He had not been on the job long enough to gain respect for these captains who brought the 630, 730 and 850-foot monsters through quick storms and treacherous narrows and whispered them up to moorings as gently as canoes without carrying away half the dock, which they could easily do if a wind caught them broadside when empty, riding very high in the water.

The *Moran* passageways gleamed under the storied sheen of a hundred coats of paint. She was one of the 630-foot workhorses which had fed Minnesota iron ore to downlakes furnaces to make steel for wars.

Now ... a soybean crib?

The mate told the cleaning crews to slow down the cleaning.

Evenso, Brinkman came aboard at 5:00 p.m. "Ready yet, Captain?"

"No, sir. And by the work rules, I can't keep the crew working through the night unless we're loading, unloading, or underway. So we've got to quit."

"Captain, I get the feeling you're not pushing this job. The company gets paid per diem on this grain storage contract."

"Yuh."

"And one day's earnings ain't hay."

"Yuh."

"I don't know why you should be bitter. You got to admit the company's early retirement plan for captains is pretty good."

"Yuh."

"Do start promptly in the morning."

"Yuh."

But in the morning Emile Hoffstetler of Dart Cube had not arrived. Brinkman did. "I don't see any action, Captain. You could have shore leave now and the mate could scrub down."

"Mr. Brinkman, I've studied the new rules on ship cleaning for receiving grain. On riveted hulls built prior to 1950, we're required to paint the hold before receiving

199

grain. We're starting to paint, but we'll run out of paint. I've ordered more out of Sarnia."

"Sarnia? Why from so far?"

"Special kind of paint."

"Captain, I never heard about any special paint."

MacDougall was looking over Brinkman's shoulder. He saw a car arriving. Out of it stepped a tall man with a gray brush cut. MacDougall said, "Well, Brinkman, maybe we don't need special paint. If you have the authority, you go ahead and procure us some paint. Three hundred gallons."

"Let's skip the paint."

"You better check with the grain people."

MacDougall walked toward the arriving newcomer.

Emile Hoffstetler, the aging metal bender who used to fabricate whatever machinery Dart drew on the cement floor of the quonset hut, was now vice president of manufacturing at Dart. He brought two young men with him. "Captain MacDougall, I'm Hoffstetler. Jason Dart told me the story. How long we got before the ship is all soybeans?"

"Maybe two days, I hope."

"Lead. We follow. Start at the front." He turned to the young men. "Make drawings. Think hard."

They moved quickly through the ship. As they strode the whole deck, then through the inside fore and aft walkways, looking down into the cavernous compartments, Hoffstetler threw out questions:

"How much power this ship makes? AC or DC?

"What happens to the ship if we burn passageways for a crane through these bulkheads?

"In a river ... this ship stays level? Or rolling all around?"

Part of the tour went through the galley. The steward brought them coffee. One of the men shook his head and said to Hoffstetler, "This would be disastrous for precision manufacturing."

Hoffstetler nodded. "True. But precision manufacturing we're not talking about. What we talk about is precision foreign politics. You boys want to turn on your thinking brains. What you don't want is telling Mr. Dart you MIT Ph.D.'s don't have any ideas for this."

Hoffstetler turned to MacDougall. "Mister Captain, we

tell Mr. Dart what we saw. If he says it's a good idea, it's a good idea. But we're needing *time* to make planning. You can hold off the soybeans how long?"

MacDougall looked out the porthole and up at the grain elevator chutes which extended out over the boat. "I don't know."

MacDougall had lived two years with a nightmare. He knew the company kept score on the tonnage hauled by the ten boats in their fleet. By pushing the *Moran* and the crew hard, he had kept the vessel's profit productivity up. He pushed the fuel stops as fast as possible, pushed the cargo loading and discharge crews for speed, and ran on standby gear when he should have laid over for repairs. He bulldozed the lock master at the Soo to let him go through ahead of others when he was underway and others were parked.

But he saw the foreign steel unloading at Cleveland, Detroit, and Toledo. He saw the ore stockpiles building up at those same cities, and he feared the day they would order the *Moran* to tie up under a grain elevator to be a storage box. Therefore he read everything pertinent in the news.

He read about the shutdown in the Lakes shipping of Canadian and U.S. grain. He even had a fat file of clippings which included one he now retrieved:

BUCYRUS FARMER ATTACKS
TOLEDO ELEVATOR TO
RECLAIM HIS IMPOUNDED SOYBEANS

Arrested Were Benjamin T. Ruoff
And Three Neighbors

MacDougall went to a dockside pay telephone and asked information for the number of Benjamin T. Ruoff. He didn't reach Ruoff, but he reached Sheila Ruoff. He told her that soybeans from Toledo Elevator were going into an iron ore boat for storage. "And what does that do to soybeans, Mrs. Ruoff?"

"I don't know. But it doesn't sound good to me. We don't own our stored soybeans anymore. But whoever owns them, they shouldn't be spoiled. There's a lot of work in beans. I'll try to find out."

Sheila called Steve Varney. Varney called Warner Schlicter. Schlicter called Dick Lempke in Toledo Trust. Lempke called Toledo Elevator. "You're a good loan client of ours, Mr. Jay, and we think you know your business. But before you store any soybeans in an ore boat, we'd like to see how clean it is, what kind of paint is being used, what is the effect on the beans stored below the waterline and a few things like that. So will you boys hold up for a while on loading any of our beans into any ship?"

(Foreign Trade Digest)

The Vessel *Moran*
A Factory Without A Country
Is Defying National Trade
Boundaries in South Atlantic

The *Moran* Works Three Shifts
Attempting to Keep Up With Demand

Chiclayo, Peru - The vessel *Moran*, equipped as a floating factory to build the Dart Utility Cube (see photos overleaf), is lying offshore, taking aboard materials from shore at the bow and delivering Utility Cubes astern.

But while the ship is a manufacturing novelty, the vessel's great achievement is a living demonstration that the people who have really been deprived by protectionist restrictions have been the natives of the nation with the highest tariff barriers.

The mayor of the devastated city of Kajtec said, "Our people, who have been living in our miserable houses and dying from exposure, could have had these Utility Cube houses all along had it not been for our own government's stupid trade barriers.

"Our government has been our enemy. This ship only proved it."

The man who sold the Peruvian ambassador on permitting the *Moran* to run this operation was a blustering marketing manager, Thomas X. Dougherty, with the assistance of Senator Knute Boar.

Senator Boar put down his copy of *Foreign Trade Digest* and asked Ellen Brewster to reach Tom Dougherty in Seville, Ohio.

Shortly thereafter Dougherty walked over to Dart's office. There was a backlog cluster of new young executives waiting to see Dart. Dougherty went back to his office and dialed his way in past the anteroom crowd. "Jason, when you're ready to go home, I'll drive you."

"No, Tom. Ned White will drive me."

"Well ... I need to talk."

"Why didn't you say so? Are we so big now we can't talk?"

"Well ... it's not business, so ..."

"All right. Drive me home." Dart hung up but left his hand on the receiver. Suddenly he said to his comptroller, "Excuse me briefly." He pushed himself up out of his chair and transferred to his wheelchair, then rolled out of the office and down the corridor to the marketing department. A couple of young marketing managers U-turned to hold open the double doors for him. He rolled to Dougherty's office where an advertising agency woman was presenting a campaign. She started to leave. Dart signaled her to stay and explained, "Tom, you said it wasn't business, so of course I know it is. What?"

"Well, Jason, Senator Boar wants me to ask you if it would be okay for me to go on leave of absence here and go on his staff six months to help sell the free trade campaign."

"And?"

"I don't owe him anything, and I can't sell an intangible anyway."

"Number one — we owe him a lot. Number two — you

203

can sell *any*thing."

The ad woman nodded corroboration.

Dart asked, "So where does that leave us?"

"Well ... what does it do to our marketing program here?"

"Dougherty, you've got us stuck with a 12-month backlog already. And you've built a staff of more marketing types than I can count. Who needs you!"

The ad woman laughed, then clapped her hand over her mouth.

"What it gets down to, Tom," — Dart studied the floor — "is that you and I both don't want you to go; and we both know why. Washington runs on distilled grain alcohol, and we're both scared of that."

"Yuh."

"If you could help them sell free trade, the benefit is ... it would be a national milestone. But you might lose everything personally ... if you're not ready. Have you got it licked?"

"How does anybody know?"

"Tom, your decision. But if you elect to go, come back to Seville every weekend."

Dart wheeled out.

BOOK 3

23

DRUMMOND

There were not a lot of surprises left in the world for Dougherty, but this was one of them.

He paused at the top of the stairway, looking down on the well-groomed heads of the lunch crowd in the sunken dining room at Hal Boklin's Capitol Restaurant. A half-hundred faces turned up briefly to see if he was anybody.

Boar had told him his first job was "Eat lunch at Mel's to see Washington at work." He had his A.A., Jim Veitch, make the reservation and now meet him here.

As Dougherty descended he recognized news-worn faces, including one former presidential candidate. Scanning the crowd was like paging through *People Magazine*. A high-performance salesman is a walking radar, picking up a myriad of trivial signals. Dougherty recognized $1,500 suits and knew a power club when he saw one.

Being led to Veitch's table, he passed a bar setup and walked through the delicious bourbon aroma.

Being a man of the world, Veitch recognized another. They greeted with neutral smiles. Veitch raised a drink to the waiter and pointed to Dougherty who waved him off. Veitch shrugged and began abruptly, "Tom, the senator sent for you too late."

"Oh?"

"The protectionist drive on the trade bill has turned into a rout. And the quarterback who did it is sitting right over there."

Six dark suits at a large round table focused on a huge tan suit whose back was to Dougherty. The tan suit stretched tight across authoritative shoulders.

"Looks more like a halfback to me."

"He **was** ... Michigan."

"Looks familiar."

"Of course. That's Drummond. Senator. Michigan. He's suddenly grabbed the protectionist ball and he's going to run right over us with it all the way into the Oval Office. The power of the man is — he *believes* in it."

"Which? Protectionism? Or becoming president?"

"Both."

Dougherty watched Drummond rise and the eyes of the crowd follow him and attached entourage all the way up the stairway. Veitch watched Dougherty, "A new power is born."

"Well, Senator Boar must think we can tackle him."

"With a salesman?"

Dougherty grinned. "Now, Mr. Veitch, a good peddler can surprise you."

"Then surprise me." He handed Dougherty a ragged newsclip:

(*Washington Post*)

DRUMMOND BANDWAGON DRAWS FREE TRADER CONGRESSMEN TO DEFECT

The thousand-page omnibus trade bill now tidal waving through the massive Joint Committee could become history's biggest surtax on American citizens.

It will practically shut U.S. ports to most nations. Consumer prices will skyrocket.

Will It Pass?

Senator Knute Boar (R., MA) said "Before Drummond seized the leadership, the answer would be no. But he's got staunch free trader congressmen now crossing the line. He helped Wyoming and Montana delegations, strong free traders, punch through a proposed amendment to protect their lamb sales from Australia and New Zealand imports."

The Australian embassy's commercial minister protested, "The U.S. actually runs a trade surplus against Australia. Is this a way to treat one of your best customers? What does that tell the world about U.S. balanced trade intentions?"

Oklahoma has been for free trade, but it now wants an amendment against wire mesh and fence panels from Mexico. Oklahoma Steel & Wire's government affairs officer testified, "We just cannot compete with Mexico now."

Washington State wants to shut out imported grooved plywood wall panels.

Sugar Again

Senator Boar complained irritably, "Lobbyists from the sugar states are crawling all over this building to raise sugar quotas and tariffs against the Caribbean."

Senator Justin Forte, intellectual center of the free traders, could not be reached, but an aid, John A. Visconti, said, "The only reason legislators can get away with these special interest tariffs is ... **they concentrate the benefits and spread the costs.**"

The Same For Every Product

"With every senator claiming to be a free trader, but only wanting one or two exceptions for his own state," Boar said, "we are headed for a gorilla protectionist trade bill as brutal as the Smoot-Hawley 1930 tariff." Europe's finance ministers are warning that, if this bill passes, they will not be able to stop retaliation. Congress knows this, but the priorities of men seeking re-election, and one seeking the presidency, do not include the public's well-being.

Before Dougherty finished reading, Veitch interrupted, "How does that grab you so far?"

Dougherty smiled, "You boys play rough down here."

* * *

"Success is the child of audacity" — Disraeli

Top staffers in the offices of Senator Drummond knew that aphorism was posted above the mirror inside the coat closet in Drummond's office, reminding him every time he opened that door how he had reached a seat among the top hundred legislators in the world. Beside the lessons he learned on the football field, those six words from History 108 were the basic education Drummond took away from four years of University of Michigan. But they were golden.

Those six words had been his master theme in rising from three generations on automotive production lines.

As a very junior Detroit councilman, he had spotted a rare situation where an aging incumbent congressman, under temporary fire for opposing automotive sanctions against Japan, fell sick prior to his November re-election effort. With only moderate expectations, Drummond audaciously threw his hat into the ring. The aging congressman had wisdom, but Drummond had energy. He pulled off a squeaker win, becoming the youngest freshman representative in the new Michigan delegation in the U.S. House of Representatives.

He studied his new trade, kept his nose clean, and answered all constituents' mail personally in a massive correspondence.

After two terms in the House, he ran for the Senate and won. He served on minor committees ... Monuments, Arts ... until a weak member of the Labor Committee resigned in a conflict-of-interest scandal. Drummond immediately phoned a newly elected head of UAW saying, "If you act fast and in big numbers, you have a chance to force a Michigan man onto the Senate Labor Committee. Me." The Senate majority leader was deluged with union pressure. Drummond got the seat on Labor.

He did not stir up dust in the Senate, but concentrated on building up a huge credit balance of favors done for other senators. When he did move, it was with planned audacity, backed by 99 called favors.

Today he announced to five staff members, "We have a chance now to push the omnibus trade bill through the Joint Committee and bury the free traders. We are going to try to raise one swift decisive public outcry." He pointed to his assistant for constituent relations. "Bill Bryan has found a way. You'll see the plan in a minute, but first get this picture: It has got to happen fast. It is going to take a lot of arranging on our part. And the arrangements have got to be kept secret until it breaks so it won't be tagged a stunt. Understand?"

Staff curiosity was obvious. Drummond said, "O.K., Bill. Bring in your man."

Bryan left the room and returned leading a wiry, poised young man, about 33, unawed by the paneled office or the presence of a United States senator.

Bryan introduced him, Red Graves.

Graves yielded a nod at each introduction, then seated himself. Drummond nodded. With hands in repose on the chair arms, Graves said, "Gentlemen and Miss Buford, the deluge of goods into this country enters through so many ports that its huge mass is visually diluted to the public. Not disturbing. Published trade deficit figures in billions mean zilch to the man in the street."

Debra Buford nodded, "Amen."

Graves said, "But there is one place in the nation where the view of the import flood is awesome. All free trade economics lessons fly out the window when you see it. If we can show this sight to 36 of the nation's leading business newspaper people, they will be compelled to print it. The public will turn it into the conversation piece of the month like NASA's nine-hundred-dollar hammer. The pressure on Congress will blowtorch their feet.

"I will need a lot of help. Before you will believe in this effort and give it the full shot, this group must see it for yourself. Therefore meet me tomorrow at ten p.m. for a dry run at KAL Air Cargo concourse, Kennedy International."

Dougherty's first exposure to the Three Musketeers together, as Washington now dubbed Forte, Boar, and

211

Bain, was at a meeting in Boar's office. Some top staffers were present, including Visconti.

Boar said, "You all know we just lost Minnesota, Montana, Wyoming, Arizona, and Oklahoma on the free trade side. Drummond is pulling out our support like a magnet. We have got to have new power, or we're dead."

They looked to Forte, the strategist. Forte spoke to the carpet. "And that power has got to be either a **man** ... or a new picturization of free trade."

Bain said, "Justin, we've pictured it every **possible** way. They just do not get it. So we've got to have a **man**. A super influence."

"Correct. So that means...you know who."

Boar's cigar fist hit the desk, powdering it with ash, "The president."

Forte objected, "He can't come out flat for free trade."

Boar was wounded, "Why not? He wants it!"

They all looked to Bain. They had previously sent him to the White House because he had the deepest credit balance with the president from the time he recruited the Senate behind the president's unpopular austerity program. Bain said, "This president has the most sensitive radar for the public sentiment since FDR, plus a P.R. instinct that makes Madison Avenue amateur. He says he should not spend his popular clout on this one. We should better save him for a possible veto of the trade bill."

"He couldn't sustain a veto."

"Don't underestimate the boss's clout with the people. Remember the compact autos edict?"

They did. The week this president moved into the White House, the public nicknamed him "The Boss," a term he allowed to grow. It started because in that first week he issued a directive which caught the public's affection. He told his chief of staff, "You find the right binding language, but the first thing I want done around here is ... get rid of these goddam government limos hauling around generals and cabinet officers and hotshots down to G-18's. The government .... all levels ... will drive Fords, Chevys and Plymouths, etc."

"Yes, sir."

"And I don't mean custom jobs."

"Yes, sir. But what about the State Department cars for hauling visiting dignitaries?"

"Same thing."

"And ... uh ... the president's car?"

"That'll be the *first*. Make it a Ford." Then he grinned. "But with the sun roof."

When the press asked the media secretary where that edict came from, he replied, "Straight from the boss." The public loved it, and from then on the president was the boss.

Chris Bain concluded, "The boss is not going to chuck all that good will for free trade. But he's a president who will make a gutsy veto."

Visconti had taken to driving by the Japan Ministry on his way home from racquetball to his apartment certain late nights.

Visconti had talked Dougherty into joining the B Street Racquet Club so he'd have somebody to play with. He had carefully avoided the top-notch clubs. The B Street was difinitely Class B, but it had just men who wanted a quick brutal workout. The two men were intense players of a different sort. Visconti played with a grim determination to win, Dougherty with an equally fierce and exhilerate joy.

It was midnight when he and Dougherty, from Boar's office, were driving home. Visconti pointed to a second-floor room with a lighted window. "Ever since Drummond stepped up the protectionist heat, those lights have been on past midnight. That's their trade information clearinghouse room. Room 713. They know everything Drummond is thinking before he thinks it."

Room 713 was a large spartan office with scarred gray metal desks, filing cabinets, harsh overhead lighting, and a dozen driven people.. Here, the best of Japan's Washington commercial corps labored late. The whole job of three of them was assembling reports on the trade bill progress. These reports were extremely detailed. Daily the chief trade negotiator was given an estimated head count of Joint Committee legislators for and against amendment proposals affecting Japan and Japan's competitors. The information net created by the Japanese topped that of any foreign office in Washington. A platoon of lobbyists, including former U.S. trade negotiators, had wires reaching top men on the Hill and deep into the administration and even mobilizing help from large U.S. industrial customers needing Japanese components.

Hundo Sukuto walked into Room 713 and motioned certain people to join him in stand-up conference. Because one of them was American, he spoke in rapid unsmiling English. "We have an urgent problem. Get all the information you can, quick, about the following. Senator Drummond is planning a major nighttime media tour of the Kennedy Airport cargo tarmac. We need to know which night? Which journalists? Probably just print media. No TV. But find out.

"Most important: When we find out when the tour is, we need to see if JAL cargo arrivals could be drastically rescheduled or the whole affair will turn into a Pearl Harbor II festival. We can't afford that at the very moment when Tokyo has infuriated Drummond."

The American staffer grinned, "What did we do to him...lately?"

Sukuto frowned. "Toyota made him look very bad in Michigan. They skirted the passenger car import quota, sending in a boatload of 4-WD vehicles they claim are not cars. They label them 'farm service carts'— no seats. But... Drummond's Michigan voters call them cars."

In Miami, in response to Ed Fash's call, Mike Knox entered his boss' cubicle. "Michael, we've been invited by Senator Drummond to accompany him on a mysterious business tour."

"And I'm elected to RSVP."

"Bingo." Fash handed over a telephone message slip. "Send back your story by modem so I can make Sunday edition."

* * *

(*Miami Herald*)

DRUMMOND FUELS PROTECTIONIST FIRE WITH MIDNIGHT TOUR OF KENNEDY INT'L IMPORT CONCOURSE

Senator Escorts Free Trade Press On Staggering View Of Import Onslaught

New York — Senator Drummond launched a media coup, personally leading business reporters from 36 major free trade newspapers on a nighttime tour of the avalanche of foreign cargo smashing into Kennedy Airport.

You can talk all you want about the import imbalance, but until you see the cartons pour out of the jumbo jets, you don't really get the picture.

Here is how it goes at the port.

At 11:50 p.m. the passenger side of Kennedy International is nearly deserted. But on the cargo tarmac a KAL jumbo from Korea cuts its engines. No passengers get off. But when the belly doors open in the floodlights, a phalanx of fork-lifts attacks the aircraft, pulling out a quarter of a million pounds of microwave ovens, cameras, VCRs, electronic circuit boards and hundreds of other products.

The journalists watch awestruck. Drummond has the show business sense to let them view the entire spectacle. Off-loaded goods rose in stacks 20 feet high.

Korean cargo manager, A.L. Park, not yet aware of the reason for this media visit, bragged, "This month we brought 5,080 tons into New York. The planes are loaded to 99.2% of legal cargo weight."

At one point, with an electronic megaphone, Drummond instructed the crowd, "We'll come

back this way at the end of our tour. I want you
to see that same Korean aircraft when it leaves
here. They don't linger, they have relief crews
aboard for the return trip."

With the journalists still open-mouthed,
Drummond led them to some other airlines,
explaining 125 foreign cargo flights per day
come into **Kennedy alone**, "to say nothing of all
our other ports of entry."

They stopped at one of the customs stations.
The uniformed officer picked up one bunch of
manila folders and read off the products coming
off a Lufthansa flight from West Germany. They
all sounded like American products, aerosol
valves, plumbing supplies, hand tools, gauges.

In a short walk the reporters saw leather
belts from Brazil, $60,000 worth of designer
phones from Hong Kong, stacks of clothing from
China, Philippines, Hong Kong, globes from
Denmark, sweaters from Scotland.

At one gate the Alitalia cargo manager let
them watch the unloading of seven Lamborgh-
inis. "It costs $4,000 each to fly them over, a
dollar a pound, but then ..." — he shrugged —
"the sticker price on each is one hundred thou
per."

At Japan Airlines the freight manager was
directing the stacking of rows of cargo 30 feet
high ... film, specialty chemicals, lathe parts,
Toyota parts. As fast as trucks can haul this
away to spread it over eastern U.S., JAL's twice-
a-day flights to Kennedy push a thousand more
tons into this warehouse weekly.

India imports have grown so vast that six
customs men tend to nothing else but rayon
imports from India, another six do cotton. Evenso
they can't keep up. Drummond pointed to a box
full of unprocessed shipment folders.

The Empty Return Syndrome

Drummond brought his group back to the Korean warehouse at 1:00 a.m. where he had some coffee and doughnuts waiting. There he explained, "Now I want to show you this warehouse for a reason. Mr. Park originally divided this space 50/50: half for storing imports, half for exports. Now if you look over there you will see, by those yellow lines on the floor, a tenth of the space is now allotted to U.S. exports storage; nine-tenths is now full of imports. Now let's look at the nature of the exports. Are they heavy industrials? Mike Knox of the *Miami Herald*, can you read the labeling on those cartons?"

"Yes, Senator. Cigarettes, cigars, cola mix and videotape movies."

Drummond did not hammer the point, "Now let's go watch the reloading of that flight we saw arriving from Korea."

The reporters were allowed out on the tarmac to watch the loading. When the belly doors closed, the jumbo was practically empty. At 2:30 a.m. it lifted off for Korea. Park explained, "We have to keep them in constant motion because we need three more cargo aircraft. No other Asian airline will sell one to us because they need them. Delivery time for new planes is too slow."

Mike Knox said, "Well, at least I'm glad to see you're using good old American fork-lifts by Caterpillar."

Park smiled, "Yes, sir. They're the best. We use nothing but Caterpillar."

Drummond cut in, "Mr. Park, I can't let your comment stand. Please tell my guests where those Caterpillar lift trucks were assembled."

Sheepishly Park said, "Seoul, Korea."

Not satisfied, Drummond pressed, "Tell the whole story, Mr. Park."

"All right, sir." In resignation Park beckoned one of the lift truck operators over. He pointed to the various components. "These hydraulic masts are from England. The engine is Peugot, France. The tires ... Sri Lanka. Battery ... Japan. The hoses ... Italy."

The journalists were stunned.

In Forte's conference room, Mrs. Rider had 22 newspapers spread out on the table, open to Drummond's Media Tour of Kennedy imports. Forte, Visconti, and two staff members bent over the table, moving from newspaper to newspaper clockwise around the table.

A majority of the headlines picked up two phrases Drummond had belabored: "Economic Pearl Harbor" and "Past Time To Fight Back."

The *St. Louis Globe Democrat* worked both into the headline and added a jab at Forte:

KENNEDY AIRPORT IMPORTS
REVEAL ECONOMIC PEARL HARBOR

Sen. Drummond Charges U.S.:
"Past Time To Fight Back"
Many Say: "Time To Recall Forte."

Mrs. Rider said, "Senator, the phones are jammed. Can I call in the extra telephone people?"

"Yes. And in an hour, give me a one-page digest of the drift of the calls."

Forte scanned the articles with lightning mind, expressionless. He spent a little more time on one particular newspaper, then left.

Visconti moved over to read the one Forte had dwelt upon:

DRUMMOND VERSUS FORTE, THE PRO & CON IN BATTLE OF THE DECADE OVER THE OMNIBUS TRADE BILL

Drummond, respected as a legislator with character and daring, is betting his future on the severe Trade Bill.

Totally committed against the bill and even more at risk is the cerebral Senator Justin Forte, dedicated to thwarting the bill or pulling its teeth.

FOR

Arnold Drummond, son of a UAW shop steward in the Rouge Ford Plant, rose to the U.S. Senate. Particularly powerful on labor's behalf especially because he has miraculously avoided being tagged "UAW's man," his reputation is formidable and credible. He has opposed Labor's positions on seniority and check-off at risk of his re-election.

Now among the Senate's most influential men, he told the Joint Committee, "I'm well aware history shows the world's swift retaliation against U.S. tariffs. And we should heed that lesson.

"But ... we are not *teaching*

AGAINST

Justin Forte, acknowledged even by his enemies to be the brilliant mind who probably knows more about international trade than any legislator, opposes the Trade Bill's severity.

He may never be re-elected because his Missouri constituency is labor intensive ... metallurgical, automotive, brewing, leather, garments, and farming.

Keenly aware of the damage his voters suffer from imports, he still warned the committee, "The damage so far suffered, will be nothing compared to what this bill will bring down on us ... *because* despite our trade deficit ... now approaching three hundred billion ... *we are still the world's*

219

(Drummond)
that lesson to the rest of the world by letting them put up barriers against our products *without* retaliating.

"Europe and Asia don't call their barriers tariffs. They call them inspection fees or special standards.

"So ... clinging to free trade, we sit here like Patsies and let them destroy our shoe industry, our farming, television, steel, sporting goods, bicycles ... and the auto industry, leaving us to grease the cars, pump the gas, run the car washes, and the drive-ins.

"How can you let us do this to ourselves?

"How *can* you?"

When he finished, smart men had long thoughts.

(Forte)
largest exporter! We will be hurt first and most when the world retaliates against this protectionist law.

"We will shut down the world as we did in 1933 with the Smoot-Hawley Tariff! Nothing will move in international trade!"

Before noon a small eight-page newsletter dropped onto Visconti's desk, the lead story circled.

(D.C. Backstairs Digest)

SENATORS FORTE/DRUMMOND
SQUARE OFF TO POLITICAL
DEATH OVER ULTIMATE TRADE BILL

The Loser Will Go Down In Flames

Drummond, (D., MI) has staked his political life on a "Berlin Wall" tariff bill. Forte (R., MO) is dedicated to stripping it. Each is using up all political IOU's. When dust settles, one of them will be a dead man politically because ...

Visconti stopped by the telephone desks and listened to the responses the women were making. These part-timers were from a corps of Washington women seriously interested in political affairs, some political science college majors, quick studies, who free-lanced on various sophisticated government assignments. To hear them respond to the calls you would think they were regular Forte staff members.

Visconti could tell by their responses that they were fielding angry constituent complaints. He walked to Mrs. Rider's office, "Has the senator lived through many other hassles this bad?"

"No. Maybe three. But none this bad."

"Physically, can he handle ... I mean, he's not young."

"He has a remarkable stress protection, rare in Washington."

"What?"

"He lives by a code. That eliminates stress."

How?"

"Every act is either in or out of the code. So — no hard decisions to make."

Drummond ordered the Joint Committee professional staff to reserve the big committee room on the third floor "because Forte is going to give his estimate of consquences of a severe bill."

Drummond knew there would be a large crowd of spectators, not the politically effective heavy hitters, but the intellectually concerned and media types wanting beats in general. They would want to hear Forte.

The committee staff head, Battaglio, grinned, "Won't the big room concede Forte's stature and enhance it?"

Drummond was unusual in never letting ego dull his shrewdness. He winked, "You're damn right, but not as much as that small room. There would be SRO and lines in the corridor to hear the oracle. In a big room, they won't seem so many."

Drummond was even shrewd enough to lower his silhouette at this session, very graciously turning over the floor "to the distinguished senator from Missouri."

Forte's tired manner strangely had the compelling power of a senior professor who believes half this new class can never pass the course. His bluntness, they could tell, was not the planned attention grab of a Drummond. It was a worried man racing the calendar, "Congressmen and women...you are not reading your foreign papers. They are available only one day old downstairs. Many of them in English. You are featured in those papers. We are not building this trade bill in secret. What we do here by noon will be in the morning Paris *Herald Trib*. Europe knows our every move on this bill. But obviously we are not reading *their* newspapers.

"If we were, you would be scared to death of this bill we're building...this Berlin Wall."

"Why?

"Europe at this moment is preparing against it...working to have free trade among their big twelve in three years...a free, no borders, 360-million consumers market. They are already standardizing industrial parts sizes. France is already scrapping its cumbersome border-crossing procedures. Governments are changing lending laws so that their banks can loan across borders easily. Europe's cool attitude toward the Channel Tunnel is warming up. Border paperwork is being slashed so that long-distance lorry drivers won't be delayed at checkpoints."

Forte spoke without a note. "Even reluctant Belgium is getting ready. Societe Generde de Belgique is buying warehousing in Germany, of all places...to be ready for free trade in Europe.

"Sure Holland and Spain are nervous lest West German companies flood them with goods, but the more they read about this severe U.S. trade bill we're building, the more they favor the European free trade. Italy's businessmen are moving for free trade ahead of their own government. Olivetti's president said in this morning's paper, 'Free European market means we'll no longer depend on the American market.'

"England, always suspicious of European finance, is now busy turning Europe into one big free market.

"Nations there are already conferring on common rules for price labels in stores and for mutually acceptable pesticide residue levels on produce."

Forte pictured a huge free-trade Europe, self-sufficient within itself. Then he asked, "If we now come out with this trade bill which will shut their products out of the U.S., are we naive enough to believe that within 48 hours they won't shut Europe's door on us?

"My colleagues, would you expect so much as a half-priced Mickey Mouse watch to move in trade to Europe?"

Drummond was shrewd enough not to gavel down the out-of-order visitor applause.

24

CHESTERVILLE

Ed Fash, business editor, *Miami Herald*, handed the clip from the *Globe* to Mike Knox. "Read this."

(*Boston Globe*)

BOAR CONCEDES SENATE FREE TRADER HARD-CORE "CRUMBLING"

Rear Guard Overwhelmed By Drummond
Momentum For High Tariffs

Washington, D.C. - Sen. Knute Boar (R- MA) today expressed angry surprise at the sudden about-face of the prestigious Business Round Table.

This organization of presidents of the nation's hundred largest corporations, once the bastion of free enterprise and free trade, suddenly reversed itself, presenting a menu of fiercely protective additions to the Congress for the hardnosed trade bill now accelerating through Joint Committee of Congress.

The Round Table's L.K. Braxton requested a meeting with Boar. The senate bulldog first refused, then agreed, but said the meeting would have to be in his office at 10 p.m. Friday or ...

Knox asked, "So?"

"So our Washington bureau won't cover the meeting for me because it's after hours."

"Of course. They claim nothing ever happens inside the

Beltway on weekends. Right?"

"Right."

"But you think the Business Round Table might get Boar to cave, then the whole free-trade rear guard would collapse."

"Bingo."

"But Boar doesn't cave."

"Not usually. But they've got new leverage against him. The Massachusetts white-collar tech specialists started a huge union, MTS, to fight high-tech imports. They're battling Boar's re-election."

"So I go up to Washington and try to find out what happens in the meeting."

"Bingo."

"How do I get in the Senate offices at night?"

"Challenge our fat Washington bureau to show you some clout."

* * *

A man who doesn't need money is a problem.

Senator Knute Boar was a problem for the trade bill lobbying committee of the Business Round Table. His election campaigns were well financed in Massachusetts. He refused all bloated honoraria for speeches. He could not even be inveigled out to business dinners on Potomac yachts. "The people supply me an office for my work, so that's where we'll meet." His late Friday night meetings loused up a lot of supplicants' yachting and golf.

Boar's vast white-shirted torso hunched, sleeves rolled up, over his desk, a paperwork battleground. A .50 calibre cigar aimed dead ahead like a tank gun. The worldly spokesman for the committee, L.K. Braxton, president of the giant machine tool builder, Millitech, was a match for Boar in directness. He summed up their case for the inclusion of a farrago of metallurgical protectionist provisions, "In short, Knute, we and the new MTA are just looking for a fair shake against Japan's closed markets and trade cheating. That's all we ..."

Boar held up the flat of his meaty cigar hand, "Brax! Cut

it with the cheating and the closed markets! Sure that goes on. But you're beatin' on the Japs for their very merits — good quality and good price. You guys have better research, but the Japs are faster translating theirs into products."

Braxton reddened, "That's because you hogtie us with rules!"

"Some of that, Brax. But face it: Your sudden flip-flop is because they out-hustled you guys. They got the jump on you on machine centers, robotics, microchips, fiber optics, and they're about to jump you on superconductors and telecommunications. Now you boys have got to can your goddam golf playin' and get the lead out!"

Braxton growled, "Knute, you know damn well Asian governments pay for research. Unfair competition."

Boar put his massive head in his hand and talked to the desk blotter. "Brax, give me credit. A huge bunch of that so-called unfair Jap competition is you guys."

"Huh?"

"Americans bought seven million bicycles last year. Eighty-three percent from Taiwan. And you know who shipped them in? *You* guys. The largest Taiwanese companies are G.E., Texas Instruments, Digital, Wang, Mattel, and TRW. And you're shipping Fords in from Mexico and Brazil. And you knew that when you walked in here."

His phone rang. He answered it and said, "Not tonight, Ellen. No calls." He was about to replace the receiver but stopped, "My father?"

He headed for the outer office. "Excuse me, gentlemen; he's ninety-six and broke a hip."

He snatched up the outer office phone, fearing the worst.

But it wasn't the worst. Sven Boar, former chairman of Boar Dock and Forwarding in Boston, had lived through the Smoot-Hawley international depression of the 1930's and had schooled his son since childhood on the devastation of tariffs. He monitored Knute's free trade work closely in three newspapers with a thick reading glass, firing off memos of advice, outraged that his own weakened flesh could not keep up with his ideas for selling free trade to the world.

To conserve strength, he spoke very shortly, "Yes, I'm

okay, except for ... never mind ... listen! I now know exactly what you got to do to get this free trade across to the public."

"Dad, I'm right now meeting with the Business Round Table, about ..."

"They're half the problem. Now listen. I'm tired. Don't interrupt." Ellen saw the awesome bull regress before her eyes to a young man and then to a young son, listening.

"Knute, your approach to the public has been all wrong." Telegraphically the old man explained that nobody under 70 really remembers the big depression or Smoot-Hawley tariff disaster. And the man in the street who lost his job to imports doesn't relate himself to balanced free trade. But he does relate himself to the earth. "And he's right. And that's what you boys should all have realized. You are too narrow on this thing."

"I don't get you, Dad, and I'm pressed for ..."

"Breakfast doesn't come from the grocery store; it comes from the land. Heat doesn't come from the furnace dealer; it comes from the land ... coal, gas, oil."

"Dad, I don't have time for philosophy; I ..."

"Not philosophy! *Basics!* Your balanced world economy is only a part of the balanced world ecology."

"Dad, I don't have time for ecology."

"That's been your trouble! Now, here's what I want. Go to Chesterville, Ohio. Now! I'm paying part of a balanced economy study out there. The finest thing I've ever funded. And just what you need. Go there. I told your secretary the address."

"I cannot just pick up and go to Ohio."

"Knute. You're too big for your father now?"

"I've got the Business Round Table here."

"Perfect. Have them meet you there."

"I cannot do this."

"I'm going to put it this way, Knute. This is a lifetime request."

The line went dead.

Boar stared at the dead phone. Then he noticed Ellen had caught him naked. His voice was tired, "Ellen, tell the men — an emergency. We'll reschedule. I'll call you from ... from some ..."

She handed him a slip with an address. "There's a flight to Columbus, Ohio, at 9:30 a.m."

The phone woke Ed Fash at 2:00 a.m., Saturday. It was Knox. "Sorry to wake you, Ed, but I wanted your okay to grab the early bird flight home to Miami."

"Sure, if you got the story."

"There's no story."

"No story?"

"No. Boar broke off the meeting."

"For what?"

"Nobody knows. He got a phone call. And booked a flight to Ohio tomorrow morning."

"Oh. So a tough free trade Massachusetts senator stands up the Business Round Table Friday night to go to Ohio someplace. And there's no story?"

"We-ll ... uh ... I guess I'm going to Ohio, huh?"

"Bingo."

Boar was driving the rental car while his two staff men spelled each other reading to him extracts of the Business Round Table proposals.

Far north of Columbus, they turned off I-71 where the sign said Chesterville - 6 miles, Pop.254. Boar was stunned. Chesterville was an acreage of early America bypassed and isolated by time and I-71. The fields rising on land swells astride the high-crowned tar road were beautiful. The occasional buildings were an ugly calendar of the descent of a town. Grand old white farmhouses with lace millwork and floor-to- ceiling windows from a prosperous farm generation now had asphalt shingle extensions and skeletal barns and rusting machinery randomly parked.

The sidewalk began at West Third Street. Dead center of the town, the buildings were vacant except for a windowless grocery with porcelain enamel siding spelling Coke, Kodak, Hires, Bull Durham.

Inside, by contrast, a country-courteous young woman helped the customers. Boar noticed the customers looked his way with smiles when he inquired for Custice Laboratory.

Afterward, the door wouldn't let him out. "It wants you to lift up on it, sir."

A customer helped him, volunteering, "You'll really be impressed with the Ecosphere."

"The what?"

"The Ecosphere. Isn't that why you come?"

He nodded and left.

The sidewalk stopped at East Third. Two miles more brought them up to a farm mailbox: Custice.

They were expected. The weathered woman in khaki shirt and pants shifted a stilson wrench to offer a hand. "Senator." She turned out to be a Dr. Grayson. She explained that Dr. Custice was due back tomorrow from Battelle Research. She led the way up to the barn. Her conversation displayed appreciative knowledge of the senator's main work, but as an equal, one who also had a large mission.

The barn was ordinary, disintegrating in front. But Boar's group was led up a new plank stairway to the back of the loft into another world, expensively remodeled. The roof over the loft had been cut away. The loft floor was new planking with reinforced supports. A new roof of glass had been built, with some venetian-type vanes which could be adjusted electrically. This large atrium contained laboratory counters and sinks and desks. An assortment of lights reached down from the glass roof.

Boar suddenly decided his father had sent him to some artsy economics boutique, possibly run by a nut. "Look, Dr. Grayson, my father said you had a balanced economic model out here I should read. For some reason you couldn't mail it to me. I brought our legislative assistant, Jim Veitch. Can we get at it?"

"Yes, Senator. You're looking at it." She nodded to the center of the atrium. There was a very large glass hemispheric dome three-quarters full of water. Through interruptions in a green slime lining the insides, Boar could see fish swimming. "That is a balanced economy. Our mission is to see if it will sustain for ten years, twenty, thirty ...

forever.

"Professor Custice spent six years getting it in balance. Then it was sealed forty-seven months ago. It's been running ever since on its own. No food. No new water or plants.

"Now I have to meet with a contractor. But coming on duty for the two o'clock readings and to answer your question is Maybeth Harlow, my successor."

"Your *successor*?"

She now smiled broadly. "Senator, if the Ecosphere endures as long as we hope, we need a relay of generations.

"Professor Custice is seventy-four. I came on the project at thirty-seven. The professor started training Maybeth in aquatic biology when she was sixteen, getting her commitment to the project until she is forty-five. Then she must recruit a ..."

Boar smiled and nodded.

Maybeth Harlow was a stunning surprise in blue denim shirt and jeans and boyish-cut nearly black hair. Reading some gauges and penciling the readings, she was unaware of her striking presence. The knowing eyes, set wide, were only shallowly recessed, and a crescent of white *below* the pupils made them compelling. The full lips were not crisply sculpted. The pale denims were working clothes, but the small earrings were dress-up. Her sure knowledge of the project gave her feminine motions authority.

Her pencil pointed out the twelve-inch-thick rubber pad under the ecosphere. "In case the road ever becomes a highway with heavy truck vibrations."

"Why Chesterville?" Boar asked.

"Dr. Custice studied that carefully. He thinks industrial development will never come this way, to cut off sunlight and jar the ground."

She explained that once a balanced economy is achieved in the ecology of the sphere, it should theoretically continue indefinitely. "That's what we're proving, we hope. If we do, we can show mankind how to sustain the balanced earth ecology ... and economy ... which is the same thing."

"The same thing?"

"Of course, sir. Ecology, economy. In the ecology, every organism supplies something *to* the others; and uses something *from* the others. The business economy — same thing."

Boar looked to his two staff men, slowly turning up his palms, as if discovering a truth. They honored his mood, nodding. He breathed, "So obvious. So obvious." He studied the sphere. "Yet obscure."

Embarrassed, Boar broke the spell, "Where's the air pump?"

She turned on an impish smile, "Senator, what did I just tell you?"

"No pump?"

"Shouldn't need it," she grinned, "if we have truly balanced the sphere. It's a closed system. It's a world. An earth. This is the original water. The only outside influence is the sunlight and temperature. Our big problems." She pointed to the mechanical shades. "That may trip us up."

Boar's delegation now studied the Ecosphere. Washington, D.C. shucked off them like their suitcoats as they peered in some awe. Miss Harlow explained that, though the execution is infinitely complex, the theory is grade-school simple, "A kid can make a sealed world that will last a long time. Put an inch and a half of sand in the bottom of a gallon jug and fill it to within two inches of the top with pond water that's got plankton, tiny plants and animals. Let the water settle a week, put in a snail and two minnows. Screw the top on, seal it with paraffin, and give it sunlight. If the kid's got it balanced, that sealed world will sustain itself for months. The plants supply the food and oxygen the fish need. The fish give off CO_2 and fertilizer that the plants need."

"Why not forever?"

"Nature is complex. If you simplify complex systems, you can get disaster ... like removing the wolves and pumas from the Kaibab plateau in Arizona, or importing the *Endothia* fungus from China which killed the American chestnut trees."

"Huh?"

"For example, the child's glass jar and lid become part of that world inside it. The lid will rust and intrude foreign substances. We needed something in the Ecosphere to provide against that. Dr. Custice and Battelle Research finally came up with a special kind of polished plate glass, but we don't know ..." Her voice faded.

While continuing to read gauges, she explained the complication of getting the proper balance that would endure if the population ... the animals ... in the closed environment change themselves by adaptation.

"The plants we have there are high oxygen producers. The squiggly ones are Vallisneria. The broader leaf, Sagittaria, and some Anacharis. If too many fish use more oxygen than the plants produce, the fish begin coming to the surface to gasp for air."

Boar's attention drifted long enough to note that the expression on the face of the wordly Jim Veitch for once betrayed naked wonder. However, Boar detected that it wasn't for the Sagittaria or Anacharis. It was for Miss Harlow.

"But you have to have enough animals," she explained, "to keep the plants eaten back so they don't go into explosive growth. Balance is *everything*."

She cited another complication. Plants produce more oxygen than they use, except in the dark ... at which time they are in direct respiratory competition with the animals.

"Also the quantity of animal life and plant life must relate to the water volume so they can survive indefinitely by gaseous exchange.

"And you need the kind of bacteria and plants that consume most of the waste from the fish as fast as produced ... so you don't get a toxic build-up."

She added that Dr. Custice was concerned that ammonia, which is poisonous, must be rapidly consumed by bacteria and converted to nitrite, then to nitrate.

Animal wastes want to increase the acidity of the water. This must be countered.

Boar asked, "What do you expect to get out of all this?"

"Answers to a hundred questions."

"Like?"

"How large an imbalance can the system counter?"

"What do you mean?"

"The system can assimilate how many dead fish before

poisoning itself? Or without a biotic growth explosion that upsets the whole balance?

"Does the upward migration of plankton with the rising light and then downward with the dark have any function? Signaling or controlling?

"Will deaths versus new births balance?"

Veitch, Boar's head of staff, studied his boss in surprise. Boar was no longer a senate giant, he was a kid at a mill pond. "Young lady ... what was that bit about Kaibab plateau and the ... uh ... fungus?"

"Senator, when legislation interferes with a balanced ecology — disaster time."

She told of the deer on the Kaibab plateau north of Grand Canyon where about 4,000 deer were preyed upon by pumas and wolves. Since the deer had the better public relations, men set out to reduce the wolves, and did. The deer population exploded then to about 100,000, far beyond the capacity of the prairie. The region was grazed clean of grass, tree seedlings, shrubs. In two winters 40 percent of the herd starved. "The damage to the forest is still visible."

She explained that the competition in nature keeps the balance if man doesn't interfere.

"Interfere?"

She cited the half-billion-dollar Narmada Valley Development, a massive scheme to dam India's largest river, thereby displacing two million people, wiping out 33,000 hectares of India's forest cover, including its teak and bamboo. "Dr. Custice looks for it to create epidemic malaria, cholera, and encephalitis."

She told of the environmental disaster expected from Brazil's $450-million hydroelectric project. She explained the destruction expected from the $600-million-dollar deforestation of Java. She told of the death of hundreds of thousands of animals in Botswana resulting from the attempt to create more cattle range land, which instead created a desert and starving natives.

Veitch looked at his watch. "Senator, the flight schedule ..."

"Change it."

"Senator, we're not in the biology business."

"The hell we're not. You know who financed those disasters just named? The World Bank. You know who the World Bank is? It's us. And it looks like we're screwing up the world."

"I thought we were here about free trade."

"We are. The world economy is part of this bigger thing ... the world ecology. We get that out of balance, everything dies. If there's no cross transfer of nutrients and gases, we die. If countries can't import and export ... we shut down the world."

Boar looked into the murky interior of the Ecosphere. "Young lady, is there a motel somewhere ... twenty-thirty miles?"

"Yes."

He turned to Veitch. "Get our office to contact Braxton. Tell him if they want to resume our meeting, it will be here. Monday. Ten a.m."

"How are they going to get here by then?"

"These guys aren't presidents for nothing."

Dr. Grayson gave them directions to the motel. Boar finally smiled, "Tell me, Dr. Grayson, didn't you make a tactical error — choosing such a beautiful successor? Won't she get married and fly the coup?"

"Extreme beauty was one of Dr. Custice's specifications."

"Why?"

"So that she can dictate to any fiance that she's going to live here."

"Where would any future husband find work in Chesterville?"

"Dr. Custice says we need every kind of skill. We'll make him a job."

Across the U.S., chain-reaction phone calls connected the Trade Bill Task Force of the Business Round Table. The angriest protester, Lockhart, head of Gould Ocean Systems, snarled, "Where the hell is Chesterville, Ohio?"

Braxton laughed. "On the map it shows between Amity, Mount Gilead, and Pulaskiville."

"Oh. Thanks."

"There's a private landing strip at Ankenytown."

"What is Boar trying to do ... humble us?"

"Don't think so. He wants us to see something in Ohio."

"Well, Brax, you're going to have to do Chesterville without me."

"You I need *especially*."

Lockhart had risen to the top of Ocean Systems, Inc. because of his rare combination of marine engineering and marine biology. Braxton knew from Veitch's message there was some kind of ecological implication in Boar's trip. He explained that he needed Lockhart's scientific background.

"Is this some precious kooky environmentalist deal?"

"Don't know. It's run by a Dr. Custice."

"Oh-oh. Custice?"

"Yes, why?"

"It's not kooky. Custice is Mr. Ecologist. But with clout. With only two phone calls, he raised six million to save four million acres of Bolivia forest from slash-and-burn developers."

"He's that big?"

"Bigger. He headed the Oxford Marine Biology Division. He headed Conservation International. We tried to hire him for three months at quarterback wages. He had his assistant phone us — 'too busy.'"

Braxton asked, "If Boar is going to sic him on us, will we be able to follow the conversation?"

"Maybe not, but we'll sure learn something. How long is that Ankenytown air strip?"

(*Miami Herald*)

SEN. BOAR STIFFENS OPPOSITION
TO PROTECTIONIST TRADE BILL

CLAIMS NATURE FAVORS FREE TRADE

Holds Offbeat Seminar For
Business Round Table In Boondocks

by Mike Knox

Chesterville, OH — Who was more startled? The 254 residents of this town or the seven distinguished visitors arriving in rental cars? Each stopped at Chesterville Grocery to inquire for the Custice Laboratory. And they later took their meals at the Grocery (potato chips, Hostess cakes and Coke).

Sen. Boar left the Business Round Table trade committee no choice. If they wished to continue the meeting he broke up in Washington, they were to meet him here on a farm at the Custice Laboratory.

Under Boar's direction, Dr. Custice, renowned ecologist, explained a long-running experiment called the Ecosphere, which is a balanced ecosystem, which Boar claims is the same as a balanced world trade.

Patronizing and cynical at first, the corporate presidents later became attentive under the spell of the aging Dr. Custice who has spent a lifetime trying to teach mankind that we humans are not owners of the earth. We are part of it. We are not outside looking in; we are in it. And the earth is a balanced economy.

The committee is still in Chesterville (though they have found a better restaurant 30 miles away), and they have sent for other Round Table members to join them at the Custice Ecosphere.

The residents of Chesterville have seen many distinguished visitors come to the Custice Farm, but never such a concentration as this. They have made available rooms and they ...

In Washington, Boar projected to Forte and Bain his conviction that balanced free trade was an imperative of nature. "We have got to get the public to stop thinking and talking U.S. ... and think global. So I think we've got to enlist that worldwide network of environmentalists."

236

Bain countered, "Anybody can see you're affected; but politically the environmentalist crowd has no punch."

"But they did once. You're forgetting the whole emissions legislation, the oil spills legislation, the drainage and sewering legislation. They had billions of dollars worth of clout. If they go on our side on balanced free trade ..."

Bain nodded, "You've got a point. But how can we reach them ... quick?"

Forte said, "I'm going to send Visconti out to Chesterville. If he gets the religion like Knute, he'll find out how to enlist them."

When given the assignment, Visconti said, "Senator, we don't have time for that long-range type action."

Forte asked, "Do you have a short-range plan?"

Visconti flew to Columbus and drove to Chesterville.

Visconti's reaction to surprise, which seldom happened to him anymore, was alert silence. During his stay in Chesterville he did not meet the absent Dr. Custice, but he gained a picture of the man by reflection from the ecosphere staff. They were relaxed and natural with a visitor from Washington, quietly confident that they were working on the most basic subject in the world. Despite the rural Chesterville pace, they seemed to be racing some invisible clock. They answered questions with a minimum of words and went on to their chores.

Visconti found himself surprised and compelled by the ecosphere. He studied it alone for long periods.

The second surprise for Visconti was not scientific. An alumnus of one marriage, with a subsequent bachelor social life, Visconti was at ease around interesting and exciting women. But in the presence of Maybeth Harlow his feet were suddenly too big, his hands stuck way out of his sleeves. To remain effective he looked away when asking questions, which he kept brief but pointed, "If there is a single concise theme that draws all environmentalists, what would it be?"

"You mean packagable and promotable?"

Was the question sardonic? Maybe so, maybe no. He

risked a direct glance. Now the placid brown eyes under heavy gull-wing brows met him straight on. The eyes, not deep-set, were extra crisply defined and lidless. If there was challenge, it was the mouth below small flared nostrils. Generous lips, not finely molded, seemed to need to be consciously closed to hold in ... what? Tiny parenthesis etched around the mouth could be a grin. He thought the Maker must have said, "Now I'm going to carve me a heroine." A straight-sided face to the jaw angle; cut squarely toward a rounded chin above a vulnerable throat. She was royalty in a barn in Chesterville. He looked back at the ecosphere.

"There is one theme," she said. "The only one."

"What is it?"

"One earth."

"What?"

"One earth. That's what it's all about. Nature didn't break up the world with boundaries. Man did."

"Explain, please."

She pointed to a gap in the scum that lined the ecosphere. "When I tell you, you look through that one gap." She took two flashlights and placed them at two other open spots so that the beams crossed, then nodded to him to look. "Suppose we put partitions ... boundaries ... where these beams shine. What would happen?"

"Those fish that are crossing the beams would be stopped."

"Yes." She abandoned the flashlights. "So they couldn't get to the various plants they need, nor to the depths they need at certain times. Now ..." Involuntarily in the interest of speed, she took his elbow impersonally and drew him to a large world globe... "Same thing here."

Her large slim hands traced an odyssey from Alaska to California and back. "The whales need to be free of boundaries to make this breeding trip yearly."

The hands traced a sweeping curve from South America up along the Carolinas and east into the Atlantic. "The Gulf Stream is not blocked by man-made borders." Her eyes were on the globe so he could look at how her motions made a blue denim jacket into a royal cape. The hands swept down overland from Alaska and across the U.S. and up to

Hudson Bay. "The weather from the north that regulates plants and animals has no boundaries."

Her hands did the same thing for the Canada geese migrations. "The big flyways."

"Are free trade lanes," he said, "one earth?"

"All scientists always know this," she said. "Politicians seldom. One did, Wendell Wilkie. He called it 'One world.' But 'world' is political. 'Earth' is right."

"One earth."

She smiled. "So you got what you came for. Will that be ...it?"

He nodded. "Except I ... was wondering if you ... uh ... would be free for ... uh ... supper?"

She looked at her watch. "I'm brown-bagging dinner because I take readings at six-thirty."

He nodded and extended a hand. She had a thin firm grip and she handed him his briefcase. As he started down the plank stairs, he turned to look back. She was in fact opening a brown bag. "All right," she said, "you could have half."

Forcing himself not to smile or hurry and spoil anything, he came back.

As they dined on peanut butter sandwiches, he asked why the time pressure. She explained they were balancing two other ecospheres. In case this one failed, in case they hadn't got it balanced right, they need to start over, and it takes time to get one in balance before sealing it.

Then she asked him why he had come way out here for information available right next door in Washington at Committee on Resources of National Academy of Sciences. "They have a hundred publications begging the world to understand it is one earth."

"Would they have the ear of the environmentalists?"

"Totally. All over the world." She pulled from a desk a 400-page book filled with addresses, titled "Environmental Organizations Directory". He wrote down the title.

"What could free traders do for them ... to get them to enlist the environmentalists behind free trade?"

"Make the world aware that your free trade goal is a natural phase of the one-earth truth."

"Don't their hundred books do that?"

"Nobody reads them."

Vincent Treadway, director of Committee on Resources, received Visconti so guardedly that he assembled a group of five of his staff for the meeting.

While they studied him, Visconti laid out his plan, requesting the mobilization of the environmentalists nationwide to pressure for balanced free trade...as a route to *one earth*.

"We're already pressing that concept, Mr. Visconti. How does pushing balanced free trade further our cause?"

"It connects it, in the minds of millions, not with bird walks, but with the main concern of millions — making a living and buying groceries."

Treadway said, "Crude as that proposition is, it has a great deal of merit. But we have to view it with enormous suspicion."

"Why?"

"Many have enlisted us, claiming environmental concern, only to later act exactly opposite. The Corps of Engineers, for example, uses us to sell large projects, claiming environmental benefits. Then, when they get funding approval, they proceed in total ignorance of the environment. There are a dozen others who have used us. Then betrayed us."

"I think if you would talk with Senator Boar, you would not fear that."

"Probably you're right. But, Mr. Visconti, across the country thousands of environmentalists are now gunshy of such alliances. To get them up for this would be an enormous mobilization effort. Why should we undertake that?"

"I have your answer...if I can talk to you alone."

Treadway was astonished. "Why?"

Visconti was tired. "Because I'm going ahead with or without your organization. I think you would want to hear my alternative alone. Then decide who to tell."

When the two were alone, Visconti rose and leaned over the director's desk. "Mr. Treadway, your environmentalists are not *your* environmentalists. They're divided a hundred ways — the marine guys, the bird types, the oil spill crowd, the whale people, the seals. You can't even get them to agree on a picnic. But here's your chance to get some unity. And with *you* in charge. And *fast*. Why fast? Because Boar and Forte are out of time. So this won't be another hundred-year struggle. Twenty-six weeks! Maximum! Call me tomorrow by noon. Let me know if it's you or if I should be talking to the Audubon or the Greenpeace or the _____."

NERVOUS ALLIANCE BEGINS BETWEEN ENVIRONMENTALISTS AND FREE TRADERS ON "ONE EARTH" CAMPAIGN

While unbridled free trade can bring misguided overdevelopment, it can more often allocate limited resources to fit the demand or need ... as opposed to government subsidized operations which stimulate gross overproduction far beyond the demand, resulting in massive waste and destruction.

The free trade leaders in the Congress are enlisting environmentalist support in talks with the National Academy of Science. Should agreement be reached, swift and massive action by the vast army of ecological organizations may bring a breakthrough for both balanced one-earth laws and balanced free trade with ...

25

SUKUTO

(*Lansing Times*)

CONGRESS SEIZES PUBLIC OUTRAGE
TO STIFFEN TRADE LAW

Drummond's Airport Tour
Ignites National Anger

Washington—Responding to a crush of angry citizen mail following Sen. Drummond's media blitz on imports at Kennedy Airport, the Congress is in a mood to "stick it to" the foreign imports with gorilla tariffs, quotas and domestic subsidies.

The huge Joint House-Senate Committee numbers 160 legislators from eight senate committees and 12 house committees.

The protectionist ardor is so hot that at present the Joint Committee is even leaning toward increasing the farm subsidies to help farmers against lower-cost foreign produce.

Once Drummond uncovered the foreign deluge into Kennedy Airport, media descended on other U.S. ports to document the astounding inflow of goods with pictures which fired the protectionist boiler.

(*Detroit News*-Editorial)

HAS MICHIGAN LOST DRUMMOND?
What About The Home State Problems?

Our senior senator is making a name for himself nationally, but he is worsening our rising home state problem ... housing. Federal funding for Michigan's serious housing deficit in five cities has dried up. Our man in the Senate, with the most clout, has not only shorted the problem, his protectionist drive is working against low-cost housing for Michigan, raising the cost of building supplies. The shelter emergency in Michigan has reached ...

Drummond's domination of the Joint Committee open hearings was masterful. While maintaining authoritative control he gave the appearance of wide-open objectivity. When the free traders had a weak witness, he was gentle and courteous and let the witness ramble. While other committee members busied themselves with paperwork, the TV cameras never caught Drummond in any posture but rapt attention to the witness. When the free traders had an effective witness, Drummond enforced strict rules of order, insuring against any free-flowing oratory. While some committee members were obvious in playing to the cameras about lost American jobs, Drummond's showmanship was too subtle to get caught by any but the most perceptive camerawomen.

Forte instructed Visconti to get quickly a farmer witness to counter farm subsidies, and a consumer witness, and "get Sukuto to come as a witness to counter that Drummond Kennedy Airport stunt."

The president of the Alliance of Consumer Associations agreed to be available as a witness. Sukuto said he would need to talk to his Commerce Ministry. "I think they will feel that my appearance would only escalate Japan bashing."

For the farm representative, Visconti phoned Toledo, Ohio. "Mr. Lempke, I'm calling on behalf of Senator Forte. You once called the senator's office after hours and got me instead."

"That was a dog's age ago. But I remember it. I was so shocked to find any of you Washington fellas workin' after

243

happy hour."

"You alerted us to watch the Midwest farm news, especially Ohio, for ammunition to bolster our free trade position."

"True. But I never heard from you, so I decided for you fellas the Midwest is C street."

Visconti was wondering what kind of man he had on the end of the line; but he continued, "Then it will surprise you, but we **did** send for that newstape where you were testifying before an Ohio legislative committee."

"That wasn't what I wanted you to see."

"Let me finish, please. We were impressed with the way you presented certain farm economics. We would like it if you would come to Washington to testify on the free trade side before the Joint Committee on the omnibus trade bill which is getting out of hand."

"Young fellow, I'm honored by your invitation. But that won't do you any good."

"We think so. You have the credentials ... agricultural, financial, and at a high level."

"Those credentials will kill you. Only thing everybody hates more than a golf-playin' doctor is a bank vice president."

"I'm sorry you're turning us down."

"I'm not. I've got you something better."

"Who?"

"There's a young farmer down here knows more economics in his blind eye than half the bankers. That's not unusual, of course, but the thing about this young fellow ...he can explain it so even bankers understand it."

"But can he do it in front of fifty-sixty hostile congressmen and a battery of TV cameras?"

"If you can give him big enough questions to keep his mind off that circus."

"It may take a week of standing by — can he be away that long?"

"Nope, you'll have to fly him back home a couple times."

"Our budget rules don't permit that."

"I'll get our bank to spring for his extra trips. After all, we fund the theater here. This'll be a better show."

"Tell me about him so I can decide if we want to bring him on."

"That isn't the decision. It's ... will he come? He's got a lot of acres to manage. Better let me talk to him."

Visconti found himself laughing as he hung up. It had been a long time since anyone had called him "young man," even if he was.

Mrs. Rider told Visconti a man from the Consumer Alliance was here to see him. The man who entered said, "I came in person because my message is difficult."

The difficulty was that a quick telephone scan of their affiliates showed the regional groups had a high content of people unemployed because of foreign imports. "So I'm afraid we have to back off on appearing for free trade. Your Senator Forte will surely understand that."

"No," Visconti said. "He won't." And he waited.

"He won't?"

"No. What he will understand, Mr. Reiker, is that you big consumer bleeders are ducking the biggest rip-off facing your consumers today ... protectionism. Import restrictions cost your American consumers over a hundred billion a year, and you guys say nothing. Twelve hundred extra just for a car. Americans paid an extra billion just for shoes because of quotas against Italy; 25 extra billion for clothes, five billion extra just for cheese, butter and milk.

"And it's regressive tax. Like a 40% surcharge against families with under $13,000.

"Protecting one TV assembly job that pays $23,000 costs your citizens $74,000 in raised costs.

"But you guys won't testify. I'll try the other consumer organizations. Maybe they have some guts. Good day."

Sukuto called, "The Ministry says no."

"No what?"

"They don't want me to testify."

Visconti said, "Mr. Sukuto, I know you guys are plugged in all over Washington at high levels, but did you ever get turned down by Senator Forte when you wanted a fair listen...like on the compensation for the California war-displaced Japanese?"

There was silence on the wire. Visconti knew he had

handed Sukuto a soul-wrencher. Finally Sukuto asked, "Mr. Visconti, does the committee have the subpeona power?"

"Yes."

"Use it."

The grapevine signal that Sukuto would appear as a witness before the trade bill committee crowded the spectator section with visitors from trade associations ... automotive, electronics, off-highway earthmovers, lift trucks, machine tools, and steel men.

Sitting astride Sukuto were two Japanese Americans. In front of them were stacks of U.S. tariff laws. Drummond let a congressman from Detroit lead the questioning, which began about Japan circumventing steel pipe import quotas by sending unthreaded pipe to Thailand where it was threaded and entered the U.S. as a Thailand shipment, not Japanese. It was obvious that Sukuto was struggling to find polite language for his reply. His two colleagues scribbled suggestions. Finally he shrugged, "Congressman, respectfully ... *very* respectfully ... I have to say ... **your** people ordered the pipe. It is only supply and demand. Nepal has no steel mill, yet you are receiving steel from Nepal."

Drummond's gavel struck, "Mr. Sukuto, we did not ask you about Nepal."

"I apologize."

Interrogation turned hostile. Sukuto kept his answers shorter until the Detroit congressman challenged, "If you folks are for free trade towards us, why don't you open up your market to us?"

Sukuto was exhausted. With resignation and carelessness he said, "You don't realize your own laws prevent you selling to Japan. You have not told your people that you could wipe out one-third of the Japan deficit overnight if you would sell us petroleum. You don't realize that on 70 percent of our exports to you we pay an average of 50 percent tariff. In addition to your federal, we face barriers from your states, counties, and cities."

Drummond's gavel struck. "Please refrain from assumptions about what we don't know. I believe this subject is now completed."

However, the Japanese American senator from Washington state said, "Mr. Chairman, I request that we hear the rest of Mr. Sukuto's informative reply."

Drummond shrugged grudging agreement.

Sukuto ignored his two companions who were pushing open tariff books in front of him. Seeming oblivious to the entire audience, he said, "What I should think would trouble you most ... ironically ... you punish us for delivering what Americans ask us for ... quality products at lower prices so that you can enjoy even higher living standards. I could understand if you hated us because we were shoddy and overpriced. But ..." He turned up his palms, ending the interview.

The insiders knew that last 30 seconds would be the "select" for the six o'clock news.

The media section was sandwiched between the witness table and the raised triple-tiered committee dais. The journalists found themselves compelled by the earnest face of Steve Varney, the farmer with the black eye patch who sat with no papers and no briefcase and no assistants.

They stopped handing back and forth batteries and cassettes and adjusting lights and cameras to study him. He seemed such a central-casting farmer. The new suit hadn't been much worn. The white shirt was so new it was bluish and still had the packaging creases. So they expected him to muff his lines. Then they were sure he would because, after listening to Drummond's question about his opposition to farm subsidies, he thought about it forever. The farmer had choked up.

Suddenly an audible relief pervaded the chamber. Quietly, Varney was saying, "Whenever you try to help us with subsidies, gentlemen, you hurt us. Canada and Europe raise their subsidies to overmatch it. We all end up selling our own products to our own governments at support prices. The public pays a premium and the poor nations go hungry. Then farmers plant more to get more subsidy money. And we wind up short of storage. The world could feed ..."

"Mr. Varney!" Drummond was suddenly uneasy with this articulate farmer. "Do you consider yourself not only a farmer but a world economist?"

The cameras swiveled to Varney who studied his folded fists, thinking. Without looking up he said, "They're both the same, sir."

"Oh? Enlighten us, please."

"A farm is a small planet. Your grain field is a small nation which must supply enough fodder for the farm's dairy nation. Plus extra ... for next year's seed. And the dairy, as a nation, must supply enough manure to renew your fields. And if you have more cows or hogs than your fields can fodder, you've got to borrow into next year's seed for feed ... which leaves you less seed for next year. So a still smaller crop follows, leaving still less seed for the third year and ..."

Drummond snapped, "Mr. Varney, I'm sure this homey little homily is supposed to enlighten our national problem in some way. Exactly how?"

"Yes, sir. If we eat our seed corn, we go down. The U.S. is eating its seed corn."

Drummond, noting the earnest attention of his colleagues, said, "Congressmen, it is eleven o'clock. I feel it is time for noon recess."

A congressman from western Ohio said, "Mr. Chairman, with your consent, there seems to be keen interest in this testimony. I suggest we pursue this another hour?"

Senator Forte addressed the chair, "Senator Drummond, Mr. Varney was promised that at 11:15 he could be excused to go outside and listen three minutes to his radio which they would not allow him to bring into this chamber." The infrequent visitors started to laugh but ceased when they noted that Forte did not. "He needs the Chicago WBBO farm report especially today in making a decision to sell or not sell a considerable number of livestock."

Drummond agreed. Questioning continued.

Seeking to show that the farmer's Bucyrus, Ohio, answers were too provincial for national consideration here, Drummond asked, "You say subsidies have hurt Bucyrus,

Ohio, but in this body we are concerned with 270 million Americans and many world governments who consider subsidies beneficial. Do you set yourself up as saying what is bad for Bucyrus is bad for the world?"

"No, sir. The Harvest Farm Papers say so."

"Say what?"

"Say that the Japanese are paying forty dollars a pound for beef and six times the world price for rice. And that in the last seven years subsidies added a third to the cost of all farm produce in 23 nations. OECD figures."

At 11:10 Drummond eagerly called a ten-minute break so that Varney could get his radio report. The committee busied itself with paperwork, some left on brief errands. The spectators conversed in a low hum. Some of the media followed Varney into the corridor to catch the broadcast. The guard handed over the radio. Varney took notes from the rapid-fire broadcast:

Don't carry feed cattle past 1,000 pounds unless they'll move up a grade.

Move wool on any price rise.

Sort and sell hogs as soon as ready.

Hold small red beans for possible price rise.

Buy feed cattle now.

Hold oats and barley.

Buy mixed feeds now.

Hold onto your rice.

Store grain sorghum for higher price.

Eggs 49, medium 52, large 60.

Hold ready beef cattle for rally.

Varney snapped off the radio and did some penciled calculations. Then he nodded to the guard to take away the radio.

Drummond resumed the hearings. Quite aware of the media's interest in Varney's radio business, he did not waste the opportunity to become part of it. He smiled, "Mr. Varney, as a result of that broadcast, do you need to make a phone call to Ohio?"

The crowd knew they could now laugh and did so.

Varney said, "No, sir. I'm going to hope for better tomorrow ... like all farmers."

Ed Fash switched off his office TV and dialed *Miami Herald's* Washington bureau, asking for Mike Knox. "Mike, stay there the whole week instead of coming home."

"You want me to cover the 'Mr. Farmer goes to Washington' ... right?"

"Bingo. Like a blanket. I hear he goes home to his farm some nights. You go, too."

"Ohio again?"

"Buy some work gloves and boots."

(*Miami Herald*)

"U.S. EATING ITS SEED CORN" OHIO FARMER TELLS CONGRESS

Unusual Attention Of Trade Bill Committee Focused On Ohio Farmer

by Mike Knox

Bucyrus, OH — On instructions of my newspaper I came to interview Steve Varney, a general farmer, regarding his view that subsidies are bad for farmers. A man who cannot bear the thought of wasted manpower, he said, "If all we're going to do is talk, we might as well change the bedding straw." He handed me a pronged fork and went to work in the dairy barn. I couldn't take notes, but I learned volumes.

Varney is a leader here, and neighboring farmers came to ask counsel.

What I heard was ...

In White House conference room C, seated around a boat-shaped table, were top administrative staff. Full of curiosity, but not wanting each other to know that they didn't know the purpose of this surprise meeting, they waited for the chief of staff. He walked in carrying under-arm a thick stack of *Miami Heralds*. Wordlessly he walked around the table, placing before each a newspaper folded so that one headline circled in red dominated:

"U.S. EATING ITS SEED CORN"

He then took his seat. "Gentlemen and ladies, I obviously could have had these distributed to your offices with a memo. I called you together like this on the emphatic orders of the boss. You well know that he is always emphatic; but this time he is double-rectified 100 proof emphatic.

"Before you, circled in red, in five simple words ... is the complex message we have been trying unsuccessfully to get across to the population and to the Congress. The boss wants these five words ... without any improvement or elaboration ... to become the theme or tag line of every communication which goes out of this office.

"The boss says this explains the budget deficit, the trade deficit, and the character deficit of this nation."

26

BOOMERANG

Visconti was a thorn in Forte's staff.

He was capable of correcting that; but caught up in the importance of the Trade Bill war, he would not take the time for the staff games.

What rebuffed them early was that when he first came aboard they were prepared to help him, indoctrinate him into the ways of working the government labyrinth of overlapping jurisdictions and jealousies. But amazingly, Visconti did not need it. With some cynical instinct he seemed to grasp gambits no one told him. Some antenna picked up faint signals, untutored.

On his very first day, reporting to join Forte's staff for the duration of the Trade Bill war, Visconti grasped the environment he was entering from fragments of dialog in the ascending elevator:

" ... he can't if he doesn't know about it; so keep it in processing until ..."

"No-no. Put in on your B budget to underfly the audit."

"... so don't go through Murphy. Go through Boar's office when he's away campaigning. Veitch will grease it through."

In dealing with other governmental agencies, Visconti early projected the Washington-weary ennui of an old government hand. He radiated an underlying threat ... as if he knew how to *use* government to reward ... or punish. The sense of threat was compounded by the fact that one suspected he was reckless.

What bothered the Forte staff most, however, was that the senator leaned on Visconti. The rapport was not from any mutuality of background. In fact, the reverse. The only bond was their intensity about balanced free trade. It was a mission with Forte. But why should Visconti give a damn?

Maybe just the contest. Who knew?

Worse — the staff had no handle on Visconti because he considered his job here temporary and conducted himself with the candid abandon of a man expecting to quit or be fired any hour. That enabled him to provide Forte with a rare Washington commodity ... blunt candor. "Senator, you've got to quit persuading and lobbying. You've got to terrify. Terrify the leadership. World leadership. That they're about to recreate 1933 ... but worse."

"John, the leaders are too young. There's no way to make poverty that personal to them."

"Let's **show** them poverty."

"Won't work. They see desperate poverty on their vacations in Mexico. Haiti. Jamaica. Doesn't reach them."

"Justin, that's because there's no fear involved. Only pity. And no personal self-blame."

"What good is fear?"

"Fear of retaliation is all that holds off World War Three."

"Why aren't brilliant men already afraid of protectionist retaliation?"

"Because they don't see the whole chain-reaction network of disaster that goes into motion ... finally coming back like a boomerang. That's what they've got to discover. And they've got to discover it for them*selves*."

Forte thought about it. Finally he charged, "Is this one of your prefatory build-ups for presenting the plan of action?"

"Yes."

"Well for God's sake, spit it out now."

"Not now."

"Huh?"

"I'm not going to throw it out on the table five minutes before you leave for the Joint Committee."

"Why not?"

"I don't want it scrapped because you hear it on the run. I need your undivided attention for forty minutes. Otherwise, I might as well quit."

Visconti had learned the hard way. In his younger days at union headquarters, he threw out solutions so glibly they were dismissed as coming too easily to be good.

"John, don't play games. This is urgent."

"Damn right. So it needs urgent attention."

"You mean you've been sitting on some idea without telling us? Why?"

"You weren't ready. Your back wasn't quite to the wall ... ready for this big of an effort."

"How big?"

"It could cost thirty or forty million."

Forte grabbed up an armload of papers for the Senate-House Joint Committee on the Trade Bill.

* * *

JOINT COMMITTEE SESSIONS ON MASTER TRADE BILL BECOME STAMPEDE TO SUPER PROTECTION

Free-Trade Rear Guard Overwhelmed

Washington - Every morning in the Senate Office Building three senators, Forte, Boar and Bain, meet urgently for one hour before the Joint Senate-House Trade Bill Committee meets.

They are the three musketeer core of resistance to the protectionist grass fire sweeping the capital. Their support corps has dwindled to 32 senators.

The three senators have had no time in the past year to tend their own election fences because ...

The following Tuesday morning meeting of the Three Musketeers and some of their staff people was in Boar's office. He said, "We've lost the Senate. We're losing the Joint Committee. We've got to go *outside* the Congress. We're out of time for going to the grass roots about this disaster course, so we've *got* to find and persuade one super leadership organization which can swing other leadership groups. We've got to choose *one* organization and focus on it every influence we can muster." He nodded to Veitch. "Bring out the list, Jim."

Veitch uncovered a chalkboard with a long list of the world's great commerce-related organizations.

He pointed to G.A.T.T., General Agreement on Trade and Tariffs.

Forte said, "It's become only a debating club."

Veitch pointed to OECD, a 24-nation group. Boar said, "Too remote."

Veitch pointed to BIS, Bank of International Settlements. Forte shook his head.

The pointer hit UNCTAD, United Nations Conference on Trade and Development.

Boar grunted, "Just a wailing wall for Third-World finance ministers."

Looking for one organization with enormous leverage, influence, and the ability to move fast, they went through European Common Market; IMF, International Monetary Fund; Finance Ministers' Summit (9 nations); Inter-American Development Organization; World Bank; UNCTND, United National Conference on Trade (168 nations); OPTD, Organization for Pacific Trade Development.

They considered 70 powerful organizations, but at the end of the list the meeting went silent.

Finally ... Veitch ventured, "Gentlemen, that takes us back to the start — the most powerful organization in the world."

Boar grunted, "What the hell is that, Jim?"

Veitch, a veteran of many meetings, used a subdued showmanship. He slowly replaced the cover on the chalkboard, and as if saying the last word he asked, "Gentlemen, and gentlewomen ... what is the world's most influential body? Ninety-one men and nine women who can be assembled quickly in one place and can act?"

Forte nodded. "He's probably correct. The U.S. Senate."

Boar grunted. "That puts us right back into Custer's Last Stand."

"It's enemy country," Forte admitted. "But he's right; it *is* the world's single most influential body."

"But," Boar objected, "we've exhausted every device to persuade them. We're dead."

"Maybe not. Gian Visconti is checking out an idea he hopes to have ready next week."

* * *

Visconti had asked Mrs. Rider on Forte's staff if she could arrange an appointment with the second in charge of the NASA Computer Center. She said she could do much better. Senator Forte had an IOU from the top man at the Computer Center. "He would be glad to help the senator."

"No. I want the number *two* man."

"Why?"

"The top man probably spends a third of his day on job security. The number two guy probably knows operations."

At ten o'clock the next morning, Mrs. Rider stood in Visconti's office doorway with a trace of a grin, like she knew the joke and it wasn't on her. "The number two is here. Shuva. Are you ready?"

"Yes."

Mrs. Rider beckoned down the hall.

When Shuva walked in, Visconti rose slowly, one of the rare times he was caught off balance. Shuva was a handsome, short woman with prism-thick glasses on the face of Asia.

Visconti motioned to a chair and sat down slowly, "I ... uh ... didn't ..."

"Does it make a difference?"

"No."

She nodded. Her eyes radiated sheer intelligence. Visconti could imagine that she probably owned genius-grade brilliance which had probably supported a relay of department heads, without threatening them for their jobs.

"Mrs. Shuva ..."

"Miss."

"Miss Shuva, don't give me an education in computers. Even if I could follow you, I'm out of time. Just tell me whether computers can do this, and where in the government I could find such a setup."

"We may be able to find it," she ventured, "but *borrowing* it is something else. The departments have become totally computer dependent. Also highly protective. They won't lend. I know your senator has great power, but ..."

"One step at a time. Can you find it?"

"That depends on how much of the mission you can tell me. Usually it's so confidential that ..."

"I'd *like* it confidential, but a leak probably won't matter. People will laugh it off anyway."

"So what's the joke?"

"I need for the computers to be able to replicate in tremendous detail worldwide financial chain reactions in response to entry of particular tariffs and quotas which the operators hypothecate them*selves*."

She did not smile. Just waited. Visconti could imagine everyone had the same problem with Miss Shuva, wondering what she was thinking, and suspecting it was judgmental.

"I want to be able to seat 50 men from 50 states or 50 nations on the outside of a large U-shaped table, facing inward, with individual CRT's and keyboards. Each state or nation can hypothecate a tariff or import quota or restriction against any import of his choice and enter it into the central computer. He can then request that the system calculate and display the resultant effect ... consequence ... of that protectionist move on any other industries in his own state or nation."

Visconti explained that he wanted any of the 50 men to be able then to track the chain reaction of consequences of a specific protectionist move, on a current status screen, as that move would affect prices, shortages, job displacement in interdependent industries. "For example, if the U.S. raised the import quota against foreign sugar, what happens here to the price of soft drinks, chocolate, jelly? What kind of unemployment among candy and food process employees, brokers, and dock workers? What would be the effect on the economies of Haiti, Jamaica, Cuba, Nicaragua? How would that hit their purchases from us of appliances?

"If we raise the tariff against Italian shoes another 30 percent, what happens to our leather hide exports to Italy? How many U.S. leather workers get laid off?

"If we put a 100 percent tariff on microchips, what happens to the U.S. home appliance and machine tool and auto and computer industries?"

She finally spoke. "You're telling me everything except what you're really trying to accomplish."

"I want to recreate in enormous detail a modern version of the worldwide depression of 1933 caused by the Smoot-Hawley Tariff bill."

"What was that?"

Visconti spoke to himself, "That's our problem." Then to her, "Didn't your father ever tell you how it was in '33?"

"My father wasn't born then."

"Of course."

She asked, "Who tells the computer all this data you want it to retrieve? Who develops the software model? How do you accomplish building the massive data base required? How do you even test its validity?"

"I hope ... a multimillion-dollar research crash program by six universities will develop the information ... based on the best data and assumptions ... and guesses. Some of it is already done from previous work."

"If you can get the data, what's the point of the computer? Just print it." Visconti stared out his office doorway. How could he explain such a book would weigh 500 pounds and never get read? Each senator is only interested in certain few imports. How could he tell her the participants would need to create the depression with their own hands to believe it, actually simulate the devastation using the computer for their own specific interests? How could he explain that they must act out their own selfish protectionist measures, and be shown by the system how it would affect other specific parts of their own specific constituency? How could he explain that leaders have no time to read massive documents? Finally he looked at her, "Miss Shuva, the leaders of the world had in front of them the written data forecasting World War Two in a slim volume named *Mein Kampf* by Adolph Hitler. They never read it."

She asked, "How many industries, products, facts, and relationships are you talking about?"

Visconti looked out the window with uncharacteristic uncertainty. Finally he plunked down in front of her a five-inch-thick directory. "Here is the Commerce Department's directory of U.S. products."

She leaned forward to fan its pages.

He plunked down in front of her a half-inch-thick paperback. "Here is just the fastener industry's directory of products. Over 2,000 kinds of bolts, let alone screws, spring clips, shackles, anchors, grips, retainers, manacles, pinions, yokes, and you name it ... in steel, brass, copper, and plastic."

She pointed out the language problem and translating all prices to dollars, and the computer illiteracy of distinguished men. She folded up her small notebook, not having taken a single note. "Since neither of us know," she said, "let's say we're talking fifty million possible combinations, to be made quickly. I don't think this exists. Wright-Patterson Air Force Base has a new computer that simulates how metals will react to various stresses, temperatures, and treatments. It uses enhanced VLSI technology and, by multi-tasking and concurrent processing, it's three times faster than anything put out by IBM or Cray in the last six years. The work-station, I hear, is a Microvax II tied to an Intel IPSC Hypercube. And the submarine service has a BC-10 set up with bubble memory which I understand can ... " She saw boredom curtain his eyes. "But you expect too much. And even if I could find it, who will develop the software for this monster? How will it accommodate the unpredictable ... strikes, crop failure, war?"

"One step at a time, Miss Shuva. Give it a try."

"Don't hold your breath."

The morning meeting in which Visconti presented the computer simulation plan to the Three Musketeers and their top staffs in Forte's office was tense.

Forte paced before the seated group. When he turned to a formal mode of address, they knew it was make-or-break time. "Ladies and gentlemen ... we're out of time, out of choices, and out of ideas, except the one we're here to consider this morning. When you hear it, speak your candid opinion. This is no time to wait for your bosses to speak first. I personally like the plan, but we don't have time for another failure.

"We have concluded just one thing ... that we have got to focus all our ammunition on the U.S. Senate. Today we're here to decide whether or not we have a plan to do that. Mrs. Rider, no phone calls for anybody until we're done. That okay with you Knute? Chris?"

The senators nodded.

"When John Visconti presents this plan, you'll note it involves a huge expenditure ... for a massive, crash research program by several universities. Don't let that be a hang-up. Senator Boar has found a consortium of forty institutions who would fund part of it. Commerce Department will give us something for access to the data. And the universities will shave costs for certain benefits."

He turned to Visconti, "Go, John."

Visconti had the poise and relaxed delivery of an exhausted man. Lining up the pieces of the plan had put him on a dizzying merry-go-round. "We've given this proposed demonstration a name here in the office," he began. *"Boomerang."*

He proceeded to outline the plan in which fifty senators seated at individual CRT's could, with a computer operator assistant, establish a tariff or quota or subsidy against any import of their special interest ... and call for the resultant response to that action in terms of foreign retaliation, other prices, shortages or surpluses, or probable employment decrease or increase in dependent industries, and other reactions on a current status screen with a list of variables. A conversion mechanism for various world currencies would be built in.

The staff audience present was nervous because they wanted it to work, but they could see so many roadblocks and hitches.

In the other offices in Forte's suite, other staff members were sensitive that they had not been called into this particular meeting. Ed Mercer, Forte's constituent liaison specialist, had a visitor from the Arizona senator's office who asked, "Where is everybody today? This some Missouri holiday?"

"No. All our movers and shakers, and those from Boar's and Bain's offices, are in with the boss."

"What are the Three Musketeers up to?"

"Saving the world for Honda via balanced free trade."

"Huh?"

"They've got a plan for staging a huge morality play for the Senate ... 'The War of the Nations' by 3-D computer."

"You're kidding?"

"I'm not. This is real."

"What's the whole scenario?"

"You buyin' lunch?"

"Sure."

Visconti explained to the group that a Northwestern U. skunkworks group felt the software would be costly, but not impossible. The software model might be able to interact on 30 years of information, borrowed, stolen, and developed by a battalion of economists headed by a referee, so the model would reflect historic patterns. Then the participants in the Boomerang war game would use the software to create the future.

Visconti concluded, "So that's Boomerang."

The three senators held back their comments deliberately. The staff was silent, not out of timidity nor disappointment, but from the enormity of the undertaking and the staggering problems.

The room was also tense with the disparity of personalities and their approaches to life ... and the two dominant new intruders ... Visconti, on Forte's staff; and Dougherty, newly aboard Boar's team.

Visconti, trim, controlled, laconic, and authoritative, sat opposite the big Irishman who overfilled his chair, and had a smile on his face, and socks drooping around thick ankles. Dougherty was the first man to speak. "John, I still think it's fantastic. The more so now that I hear the full details.

But it's got one whale of a gopher hole in it."

The staff watched Visconti. The opposite approaches of Visconti and Dougherty had been the coffee-break subject for all observers. Visconti turned up a palm, ready to hear it.

"John, I've been selling all my life. I sold by offering an **incentive**. I never made a nickel with a *threat*. And the way we've got this thing packaged, it's one big threat." Dougherty's right fist hit his chair arm. "Boomerang."

Visconti answered, "I've been negotiating most of my professional life. I never made a nickel for the workmen ... unless I had a big stick."

With the ice broken, a half-dozen people jumped in on one side or the other. In the cross talk, Forte looked at Boar and found Boar looking at him and grinning. Boar held up his cigar hand. "Hold it!"

The room hushed. Boar's gravel voice stayed on low volume. "You're both right. That's exactly our proposal to the world."

He walked to the chalkboard and scrawled powerfully, *"You can sell to the U.S. as much as you buy ..."* The chalk broke, he grabbed another. *"... otherwise we go protectionist in 18 months!"*

Boar faced the group. "We give the **incentive**. We show the big **stick**."

Forte said, "The Boomerang demonstration will show the consequences both ways."

The mood in the room rose until Veitch stood up and dampened it. "John, this mass of calculations, assuming the universities can prepare even a fraction of what you're asking, sounds to me beyond the capacity of any computer setup I ever heard of. We could be building a plan that's dead before it starts."

Visconti said, "That's why I asked Miss Shuva to come." He gestured to the petite, composed woman who stepped forward and placed on Forte's desk a briefcase with a projection screen in the side of it. With a remote control unit, she brought up a photograph of a computer system which looked like a miniature of the Manhattan skyline. "I find that the Defense Department, under its program of supplying the tooling to defense contractors, owns a computer system in a Boeing plant called a Time Line. It has nowhere near the capacity you need. Defer the question whether that could be enhanced. But it has a very similar function. Boeing has a roomful of CRT's which display instant status of production of any subcontractor component for any aircraft under construction. They use 500 subcontractors who supply some 6,000 parts. This setup will tell if the part is completed, in inventory, where, or in transit and time of arrival at which Boeing plant. If any component is behind schedule, Time Line changes the entire completion date schedule for any aircraft.

"You need more function than that and more capacity. But perhaps this system could be modified... if ... you have a trainload of money.

"But you'll never get that system away from Boeing."

Amid the sudden silence, Boar turned to Dougherty, "Tom? Any ideas?" Boar had been impressed with Dougherty from the day the stout salesman came into his office for help on getting the Utility Cube into Mexico. He shanghaied Dougherty onto his staff just for the duration of the Trade Bill war, and put a big load on him.

When Dougherty blew onto Boar's staff, he early discovered the shadow senate ... an invisible echelon comprised of the men and women who ran the senators' offices. They had different titles. Some were simply called the office manager, some staff executive, some legislative aides, some administrative aides, AA's. Pompous Senator Mulligan of New York, head of Senate Rules Committee, called his top office manager his *chief of staff*. These first mates, working with each other, made more profound senatorial alliances and influenced more legislation than the public would want to believe. They also moved easily around the top levels of the bureaus, achieving their senators' objectives.

They wielded enormous power, wearing two faces. They could be humble, "I'm only a messenger from the senator" ... or threatening, "I can only advise you, sir, that the senator would be most disappointed if ..."

From his work in marketing building products, Dougherty had outdistanced his competition, not by selling to owners and general contractors, but by selling behind the lines to the hidden network of architects, designers, and specifiers who had no power to place an order ... but who specified materials by brand long before the orders ever came up for bids.

When he got to Washington, Dougherty looked for the hidden buyers and found this phantom senate network.

He now replied to Boar, "I was talking to the Washington State senator's man, Dan Murphy. He tells me the senator's office is very concerned about Boeing's battle against Europe's Airbus Industries. Their hundred fifty seater could beat out Boeing's 7J7 propfan for the Europe airlines business. Boeing is betting the company on their 7J7; but Europe Airbus is heavily protected by tariffs. Why don't I drop over and chat with those fellows about free trade in the aircraft industry?"

Even Visconti grinned.

As the meeting broke up, Forte cautioned, "Let's keep all this quiet until we see if we can get it on track."

It was only two days later that the little four-page underground sheet *DC Backstairs Digest* appeared on desks inside the Beltway:

THREE SENATORS PLAN
FAR-OUT "WAR OF WORLDS"
3-D COMPUTER DEMO
FOR SENATE

Behind closed doors the staffs of Senators Forte, Boar and Bain are designing a mega-million-dollar computer demonstration for the U.S. Senate to simulate worldwide disaster they believe will result from passage of the upcoming Trade Bill, rapidly shaping up as the U.S. Berlin Wall. The so-called "Three Musketeers" apparently have rounded up tens of millions of free trade dollars for this extravaganza to be played to the full Senate as soon as ...

The three senators with some staff were meeting that same day in Senator Bain's office when a call came in for Veitch from Senator Mulligan's "chief of staff." Veitch looked a question at Boar. Boar nodded ... take the call. Veitch did so and shortly hung up. He said to Boar, "Mulligan's man says the Senate rules chairman read the *D.C. Backstairs Digest*, and there's not going to be any Disneyland show-and-tell extravaganza put on in the United States Senate. And that applies as well to the Joint Senate-House Committee on the Trade Bill. Said it would open the doors to every special-interest circus and extravaganza."

Forte said, "That pompous ass."

"Damn!" Boar's cigar hand hit the table. The plastic "Thanks For Not Smoking" sign jumped. "Down the tubes before we start!"

Forte turned to Visconti. "Welcome to Washington."

27

BREWSTER

Against many pressures, Jason Dart resisted moving the headquarters of the now enormous Dart Industries holding company to Chicago or Atlanta or New York.

"Staying in Seville, Ohio, keeps our people's feet on the ground. Gives our suppliers' salesmen a nice trip into the country." He did make a concession to the corporation's size, a large new office complex. His personal office was very spacious. But most of the four hours he worked each day he spent in a Spartan cubicle just off his main office. It had bare white plastic laminate walls on which he diagrammed apparatus as he had once done with chalk on the cement floor for Emile Hoffstetler. But now young engineers came in late afternoon, photographed the sketches, then erased the walls and rendered the photos into engineering concept drawings. The room had a cot and a chair in which he now sat as Tom Dougherty explained how the Boomerang System demonstration was roadblocked. Dart listened with his forehead on one hand, a stack of disheveled newspapers on his lap and more around his feet.

"So here we are," Dougherty griped, "with this fantastic demonstration plan, and the Senate Rules Committee blocks it."

Dart thought about it. "Tom ... you may be better off." Dougherty did not interrupt the ensuing silence. He had watched Jason's kind of concentration many times. Dart rose and reached for his walker, dumping the newspapers onto the floor. He paced. "That refusal may be just the break you need." Dougherty still held silent. "Those are the wrong people. Good intelligent people; but locked to narrow constituencies. You need somebody with a selfish interest in the whole world."

"There isn't such — since Jesus Christ."

"There may be now."

"Who?"

"You've seen the *Buy American* sentiment spread like wildfire, right?"

"Hell, yes."

"But what few have noticed is the parallel in Europe. They're creating Fortress Europe. But to do it they had to create a single European market to get enough customers, thereby destroying their national protection boundaries. Businessmen did it ... led by France's Banque Indosuez. They're collapsing the protectionist borders so companies will have a market of nearly four hundred million consumers. A single European market.

"European executives finally had to dump the ancient notion that prosperity came from protected national markets.

"The government statesmen could not do it. They'd be called traitors. But businessmen did it ... out of *incentive*. France's St. Gobain ... building materials ... has got building codes in the different countries standardized more so they can sell to the entire market."

"Jason, how come *their* businessmen have so much clout suddenly?"

"*Incentive*, I repeat. When governments denationalized industry, and companies had to compete in a deregulated Europe, businessmen had to make it work. The only way was — destroy trade barriers to get more customers. France no longer requires yellow headlights on cars, for example.

"Now the same thing is happening somewhat among the Pacific rim countries. And between the U.S. and Canada."

"So how does that help our Boomerang?"

"You now have a bunch of European businessmen who found out for *themselves* national protection boundaries were killing them. Erasing the local boundaries helped them. Raised employment, too."

"So?"

"So these men are more likely than the U.S. Senate to see that smashing the protection across oceans is just *the next logical step.* If a total European open market is good ... a total open global market is better. Who you need at that computer round table is not fifty senators but fifty of the world's top businessmen."

Dougherty hit his forehead with a meaty hand, vibrating his coarse grey hair, "Jason! Would you come to Washington and repeat that to Boar and Forte?"

"You can tell them."

"Jason, I'm just a peddler."

"Tom, never ... never ... say 'I'm just a peddler.' You are the one who spread the Utility Cube ... and the Dart Utility House into South America and into Asia. You!"

"Me? Hell Jason, *you* built the Cube!"

"I assembled a bunch of components. It isn't even patentable."

Dougherty grinned, "Except for that little doohickey controller that controls the components."

Dart chuckled. "Just sell Boar and Forte the way you sold Mexico the Utility Cube."

"Jason, they've got to hear this from you ... because of what you stand for."

Dart manipulated the walker leg to uncover some papers on the floor. "See that journal ... *The Economist*? Take that to them. Most of the story is in that."

"And nobody paid any attention to it, right, Jason? You've got to go ... in person."

"Tom, my bones are giving me a very hard time. Any chance they could come out here?"

"You don't believe in giving me a hard problem."

Dougherty was showing the wear from shuttling between Ohio and D.C. He kept seeing a deep amber liquid over ice in a short glass. In Washington, he asked Ellen Brewster how soon he could get in to see Boar. She said there'd been a schedule shuffle. Veitch had the latest. Even getting to see Veitch was a problem, but Dougherty got in to see him at quarter to five and asked how fast could he get to see the senator.

Veitch said, "For the next two days he's up to his hips in hornets."

Dougherty explained his message was a red alert.

"Well, he's going to phone me late tonight. Give me the message. I'll tell him."

Dougherty smiled, "Jim, I'm not a peddler for thirty years not to know the difference between the telephone and face to face."

Veitch never had understood why Boar had brought Dougherty on staff. He knew Dougherty's strengths, also his non-strengths. "Tom, a couple of us are heading over to the Green Goblet for a short one. Join us. We'll solve whatever you're trying to get done."

Dougherty thought about it. "I better not."

Veitch shrugged and left.

Dougherty talked to Ellen again about seeing Boar. She said, "He's going to phone Jim Veitch late tonight." There seemed no way to reach the senator quickly. "Then I guess I better go over to the Green Goblet and beg Veitch to get me to the senator late tonight," he told her.

"Tom ... Mr. Dougherty ..."

He grinned, "You were right the first time."

She rose and put a hand on his arm. Ellen Brewster, in a city of tigresses, remained a tender woman, "Tom, don't go there. I ... I know about you."

"Ellen, thanks. But I always order ginger ale."

"Is it so urgent?"

"Yes. They're going to scrap Boomerang if I don't get a message to him."

In the Green Goblet, Dougherty heartily joined the staff. Veitch signaled the waiter. Dougherty resisted the wonderful bourbon fragrance in the air. "Ginger ale."

Later the bartender received a call "from Senator Boar's office." Ellen Brewster could switch from her soft voice to very official. "I'm speaking for Senator Boar. There is a large man named Dougherty at Mr. Veitch's table. He will order ginger ale. Senator Boar wishes you to see that nobody switches that order on him. Understood?"

The bar man said, "Gosh, Ma'am! They already did. I didn't know..."

Ellen Brewster hung up and grabbed her raincoat.

In the dark drumming cacophony of the Green Goblet

entrance, she stood squinting into the psychedelic hive, searching. An assistant manager asked, "Can I help you?" She shook her head, "Not yet."

When her eyes adjusted she touched the assistant manager, "Now." She handed him a $20 bill. "See that very large man standing, waving his arms, and talking to that table? Get a couple of your waiters and see if you can get him to come over to me. Be careful!"

* * *

In Boar's office in the morning, the senator ignored the new interoffice phone and roared, "Ellen! Where the hell is Dougherty?"

She sat thinking of an answer. Boar appeared in her doorway, "Well?"

"Uh, Senator, he ... "

"Get him on the phone." He returned to his office.

Ellen Brewster dialed her own apartment. No answer. She asked a colleague to relieve her at her desk. "What's up, Ellen?" But she was out the door.

She unlocked her apartment. Sprawled face down on the couch was Dougherty in his shirtsleeves. On the floor lay her half-gallon cooking wine jug.

She had great difficulty in waking him.

His voice was deep and thick. "Where? Where's thish?"

Fifteen minutes was wasted in orientation.

"How'd you ge' me here?"

"I'll explain. But the point is, the senator is at the office. You said it was urgent to see him."

"Right. Gotta get there." He stood up, weaving. Then he dropped back onto the couch. "Ell'n, you gotta do me somethin'. Somethin' big."

He asked her to tell Boar to phone Dart. "Jus' 'ave 'm say 'Tom Dougherty said you had a message. Importan' message.'"

"I don't think the senator will take that from me."

She checked the kitchen, pouring a liqueur down the sink. "Don't leave here, Mr. Dougherty ... Tom. Don't leave."

270

* * *

Before she had replaced her purse in her desk, Boar came in, "Where were you?"

"Out."

"You find Dougherty?"

She stared at her desk.

"Well? Yes or no?"

She did not look up.

"Come on! It's yes or it's no!"

Head down, she moved a folder from one side of her desk to the other. Then moved it back. A blue vein in her temple throbbed.

Boar slapped the side of his jaw and said softly, "Boar, you idiot!" He pressed a button on her phone and said, "No calls for fifteen minutes." He closed her office door and sat down, "What's up, Ellen?"

"Senator, I have an important message from Mr. Dougherty that I think you ought to hear. But coming from me, I doubt you'll seriously ..."

"Stop." Boar leaned across her desk and pointed a stubby finger. His gravel voice was low. "Although I never mention it ... there is no one ... *no* one .. in this whole D.C. circus I should take more seriously.

"Except for my wife, there aren't five people in this city who will beat you to my political funeral."

She stared at her hands in her lap.

He laughed, "Didn't you know that I know that?"

Her laugh fought tears. "No."

"Well for cryin' out loud, find ways to remind me!"

Her laugh exploded the tears. She gave him the message from Dougherty.

"Why in hell is everybody having me call Ohio, for cryin' ..." He corrected. "Excuse me. I will do it." He picked up a dead cigar, "Now where the hell is Dougherty?"

Her eyes pleaded.

He immediately held up the flat of both hands to her. "Question withdrawn."

As he opened her door to leave, he stood, "And, Ellen ... I meant what I said."

"Shall I put through the call to Mr. Dart?"

"Yes."

In Seville, Ohio, Jason Dart made his way on his walker out to the parking lot. The lobby guard came running after him, "Mr. Dart. A call from Washington."

Dart waved. "Get the name. I'll call tomorrow."

As he left the office, Boar told Ellen Brewster, "If Dart calls back, forward the call to me. Meanwhile, tell Jim Veitch to draft me a letter to those foundations suitable for aborting Boomerang."

* * *

It was ten p.m. in Forte's office. Visconti remained silent, letting Forte and the rest of the staff hit bottom. The senator's face was gray with fatigue and depression. "Rules Committee rejected Boomerang way beyond the nine-seven party split. What does that mean?"

Mrs. Rider suggested, "It just might mean they suspect the power of it. And Rules chairman is beholden to Drummond."

The meeting went silent. Forte's gesture told them to go home and they filed out, except Visconti. Forte started to stuff his battered briefcase; then he quit, took his jacket off the back of his chair and headed for the door, flicking off the lights. "Lights out, John. We're out of business. God help the world."

Visconti flipped the light back on. "Not yet."

"Huh?" Forte halted.

"The turndown by the Joint Committee is a blessing."

"Meaning?"

"There's a better group for the Boomerang story."

Forte snapped, "We just had the staff here. Why didn't you speak out?"

"Because I'm still the new kid on your block. Quicker if you tell them. And we're out of time."

"Tell them what?"

"Come down to my cage."

In his own office Visconti unfolded the top sheet on a large easel. "There it is, Justin." In the dark office Visconti had only turned on the one eyeball spotlight that hit the easel.

In heavy black crayon were eleven names:

U.S. - AFL-CIO
U.S. - Machinists
U.S. - Garment Workers
Germany - Bundinis Anstrengung
France - Alliance Labeur
England - Working Men's Coalition
Spain - Alianza Labor
Italy - Fatica Alleanza
Italy - Legione Lavoro
France - Ouvriers de France
Japan - Nippon

Visconti flipped that page over, revealing twenty more labor unions, guilds, and fraternities of twenty more nations. "There's our target."

Forte tossed his jacket across Visconti's desk and sat down slowly, facing the easel. He motioned Visconti to flip the next page. It revealed twenty more unions.

"John ... " Forte walked, "Why didn't we see it? These are the guys screaming for protection. And their members are going to pay seven bucks for a loaf of bread."

Forte asked Visconti if he thought they could get a top man from each of those unions to meet in the U.S., and why had he selected those particular unions?

"Because they are already scheduled to meet in the U.S., Boston, on matters of their own."

"Could we get Boomerang on their agenda?"

"That's the hooker."

"You could start working on the Machinists."

"You forget I got thrown out of the union."

On a Friday morning the Three Musketeers with some staff were meeting in Boar's office. Forte and Visconti had explained the merit of a world conference of labor leaders for the Boomerang operation. Boar and Bain and their staffs were arguing about it; the language problem, the impracticality. Bain said, "And even if the labor leaders are overwhelmingly convinced, do they have the clout in their countries to force action from the politicians and the business leaders?"

Ellen entered the conference and put a slip of paper in front of Boar. He said, "We made a rule. No calls."

She placed another slip of paper in front of him. It read: "You told me to remind you to listen. Take this call."

Boar looked at Bain and Forte, "I think it's pertinent." It was Dart, returning the call.

Boar explained into the phone that he placed the call to Dart only because a message from Dougherty had told him to call. "I don't know why, and I don't know where Dougherty is to ask him why."

"That concerns me ... that you don't know where he is, Senator. I'll get to that. But first I know what Tom wanted me to tell you."

When Dart was just barely into it, Boar turned on the speaker phone so all could hear.

The voice ... so relaxed ... yet so faint ... and obviously thinking its way through the subject ... without preparation ... compelled the group's attention.

"And so, Senator ..." the voice concluded ... "I feel that the time is right to prove to the world's businessmen that what they already learned in Europe on a nation-to-nation basis ... is even more true on a continent-to-continent basis. Let them put the heat on the U.S. Congress.

"Now, if you'll forgive me, I'm running a little low on energy as I don't speak with senators every day. But I have one request. Much of Dart Industry's success is owed to Tom Dougherty. I am concerned that you have lost him... for reasons which you may know. Can I speak with someone on your staff who saw him last?"

Ellen pointed to herself.

Boar said into the phone, "Yes, in a moment I'll connect you with Miss Ellen Brewster. But first ... thank you for this discussion. I will be in touch." He pointed to Ellen who went out to her own phone.

The meeting continued. The argument now heightened as the staff took sides on whether to go with the labor leaders or the business leaders.

Forte said, "If the American Business Round Table is

any sample, they have flip-flopped all-out protectionist."

Boar pointed out, "No more than Labor."

It was at that point that Bain, the iconoclast, said, "What are you arguing about? If we stage Boomerang for *both* the labor leadership **and** the business leadership ... we've covered the two most powerful activist constituencies in the world. One has the money; the other has the votes. What else is there?"

There was some optimism. But suddenly Veitch said, "But what if Boomerang doesn't prove what we think it will?"

28

GEN. GEORGE MARSHALL

Forte, Bain, and some staff were in Boar's office. Bain decided, "The man we need aboard the Boomerang planning is that fellow Dart. He understands this."

Boar explained, "He won't come to Washington. Very, very hard for him to travel.

Bain said, "Sure, but Dart's name associated with Boomerang is important to us. What this man has accomplished in exporting to the world commands respect in Europe and the Pacific. He's the legend. The new Henry Ford."

Washington was a city in which reputation was more of a solid than cast iron. For certain purposes it had worth beyond measure. The wrong name to the right project or vice versa was success or failure.

Forte said, "Knute, I know his disability. But this is heavy enough to ask *any* man to ..."

Boar cut him off. "Of course." He arranged the call on the speaker phone, explaining to Dart the objective had to override the pain of traveling to Washington to help. Boar softened his voice. "Fact is, Mr. Dart, we're drafting you. There's everything at stake."

Boar stepped up the volume to bring in Dart's thin voice, "Senator, that part's right. But the man you need is the man you stole from me. Tom Dougherty."

Boar said, "He's very useful to us, but ... as he says himself ... he's a magnificent ... uh ... peddler. We're talking to world leadership."

Dart's voice cut in, "Senator, that's his way of talking. But Thomas J. Dougherty is probably one of the ten shrewdest marketing men in the United States. Did you ever ask yourself how Dougherty won those foreign markets ... so quickly?"

"I suppose he just pounded down doors."

"No. Dougherty does not believe in selling upstream. He went to your state, Senator, and found on Circle Pond Road in Cambridge ... the Center for Short Lived Phenomenon, a division of Smithsonian Institution, and he made a connection with them."

"What in hell is the Center for Short Lived ... whatever?"

Dart explained. The Center was a small organization housed in an undistinguished cement block building in rundown Circle Pond Shopping Center, staffed by enthusiastic underpaid young scientists. The organization had contacts with scientists around the world through a complex, comprehensive communication system ... a lash-up of phone, satellite, radio, and horseback. The object: to immediately, upon occurrence of any major natural phenomenon , dispatch scientists to study it before causal evidence was destroyed. Events like volcanic eruptions, earthquakes, whale strandings, mass appearance of large sink holes, lake drainings, sudden animal migrations, landslides, tidal waves, fires, flash floods, huge fish and bird kills, predator infestations. In return for investigating the disasters immediately, the scientists used the resultant information for their own scientific work.

Thomas J. Dougherty heard about this organization, flew to Boston and ambled in, smiling. The walls of the large circular central "war room " were lined with clocks showing the time of day around the world. Below the clocks were desks with teletype CRT's. There was no receptionist. He wandered into the big room and watched. Then he made his deal. He persuaded Dart to make a modest donation to the Friends of the Smithsonian Institution. In exchange, the Center would notify Dougherty's office whenever there occurred someplace in the world a natural disaster which destroyed very large numbers of houses.

"Disasters overrode a lot of import-export rules," Dart explained, "and we shipped Utility Cubes. That is just one of the marketing devices invented by Dougherty which put us into the world market. Made jobs. Made money. Built plants. We can't keep up with demand. Dougherty did that. Put him in charge of selling your Boomerang."

277

The listeners were silent.

"Are you there, Senator?"

"Uh ... yes, Mr. Dart. We ... we'll find him."

"Find him?"

"Well ..."

"You said that woman, Miss ... Brewster, would know where he is."

"Well, she has been out sick for a week."

"You've lost Dougherty for a week?"

"Yes."

"Is Miss Brewster often out sick for a week?"

"Never before."

"I will be in Washington in the morning."

Dart, with two canes and two young executives in tow, checked into Silver City Hotel, Washington.

By phone they tried three "E. Brewsters" before they reached Ellen. Dart identified himself and, "Are you the lady I talked to about Tom Dougherty?"

"Yes. And I need your help. He got away ... again."

From Miss Brewster's apartment, Dart sent the two executives in concentric circles, checking bars. With great difficulty they brought the big man back to her apartment. His suit was a damp wrinkled bag. She had apparently bought him some shirts, too small. The shirt had ripped at the shoulder seams.

Dart reached Boar by phone. "I'm taking him back to Seville, Ohio, for a while, Senator. You folks don't take very good care of valuable people up here."

Boar asked for a meeting. Hence the next meeting of the Three Musketeers, and some staff, was held in Ellen's apartment. With a thick tongue and slurred speech, Dougherty made a few points.

"Firs' place ... if y'r sellin' a real big ticket item, y'don' sell to a big group all at once. Firs' y'sell one to one. Get a li'l practice with it. Tes' the water. Get a li'l talk started. Li'l curiosity.

"So your Boomerang gotta star' small. Build up."

Forte interrupted, "Wait a minute. The whole concept of Boomerang was a group sell. One smashing impact, hitting everyone at once. That's the whole idea."

Visconti said, "Justin, you remember my first visit to you? Representing the Machinists?"

"Sure. What's that got to do with it?"

"Your top staff was present at first?"

"Oh, yes. You insisted on talking to me alone. That's always been your way, but this is a big worldwide sell."

Senator Bain cut in, "Exactly, Justin. And you remember hearing how George Humphrey sold Europe's leaders on holding up the stripping of Germany so we could pass the Marshall Plan?"

"I'm not that old, Chris."

Bain explained how Truman was trying to get the Marshall Plan through Congress. Congress objected to sending goods to Europe with one hand, while stripping Germany with the other. Truman drafted George Humphrey, the iron ore executive who had a magnetic leadership with men and horses, to go over to Europe and get the other 12 Allies to stop stripping Germany ... while Congress debated the Marshall Plan. General Lucius Clay... headed the Allied organization in charge of reparations. He was sick and tired of world statesmen persuading him to a stop-go policy on the dismantling of Germany. It had all Europe confused and cynical about the postwar policies. Clay had decided firmly ... no more policy changes.

In a windswept, candle-lit tent at Templehoff Airport, Clay told George Humphrey that, adding, "I do not work for the U.S. I have a contract with 13 Allies to execute this agreement."

Humphrey had an ingratiating smile and a very quick mind. "General," he said, "I see your point. But in my lifetime, I have made many large contracts, and I have never hesitated to ask for a change of contract so long as I was willing to pay for it. The American people are considering paying nearly 17 billion dollars for a change of contract."

The stern Clay broke out a grin. "You have a point."

Next Humphrey went one-on-one with Churchill, bringing him a box of Havanna cigars. Then Schumann of France. Then the others, one at a time. He came home with a European agreement to stop the dismantling of Germany. The Marshall Plan passed Congress.

Forte nodded, "You've got a point." He turned to Dougherty, "What's next?"

"Secon' place .... y'don't start sellin' to y'r front guy," Dougherty slurred. "Y'go backstage. Y'sell to the guy the front man *trusts*. And somebody that needs an idea to ride. Needs a vehicle."

Veitch asked what he meant by backstage.

"If y're sellin' building materials, y'don' sell to the owner of the buildin'. He doesn' understan'. Y'don' sell to the contractor. The owner doesn' trust him. Y'sell to the architect. He can't buy it, but he'll tell the owner to buy your brand. Then ... you go see the owner, an' make your pitch, an' it's a shoo-in. You men gotta find that backstage guy. Who is he?"

"We probably don't know. We've got to study that one."

"Third place ... the man you put in charge of presentin' y'r Boomerang ... gotta be hunnert percen', absolute, damn sure sincere."

Bain and Boar looked at Forte. "That's you, Justin."

Dougherty's large head slumped down on his chest.

When the senators had left, Dart said to his two young men, "Get him to the airport."

They did so with difficulty, but Dougherty braced against walking. "Jason, I'm going to stay here awhile. Miss Brew'ser's gotta spare room ... an' she can hannel me pretty good. Gonna be okay, I c'n hannel everythin' now."

Dart looked at Ellen Brewster. She nodded.

Outside, Dart said to one of his men, "You stay in town a day or so. Keep me informed."

Before the week was out, Dougherty was shaken but presentable, alert, and into the planning with the Three Musketeers.

Forte's man, Mercer, said to Boar's aide, "Why don't they get the Irishman to write down his ideas in a plans book instead of yakking about it?"

"He's not that kind. Said he never sold a nickel's worth with a piece of paper. He's a real ..."

"I know. A peddler. Come on, we're late for his valedictory."

When the staff men entered Forte's conference room, the three senators were listening intently. Dougherty was pacing, thinking as he talked. "So let's see what we have so far. We're going to stage a few small trial Boomerangs first with selected business and labor leaders. Then a second round with a larger number. Then ... if we get that far with results, we stage the two large demos with labor leaders and business leaders. Now the chances are, before we get that far, some congressmen are going to want to sit in, off-the-record. Question: Do we let them? We decide that after we see how much word of mouth we're generating and how favorable.

"Now our hope is that those leaders will go home and lean on their colleague leaders. But that's a big load for them. We need to back them up with a worldwide pronouncement by some giant ... spelling out the balanced free trade proposition clearly ... so it is heard around the world in the very same language ... on the very same day: 'You can sell to us as much as you buy. And you can do that in groups of nations formed by yourselves.'"

The senators nodded to each other. But Veitch cut in, "Where do we get an international platform like that? Disneyland?"

Ellen Brewster watched Dougherty. She could see him thinking. Then he pointed to Senator Bain, "Visconti told me your story about Humphrey and the Marshall Plan. But wasn't that plan announced some crazy way to the whole world on the same day?"

Bain squeezed his forehead. "You're right. There is one podium in the U.S. from which a man can talk to the entire world on one day of each year. It has been the launch pad for big ideas. That's the Harvard commencement address. The whole leadership world listens. That's where General Marshall launched the Marshall Plan on June 6, 1947. Sprang the whole scheme at once."

Bain recapped Marshall's famous speech. It explained that before the war Europe was one big assembly line with each nation a subassembly feeding in components ... electricals from France, coal from England, machine tools from Germany, and so forth. The war broke up the factory. The U.S., Marshall said, is willing to help put that factory back together again for the survival of Europe. But you nations have got to tell us what you need, and not **separately**, but consulting **together** to make a **consolidated** wish list.

"Schumann of France immediately phoned Churchill in England, 'Do they mean that?' Churchill said, 'Yes.' He jumped out of bed and started organizing the nations."

Dougherty turned up his palms. "We're now proposing the same for the whole world. The world is now one big production line. Our automobiles have parts in them from six nations. If we get into retaliatory trade barriers, we shut down that world factory. So the U.S. will drop trade barriers toward any major nation or group who will buy as much as they sell to us."

Veitch asked, "And just who is this Messiah who can say this with authority?"

Dougherty said, "You boys have got to come up with the right man."

"And if we do, who says Congress will back up his offer?"

"Nobody. He's got to ask for the order ... in the same speech."

"And who says Harvard will give us their podium for this?"

Boar turned to Veitch, "You! That's your assignment. Get it?"

"Commencement won't synch with our timing."

"Have them hold another commencement when we're ready. They can award some honorary degrees or something."

Veitch objected, "Our present secretary of state is highly regarded, worldwide; but he won't make that speech."

For the first time, Visconti spoke. "I think he will." All eyes focused on Visconti. "The three senators will visit him as a group and explain the situation, and he will agree."

"Without instruction from the president? Senators don't make foreign policy."

"Officially, no. But this time ... yes."

Forte grinned at his brazen assistant. "And just because

three highly disfavored senators ask him, why is he going to do this?"

"Because you're going to give him a choice. Either he does it, or **foreign** leadership does it."

Veitch and Bain in unison exclaimed, "Foreign!"

"Foreign," Visconti said. "Maybe the foreign ministers of Japan and the heads of West Germany, Canada, and France."

He let the silence lie there awhile. Boar's fist hit the table. "Beautiful!"

Dougherty grinned.

All eyes now turned on Boar. Bain asked, "Knute, you're not serious. Why would they?"

Boar dropped his voice and leaned across the table, "Chris ... think about this: Can Europe and the Pacific countries and Canada really afford a bankrupt U.S.?"

"They might like that."

"A U.S. that can't buy? Can't repay their loans?"

"When did any nation ever speak for another?"

"Nineteen forty-seven," Boar said.

"Who?"

"We just discussed him. General Marshall. He put this country on the line for Europe."

"Sure," Bain countered, "but for selfish reasons ... to save Europe from Russia."

"True. So for selfish reasons what's wrong with saving their biggest market?"

"The U.S. market may not be enough of an incentive."

Visconti let the debate deflate, then he said, "Whoever makes the presentation to the world ... must offer the carrot and hint at the stick."

They waited. Visconti pulled from a slim briefcase a long list of nations with dollar numbers assigned to each. He held it up. "Here's the stick. U.S. re-evaluates its excessive share of foreign aid ... such as the hundred eighty million now being discussed for Brazil. And ... the U.S. re-evaluates its excessive share of the world defense."

Bain said, "Whoa, boy! Who do you think we are? We don't make these policies in this room ... which the secretary of state will point out ... while laughing."

Forte said, "True. But we can **talk** about it. **Loud**. So Europe hears. Even Drummond might help us do that."

Forte amplified, "Send a few congressmen abroad studying results of foreign aid and evaluating our disproportionate share of world defense. It will stir up plenty of worry."

* * * *

The secretary of state was professionally cordial ... at first. He came out from behind his desk and sat among the three senators.

"Senators, I know you are dead serious about this. I know a lot of thought went into it before you came. But I could not make such a world announcement unless the boss told me. And he can't tell me to do it unless balanced free trade becomes the official policy of the United States, which does not look promising." Boar started to rise. "But ..." Boar sat down. "But from someone other than me, why can the speech not be made as a **suggestion** for the world? The trick is getting the right person. Think about that."

* * *

Veitch said to Boar, "This thing is going down in flames."

"Why do you say that?"

"We're drifting. Zigzagging. We try this. We try that. We change course. We change strategy. Why?"

"That's how you make any big sale."

29

POTOMAC RAIN

Rain turns Washington bleak. The monuments are ghosts. In rain, coupled with bad news, career Washingtonians reflect on why they left Kansas or Nebraska.

Visconti received a call from Miss Shuva, "You're a great one. You interrupt my happy career for your **Boomerang**. Then get me to supervise the tech part of the dry run. I send you a detailed report that the dry run worked beyond belief. And from you ... I hear zilch."

"You're right to be mad, Miss Shuva."

"After all this ... I'm **Miss** Shuva?"

He apologized, then explained, "Lee, I couldn't face you."

"Even to say thanks? Why?"

"It looks like it's my first million megawatt failure."

"Failure?"

"The people we want to do the exercise are turning us down."

"**All** of them?"

"No. But the big ones."

"**Boomerang** is scrapped?"

"In fifteen minutes, I go into a meeting with the Three Musketeers and their staffs. I'll let you know."

The meeting was in Forte's office. Mrs. Rider finished the roll call of the negative RSVPs for the **Boomerang** demonstration.

Silence hung like Potomac humidity. Boar turned up his palms and shrugged. "We built a **Titanic**."

Forte nodded.

Bain built a steeple with his hands and blew it down.

Veitch seemed not depressed.

Mrs. Rider's head inclined forward, but her eyes looked out at Dougherty.

285

Dougherty looked around the room.

Then he shoved his bulk up out of the chair. "What in the hell is wrong with you men?" He walked around. "How did you survive this long down here? Don't you know what it took for Roosevelt to sell the U.S. on entering World War II? What it took to sell the Marshall Plan? What it took to sell the tax bill?

"When I tried to sell distributors on taking on the Dart acrylic skydomes, they laughed me out. Said domes leaked, weren't code approved, contractors didn't know how to install, and they were too expensive.

"I had to find some small struggling distributors who needed something unique in the market. Later the big boys wanted to handle them, too.

"Same thing with Boomerang. We don't do it in one big bang. Start small. Put it on first for some select small fry — even if it's a few distinguished professors, a handful of foreign businessmen, a few brainy editor types, some minor league union guys, a couple maverick congressmen. Start some curiosity. Try this, try that. Fail here, fail there. What do you expect...a hole in one?"

Forte and Bain were studying Dougherty. Boar's face betrayed rapt attention.

Dougherty asked, "What big thing ever got sold first time out? Name one."

Boar was on his feet. "He's right."

Bain and Forte were reserved. But Boar carried them up on his back. "The fact is ... we either do it, or throw in the towel."

They spent an hour coming up with a lesser list of people to invite to **Boomerang**. In discussing which senator should actually conduct the working part of the exercise, Visconti shocked the group. "None of the senators. Dougherty should carry the ball."

There was some discussion, but it ended when Visconti said, "Am I right?"

Forte said, "Amen."

Mrs. Brewster bent her head to her notes.

On the first day of **Boomerang**, rain pelted Washington. The interior of the vacant auditorium on C Street, made available on lease from GSA, was a depressing government green.

Thirty CRTs around a U-shaped table glowed green. Only 21 of them were attended by small two and three person groups, usually a computer operator, an interpreter, and the principal guest.

Although the room was gloom, it must be said the guests were alert. Not first magnitude stars, they were nevertheless men and women who each had a cause and a constituency.

There were two American and two foreign economics professors. There were seven editors as disparate as DeLong of *Wall Street Journal* and Webster of *Kenyon Review*. There was a brace of congresswomen, a trio of TV news producers, Braxton of Business Round Table. Kosicky of UAW did not come, but he sent a top staff man. The Computer & Business Equipment Association sent a representative only to observe this special computer application. Sussen of United Steel Workers was present.

With what passed for graciousness with Forte, he welcomed them, then plunged right in, "Our problem is that the human being cannot feel history he did not live himself or hear from an eyewitness. We can't smell the stink of poverty, of worldwide depression. We can't envision the consequences of an action — the myriad of retaliatory reactions it triggers — unless we do it our**selves**. Therefore we have created a system whereby **you** can initiate a trade act, and then ask what reactions that would trigger, what chain reactions would occur..."

He explained how the system was created. He said the managers of the software project were present "for you to interrogate at your pleasure.

"We will conduct two rounds of the exercise. After that, each of you is free to direct your own computer operator to feed in any protectionist tariff or quota or restriction or sanction, and call for its effect on whatever you wish."

He turned the meeting over to Dougherty who strode into the U of the table. His presence changed the room, charged the air, "Gentlemen and gentlewomen ... before us this morning is an historic first!"

In a corner of the room, an exhausted Professor Warner elbowed a colleague, "My God, we built this whole magnificent thing ... to be put into the hands of a goddam pitchman."

After building some suspense, in more sophisticated language yet basically the same as he had done 30 years ago selling nail guns to hardware dealers, Dougherty said, "Senator Magurn, will you lead off? Your computer, for demonstration purposes, will project up onto the big screen here. Please feed in a protective tariff of 30 percent against Canadian soft wood."

They allowed time for this action. Then, "Thank you. Now will you call for the effect of that on the price of a daily newspaper in Chicago?"

Magurn spoke to his computer operator. On the large screen appeared the lettering ... $2.25.

There was a slight chuckle in the room. But Dougherty said, "Will you now call for the resulting reduction in circulation of that newspaper?"

The senator did so. On screen appeared the result ... 54%.

There was no chuckle.

"Will you call for the resultant percent decrease in advertising rates?"

On screen appeared ... 64%.

"The economists told us they had no good way to calculate the resulting negative effect on retail commerce. But would you call for the percent reduction in employment in the printing industry?"

The room grew silent as the exercise continued.

Dougherty called upon labor delegate, H.L. Hague. He led him through an exercise on restriction against Italian shoes, showing a rise in price in the cost of shoes in America. A pair equivalent to the bottom of the line of Thom McCan, rubber-soled high-topped work shoes, priced out at $310. Dougherty asked Hague to call for the effect of that on U.S. leather hide exports to Italy. The computer slashed exports 76 percent. Dougherty asked Hague to call for the effect on leather worker employment in the U.S. The computer laid off 5,700 leather workers.

Dougherty continued the model workout featuring the labor-intensive industries in Congressman Hulvane's home state of Indiana.

The room had come to a hush.

Dougherty announced, "Ladies and gentlemen, you may use the next 90 minutes to feed in any type of protective information and call for the reaction against any other product of concern to you, or price, or employment in your state. And the effect against any other country, and against any other country's ability to buy the products of your state. Even though this computer model was constructed at an enormous cost, some answers are beyond it.

"At eleven o'clock this morning, I will interrupt the exercise to ask your support of a very specific proposal. Some of you know about it, of course. But by eleven this morning, you may want to hear it again."

The players and their staff assistants went to work on their individual computers.

Dougherty walked among them, watching the screens to see what questions were being put. Halfway around the circle he encountered Visconti doing the same. Forte said, "Do you hear what I hear?"

"Nothing. It's a funeral parlor."

"That's what I mean. Even Buckholtz is quiet."

They continued circling in opposite directions. Forte noticed that the quiet instructions from the delegates to their operators, punctuated by light clicking of keys, gave the room the hush of a high-class casino. He said so to Boar. "Well, hell," Boar grumbled, "why not? This is the biggest gamble since South American loans."

The questions the system could not answer increased its credibility.

Occasionally there would be an involuntary exclamation. Clarke of Atlanta was probing the result of increased sugar quotas against the Caribbean. He checked against what that would do to the Caribbean economy and the increases that would be required of the U.S. Caribbean Aid program. Then he called for the effect of sugar prices on the price of an eight-ounce cola. "Cripes!"

The screen read ... $3.50.

Other discoveries were being made around the room.

An additional 20 percent duty against importing Mexican wire-reinforcing mesh boosted the cost of U.S. highway construction (four lane) to $4,000,000 per mile, reducing U.S. highway construction, disemploying one third of the road-building workers.

United Steel Workers' man then raised the tariff against Asian Steel to protect the 200,000 remaining U.S. steelworkers. Then he tracked the rise in steel prices and the unemployment repercussion against U.S. people in steel-using jobs. He worked his way through automotive, white goods, appliances, plumber supplies, industrial and marine engines, then suddenly grunted to his operator, "Stop."

"Why? You wanted to check structural steel, steel belted tires, shipbuilding, and so forth."

"Stop."

The German professor raised his hand for assistance from Ms. Shuva. "Cannot be correct ... this. Shows our German subsidies of our dairy farmers' butter at five times what New Zealand sells it. What are we doing wrong here? My operator?"

Shuva keyed up a cross-check menu and tried it another way. "You left out one step, sir. You're paying **seven** times the New Zealand price." She moved on to another raised hand.

Braxton fed in a ban on electronic imports from the giant Toshiba Corporation and called up the effect on G.E., AT&T, Hewlett-Packard, IBM, Honeywell, Rockwell, and Xerox. "Holy Hell!"

One delegate fed in a blanket 40 percent duty against all Pacific rim nations. Scanning the possible retaliations against various U.S. industries, he didn't see much damage until he came to the paper industry. These fast-growing Pacific rim nations buy about 20 percent of the U.S. paper output. They have few trees suitable for paper production. The operator asked the Boomerang system where else these nations might shift their paper business. The answer came: Brazil, where eucalyptus trees are ready for pulping after only five years compared to fastest-growing U.S. southern pine. Eucalyptus is excellent paper. The operator asked for U.S. unemployment consequences.

The editor of *Kenyon Review* raised his hand to get Ms. Shuva. He asked help on converting dollars to lira and rubles. She showed him how to call up the conversion menu for:

marks	rubles	pounds
krones	dollars	lira
francs	pesos	drachma

The surprises caused some participants to violate the procedures established in the briefing, raising their hands to summon Ms. Shuva. "Didn't you have to make enormous assumptions to create this software?

"No. For the details, ask Professor Warner's staff over there."

One hailed Justin Forte, "Senator, isn't there a big danger here?"

"How so?"

"We're creating the future here. One of the protections of man is not knowing the future."

"True, we're creating the future; but if we don't like it, we can erase it before it strikes ... if we're smart enough."

Marotti, maritime labor, was stunned. He restaged a worldwide protectionist war which, when carried to the ultimate, showed only one American flag bulk vessel moving on the Great Lakes in international trade. Only twenty-two American flag vessels moved on the Atlantic, only nineteen on the Pacific. The Seamen and Longshoremen unions were wiped out. The entire dock and warehouse business would cease, including the container shipping industry and the huge portion of the trucking industry involved in containerized shipping. Caterpillar's plant for building the one-hundred-ton dock lift trucks would close. Overseas cargo aircraft would be mothballed almost totally, discharging 78,000 ground service personnel.

"Jesus! The world will shut down. Nothing is moving."

At 11:00 a.m. Dougherty rapped for attention. "Five of you have asked if you could continue another hour. A simple show of hands if a majority prefer that."

All hands went up.

Some delegates remained at the computers through lunch. Conversation was nearly absent among those delegates who went to lunch.

When the delegates reassembled at 1:30, Forte said they could work the system until 2:30. "If it is saying to you what it says to us, what should you do about it? Use your influence to: One — kill the U.S. Pro America trade bill in favor of a one-earth bill. Two — work toward a U.S. trade policy that says to the world: **You can sell to the United States as much as you buy. No strings. No restrictions. No quotas.** There will be an 18-month cease fire of protectionist legislation while you accomplish that."

Forte explained that, to reach that objective, regional groups of emerging nations could band together to act as a single trading partner. Europe could act as one trading partner if it wished. Pacific rim nations could do so. And there would be no scorekeeping on what products exchanged. Only the dollar gross. All barriers should be lowered to less developed nations so they could grow into attractive markets. "We want to give the world a simple, workable plan:

You can sell to us as much as you buy."

Several delegates asked if they could send other members of their organizations to do the Boomerang. Dougherty was gracious, but he said, "I'm sorry. You see we have a very limited capacity. We have to be selective ... inviting only the most influential and pivotal people from each organization."

Professor Warner elbowed his colleague. "The damn fool is blowing it."

(*Backstairs Digest*)

THREE MUSKETEERS'
DISNEYLAND SHOW
ATTRACTS SMALL FRY

The enormously costly computerized Show-And-Tell mounted by the senate free traders opened to an enthusiastic but cloutless first night.

None of the European biggies arrived for the show, and few congressmen showed up or even ...

The Three Musketeers and some staff reviewed the low-level showing, and the depression in the room focused on Dougherty who looked wounded. "I don't believe this. Were you putting all your eggs on one pitch? I've had salesmen pushing their cars over the freeways through the snow from town to town hearing nothing but 'No,' 'Sorry,' 'Don't need any,' 'Your price is too high.' But they keep pushing. Why? Because they know they're going to win. Not on one pitch. If they can't sell the product, they'll sell the service, or the make-good record, or the price or the credit plan. Then they watch for the unexpected break ... and capitalize on it.

"But here you sit, giving up when one pitch doesn't break records the first time out.

"You've got to keep all your programs going, **including Boomerang** ... then recognize the unexpected break when it happens. You've got so many things going for you, one is going to break through."

Boar caught a naked smile on the face of Ellen Brewster, but he growled listlessly, "Tom, cut the cheerleading. What the hell do you mean, 'so many things going for us'?"

Dougherty looked at his watch and strode to the chalkboard. "Add it up!" He grabbed chalk and scrawled a '1.' with an illegible scriggle after it. "One — you've got basic truth on your side — proved by the Smoot-Hawley depression of '33. Two — the 'One Earth' campaign, just now working its way through the environmentalist network.

"Three — you've got the possibility of the worldwide broadcast from the Harvard commencement. Four — the bargaining chip of suggesting that if the other nations won't go for balanced free trade, the U.S. **should** re-evaluate its foreign aid programs and start over on a merit plan basis. Five — a second bargaining chip: Buy our balanced free trade program ... **or** ... start paying your own way on defense."

The chalkboard list was illegible but the staff stared at it.

"Six — we've got Visconti's superb Boomerang program with four potential leadership audiences for it — labor, business, media, and government types."

"But they're not coming, Tom." It was Chris Bain.

"The first time? Of course not. Hey - it's got to build. You got to keep it going." He sat down and lowered his voice. "Let me tell you something about selling. What really wins big is not brilliance. It's persistence. Dart Industries was flat on its can five times. There are far smarter guys than Jason Dart and me on unemployment. Persistence was our main ace. Keep all those programs going, including **Boomerang**. And — watch for the unexpected break."

Forte said, "That may be okay in the Midwest, Tom; but in Washington there may not be time for persistence."

A young woman apologetically entered the room, handed a note to Ellen Brewster, and vanished. Ellen read the note and walked it over to Knute Boar. He read it quickly. "Wow." He read it again. "Gentlemen and ladies, the president wants a private and secret showing of Boomerang for five of his top staff."

30

HOLLINGSWORTH

Ms. Shuva had been brought over on extended loan to Forte's staff and elevated to director of the Boomerang facility.

She called Visconti, "Something's happening. Can you get over here?" Some who had turned down the first invitation were asking if they could come now.

Shuva reported that every think tank and university seemed to have a little basement room called Foreign Trade Studies Division which wanted to come. The cost per head to put one person through Boomerang was high. Should she admit them?

"Not yet. Let them clamor awhile."

Then the day after the president's staff tried Boomerang, Chris Bain called Forte. "The president wants Drummond to attend Boomerang."

Drummond capitalized on the invitation.

(Lansing Times)

DRUMMOND SNUBS PRESIDENTIALLY INSPIRED INVITATION TO SUPER DEMO ON WORLD TRADE

"The Boss Is Not Boss Of The Congress"
— Drummond

Washington-Michigan's senior senator, now chairing the Joint Committee on the trade bill, emphatically declined Sen. Forte's invitation to participate in the rather spectacular multimil-lion-dollar Boomerang exercise now being hailed by many economists as a stunning demonstra-tion of the consequences of protectionism.

However, Drummond, dismissing Boomerang as a "costly computer game," told us, "I know Forte was the conduit for the president on this invitation. But I say to the president, the Joint Committee is not the theater for any sideshow that is probably rigged. I will not ..."

Boar handed the newsclip to Dougherty. "Tom, got any ideas?"

Some had noticed that Jason Dart was getting short with people. He had told Emile Hoffstetler, "Send me one of your young MITs."

"Mine? The whiz kids were your idea."

"Okay. But I need one that's a quick study, very quick, and can work around the clock. Something Tom Dougherty needs fast."

"All right. The one I'm going to send you is Harvey Hollingsworth. He's the brightest, but a little nervous. Don't bulldoze him around."

"Me?" Dart looked wounded. "But hurry."

Harvey Hollingsworth came in. His diffidence was not a lack of confidence, but excess awe of the legend of J.W. Dart, not relieved by the fact that Dart, with his back to the visitor, continued studying a sketch on the wall without even looking at the newcomer. After many seconds, still without turning to his visitor, he started instructing. "Harry, take our smallest Utility Cube design, and design around it a do-it-yourself kit that'll make a house of a thousand square feet of living space. Minimum of ..."

"I...I'm sorry, sir, I didn't know you were beginning already. Could you ... uh ... restate?"

Dart swung around and saw a surprisingly young man with notebook and pencil now poised. "Harry, what I want is ..."

"Harvey, sir. Harvey Hollingsworth."

"Harry, I want a do-it-yourself kit designed ... fast."

He outlined the kit's objective in some detail: A minimal house that could be assembled by a family of moderate skills. Wood and plywood. Nothing exotic. Not counting the land and labor, it should go up for $25,000. He needed the plan in seven days, including a dry run of building the house to insure workability.

"Get help from a local contractor, Bob Morton. Listen to what he says, don't instruct him on modern technology. Let me see the drawings in two days."

Harvey could not believe the interview was over already. "Is that it ... sir?"

"That's it, Harry."

"Harvey, sir."

Dart nodded.

Hollingsworth knew a career opportunity when he had one in his hands. After 48 hours of study and interviews and using the design department resources, he had a drawing he put in front of Hoffstetler. Hoffstetler nodded. "Very good. Very good."

"But would you take it to Mr. Dart, sir?"

"You got nothing to worry ... except yourself. You walk in. You lay it down. You say nothing. Then you answer questions. When you don't know you say, 'I don't know. Need another day.'"

Dart studied the drawing in excruciating silence, occasionally using a magnifying glass. Finally he pointed to a joint on the drawing. "How is an ordinary man with ordinary tools going to swage that collar onto that pipe?"

Hollingsworth studied the juncture in embarrassment. Then suddenly he said, "I need another day."

"Harry, can an average fellow really put this together?"

"It's Harvey, sir ... and ... I think so, but I need another two days."

Dart sank back in his chair and studied Hollingsworth. "Take another day." Then he smiled. "But first fax a copy of that drawing to Tom Dougherty, Washington."

"Yes, sir."

Dart dialed Edith White, whom he called vice-president-at-large. He put her in charge of whatever he wanted. The new sophisticated management now understood this and gave her plenty of room. "Edie, do you remember there was a fat country-boy banker on the TV news appearing at state legislature farm hearings?"

"Yes. He was fun. Why?"

"I want to put together a kind of a customer financing plan. Do you think you could find that fellow and have him call me?"

"Sure. But, Jason, what have we got a big fancy finance department for ... if not for that?"

"Too fancy. That fellow on TV made a lot of common sense."

"Mr. Dart, Dick Lempke. Honored by your call, sir. I'll be happy to drive over there to Seville to talk."

"Not yet. Wait till you hear whether what I want is crazy." He explained that he wanted a financing setup whereby a man could put $5,000 down on a $25,000 kit to build a small house and then have very reasonable mortgage payments. Dart Cube, Inc. would furnish an instructor and an inspector and would be guarantor for the first hundred loans. "There are details to be worked out, but what do you think so far?"

"Mr. Dart, I think this is the kind of deal that a young downtown-type career banker would love to take hold of. I'm kind of a country banker. But we have on staff here a whole platoon of the other kind."

"So have I, Mr. Lempke. But when my ox is in the ditch, I call a country doctor."

A huge laugh broke out. "I'll be there tomorrow!"

Tom Dougherty slid a fax copy of the kit house across the desk of Drummond's political aide. "The senator might see me and he might not. But I figure you will know the value of what I'm going to give you, and whether you want to take me in to see him."

Dougherty pulled out a spread from a month-old *Detroit Free Press*.

FEDERAL HOUSING SUBSIDIES
FOR MICHIGAN DRYING UP

State's Congressional Delegation
Ineffective. Drummond Efforts Fail.

The feature explained that, despite the best efforts of the Michigan congressional delegation, housing aid for Michigan, especially Detroit, for many good reasons, was exhausted. Housing had become a top crisis in four Michigan cities. The Detroit mayor said, "Our now-distinguished Senator Drummond has forgotten what state sent him to Washington."

Dougherty said, "Drummond can become the hero and get re-elected. If he can get some union and code concessions, we will build these do-it-yourself kits, thousands of them, called 'The Michigan House' ... which a family can put up itself ... cheap." The political aide studied the drawing. Then he rolled his eyes to Heaven, "Oh boy!" He studied it some more, and picked up the phone.

In the senator's office, Drummond rotated his chair to face the flag in thought. "Oh boy!"

Then he turned severely on Dougherty."Dougherty, the price to me? Personally?"

"Come to the Boomerang demonstration."

Drummond shook his head. "But I'm willing to send some staff."

With a smile, Dougherty shook his head. He slid in front of the senator a one-paragraph, easy-financing plan. Drummond grasped it. "Oh boy!" He thought a long moment. "Mr. Dougherty, I'll send my staff and three other senators."

Dougherty shook his head.

"Me? Personally?"

Dougherty nodded. "In person."

"Can it be in private?"

"I think so."

"And then?"

"And then, Senator ... just follow your conscience."

31

YAS NABU

Unknown to Susan Hamilton in Dayton, Ohio, the Hamiltons were not going to dine this night at Fairlawn Country Club. It was in a window booth at a clangorous restaurant named EAT-LIQUOR where the menu was pictures. She laughed, "What are we into — a populist phase? Or nostalgia about our hard beginnings?"

"The latter, maybe."

She had kept the books and cleaned the office in the converted garage phase of Hamilton Machine. Although humorless lately at work, Hamilton usually joked with his popular wife. Not tonight. "Sue, I had to get you away from the kids and away from friends at the Club. We've got to talk."

"Oh-oh. You are going to borrow some big dollars again and put our house back in hock."

"No. The opposite." He leaned across the table. "Sue, how would you feel if we sold out?"

Even the dinner plates klunking down in front of them didn't break through her stunned silence. Finally, "Is it getting old to you, Ham?"

"The opposite. More exciting than ever."

"Then what?"

"Something funny is happening ... that's beyond me. In the shower at the gym and on the street, four separate days, guys asked me if they could buy stock in the shop. Two fellows at the bank and two from Merrill Lynch."

"We're not listed anywhere. How do they know the value?"

"Book value is easy to find. And earnings. The bank knows our assets. But listen, one offered half again over what Max says it's worth. Didn't even ask for a P&L!"

"Isn't that just because that's what the whole country is doing? The stock market spree? No relation to the performance of the companies. Just boom the stocks. The traders don't even know what the companies' products are."

"Maybe. It's over my head. We've had three not good years. They know that; but they still want to buy." She had seldom seen him so unsure. "So these offers have no relation to the company's performance. But we could get out now ... profitably. We may never get another chance."

"Eat your dinner and forget it. You'd die of boredom at home."

He grinned. "You realize we'll probably have to die in harness."

"So die in harness."

They finished in silence. He was scooping up the check to leave when she put a hand on his sleeve and smiled, "But, Ham, sell one fifth. Use the money to buy the other CAM machines."

A smile stretched his face. "That ... is why I married you!"

The next morning Hamilton phoned the four men. "If you can sweeten your offer by next Friday, we're considering selling a few shares."

The men were pleased.

Unknown to the Three Musketeers, Hundo Sukuto took JAL flight 369 to Tokyo, summoned to a private conference with the foreign trade minister's staff. They wanted a firsthand eye-to-eye assessment of whether the tough U.S. trade bill would pass.

"Yes. It will pass."

"Why are you so sure?"

"Too many legislators, too committed."

"Do they know the consequences?"

"Mostly no. But even if they change their thinking, the legislators cannot back off now and be re-elected."

U.S. CHINA WALL TRADE BILL
CERTAIN TO PASS

Hundo Sukuto, Leader of Japan's Elite Corps Of Trade Negotiators, Returns From U.S.

Hong Kong—*Asia Week's* best source believes that the capable Hundo Sukuto reported directly in person to the highest levels of Japan's Foreign Trade Ministry that the gargantuan U.S. trade bill will pass Congress.

It is believed it will effectively close the U.S. market to nearly every product.

World Retaliation Expected

Winston Rollins, publisher of the respected *Pacific Economist* reacted promptly. "Sukuto's anticipation of U.S. trade legislation has been nearly perfect for six years. If he indeed told his ministry to expect passage of the brutal U.S. trade bill and defeat of the free trader group, batten the hatches. There will follow immediate closing of world borders to the flow of goods and

...

In Miami, Ed Fash flapped his exchange copy of *Asia Week* onto Knox's desk and fingered the Sukuto item, "Get on the horn and see if this fellow, Rollins, will talk to us. Will he spell out the expected scenario?"

Unknown, even to the pedestrians on Water Street in Lower Manhattan, is a building containing a gymnasium-sized room full of 300 Tandem TNX and TXP mainframes, stacked. This is the action heart of Financial Transactions Services, Inc., FTSI. It serves the stock exchanges and the foreign departments of several large banks whose transactions depend for success on ever-faster financial transfers. Small margins, huge volumes. This state-of-the-art complex is capable of 100 transactions per second. And it has standby redundancy for overload. It is manned by youthful geniuses, mostly women.

At one free-standing console with central monitoring display screens sat precocious Artha Kilfoyle, with two red tassel academic degrees and a brown bag lunch. While watching the monitors, she was listening to her boss, W. A. Jarmual, who stood behind her speaking. "Five congressmen from Senator Boar's trade bill Joint Committee group have been up touring the stock exchange. They learned about the existence of FTSI and they want to come for an unannounced quick tour an hour from now. Are we ship-shape?"

"Is it a media extravaganza like Drummond's Kennedy Airport visit?"

"No media. Just five congressmen. I don't know why."

"I'd get them to postpone it."

"Why?"

She pointed to the transaction counter. "Something sort of funny is going on. Look."

He looked at the transaction counter monitor. It usually strummed along at a stately gavotte of five transactions per second. But now its soft symphony of musical beeps was purring along at ragtime.

"An hour ago it was registering ten trades per second. Now fourteen, fifteen, sixteen."

Unknown to anyone in Dayton, Ohio, or Massillon or Upper Sandusky or Selina, Yas Nabu in the central trading office of Hartman Equities, Tokyo branch, wrestled the biggest problem of his career at 7:30 a.m., Tokyo time. A Columbia University and Wharton graduate, he knew that he was slated to be promoted to the London office. But if he misinterpreted what he thought he saw on his screen, he would be lucky to avoid demotion to South Africa. Yet if he waited for confirmation at 9:30 a.m. when the Nikkei index of 225 international equities was recalculated, he could lose great advantage for his London and New York offices

... which they would note loudly, and in his 201 file.

If he phoned the New York office, it would be 5:30 p.m. yesterday. That office would be closed, although he still might reach the boss's car phone in the commuter traffic. But since it would be yesterday there, the boss would never believe this anyway.

He therefore elected to call the London office .... where it would be 10:30 p.m. yesterday. His bosses there would probably be in bed, but they were more worldly and less naive than New York. They might believe him. He dialed the home of Edmund Worthington III. "Sir, this is Yas Nabu. Tokyo. Are you awake?"

"What is your best guess?"

"Well, I'm either going to get fired or promoted."

"Can we decide that later? Shoot."

"The Nikkei has been rising so beautifully that yesterday I turned my desk over to Dan, and I played golf with our good investor customer, Tokyo Marine."

"So you called to give me your golf score, no doubt. Can we get to the point?"

"Well, when I got in here this morning ... tomorrow your time ... Japan is raising interest rates. In overnight trading, Tokyo Marine fell nineteen points. Others are dropping. The Nikkei is down ten ... and it looks like everything's going to hell here... worse than '89. Am I crazy?"

With a shoulder lock on the phone, Worthington was out of bed tearing off the top of his pajamas. "No! We suspected we were in Fairyland. Call in some extra help. Monitor the Hartman Equities book closely. Start calling our largest investors on any two or three point drop on their stuff! Keep one phone clear so I can reach you 20 minutes from now!"

"Mr. Worthington, what shall I ..."

"I'll call you! Let me off this line!"

Worthington dialed Stamford, Connecticut, home of the new Hartman Equities chief, and left a message: "When he gets home, tell him **immediately** three words ... 'London says Mayday.' Repeat that, please."

The Hartman chief received that message at 6:15 p.m. in Stamford Connecticut. It would be 6:30 before he could reach the office manager's home in New Jersey, but it would still be only 5:15 in the Chicago office. There might be somebody there. Without taking off his hat, he dialed Chicago, "Mayday. Call in extra people and call Dallas, L.A., and San Francisco offices. I'm going back to New York right now."

By midnight New York time, which was breakfast next morning London time, the men who push money around the world for a living in multinational brokerages had been rung out of bed and were jamming international circuits.

By noon in New York, daytime TV programming was interrupted every ten minutes with financial news bulletins.

By midafternoon in eastern U.S. cities, patients in doctors' tiny reception rooms found their appointments backed up two hours and nurses were calling tomorrow's patients to reschedule. Some doctors, getting constant busy signals from their brokers, left by the back exits to go to the brokerages.

At FTSI on Water Street in Lower Manhattan, W.A. Jarmul stood looking over the shoulder of Artha Kilfoyle. Both stared at the transaction counter, climbing to 45 transactions per second. She turned to look up at him, "Mr. Jarmul."

Jarmul continued to stare at the counter.

"Mr. Jarmul."

He seemed hypnotized.

"Mr. Jarmul! Time to cut in auxiliary equipment."

But he continued to stare. Artha Kilfoyle jumped up and ran to the office of the assistant director. "Mr. Kanz! Who can authorize the auxiliaries? We're going through the bottom in minutes. Not hours. Minutes!"

(*Toronto Globe & Mail*)

MARKETS IN FREE FALL
IN SINGAPORE, TOKYO, NY,
LONDON, BERLIN, PARIS.
No Buyers For Top 100
International Issues.

Toronto—The fastest falling stock prices in history began suddenly, most believe in Tokyo, triggered by nearly certain passage of the severe U.S. trade bill.

The investment community was stunned by the speed with which the drop circled the globe electronically. Some realized the intertwined world network would be set off by

...

The week that followed was an international nightmare. And as quickly as the market free fall came the post-crash diagnoses, all nearly identical.

(*Boston Globe*)

"IT'S ONE WORLD MARKET OUT THERE!"
CitiTrust Chairman Voices The
Lesson Of The Crash!
"One Market"

New York-The entire financial community had begun to suspect it. Multi-national sales managers have long known it. But the CitiTrust chairman made it official. With the disappearance of the float via electronics, the finance world is no longer a group of separate markets in separate countries, not even separate continents. The chairman told an emergency meeting of financial people that, in case they had any doubts, believe it now. **"It's one market out there!"**

He further warned that even the threat of trade restrictions...

By Friday, Frank Hamilton had had two meetings with Millitech in Cincinnati regarding the five additional reprogrammable machining centers, negotiating a good price.

He phoned one of the stockbrokers, saying that some shares in Hamilton Machine were now available.

"Forget it, Frank."

"What?"

"Where the hell have you been all week, Frank? You didn't hear of the worldwide stock crash?"

"What has worldwide got to do with a little company in Dayton?"

"Hey, haven't you heard? It's one market out there!"

Hamilton folded up the Millitech letter of agreement.

"Frank, you going to the gym tonight? Frank?"

Hamilton hung up.

32

THE BOSS

One of Drummond's strengths had always been the ability, and the guts, to recognize a career turning point. He recognized one now. How it came out would depend a lot on the president. He was banking on knowing this president better than most legislators knew him.

Some observers measured the influence of this president by a catalogue of profound results already working their way into school textbooks: enhancing the U.S.-Canada partnership, preventing the Congressional revolt from violating the Canada-U.S. free trade pact, consolidating a continental kinship between North and South America.

But if you ever wanted to really measure the man's impact, Drummond looked to less profound but possibly more telling signs. This president had spawned across the nation a generation of mid-career government people whom you could spot. Dress, mannerisms, and utterances. They stood consciously straight. There was a certain severity of expression when dealing with the peoples' business. They abjured the cute or humorous one-liners on public interviews, leaving themselves less vulnerable to later embarrassment. "Damage control," it was dubbed. They were never photographed in beach wear or Indian feathers. They frustrated the media by their formality and their refusal to be used. It was almost as if they had been to a training school. In a way, they had. That trend could be traced back to two small events which, despite their insignificance, were retold with gleeful chuckles. On one election campaign, a television newscaster of great celebrity was conducting a studio question-and-answer session. Near the end, the distinguished broadcaster looked at his watch and said to the future president, "Sir ... we just have two minutes left. Give us your proposed plan for strengthening the North-South America alliance. Quickly please, sir."

The candidate even then had the presence and profile of an eagle. To the astonishment of the broadcaster and crew and other candidates, he began detaching his lapel microphone, "Mr. Tarbell, I will be glad to answer when you have enough time. The solution to a 200-year-old problem won't fit into 120 seconds. So if you'll excuse me, I will tend to some other matters."

To the amazement of the crew, he walked off the set, leaving the broadcaster to vamp his way to the commercial.

That particular broadcaster then launched a vendetta. On the next large media conference, he rose and asked the candidate, "Sir, all candidates have taken a stand on the now-dominant movement to restrain family size to four children. But you have avoided the subject. Will you now state your position ... sir?"

"Yes."

The candidate, later to be known as the boss, delayed his answer until the suspense in the room peaked. "The president will make many decisions. But that is not one of them. That will be decided by fathers and mothers. This meeting is for questions falling within my purview."

The media hated it. The public loved it.

Political careerists, most without even knowing it, copied the boss's demeanor. Drummond was one of them, but he copied skillfully enough not to be obvious. Further, he knew something about the boss's ways that most did not. Most admirers copied the president's arrogance and daring, but knew nothing about his humility. Drummond had seen the boss in action when stakes were high, the odds were bad, and the boss needed a big favor from the Senate. The boss would crawl in on hands and knees to beg for a deal when he had to. Few knew that.

Drummond had phrased his written request for a private meeting with the president in a code to which he felt the president would respond: "Mr. President, I'm at fourth down and a hundred yards. One time out left. Need a conference with the coach. Private. Drum."

The president's staff adopted the president's enemies with more malevolence than the boss felt. So his chief of staff gave Drummond a barely civil reception. When he nodded for the senator to enter the Oval Office, Drummond asked, "Who will be in there?"

The chief smiled with some malice, "The boss."

"Sure, but who else?"

"You requested a private meeting. It is."

"No staff?"

The chief shook his head, smiling more broadly. "You're totally on your own."

Drummond masked a deep breath by pulling up his belt and buttoning his jacket. He had been with the president many times, but always in the company of other senior senators, and never with a make-or-break proposition of his own.

A staff woman opened the door. Drummond entered. "Mr. President."

The boss stood with his back to Drummond, looking out the floor-to-ceiling window at the lawn. He did not turn, nor invite Drummond to sit. Nor did he address him as "Drum." Maybe Drummond did not know this president as well as he thought.

The boss, not an amateur in the uses of the aura of this office when it counted, let his visitor absorb it for a few moments.

"Mr. President ... I have a bear by the tail."

The president turned and nodded, unsurprised. Drummond wondered: If he ever became president, would his own eyes achieve that commanding coldness for certain occasions?

"Mr. President, we ... I ... need your help. I need a ... a ..."

"A deal."

"Yes."

Drummond looked around the office. The president said, "Yes, Senator, we are being recorded. But you may shut if off yourself. Just open that louvered panel and push that 'off' button."

Drummond did so and returned to stand opposite the

president. "Mr. President, the trade bill will pass. There is no way we can stop it."

The president did not help him; made him say it. "The legislators are now committed back home. But many of us are convinced ... now ... it could bring disaster."

The president nodded.

"But, Mr. President, if you will veto it, Senators Boar, Forte, Bain and I ... guarantee ... guarantee ... your veto will stand."

"Guarantee?" The president studied Drummond. "How?"

"We have pretested privately. We *know* we can get the count."

The president held Drummond's eyes. "In other words, Senator, I take the public heat that you men won't."

"*Can't* sir. We can't stop passage now."

The president left Drummond standing as he walked once around his chair. "Senator, I'm sure you know what this would cost me. It will strain hell out of my public support for my other foreign programs. I'll certainly lose the two South American tech-aid programs."

Drummond nodded.

"But" — the president pointed — "I will do it."

Drummond did not react, waiting for the other shoe.

"And you, Senator, on your part will mount the Harvard commencement podium (which has been arranged for by Boar's man, Veitch) and broadcast to the world a message." The president riveted Drummond's eyes. "Your message will be: 'We have *one* earth. *One* market. It must be free to all. The U.S. will lead off with a balanced free trade policy. You can sell to us as much as you buy. We will hold back protectionist legislation for eighteen months while you nations work that out.'"

"Mr. President, with my past statements, I'm *not* the one to say that."

"You are *exactly* the one, and the *only* one. Then the world will know the U.S. means it."

"Mr. President, with all respect, sir, I am not empowered to speak for the United States."

"True, but ..." The president stood to the side of his desk and pointed to his own chair. For the first time he allowed a hint of a grin. "I'm aware that you would like to be so empowered in the quite near future. Would you like to try out this chair now?"

Not venturing a return grin, Drummond shook his head.

"Senator, it is all right for you to speak for the United States because you will be speaking the truth. As a powerful senator, you will *make* it truth. You will begin work on a balanced free trade law, phasing down present barriers. You will be convincing because you saw that even the *threat* of passage of your trade bill incited panic. Besides, you got the Boomerang religion."

"Yes, sir. But that doesn't mean I'm willing to do a public back flip."

The president walked around to Drummond's side. In the famous manner that made him mentor-uncle to over a thousand high-level political careerists, he said quietly, "Drum, you're trying to keep all your options open. In the Senate, you can do that. But up here ..." — he pointed to his own empty chair — "you can't."

He walked back behind his desk and faced Drummond. "Here ... you've got to know exactly *who you are*." He pointed to the portraits of Washington and Lincoln. "It's called ... growing up to the office.

"Otherwise ..." — he sat down — "boomerang!"

He studied Drummond. "So what do you want? Approval or veto? Deal or no deal? You decide ... very carefully."

Drummond now sat down. With his elbow on the chair arm and his fist over his mouth, he studied the eagle woven into the carpet. No longer awed by the president, but rather by the harsh decision offered, he reviewed the consequences ... and his life. You've got to know exactly who you are.

Drummond rose. Now in a relaxed way he extended a hand. "The veto. No boomerang."

They shook. Long and silently.

33

THE OLD RUOFF PLACE

Patrolman Braun was used to the new nightime activity in Bucyrus. A lot of farmers got up in the middle of the night to drive way over to Ottowa, Ohio. The electric motor plant there was suddenly running three shifts. Even exporting some with foreign wiring. Their parking lot was full of farm pickup trucks. There was a string of other small plants astride I-75 doing well. They found farmers, from a habit of repairing their own farm equipment, were no strangers to mechanical assembly. And the farmers found this the easiest work they'd ever done, and the regular paycheck was a real high, like church letting out.

But Braun was not used to lights in the bank. He called in, "The bank is lit up at midnight. Any known explanation?"

The answer came back that Schlicter had been working late, with some lawyers, for a week. Where else is he going to go nights? Nobody in town talks to him.

Shortly after midnight the phone rang in the Ruoff camper. Sheila sat up. She shook Moose. "Who would that be?"

"It'll be that collection agency. It's their third-stage technique. They're doing it to the Morrisons and Hallets. Don't answer."

But she couldn't sleep. She quietly dialed the police. "Jim, this is Sheila Ruoff. Our son Ben and Beth Varney are at the Pavilion party. Was any accident reported?"

"No, Sheil."

But the phone rang again. She answered. It was Schlicter. She said, "No, I'll not put him on the phone. He leaves for Ottowa at five a.m. You've ruined our family, isn't that enough?"

"Mrs. Ruoff, that's what I want to fix. And I have a plan; but I need papers signed tonight. I have to drive them to Wooster Ag Station in the morning."

"I'm sure you don't expect me to believe you're now helping us."

"Mrs. Ruoff, I do have a solution worked out. But the papers must be filed with the Ag Department by ten."

"*Mister* Ruoff has had quite enough of your papers, Mr. Schlicter."

"Then could I come out and show *you* the plan?"

"No."

"Could I come out and talk to Ben, Junior?"

"No. He's at the fundraiser dance for the Morrison farm family. And I don't want him anywhere near you."

Moose rose up on an elbow. "Who is it, Sheil?"

"Just some prankster." She hung up.

Warner Schlicter drove eleven miles to the Pavilion, a quite modern lakeside party center that served three towns around. He inquired for the table where young Ben Ruoff and Beth Varney were, and approached. The table silenced as did several nearby. Schlicter, standing, asked if he could talk to Ben somewhere quiet with more light. He had a plan for the Ruoff place. Ben Ruoff, seated, with lights from a reflecting ball flickering over his face, asked, "Why, all of a sudden?"

Schlicter shrugged.

Ruoff said, "Tell my father."

"He won't see me. And there's a deadline."

Ruoff said, "Come on, Beth." They led the way to a booth in the bar. The nearby crowd watched them go.

Schlicter arranged three stacks of forms on the table, the blanks already filled in. "This won't work for all farms. But it will for yours. There are three government programs which will make this possible. I've checked it out with Fordyce at Wooster Ag Experiment Station."

He unfolded a sketch of the Ruoff farm. "Step One: Take these acres here and retire them from production. The government will pay your father sixty-five dollars per acre per year to retire them if the bank withdraws foreclosure. And these are your poor drainage acres anyway.

"Step Two: Your father had already put these acres in your name two years ago. Just a paperwork split; but legal. And the mortgage on these acres was held not by us but by the lender of last resort, Farmers Home Administration. They foreclosed and, to partially recoup, they are renting out these lands cheap — forty-five dollars per acre. So Step Two — your father rents these acres at forty-five dollars the acre and plants. Because of that low rent, he can make out well, even if the market is soft and he sells at the government subsidy guarantee price."

Ben Ruoff turned to Beth, "You following this?"

"Yes."

"Does it make sense?"

"Not yet."

Schlicter had learned in Bucyrus you listen when farm women speak. He looked a question. She said, "It follows up until you get to the money to rent the forty-five dollar land. Ben's father won't get the sixty-five until year end. But rent is always paid in advance."

Schlicter pointed to the third stack of forms. "That's Step Three — he borrows."

Ben shook his head. "He can't borrow against rented or retired land."

"No. But he can borrow from the government on a commodity-backed certificate against part of his soybeans locked in at Toledo Elevator bankruptcy. Our Toledo bank is a major creditor of Elevator. We have some clout."

Ben shook his head slowly. "Beth ... you follow that?"

She addressed Schilicter, pointing to the second and third stacks. "Does this equal that?"

Schlicter nodded. "Or I wouldn't be here."

Ben turned to Beth, "Plant that whole row for me."

She put up three fingers. "One — you get a twenty dollar advantage between the acres you retire and the acres you rent. Two — that pays the second half of your rent. Three — you borrow against your soybeans for the first half. Four — you sell the crop at the government price to pay the new loan and ..." — she pointed at Schlicter — "to start paying off his old loan, refinanced." She looked a question at Schlicter.

316

He nodded.

Ben grabbed her wrist, "Keep those fingers up there." From his side pocket he pulled out a tiny box which he opened with one hand. He slipped a ring on her third finger.

She studied it for moments, then she smiled, took it off and handed it back.

His smile crumbled. "What?"

She held up a fourth finger. "After Step Four."

"What's Four?"

"You finish Ohio State."

"How do I know you'll wait?"

She put her arm slowly around his collar, "You were too dumb to notice. But I've waited since I was eleven. I'll probably wait another year ... or so. Will you?"

Schlicter said, "I need your father's signatures tonight. Can you two get them? He won't see me."

Driving to the Ruoff place, Ben said, "My father will want your father's opinion. Shall we go there first?"

"I don't think my father would want that responsibility."

"What if you said that your father ...?" He didn't finish.

She said, "Ben, we've got to present it strong."

Moose and Sheila Ruoff put on coffee. The four of them sat at the kitchen table in the trailer.

Beth spread out the three stacks of forms and the map. Moose growled, "What's all this?"

Beth said, "Mr. Ruoff, we're not going to back into this casually. Ben is going to explain it carefully."

Sheila pointed to Beth's flying fingers and suddenly said to young Ben, "I thought tonight was the night. But I don't see anything on her hand."

"She wouldn't take it."

Sheila's face dimmed. Beth saw it and smiled. "How could I accept, Mrs. Ruoff? He only wants me for my brainy mind."

Sheila was unsure. "Your parents?"

Beth put a hand on Sheila's arm. "Nothing's wrong. Just the timing. I'll help my dad with the farm books one more year. Ben will be at Ohio State."

Ben did not start right away. "I have to do this right, Dad." He made a few notes. Then he said, "All right. Here's the plan, and it is solid. We've got to do it." He laid it out clearly, uninterrupted; and looked at Beth. She nodded.

Young Ben said, "Dad, this plan is a soaking rain in a dry July."

Moose looked at Sheila. She looked at her hands. Moose rose and walked a circle. Young Ben started, "Dad ..." Sheila touched his hand. He stopped.

Beth watched Moose, then young Ben. Ben watched his father. "Dad..." Sheila shook her head slightly.

Moose returned to the tiny table and gave up his weight to a chair. "Ben ... I don't think so."

"No-o?"

"I don't think so."

Ben was on his feet, "How can you say no?"

"Don't know exactly, Ben."

"Schlicter's lawyers say it's okay."

"Doesn't seem right."

"Not right?" Ben was stunned. "Saving the home place is not right? Why?"

"Haven't got my hand around it exactly yet."

The only sounds were rain on the trailer roof. Moose said, "Sheil?"

She put her head in her hand. "Give me a minute with the whole notion."

Young Ben reminded, "The papers have got to be in Wooster by ten a.m."

Moose looked at the girl he would like for daughter-in-law. "Beth?"

She studied her hands. "Mr. Ruoff, the arrangement wouldn't be forever. But if you lose the land, it could be forever. Young Ben, or any young farmer, can hardly buy this farm today."

Young Ben nodded.

Moose agreed. "It's just I hate to sign my name on something that ... see, all our friends'll know we're taking with both hands. *They* can't. The hardware can't get paid for shutting half his store and then get low rent on the other half."

318

Ben said, "Dad, they haven't got one twentieth the risk of a farm."

"True." Moose nodded. "Sheil, what do you think?"

"I'm still thinking."

Moose said, "You just answered. If a thing is right, you always knew it in thirty seconds." He turned to his son, "Ben, I know you're the one we're hurting. That thought'll likely kill me. But I couldn't live with the Schlicter deal either."

"There'll be others in town *will* do it, Dad."

"I know it."

"Then why become the damndest fool in town just for some stupid, stubborn ...?"

"I was already the damndest fool, but I got stubborn only lately."

Young Ben stood up. "Come on, Beth. I'll take you home."

But she took off her raincoat. "Not yet." She lit the propane burner. "We're going to have a refill." Returning to the table with new bounce, she held up her third finger and commanded, "Benjamin Ruoff, Junior! Ring me!"

Sheila brightened. Moose alerted.

Ben was puzzled. "Why? What changed?"

She retained her smart-alec language, but her voice softened. "I want a Ruoff man. And you seem to be the only one of age not taken."

Sheila was pouring the coffee, but Moose took it from her and emptied the cups, rinsed them, and set them on the table. From the top shelf of the cupboard he reached down a bottle of Old Grandad and poured with a little water. He raised his cup and growled, "Boy, ring that girl before you lose the mother of my grandchildren."

Ben slowly slid on the ring. Without releasing the hand, he said quietly, "Beth, you'll notice the style is out of date."

"Yes. An old family ring?"

"No. Brand-new. But I bought it five years back."

Leaving the camper, Ben's nonchalance returned. "Don't leave a light on for me. It'll be dawn ... I hope."

Beth whispered, "So it's not just my brain?"

Lempke walked into the bank in Bucyrus and strained the chair opposite Schlicter. "Warney, you're a long way over your time limit and you still don't have your arms around this job."

"You're probably right, Mr. Lempke, but I guess I ought to ask your basis."

"I put up at the motel in Upper Sandusky. Been cruising around a couple days. Warney, we're the enemy down here."

"God, I've been trying."

Lempke believed him. He was looking at a very lonesome young man. "Now look, Warney, you're a bright young banker. I think you really tried here. I think you learned a lot. But you may just be wrong for this market. I'm willing to say — no penalty if you elect transfer into one of our cities."

"I'd like that. But ... I hate to leave without a win. Could I have six months?"

"Best answer you ever gave me. You can have four. What ideas you got for helping these people — without giving away the bank?"

Schlicter explained the retire land and rent land plan he had worked out with the lawyers and Ag Department.

"Not bad. How did it work?"

"It bombed out."

"Why?"

"I offered it first to Ruoff."

"Why?"

"You convinced me I need an alliance with Varney. Ruoff is his best friend and next neighbor. I figured we'd make big gains with Varney and the whole county if we could save Ruoff. It's a famous farm. But Ruoff turned it down."

"Why?"

"Said it felt like stealing."

"That's why it's a famous farm."

"Our lawyers didn't think it was stealing."

"They wouldn't. But we're not the church. As a banker you came up with a creative plan. Only trouble is you ran into a man of character." Lempke slapped the desk and laughed. "That'll kill creative finance every time."

320

Schlicter looked beaten.

Lempke said, "But your strategy that saving the Ruoff place would be a pivotal move was correct. What other ideas you got?"

Schlicter turned up his palms.

"Well, Warney, do you really want to make it work? And make this bank work?"

"Of course."

"Well, there's a way to do that right in front of your nose. Not easy. But sure fire."

"What?"

"If I tell you, we'll know *I'm* an effective banker. But we won't know about *you* .... will we?"

"H-m-m-m. But you could clue me a little."

"When I went down to Columbus ... at *your* request ... I presume you were too busy getting your butt kicked by Ruoff's friends to note what that Columbus trip was all about. Right?"

Schlicter nodded.

"Well, think about that."

"I remember. It was about ... the state buying up farms."

"Right."

"But they didn't. So how does it help me?"

Lempke sat stubbornly silent, grinning.

Schlicter put his head in his hand. Then, "Oh-h! Varney's trying to get the town of Bucyrus to buy up farm land."

"Right." Lempke shoved himself up out of the chair. "So, Warney, you're going to get yourself into local politics."

"I've never been into that."

"Learn, Warney. Learn."

"Then come up with a way this bank can help."

"You've got it."

34

MORE

To satisfy Mike Knox's curiosity, Fash of the *Miami Herald* returned the call to London, collect, a Langley Chiltenham of the *Economist*. The voice was very relaxed. "Mr. Fash! We're following your financial page most keenly."

"Mine?

"You seem to have a way of knowing what's just over the next swing before it swings. Some special insight?"

"All I've got is a phone."

"It must be a very smart phone. And you must have had some very sophisticated background."

"You could say so. I covered sports six years."

"My goodness. Then I'd better get down to the gym myself. Anyway, to the point, old man: Do you suppose you could persuade your head office to let you off for a month or so to do some pieces for us?"

"What subject?"

"Well, sir, what we consider *the* most important event of the quarter century."

"Which is?"

"The defeat of the American trade bill which we feel is responsible for preventing the world's worst depression, possibly even war. And we feel you have a certain inside picture of just what went on. We want a series of features which document that. That could give a blueprint of how to snub off protectionism when it recurs in the future ... which it probably will. Especially we'd like to know what happened to the heroes of that battle."

"I'm no big league finance or political writer. Why not a DeLong of the *New York Times*?"

"Because, Mr. Fash, we don't want somebody's preformed opinion. We want the facts. By Fash."

"Who would be my boss on the series?"

"You, old boy. No strings, except one."

"What's that?"

"The title of the series is to be 'MORE.' Meaning — with free trade, there's more for all of us."

"H-m-m-m."

"Ring me back, won't you, by Friday ... and don't get me out of bed please, like this time."

"Oh, I forgot the time lag."

"Not a *lag* old boy. We're ahead of the colonies ... as always."

Inside the Beltway and in a few places around the nation were a few people who knew that Boar came into his office a couple hours Sunday mornings. They knew he kept an answering machine lit and monitored in case Lucy called or his father or some senate friend.

This particular morning he was puzzled at the strange echoes in the office until he realized it was because so many furnishings had been removed. He wondered if the great previous occupant, Senator Dirkson, had noticed that sound. He decided to leave Dirkson's picture on the wall.

Boar opened up folded cardboard to form ten empty boxes. Moriarity, a senior security guard, kept a supply in the basement which he sold to people departing the Hill.

Boar at first tossed items roughly into boxes. He slowed, however, when he took down his daughter's painting of the old Boar Forwarding dock in Boston. He wrapped it in the *Washington Post* and placed it carefully in a box.

He threw a bunch of lawbooks roughly in a box marked "Give Away." But he carefully put in a "Save" box a four-inch-thick stack of papers entitled "Joint Senate-House Trade Bill." On the top sheet was scrawled "VETOED."

Bending over he caught himself puffing. It was a good thing ... getting out. Lucy had been telling him he needed exercise ... a lot of it. Two hours a day.

Echoing through the suite came the click-clock of his outside lobby door. Then he heard no more. Maybe security, checking.

He resumed work. The flag was government property. He left that. He swept a bunch of desk awards into a box unceremoniously.

"You should wrap those things. Boston Antiquarian wants them."

He turned. "Ellen!"

She had two cups of coffee. They sat on boxes of books.

"But I haven't been coming in Sundays, so how did you know today?"

She smiled and shrugged.

"I once told you you'd be the first one of a half dozen to come to my funeral."

"Better than that — I'm going to be custodian of your monument." She retrieved the vetoed trade bill from the box. "Fellow named Ed Fash, *Miami Herald*, wants this. He'll return it to me, and I'll return it to you later. Lucy will want it. She knows what it cost."

The phone rang. "That may be the second mourner," she said.

She pressed line one. "Senator Boar's office. Ellen Brewster." She listened a long time, then she said, "I don't think the senator would be interested, Mr. Braxton. But I'll tell him Monday."

After hanging up she said, "They want you for lobbyist for the Business Round Table."

Boar chuckled, "You answered it right." Then he leaned across and put a hairy hand over hers. "But, Ellen, I feel you should grab quickly that post at Treasury. They assure me it's yours if you don't delay."

"I knew you were concerned, Knute, but don't be."

"You hit the Irish Sweepstakes suddenly?"

She lowered her eyes in a way that reminded him of when she had first come aboard eleven years ago.

"Knute, I've accepted a different offer."

"More money?"

"No."

"Less stress?"

"No. A boss more like my role model ... in size and energy at least."

"Some senator? Washington office?"

"No. Seville, Ohio."

"You and Tom?"

Her laugh was muted violin. "We're of age. And I *do* cook."

Hamilton Machine was mostly a prestige job shop for new product prototypes. The production runs usually went to less expensive plants. However, Hamilton did have three proprietary products, the chief one being telescoping hydraulic masts for OEM heavy materials-handling equipment. Their best customers had been Caterpillar and Hyster lift trucks. But when the Japanese invaded the lift truck market with superb machines which did not leak and cost a third less, Hamilton's hydraulic mast plum shriveled to a prune.

But in anticipation of the U.S. balanced free trade proposition, two Japanese walked into Hamilton Machine. The tall, thin one laid on Hamilton's desk a beautifully polished length of hydraulic tubing. He said in excellent English, "Mr. Hamilton, we have filled the U.S. with Japanese lift trucks, dozers, and backhoes. They require replacement parts." He explained they had been supplying these from Japan. "But our government feels we'll get credit under your 'balanced free trade' edict ... uh ... policy ... if we buy our U.S. replacement parts in the U.S. Quality is our strength. We have studied your history. We do not even need to inspect your plant." He placed on Hamilton's desk a half-inch-thick document. "Here are our expected requirements on telescoping hydraulic masts for three years. How soon could you give us a firm bid on producing one-half of these in each type and size?"

He watched Hamilton open and scan the document with a sad expression and with no immediate response. Then Hamilton picked up the tube, handling it as if it were a silver trophy, admiring it sadly. Saito smiled. "Mr. Hamilton, the other bidder was more enthusiastic, I must say."

Leaning back, Hamilton closed the document with a tired smile. "Mr. Saito, four years ago I would have jumped through a hoop to bid on this order."

"And now?"

"Now ... I don't know if we could meet your tolerance specs in these lengths. We are in a transition to CAM reprogrammable machine centers. And we're having some ... problems."

Saito looked at his colleague, who smiled. Saito said. "What would you say to quoting on three-quarters of the requirements instead of half?"

"If I'm reluctant to quote on half, why would you let me quote on three-quarters?"

Saito now openly grinned. "We are overwhelmed by your hard sell." Both Japanese laughed. Saito said, "For candor like yours, we give the larger order." He rose. "Think about it, and call us."

When they had gone, Hamilton studied the document wistfully.

Sunday night Hamilton walked the darkened plant, lit eerily only through the windows from the exterior security sodium lamps, the musk of machine oil fragrant in the air. His wife's heels echoed beside him. He led her into the school section, and he looked at the mechanical drawings on the chalkboards.

"It isn't working, Susan."

"Why not?"

"The deal I made with the university branch put in here instructors who are using college methods. Doesn't work here. And I'm stuck with a huge dollar commitment. It could break us."

"That Visconti got us into it," she charged. "Tell him he owes it to get us out."

He shook his head. "He got fired by the union. He could care less."

"He stomps in, wrecks a company, and stomps out. And doesn't care?"

"There was something different about the guy."

"Then maybe it *is* time to sell out, Ham."

"Let's go home."

Next day, in the plant, Hamilton shut himself in the office, refusing calls and visitors. He finally called in Sam Hennessy, president of Machinists Lodge 111, and told him to find out where Visconti went after he was fired. "And get a phone number."

"At the head office, it's like Visconti is dead. They'll tell me nothing."

"Try again."

The staff of a lame-duck senator jumps ship early to get lined up for a job with a government bureau or a staff job with a legislative subcommittee. The best of them get hired away early by other congressmen. Forte's staff was already thin, and those remaining were in and out on job interviews. Messages were garbled and mishandled. Confusion ruled.

Two people sustained some continuity, Visconti and a damp-eyed Mrs. Rider.

Visconti received three calls for the absent senator from an L.K. Braxton. On the third one, Braxton said, "I met you at the Boomerang, Mr. Visconti. So I feel confident in your handling my important message for the senator. And I wish you'd present it with some force."

"The force depends upon the message. Shoot."

"Before anybody else talks to him, the Business Round Table wants him to assist us with some full-time lobbying."

"I'll relay the message, but don't hold your breath."

"Why?"

"The senator is not much for middle manning other peoples' ideas. Got too many of his own."

Visconti was startled to receive a call from Ed Fisher at Machinists in Chicago. After a very brief opening, Fisher was blunt. "John, we want you back."

"Me? Why?"

"John, machining is picking up fast under balanced free trade. Even some exporting. Men are being called back. But they're so beat down and docile, they're accepting bum deals from the shops. We've got to get in there fast and stiffen up work rules and pay ... before everything we've established goes to hell."

"Ed, I don't think I'm ready."

"Why not?"

"Don't know for sure."

"What are you going to do?"

"Don't know for sure."

The following day in Forte's offices, Mrs. Rider told Visconti there was an angry and urgent call for him on line 8. Visconti smiled. "Who can hurt us now?" He picked up line 8 and found out.

It was Hamilton of Dayton. Without preliminaries, he charged, "Visconti, I think you wrecked my company with this training monstrosity. These professors can't teach machinists ... or these machinists can't learn from professors." Hamilton unloaded the whole story. "You owe me some help — quick."

Visconti said, "I never claimed our union could set up the school. That was your job."

"I see. Hit and run ... huh? I should have known. Just another hot-shot negotiator." The phone died.

Mrs. Rider walked by Visconti's open door and saw him merely staring at the wall, chewing the inside of his cheek. "Somebody call the senator a bad name?"

"No. Me."

"Why should it bother you? It never bothers the senator."

"Sure, because you said he lives by a code."

"So? Do likewise."

"What if I don't have one?"

Ed Fisher was a man who started his professional union life with a flaming rage that took him to the top. He worked as apprentice machinist at Waukesha Turbine in Milwaukee where his aging father was one of a dozen top milling men assigned the tremendous responsibility of milling huge turbine shafts and propeller shafts for 600-foot ore carriers. The huge log of rust-dusted alloy steel put under the old man's charge, by the time it had been rolled, forged, and heat treated, was often worth $50,000, back when that was money. By the time the senior Fisher rough milled it, the piece had often grown in value to $80,000. By the time the senior Fisher finished his work on the now-gleaming enormous shaft with 16 different shoulders and outside diameters, the mirror-finished shaft could be worth $150,000. He was a sculptor in steel. He lived with the horrible discipline that, like a sculptor, you can't put material back on a shaft once you take it off. If you cut too deep, you've created scrap worth seven cents a pound.

One year, a week before Christmas, Fisher had nearly finished the enormous shaft for the rebuilding of the vessel *Nelson Moran*. He was working on the last shoulder. The giant Wean milling machine was running beautifully. The chips were spiraling off like fine silver hair. He calipered the OD at just six thousandths away from finish. It would be an hour before the cutting edge came to the next shoulder. He had time to step to the wall phone to return his wife's call before the tungsten cutting bit would approach the end of a pass.

He made the call. On his way back to the machine, he felt a tremor in the building. Possibly a truck hit a corner of the structure. He hurried back to the machine and calipered the shaft. As he read it, his hand shook.

You cannot put metal back on a shaft.

Fisher was fired.

That was the day his son, Ed Fisher, funneled his rage into a union career. "They're going to pay and pay!"

When he reached region presidency, it was hard to retain the rage amid administrative chores. And the politics of re-election distanced him from the shops and from his flaming cause. He became impatient with philosophy in the face of bolstering declining membership and revenue. But he needed a few on staff who were more effective in negotiations.

Therefore he was pleased when he was told that John Visconti was on the line. Visconti said, "Ed, I'm considering your offer."

"Good. What's to consider?"

"Money."

Fisher jibed, "That's the old Visconti I know. How much?"

"Ten million."

"I beg your pardon."

"Ten million."

"Stop horsing me around, Visconti."

"I'm not." Visconti explained that he wanted a $10 million union fund invested, the interest to be used for training machinists in the new CAD-CAM metalworking production, the employer to pay the men's room and board in Cincinnati, Ohio, for several weeks. "Unless we do this, you have no way to stiffen up work rules or pay. You will be captain of the *Titanic*."

"Hey, this isn't something two guys decide over the phone. This requires a major board of trustees proposal with full dress four-star research and presentation."

"Make it half dress and two stars, and get it started."

"Hey, wait a min ..."

"I waited too long already. Let me know. So long."

"Hey ... we got to talk details."

"The details are simple. Either *we* do it. Or the Japs do it. Which do you prefer?"

* * *

Visconti was shown into a small conference room at Millitech in Cincinnati. A navy blue pinstripe stood, extended a hand, and introduced himself, "Mr. Braxton will join us directly." He introduced two men, industrial relations and human resources, and one woman, public affairs.

The pinstripe asked, "Would you like to give us a little pre-briefing on your visit?"

"No. I had not expected a group."

"Is it about the Business Round Table?"

"No."

There was an awkward silence, so they talked weather and football. "Weren't you with that Massillon championship team in ..."

But Braxton came in and took the head of the table. "To what do we owe the pleasure?"

"I had only expected to talk to *you*, Mr. Braxton."

"Concerning Business Round Table?"

"No. Millitech."

"Oh?" Braxton was surprised. "Well, even so, I think

these are the right people to have present."

"I hate to tie up top-level people. But if you want people present, I suggest getting marketing in here."

Braxton sent the pinstripe for a marketing man who sat at the foot of the table, lanky, commanding, and genial. Lou Tankersly.

After a slow restart Visconti explained that he wanted Millitech to set up a training center on premises to train machine operators in the latest CAD-CAM reprogrammable machine centers.

The pinstripe said, "We already have elaborate training for our customers' operators."

"I'm not talking about your customers' operators. *All* operators."

Braxton leaned in. "Mr. Visconti, we cannot afford to pay for training operators of *competitor* machines."

"You don't pay. The union pays."

Without notes Visconti explained Millitech would provide the space and the machines and instructors right off their own production line. The union pays Millitech for that. The employer of the students pays room and board in Cincinnati.

Braxton said, "Well, for a monster like this, you've got to lay out for us a comprehensive plan, complete with ..."

"I don't think so, Mr. Braxton." His hand referenced the people around the table. "I'm sure your people can do it better than I can."

"But why should they? It's *your* problem."

"I don't think so, Mr. Braxton. It's yours."

"*Ours?*"

"Let me just ask your marketing man one single question." Visconti turned slowly to the newcomer. Lou Tankersly was a lined vertical face with a grin which broadened in anticipation of a challenge. "Mr. Tankersly, would you rather see Millitech run this school to remove your upcoming sales bottleneck from operator shortages ... or ... would you rather have the school run by the folks at my next stop ... Cleveland Machine Tool?"

Tankersly's grin widened, bowing out the vertical creases of his face. He looked to the head of the table silently.

Braxton bit off a smile severely. The heads of the staffers midtable ping-ponged between Braxton and Tankersly, puzzled.

Braxton covered his mouth with his hand and shook his head slowly in wonder.

Suddenly all heads turned to Tankersly, who exploded a huge laugh, "Visconti! You son of a gun!"

Now Braxton laughed out loud.

The staffers midtable began to smile uncertainly.

Tankersly slapped the table and roared. Braxton leaned his head back in uncontrolled laughter. The midtable people chuckled.

Tankersly sobered. "We've known something had to be done to sell robotics into smaller shops. But that it should be triggered by a blackmailer like *you*, of all people." He shook his head. "Give us six months."

"No, Mr. Tankersly. Six weeks. Hamilton Machine needs it quick."

Braxton said, "Tank ... it should be a marketing function. But strictly engineer floor types doing the instructing. Let's meet at three o'clock." He pointed a stern finger at Visconti. "You and I have another matter pending." He lightened up. "And stay away from Cleveland."

Later Visconti declined an invitation to lunch with the pinstripe, but he asked, "Can I use a phone?"

He asked Information for the number of Hamilton Machine in Dayton.

Irving Cohen, rainwear, asked Judd Hobart, sportswear, "Has GTA gone bonkers — changing the annual meeting place to Boston? It's handy to only a dozen garment makers and no textiles. Mostly there will be no-shows."

"Everybody'll show. Haven't you heard?"

"What? They got the U.S. president to address us?"

"Better. They finally got Remberg."

"You're kidding."

"He insisted on Boston so he can be driven back to Vermont the same night. Refused to be there for the banquet. He'll stay one hour only. Doctor's orders."

Hobart was right. The attendance was a GTA record.

After the banquet there were a few short announcements, including a thanks from the Israel Children's Scholarship Fund. That one quarter of one percent had built a beautiful endowment portfolio.

There was a recap by Levinson summarizing once more the spectacular industry recovery.

When Remberg finally moved to the podium, the assemblage rose in waves from front to back, applauding. Many here owed him for survival. Many of them were sons of his former associates.

"I didn't say anything yet. Sit down already." He attempted to begin his talk several times, but the ovation sustained. "Already enough." When it hit three minutes, the waxworks could see Remberg tiring from standing and nodding. Abrahms walked to the podium and waved the crowd down.

Without amenities, Remberg began abruptly, "So what did we learn yet?

"We learned that the best friend of our industry is competition. It forced innovation in design, materials, production, and marketing.

"It fought lethargy, smugness, and greed. It fought unproductive nepotism. We fired our fat, spoiled kids. The nephews had to produce or get out."

Remberg went on to tell them how to manage their future. The tremendous power of his words was that they came from a man who had nothing to sell, no office to gain, no fear of disapproval. "Stop looking at each other's ads. Get out of your offices and watch the people. Stop making new fashions only for uptown. Go already on the docks, the truck stops, the farms, the hospitals."

He told them to make pants for truck drivers with small velcro patches on the right thigh for attaching a knee notebook like Air Force pilots use, hospital gowns with some style, really interesting costumes for fast food waitresses, tough whipcord pants for driver salesmen on bread and beer trucks. "Do something about easier fasteners for the very young and the very old."

He told them to make for hunters and fishermen clothes that did not weigh like armor. "How can foreigners beat us at clothing our own people? For Heaven's sake, make a girl's basketball suit as graceful as a tennis dress!"

In the back of the hall two very new GTA associate members watched wide-eyed, McGarrity and Sheehan, formerly in the home and factory insulation business in a tiny building in Chicago. They now headed a large company manufacturing thermally treated cloth. It began with Remberg's request for gabardine impregnated with a heat-storing chemical.

McGarrity turned to Sheehan. "So *that's* Remberg!"

"I suppose he has no idea that he made our company with that first order for treated gabardine."

"I'm not so sure. I suspect he knows everything."

"What could we do for him?"

McGarrity said, "I hear one quarter of one percent of the wholesale price of all his designs goes to his Israel Children's Education Trust."

"What would a quarter of one percent of our sales come to?"

"Why? Suddenly you're Jewish?"

"As of now — believe it already!"

With the audience still wide-eyed in anticipation, Remberg paused to reach for a drink of water with a shaking hand. Some water spilled. He replaced the glass, scanned the audience from left to right in silence for several seconds. Expectations rose. But the frail figure's next words were abrupt.

"Good night...and gezunterhayt."

Abrahms escorted him off the stage.

The audience exploded. Before the applause faded, Remberg was out on Mass Ave., stepping into the back seat of a long black car which screeched for Vermont.

* * *

On Maybeth Harlow's shift at the Curtice Ecosphere on the Chesterville, Ohio, farm she received a phone call from Dayton, asking for a Gian Visconti. She said, "We know a Mr. Visconti. But he doesn't work here. As far as I know, he works in Washington for some senator."

Two days later she received a call for a John Visconti from Chicago. She explained, "We don't have a John Visconti on staff. What made you think you could reach him at the Curtice ..." But the dial tone came on.

One day later she received a call from a woman in Massillon asking for a Gian Visconti. "We know a Mr. Visconti, but he does not work here."

Two days later at dusk she looked out the window. In the drive was a vehicle distinctly foreign to Chesterville, a pickerel shaped two-door Pontiac, the kind of car that comes out at night, black and waxed and wire-wheeled. Heat waves came off the hood.

She walked down and looked at it. It was mud-splattered over an otherwise shiny body. Inside, it must be a bachelor car ... two small suitcases, a racquetball bag, two briefcases, a shaving kit, and some loose shirts. It looked as though some man had practically lived in this car for a few days.

She started back to the barn. A voice stopped her.

"Can you take time for dinner?"

She looked around. Approaching her from the road, holding up a brown bag, strode Visconti. He said nothing as he approached, nor did she. When he was close he stared ... too long. To break it, he looked down at his brown bag and opened it. "I got enough for two ... in case you didn't bring yours."

Her eyes met his straight on, studying him, humorless. However, he felt the lips were pressing shut a smile.

She nodded toward the barn. He followed her.

They sat opposite each other on camp chairs beside the ecosphere. She ate in bemused silence, he in cautious silence, a man trying not to frighten off a standing fawn. Nor did he gaze at her. Kept his eyes on the brown bag. Finally he ventured, "Miss Harlow, Senator Boar didn't send me here."

She nodded.

"And Senator Forte didn't send me."

It was in her eyes that she knew.

She took the brown bag to a wastebasket, picked up a notebook, and returned. Silence inside the barn thickened enough to make audible the lowing of neighboring cattle. "Could a city man live with that every day?" she asked.

He raised his eyes, "Yes."

"But the cities will call a man like you away."

"I've seen the cities."

"But three of them have already phoned ... before you even got here."

"That's why you weren't surprised when I came."

Unsmiling, she shook her head, "No. That's not why."

"How else could you know?"

Her shoulders lifted and fell just the slightest and she shook her head. He said, "Is it time to take the ecosphere readings?"

She ignored that. "Mr. Visconti ... Gian ... do you know ... not that it has anything to do with anything ... but do you know that I have committed to stay here until I'm forty-five?"

He was emboldened to move his chair close. He leaned toward her and looked squarely into her eyes. "I do know that."

(*The Economist*)

MORE (Part IV)
by Edward Fash

The Fash Hall Of Fame

Tracking the Destiny
Of The Unsung

Except for Abe Lincoln and the legendary Dutch Boy with his finger in the dike, there are never awards, testimonial dinners or wall plaques for men and women who *stop* something from happening.

Yet *prevention* can be far more profound than action.

Who has given an award to the government lady (I can't even think of her name) who halted the distribution of thalidomide in the U.S.?

There may be walking around among us now, unrecognized and unknown, hundreds of men and women who prevented some war we didn't have, some disease we didn't have, some animal species genocide we didn't have.

Such men and women put their lives and careers on the line like the signers of the Declaration of Independence.

Several such men have just put their fingers in the world dike and have paid a price.

Justin A. Forte

This defeated senator from Missouri returns to St. Louis. He laid his career on the line to strip the U.S. protectionist trade bill of its teeth. The bill as drafted would have rung down trade curtains around the world. Forte was offered many jobs in Washington which he declined.

Only a few in the world will know that they owe their jobs and the bread on their table to Justin Forte, who with a handful of musketeers gave the world balanced free trade.

He has told this journal that he will take a month off, and then may accept a chair at a Missouri university.

Knute Boar

Defeated for re-election to the Senate, Boar has announced no plans beyond taking a seat on the board of trustees of Ecosphere, a scientific experiment in the Midwest.

Arnold W. Drummond

This senator was on a roll for the presidency as wagonmaster of the popular protectionist bandwagon. When he failed to fight the veto of the trade bill, the wheels fell off his wagon. Though he retains his seat in the Senate and his post as majority party whip, his candidacy for

337

the powerful Rules Committee is dead.

Morton Butus

This senator tried both sides. He began as an ardent free trader; but to save his seat he switched to the protectionists. He remains in the Senate, but stripped of his committees.

The head of the Senate Rules Committee has lost power. The Boomerang computer technique for viewing cause and effect, which he banned from the Senate, has proved to be a powerful technique for seeing the future effects of legislation; and will be used as a regular tool in considering profound legislation.

Christopher Bain

Senator Christopher Bain will remain because his term is not up and his profile was low. But his free trade activity was at least prominent enough to give rise to a strong new competitor for his seat in the next election. He will lose his hoped-for seat on the powerful Banking Committee.

One interesting common denominator came out of these post-disaster interviews with these men. I asked each free trader if they would pay such a price again. Their replies were similar to Bain's answer. He drew himself up and grinned. "First time I ever amounted to anything."

Senator Boar laughed and growled, "When we threw that punch, we knew more ways than one it could boomerang."

EPILOGUE

TWA Flight 735
London to Washington National
Edward J. Fash had stayed on in England an extra week at the request of *The Economist*. As he rode west now he wished his wife and two kids could have been along.

As he walked up the aisle on Flight 735 for a cup of coffee at the amidships kitchenette, his ear caught snatches of the conversation of the men and women travelers in American and European accents; and he smiled. This plane was not filled with tourists. It was full of sales types, making international sales. Not war.

He reflected again in wonder on how fast an economy can shift. Things were looking pretty good from what he could see.

Returning to his seat he was startled, "Mr. Fash?"

It was the CBS fellow he had met long ago on the Forte flight to France. The young man pointed to an empty seat, "Red Graves. Remember? Could we talk a moment?"

Fash sat down, "What a coincidence."

"Not exactly, Mr. Fash."

"Oh?"

"A coincidence that we're both returning at the same time, but not a coincidence we're on the same flight. I called *the Economist*. They said you were booked on 735."

"Oh?"

"Been following your Fash Hall of Fame articles."

"Oh? You interested in economics?"

"Not especially. But I'm interested in those guys you wrote up. They laid everything on the line for a belief."

"Yup."

"And most of them lost."

"Depends. They think they won."

"I mean *personally* they lost."

Fash shrugged.

"Do you think they were naive? Or were they right?"

"Huh?"

"I mean balanced free trade can't really work, can it?"

"It's common sense. Why not expand world trade, increasing employment and getting more for all? Why not give working people more for their money when the product is available?"

"But I mean the *balance* part. How would we keep score?"

"Easier than tracking ten thousand tariffs. Just two numbers. How much did they sell to us? How much did they buy from us? That's all."

Graves pulled a handful of British pounds out of his pocket, "But with the instability of all these different currencies, how can that be tallied?"

"Same old way as Marco Polo did it. Translate all currencies into gold equivalency."

"That still doesn't solve the *balance*. How is a tiny nation, say Korea, supposed to balance its sales and buys against a monster like the U.S.?"

"First, let *them* work on the problem them*selves*. For example, why can't they team up with four other small nations? Create a large trade partner."

"How about big nations like Brazil, Mexico, that owe us billions? How can they buy more from us?"

"Forte says — let their loan repayments count as purchases. All we want to do is even up the money flow. And keep our own banks from going belly up."

Graves thought about that. Fash said, "Look, if the subject of trade is getting to you, there's a great book on the ..."

"The subject is not getting to me. What got to me was those guys you wrote about ... who believed in something enough to go all the way to the mat, on principle." Graves' voice lowered, "Y'see, I never did that. I've worked both sides of the street. Any street ... that paid me. And in going that road, I think I did damage ... to guys like you wrote up."

Graves fell silent. Fash felt like an intruder. He pushed himself out of the seat, extended a hand, and chuckled nervously, "Well, Mr. Graves, you're young. Maybe you can go back down that road and do some highway repair."

In Massillon, Ohio, in the garage of Gian Visconti, Sr., Frank Visconti put a handful of tools back in a box, "It won't work with that component, Dad." They stood staring at a small motorized flatbed wheeled cart which they had been trying to modify for breath operation for Gian's invalid grandson, Danny. Frank pulled from his pocket a rolled medical journal and opened it to an advertisement which pictured an electronic black box. "This is what we need."

"What do they get for that, Frank?"

"Twenty-two thousand."

The senior whistled, "Twenty-two! Why?"

"Made in Germany. Most of that price is tariff."

"Damn! That's got to change!"

Across town Margaretta Visconti walked out of her office, down a long corridor and into the office of a friend, Jack Irwin, Public Affairs. "Jack, I've got a bad problem."

"Calling men back to work is a problem? That should be the best part of your job."

"It is. Except for one call."

"Who?"

"My father."

"That's a problem?"

"Gian Visconti does not want to be given a job by a girl, especially his daughter."

Specialty Steel Company landed a five-year order for rolled girders to be embedded in pre-stressed concrete structural members. The steel was a special tungsten alloy shipped in from Korea in billets to be rolled in various sizes and shapes.

Irwin walked around his desk. "I see your point. I wouldn't want to be given my job by my daughter. How about getting your human resources V.P. to make that one recall?"

"You know him. He'll bark, 'It's *your* job.' Second ... my father is so bitter at the company, he'd tell my V.P. to go to hell. He'd rather be unemployed. Then we'll both be in trouble. And my father needs to work."

Irwin said, "Meet me for lunch in an hour."

By lunch time Irwin had an idea. "What if the president called your father in *person?*"

"Ridiculous. Why would he?"

"I'm not sure he would. But he's pretty shrewd. He knows that a big part of business today is the media. And if I ever saw a great story, it would be the president ... personally ... recalling his senior roller. A sign of the times. An image of the company."

In the garage of Gian Visconti, Sr., the phone rang. Frank answered it and then said, "For you, Dad."

At 9:30 a.m. a red-bearded outsider walked into Agnes' Hanging Limb Restaurant in Hanging Limb, Tennessee, and sidled onto a stool at the counter, "Coffee and a doughnut." He looked around the restaurant as if surprised.

"Doughnuts are all gone. Toast do?"

He nodded. "Where's everybody today?"

"What do you mean — everybody?"

"A crowd used to sit around here mornings." He grinned. "Has the coffee gone that bad?"

"Nope. Business got that good."

"How come?"

"Do I know you?"

"Probably not any more. I grew a beard since."

She poured the coffee. He said, "Where are all the Buy American signs?"

"That was a dumb idea."

"Dumb?"

"Cut off our own nose. Hanging Limb people *need* imports. Need trade. More products, cheaper and better."

"But how about the imported shirts cutting back your shirt factory jobs?"

"Japs made up for it. They're in here buyin' hardwood timber. Two saw mills are runnin' big here. Our men are workin'. Those that want. The Japs did us a favor."

"But what about the trade deficit with the Japs?"

"This country don't need to put up with a trade deficit. Why not try a simple, straight forward, common-sense balanced free trade. Invite any country to sell us all they want

.... just so they buy from us as much as they sell. What's so hard about that?

"That way we don't pay an army of bureaucrat book-keepers to score keep tariffs on a jillion products from clocks to crocks. Get 'em off our payroll. All we'd need is a computer. Everybody wins."

"Except the bureaucrats."

"The hell with them. They bled us enough."

"Where'd you learn about balanced free trade?"

"Right here in Hanging Limb. The Japs are buyin' our good hardwood oak, hickory and ash ... cut a special way. Three-by-threes instead of four-by-fours. And we buy their Hitachi fire engine and Nissan trucks for the town road department."

"You finally took delivery on that fire engine after all?"

"Damn right. Otherwise we couldn't afford one. How'd you know about that fire engine?"

He shrugged.

"Oh, you prob'ly saw on TV."

"Probably. But anyway ... didn't anybody tell your congressman to get U.S. displacement pay for the shirt factory women displaced by the imported shirts? And more tariff against import shirts?"

"We talked about it. Decided against it."

"Why?"

"The shirt works is antique. Why should the U.S. try to protect obsolete industries? I'm the one pays for it."

"I just mean for *shirts* only."

"You do it for shirts, you gotta do it for shoe people, baseball gloves, cameras. Everybody. Why let any special interests cut the rest of us off from free trade? Cuts the people off from bargains and stuff we need.

"Besides, if we're going to subsidize, we oughta do it openly; not hide it in the price of the goods. It's a hidden tax ... is what it is."

"But how's it going to work if the other countries don't buy our stuff?"

She rinsed some cups, thinking. "Y'know a lot of that's the fault of our own damn gover'ment. Makes the price too high."

"Our government?"

"Sure. You take our ships. Ruth Mallory's boy in the Merchant Marine says certain exports get to go in only U.S. ships. Raises the cost of our stuff."

The smoke alarm in the ventilator hood buzzed. "Now you made me burn the toast." She pitched out two black slices and put in two new ones. The red head said, "Stop, Agnes. I'll pay for the burnt ones, but I didn't come for the toast."

She looked a question at him.

"Agnes, would you say those things you just said in front of a TV camera, and maybe get some of the other people in town to join in?"

She put the bread back in the bag and came over to the counter with both hands on it, studying him. "Are you that guy who blew in here for a month and then ... well I'll be damned."

He nodded. "Anyway, Agnes, would you say those things again if we brought a camera in here?"

She grinned. "Hell yes. It's only common sense."

THE CAST

THE CAST
CONTINUED

ECONOMIC REFERENCES

ECONOMIC REFERENCES
CONTINUED